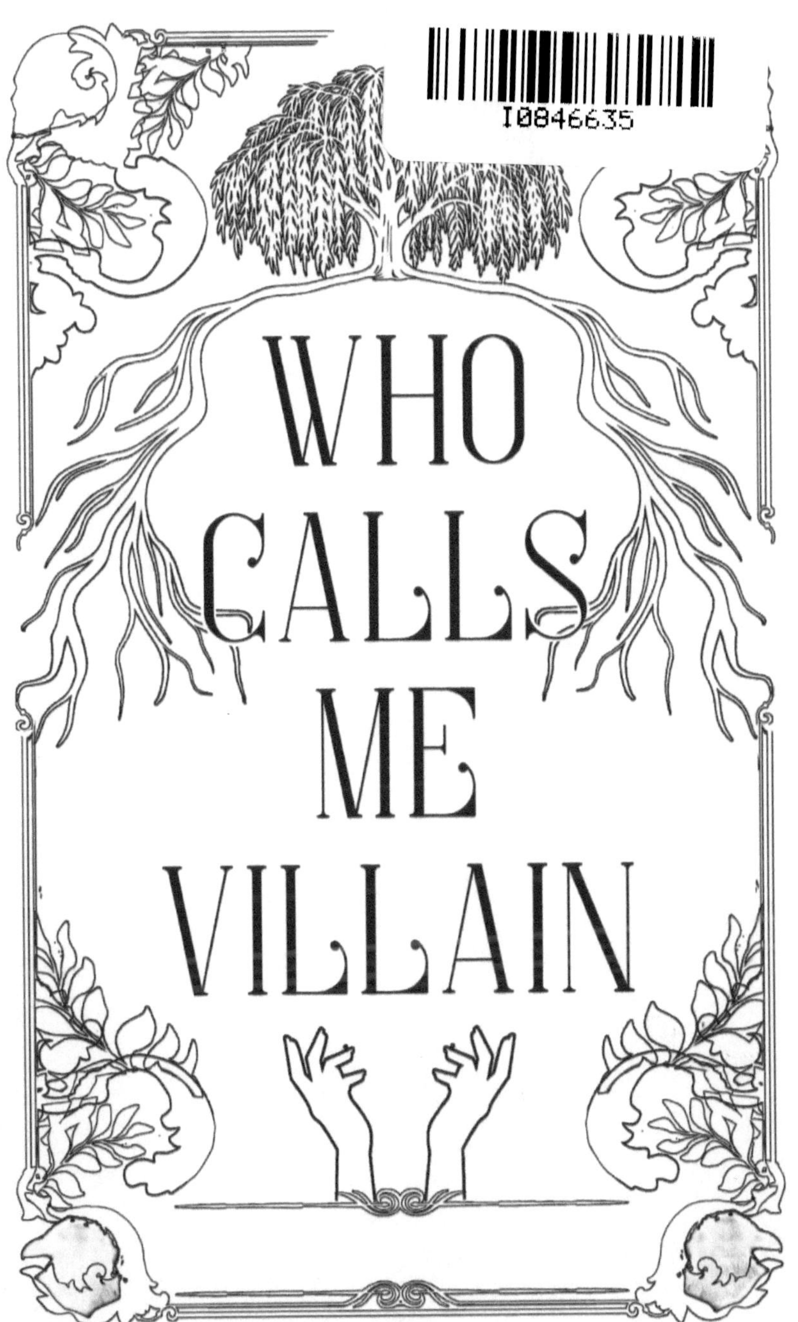

Book 1 of We Were Immortal

Copyright © 2026 by Allison Trebacz & Ephemeral Publishing L.L.C.

All rights reserved.

No part of this publication may be reproduced, distributed, or transmitted in any form or by any means, including photocopying, recording, or other electronic or mechanical methods, without the prior written permission of the publisher, except as permitted by U.S. copyright law. For permission requests, contact allison@allisonimagining.com.

The story, all names, characters, and incidents portrayed in this production are fictitious. No identification with actual persons (living or deceased), places, buildings, and products is intended or should be inferred.

No AI was used in the making or marketing of this book.

Paperback: 979-8-9906214-6-6

EBook: 979-8-9906214-5-9

Cover and Interior Graphic by JV Arts
Map by Josh at Stardust Designs
Art by Marta Into the Forest

Mirian Realm
Deadlands of Raven
Old Dover
Foria
Ernmore
Fauning Cliffs
Crystal Park
Deer Field
West Vista
Fierces Mountains
The Forgotten Shrine
Cyrlas

Belfiantw
Fiante Mountains
Avilla
Baneswood
Vharos
Malcom's Tower
Blood Hill
Forest
Fields of Reen
Vladeus R.
Linvian Ridge
Linvia
Dover
Dover's Living Watterfall
Ember
Fairview
neum
Lindon
Gates of Ersos
yrlian
ountains
Rwendeer

Author's Note

First, thank you so much for taking the time to read Who Calls Me Villain. Before you get started on Raven's journey take care of yourself. *Who Calls Me Villain* is a dark fantasy romance with heavy themes. It is the first book of the duology written in the shape of a classic tragedy.

It contains heavy themes, allusions, and some scenes that might be difficult for readers. Foremost, WCMV features an immortal main character who experiences suicide ideation and her POV may be triggering or distressing to readers.

Please read with care and know if you are struggling that you are not alone and resources are available.

Dial 988 to be connected, for free, with the Suicide and Crises lifeline 24/7 or visit https://findahelpline.com for additional resources.

For a complete list of potential triggers
with minor spoilers, visit my website:
https://allisonimagining.com/content-warnings

Content Warnings

GLOSSARY

Characters:

Raven (RAY – vin)

Orion (OH – rye – en)

Adler (AD – lehr)

Henry (Hen – REE)

Ophie (OH – fee)

Ephraim of Tyrlas II (EE – frame of TER–luss)

General Nia (NYE – ah)

Evander Devereux (EE – VAN – der | DEV – er – ROW)

Leander Morav (LEE – and – ER | MORE – ave)

Vinliana (Vin) (Vin – LEE – ahn – uh)

Pantheon:

Royal Family:
Koros – (Core – ohs)
King of Gods, God of Light.
Niany - (NYE – an – EE)
Queen of Gods, Goddess of Life
Foriana - (For – EE – ah – na)
Princess & Goddess of Death (Adopted)
Fortune – (For – TUNE)
Princess & Goddess of Prophecy (Adopted)
Armine - (Ar – MEAN)
Princess & Goddess of Love and Fate
Maxantius - (Max – an – TEE – uhs)
Prince & God of Shadow (Adopted)

Other Gods:
Malcolm - (Mal – COME)
God of War
Etta - (EHT – ah)
Goddess of Harvest & daughter of Malcom
Ersos - (ehr – SOHS) (Former)
God of Death & brother of Koros
Lucretia - (loo – CREE – shah)
Goddess of Orchards
Finneas - (Fin – EE – uhs)
God of stars and hope
Horatio - (Hor – AE- she – OH)
God of healers
Troculus - (TROC – oh – less)
God of Plenty
Leo – (LEE – oh)
God of water

Places:

Mirian Realm; Miria (MEER – ee – AH)

Tyrlas (Kingdom): (TER – lass) Under a strict, semi-authoritarian king. Understood to be isolated from most of the realm.

Miacor City: (MY – ah – core) Capital city of Tyrlas

Rivendeer (Kingdom): (RYE – ven – DEER)

Cascaade (Kingdom): (Cass – CADE) Destroyed by Raven

Verineum: (VER – in – EE – uhm) The Library state —it belongs to no kingdom.

Valley of Oslin: (OSS – lin) Between Verineum and Tyrlas

Xerxes: (ZER – seas) Southwest mountain range in Miria

Diadeus River: (DYE – ah – diss) Largest river in Miria

Reen: (REE – n) A small city along a major trade route; location of massive battle in the kingdom of

Aven (Kingdom): (AE – ven) Northern kingdom, known for agriculture

Dover (Kingdom): (DOH – ver) The trade capital of Miria & a kingdom

Linvia (Kingdom): (Lin – VEE – ah) The center city of the Linvian Kingdom

Belfiante: (BELL – fee – ahn – T) Remnant of the primordials in the North

Ember: (EM – burr) A village along the largest Xerxes lake

Avilla: (AH – vill – a)Present day city of labyrinths

Vitros (Kingdom): (VIT – ross) Old Kingdom

Vharos: (Ver – OHS) Northern City known for dark ale and it's terraced city

Vestios (Kingdom): (Vest – EE – ohs) Old kingdom before it was Foria

Foria (Kingdom): (For – EE – uh)

Palace of Niany: The palace of the Linvian King

Crystal Palace: Forian royal palace

Ettarian road: Main road through the fields of Reen to the Northern cities/kingdoms

Blood Hill Forest: Known as Etta's plains until the battle of Reen changed its topography

Ernmore: City known for it's sprawling healing palaces

Loras: The city near the shrine for the God of War
Olanoria: (OH – la -nore – EE – ah) Southern city in the fae realm

Who Calls Me Villain

PLAYLIST

Silver Venom – Brad Arthur
All That I'm Living For (Acoustic) – Evanescence
Never Know – Bad Omens
Redemption (Acoustic) – RIELL
I Feel Fine – Mitchel Dae, Lucky Dog
Who You Were – LaLion, The Tech Thieves
Is It Really You – Sleep Token, Loathe
Crossed The Line – Amira Elfeky
Specter – Bad Omens
Goddess – Xana
The Jester – Badflower
Even in Arcadia – Sleep Token

WCMV Playlist

Shout out to Aristotle.
He knocked it out of the park with "catharsis".

Who Calls Me Villain is dedicated to all the girlies
who didn't have to look that one up.
You know what you're in for.
<3

When all other gods have died, a
king will stand when Death's
darkness twines with the brightest
light—from beneath the blackened
willow, as she splits in two—new
dawn will rise.

1

His Majesty King Ephraim Tyrlas recognizes Raven of Tyrlas as a citizen of the Tyrlian King- dom of Miria.

THE PALACE OF TYRLAS echoed the state of the loathsome kingdom: questionably wet, nearly empty, and gray as the cotton robes of perfunctory priests.

"What the fuck are you doing here?"

The tip of a sword dug into my back and brought me to a halt. The ghost of my last step faded as I raised my black-clad arms, choosing not to turn around.

"Answer"—he dug the blade into my rib—"the question."

There weren't many voices in the Tyrlian capital I recognized, but I knew Orion Blackthorn.

Eighteen years ago, in the last round of a tournament, I yielded my advantage and let him win. He noticed it the moment I fell on my back and hesitated, giving him a clear shot.

He hated me for it—apparently, still does. I'd bruised his pride and injured his honor, which is all a Tyrlian knight has to live for. Either that or he was still reeling about the consequent events.

"I'm here at the Queen's request." My hands tightened; leather gloves stretched over my knuckles. "Only going to my room. Relia said one was outfitted for me."

"Queen Relia is dead."

"Exceedingly aware." I turned around, making a careful show of removing my glove, finger by finger to reveal blackened fingertips—poisoned with magic. Even bound in primordial iron, I was far from just a woman.

His sword didn't waver. Instead, he pressed the point between the folds of my coat, just above my navel and the pearl button of my silk blouse. If he wanted to, Orion could try to gut me, but knights like him were cowards, fueled by grand delusions. He wouldn't do it so I leaned in further.

"You shouldn't be here. You were exiled . . . *Twice*."

Orion was older now. Lines crinkled around his amber eyes; dark blond stubble shadowed his neck and chin; tufts of hair poked through the buttoned shirt and ochre vest that stretched across his broad chest, underneath a charcoal coat.

I shoved my gloved hand into my pocket and tugged out a wrinkled letter with the royal crest and Queen Relia's signature.

"My services are needed by the Crown."

"The Kingdom of Tyrlas has no use for a wraith and God-killer, unless you've resorted to killing kings." He cocked his head with a grin, sending unkempt ruddy blond hair to one side. "Or have you come to fuck his next wife?"

"Neither." I crumpled the note back into my pocket. "You'll find this *wraith* offers far more value than one of the king's shifter knights. Your claws don't scare me, but keep talking and maybe I'll show you mine—or have you forgotten how to lose to a woman?"

"You yielded," he exasperated. "It was barely a win when you dropped six men prior, only to throw the final."

"I was punished either way." I crossed my arms. Iron cuffs rattled against several gold bracelets with too many stories. His eyes narrowed, icy and rigid as the metal circling my wrists.

"Drop your sword and let me on my way, Sir Blackthorn. I have more to do than argue with the king's dog."

"Can't do that."

"Why not?"

"I don't believe those papers are real. Why would you come here in the dead of night?"

"First, Miacor City is more of a maze than I remember. And, second, I prefer the cover of night—part of my *wraith* sensibilities." With an inaudible sigh, he lowered his steel, the point resting at my toes. "Perhaps I'd prefer daylight if the mad old king hadn't kept me chained up at the southern border for ten years."

It was his turn to be unmoved; a shadow crossed his face. "If the histories are right, you deserved every second and got your freedom in the end."

"It's not true freedom, though, is it?" Magic trickled along the lines in my palm like a cool stream of water. "I'm still a fallen god, beholden to kings and politics as long as I'm trapped in this world."

"Perhaps you should have run faster when they came for you."

I considered punching him. Instead, I lowered my voice, feeling the low rumble of death beneath my nails become sharp chips of ice. "You're going to walk away and leave me to my room." His eyes flashed the same way his sword glinted in the sparse moonlight. "I have an audience with the king at dawn."

Blackthorn sucked in a breath and snapped his fingers. Footsteps and clanking metal echoed off the walls, gaining as guards approached.

"Guards are posted at the door."

"Flattered you know which it is." I sidestepped him as he sheathed the sword. "I don't give a fuck who watches me sleep, so long as it isn't you."

Three guards came around the corner and stopped in a sliver of light peeking through an arched window draped in cobwebs.

Orion walked toward them, whispered something, and stormed off.

I ground my teeth as the guards stared at me. For a second, I thought they might drag me to the dungeons, but nothing happened. They didn't even flinch when I moved my hand to my hip.

"I'm going to my room," I announced, receiving nothing but a cool nod from a single guard.

Fine.

The guards walked a few paces behind, watching every turn I took. The room Relia set aside was at the older end of the Tyrlian palace, where the scant marble and porous gray stone was worn, scuffed, and forgotten as the gods they once believed in.

Four hundred years ago the Pantheon was a force. No guard would have dared follow me down these halls, nor would a knight be so bold to point a sword at my back. Either they'd meet the creeping strangulation of death as my magic turned their skin to ash, or I'd raise ghosts of their dead and force a reckoning.

Now, I was a wraith, a shadow of everything that once made me fearsome. All I couldn't whittle away was the curse of immortality from a bargain with a god that turned me into one.

The room set aside for me was in the center of a derelict hallway between the statues of two gods whose deaths I'd never seen: Finneas, an acquaintance, and Armine—my sister in the Pantheon.

Like most gods, I assumed Finneas died on the battlefield . . . the way we all expected to die. As a god there was no greater inevitability than war. The only question was whether we'd die under the banners of some kingdom or the white ones of the Pantheon.

Armine's death was worse. Rumors among gods claim she died in the Pantheon dungeon, while the mortal's myths say she died on our father's dining table after an egregious betrayal.

I didn't know which was true and closed the door before guards swept in.

The room was dark, save for a single candle by the window and the pale blue flicker of a ghost in the far corner. Costly gas lamps hadn't been installed on this side of the palace. The ghost eyed me for a second longer and vanished when she realized who I was.

At the foot of a curtained bed, covered in dust was an old chest I'd left behind and sealed with blood magic. I punctured my arm with my teeth and dropped a bead of my blood on the lock. It sizzled on contact and opened with an ancient groan. Inside were a few old dresses, some raven plumes, and a stack of papers.

After centuries, I needed help remembering everything that passed between this kingdom and I. There were a few years between exiles where I'd advised the king, hoping he'd agree I no longer needed the chains. King Tyrlas, however, never changed his mind.

I shuffled through several torn pieces of paper, napkins filled with my illegible scrawl, and pieces ripped out of books with circled phrases and margin notes. None were particularly helpful, but a few were notable:

Get Tyrlian citizenship.

That was clipped to my Tyrlian citizenship with a wax seal as if I'd forget. Another note stuck to it—this one on the back of a list of names I no longer recognized.

Tyrlas despises Rivendeer, looking for any excuse to invade. Keep focus on the east side of the mountain range. You exaggerated resource availability & Rivendeer's (nonexistent) trade partnership with Ernmore. Good luck.

I didn't need the luck; I was exiled before he noticed.

Remembering one lifetime was difficult enough, but remembering centuries was worse. Monarchs and masters erased and rewrote histories I'd merely stumbled through so I wrote down what I could, shared what I couldn't, and kept a variety of personal libraries buried in several cities. Over the last hundred years, I had no use for any of it. I let my magic dissipate with that of the realm.

Now, magic only came to me in slivers, the strength depending on the positions of three Mirian moons. Then there were the iron cuffs locked on my wrists by the first Tyrlian King twenty-six years ago. They were relics from another time but the primordial enchantment still worked and sapped almost anything remaining of my godhood. But I was created for a different purpose and even the primordials couldn't save me from the curse.

No matter what was done to me, one touch could still turn men to ash and dredge up the ghosts that haunted them. Death was my true gift, forced on me when my mortal father gave me up to the King of Gods, Koros, who had a misguided fascination with fatherhood.

With all power gone, Death lived, still, on the tips of my fingers in a spreading bruise of blue and black. At its height, the barest brush of skin killed mortals, gods, and fae alike. Now, as a mere fraction of who I was, it killed them—only slower, prolonging their suffering.

I kicked off my shoes and massaged my feet. In the corridor, guards whispered as they snapped cards against the stone floor.

"Perhaps you should have run faster."

Orion Blackthorn had no idea how hard I tried.

I never wanted to live this long, but despite my best efforts, I did. Maybe by force of will—or luck. Or spite, but I believed surviving was punishment for every crime I'd committed against the Pantheon.

Never once did I hesitate to stab my brother in the back when I was offered freedom. And twice, I watched a best friend drown without blinking because I needed a mortal king to believe my power and beg for my forgiveness. Even my sister collapsed with my name on her lips and our father's knife in her chest because I made a choice.

There was no one left to blame for the death of all the gods and their Pantheon.

2

CHILLED MORNING LIGHT CAME through the window in streams of gold and blue. It was far too hopeful a morning as I knelt in front of the trunk and pulled out a simple black dress that rippled at my shins.

I tugged a pair of silk gloves over my pallid skin, dragging them under the cuffs before I clasped on several gold bracelets.

Before Tyrlas, I'd been bound in iron a handful of times, once as long as eight years, but since the day the old, mad King Tyrlas locked them on my wrists in his prison along the southern wall, I'd lost what little remained of myself.

When I had power, I had full lips and full cheeks with curves like the Diadeus River. Now, I looked more like the Goddess of Death with sharp edges, sunken features, and shadows under my eyes. My hair remained thick, the color of the darkest storm, while my eyes retreated to pure black with microscopic threads of ice blue that flared with magic.

Tyrlas rested at the base of a mountain range and it was currently caught in the exquisite grip of late fall as I rounded the corner of the corridor. Large windows stretched to a dull, gilded ceiling that hadn't been properly cared for since the last regime.

I believed these three weeks of fall were the last bit of magic remaining in this gods-forsaken world. Trees dotted the small mountainside and surrounding hills in brilliant shades of copper, crimson, and gold.

Only one hallway led to the throne room, but the palace had eighteen similar stretches all leading to different sections. The baffling design was intentional and I cursed every wrong turn as the guards from last night followed me at a distance.

A century before the kingdom fell to Tyrlas, the architect for the prior king thought it might confuse an enemy in a siege.

It was ineffective. I had the misfortune—twice—of being in the ballroom during a siege. The man who designed it lied about his experience and spent most of the construction drunk on god wine. Eventually, he was exiled not for shoddy work, but for grabbing the tit of the Crown Princess.

They were dead now and their memories had been relegated to a few paintings stored in the archives below.

At the end of the corridor, past a wide-open set of carefully carved doors in the only dusted room in the palace, King Ephraim Tyrlas waited on his unadorned wooden throne, lounging in tweed pants and a lazily buttoned shirt—the two you women at either side who must have been his daughters. Ghosts in shades of blue clung to the walls and watched expectantly. A few were nobles but most were staff killed in one of the many Miacor Massacres.

I ignored the ghosts and focused on the living. Both daughters had his wavy dark brown hair and pointed chin, but one had Relia's down-turned eyes and the other had the curve of her lips and hooked nose.

I'd only seen the oldest once, fourteen years ago, when she barely peered over the rail at the tournament. Now she was a lady in full form, following me with a sharp, assessing stare, much like Queen Relia, as I walked through the bare throne room toward the small royal family.

"*Bern pi'nde*, Your Majesty." I bowed curtly, bending only at the waist as I stumbled through the Xerxian greeting and back to common tongue. "How may I be of service?"

At the foot of the dais, his commanding general, a woman, watched me from the corner of her eye. Her brown hair was cropped short and angled around her pointed chin, adding severity to her expression.

A door blasted open, disrupting the king before he spoke.

I craned my neck as Orion Blackthorn barged toward the throne with a scowl.

"The Godkiller, Your Majesty?" he said incredulously before he'd risen from the bow he'd twisted into. "She was exiled. *Twice.* I shouldn't need to remind you what chaos she'd brought to Miacor last time, and what she's—"

"Chaos is not a tournament you won, Sir Orion," the king chided. His eldest daughter watched Blackthorn, a corner of her pretty mouth turned up.

"It isn't that." Blackthorn gritted, palming his hilt with enough friction to shine it. "She never should have walked free after she disrespected you."

"I am not free." I shook my wrists to remind the room who I belonged to. My gaze stopped on the knight's. "I'm beholden to the Tyrlian Crown the same as you. The difference is you can see my chains."

With a flick of his wrist, the king waved off the conversation.

Guards pulled the doors closed and Blackthorn continued to stare at the abomination I was. As if His Majesty were the true and rightful heir who'd never order his brother's death. Of course, I wasn't in any position to pass judgement but it didn't stop me.

"Foriana," King Tyrlas drawled. I winced at the name I wanted to forget and his brow quirked. "Well, how should you be addressed these days?"

"It hasn't changed. Raven is fine."

"Like the bird?" The king sounded unimpressed as I relaxed my shoulders. Kings were the worst version of men; they rarely remembered they were made of flesh and bone like any other mortal.

"Yes, Your Majesty. Like the bird."

"Very well." He looked me up and down twice, forefinger on his lips until he leaned forward. "Raven, if I asked you to raise a dead army for me, what would you say?"

"No."

His brow once again arched as though my perfectly rational answer surprised him.

"No? You've done it before."

"I have. When the entire realm was in danger—I see nothing worth the price. The cost of cleaning up that war was astronomical. The winning kingdom fell ten years later because they couldn't repay their debt. Decaying bodies contaminated half of the farmland and poisoned the water."

The king frowned; his crown shifted, but I wasn't done.

"The only reason the northern edge of Cascaade is habitable is because three hundred and seventy-eight years ago Lucretia was alive to pinch it back together. Now she's as dead as the rest of the gods you don't believe in."

My odd presence was an unsettling sight for him with my mottled, pale skin and the bruises under my eyes because his cuffs invited mortality and rot.

"You're saying it's expensive."

"Yes," I said. "Among the many other facets you could glean from my story."

"I see."

I was sure he didn't.

Orion Blackthorn stood beside me, breathing through his mouth with something to say that he kept thinking better of. Perhaps I'd hit him harder than I thought all those years ago.

"Your Majesty, if I may." I stepped closer to the dais. "To offer you the most assistance, let me list what I am willing to do and capable of: I can cross the veil and spin up ghosts of dead men. I am not capable of creating shades—"

"And if I order you, Raven? It is for the liberation of Rivendeer, as you know they suffer."

His lips pursed, but I moved as much as Rivendeer suffered, which is to say I didn't.

"A shade army is impossible and you forget I am not afraid to wait out your reign in these cuffs. In fact, you would not be the first king I've waited out to preserve the realm."

"This isn't about the realm. This is about the future of Tyrlas." He glowered and leaned forward, pinching his brows together. "Forget shades and other tricks. Stand on the battlefield without your gloves as you'd done for Koros—strike their army."

"Oh?" I took a step, toes bumping against the dais as a guard flinched. A tendril of magic flared in my eyes, blue and bright as the dead stars and primordials it came from. "If a shade army is a danger to the realm, my destruction is tenfold. If you believe that, Ephraim, then you know what I lost when I did it for the King of Gods."

Everything. It was the first time I lost everything, and the first time anything so precious had been taken from me. According to my mother, I still deserved more punishment, but there wasn't a deserving god in the Pantheon.

"I've heard the legends."

"Legends?" I scoffed. "Funny to hear of my own memories."

The king waved off my insubordination. "Queen Relia received a lead on your godhood. That's why she brought you here and I believe that's why she was killed."

My stomach flipped. I'd always known the pieces would find me again. Of course, this was his solution. Relia had warned me before but I always hoped she was wrong.

"I can find her ghost and you can ask her yourself. Perhaps she intended to make herself a god."

"Is that all the Goddess of Death is good for? Sending messages?" It was his turn to scoff. "I know it doesn't work so easily.

Godhood only works in full for the body it belongs to until it's fully restored. Then you can pass it on—my scholars said so."

"Your scholars can say what they want, but restoring my godhood is impossible. It is lost. Don't you think I would have taken it by now if I wanted it?"

Blackthorn's fingers closed into a fist as he glared at the king.

"Restore your godhood and return here, Raven. If you will not deliver me a shade legion, or decimate Rivendeer forces, you can pass it to my eldest daughter who knows the meaning of sacrifice. Those are your options."

"Options?" A smile spread across my face—he offered me escape, *hope*. "Even with the godhood fully intact, it will not work on mortals so easily."

"You were mortal once."

"I was, eons before mortal magic was stolen by fae. And well before Koros added three hundred gods to his Pantheon. Your scholars should have told you that magic was concentrated and destroyed."

He shook it off, the flicker of hope in his expression turning to anger. "You lie, and for what?"

"I do not lie," I said through my teeth. "I have tried."

Memories of blood and grief turned rancid as King Ephraim rose to his feet. He towered over me with a well-defined jaw and a too-narrow frame.

"I'm no longer giving you a choice. You will restore your godhood, Raven, and you will return to Tyrlas—"

"Or?" I lifted my chin, holding up a gloved hand as bracelets collided with iron and I wiggled my fingers. "You ask a goddess to take back her full power and answer to a king of men. Even if you doubt the Pantheon, you clearly don't doubt my power."

"Or?" He huffed, taking one step off the dais. "Simple. If you don't, I'll execute Sir Orion Blackthorn's sister, to whom his life is bound."

"*No!*" Orion shouted and a fellow guard hooked his arm around the knight to hold him back. From the concern on the man's wide face, they were friends and the touch only faintly calmed the storm in his amber eyes. "I do not agree with this, Your Majesty. You need me—"

"Why do I care?" My gaze narrowed on the king. "I'd cut Sir Orion down where he stands—with your permission, of course."

The king smiled. "Are you sure?"

"Yes. You'll need to do better if you want me to return to Tyrlas. Otherwise, you've only offered me freedom."

"Do you agree to do it? With blood? I'll remove the cuffs." He raised an eyebrow as mischief smoothed the lines on his face. The general smirked, scratching a red spot on her neck, below her ear.

"Yes, fine." *Easiest decision in days.* I met the king halfway on the dais. Blackthorn stared wide-eyed as the king drew a dagger and sealed a blood bargain between us. He was lucky his blade broke my skin enough to get a drop, but I suppose that's how far I'd fallen. "I vow to return to Tyrlas, godhood restored, on the life of Sir Orion Blackthorn."

"And I vow to release you from your primordial cuffs. No harm of my making will come to either of you until two months have passed."

The agreement of the vow snapped in the air—blood magic somehow remained when everything else vanished. It was untethered to any source but human will.

Blackthorn remained silent and scorned—if he weren't so opaque I'd assume he was another one of Tyrlas' ghosts.

"Now that we're settled, Lady Raven. I will have your cuffs removed *if* you do one more thing for me."

"Have I not agreed to enough, Your Majesty?"

A smile curled up the king's lips and I thought of a thousand things he might say, but nothing prepared me for what he did.

"Kiss Sir Orion."

I backed away from the dais and Blackthorn launched forward with a barrage of protests, which included phrases like "living corpse" and "ghost of her father's affection" as though I'd never heard the insults.

"Fine," I said, cutting off the knight's groveling. "I've done more to be freed from less."

Not giving it another moment of thought, I yanked the knight forward, grabbing him by the chin, forcing his lips to mine. He relented the first second, kissed back in the next, and on the third, something pulled taut—I shoved him.

He stumbled; I blinked.

Something was wrong. A flame of memory burned inside my rib cage, against my heart. *No, no, no.* Deeply and terribly wrong. Wrong enough to shift the axis of the room.

The taste of him lingered on my lips and the heat in my chest boiled into frothing anger. I took a shaky breath, then whirled back to the king as a guard shoved keys into Blackthorn's hand.

"I'm warning you," I rasped, shaking as I moved toward the king, too late to retract our bargain but ready for it to shred my gut like a hundred paring knives. "The goddess you'll restore is the reason the fae are gone, the dragons are dead, and why only mortals and shifters remain—you all are made of the same stuff as cockroaches. But you will not survive *me* a second time, not without a Pantheon to answer to."

The king laughed and sank back into his throne.

"Sir Orion Blackthorn will accompany you to your godhood and keep you in line. Once restored, you will return and serve my kingdom as I see fit." King Tyrlas leaned back. "Refuse, Raven, and I will be your executioner."

"I see." A smile twisted my face with force as I dragged on my mask of royal indifference. Magic dripped into my palm and turned to ice beneath my nails, drawing on the dead in the room as I slipped off the silk. "Fine, I'll go on your little adventure, but remember the warnings of me are written in blood by the Scribes of Nurem on the moon of Ore—or have you forgotten?"

A trickle of magic swirled, icy and poignant as a waiting winter.

"I haven't," he said.

"Good." I tried to ignore the ghost standing behind the king as I backed away, but a hundred urgent needles of magic poked the tips as my glove slipped to the floor.

The king looked around and the younger princess stared at her feet. I jerked my hand up. My bruised fingers folded into a fist and I coaxed the magic into something tangible. Gasps filled the room as the veil peeled back like a curtain and a ghost of blue light, dressed in a robe, appeared between the dais and where I stood—I was a god and I wouldn't be forgotten.

"What is this?" the king grumbled, eye to eye with the ghost.

"Don't you want to hear from a Scribe of Nurem?"

Eight other ghosts in the room slipped through, but I didn't have the energy to erase them so they lingered. This spend in primordial iron would put me on my back, but it was worth it if I stayed upright for just another minute.

The king's eyes widened and I snapped my fingers.

The apparition's mouth fell open, bald head bent at an unnatural angle as the room filled with the cacophony of a hundred thousand screams from when the world died at once.

Hands flew to ears, guards and bystanders wept, yet I didn't flinch. Another second of horrid noise, then I slammed the veil closed and the ghosts disappeared with a gust of wind.

The king lowered his chin. "Your tricks do not scare me."

"That was a warning, Your Majesty, not a trick."

"Take her to her quarters," he commanded, staring through me as I pulled my glove over my blackened fingertips. "You leave at first light."

A sliver of magic reeled back and Sir Orion Blackthorn grabbed me by the elbow, dragging me out of the throne room before I stumbled in front of the king.

Giving me an option was a mistake. I'd killed a pantheon of gods for a reason, and now a king handed me a final quest to kill the very last and turn the Pantheon to dust.

3

FATE IN MIRIA WAS nothing like the absent fae believed it to be. Their Fate was a woman with a kind smile and a tapestry softened by songs left behind.

Our Fate was a beast with scales, talons, and a thousand eyes to see every one of our thousand futures—and I hated him for everything he'd clawed away from me.

Because of Fate, my nightmares were indistinguishable from memories and now he wanted even more. His talons were a sharp pain in the back of my head as midmorning light reflected off the dusty stone floor of my quarters.

I paced on unsteady legs, not thinking about the cuffs on my wrists, or how it would feel to take back my godhood. I paced because I couldn't stop thinking about how the knight's lips felt on mine and the way my chest constricted.

Something was wrong, off—*different.*

"What the fuck was that?" Orion Blackthorn barked as the door slammed, shaking the framed landscapes on the wall.

I jerked up at the commotion. Somewhere he'd lost his coat and wore only a white shirt under the ochre chest plate. "I could ask you the same. Did you know what your king wanted?"

"No," he muttered. "I have no say in what His Majesty is thinking. I was only told your keys are mine."

"And your sister's life is tied to yours?"

The knight exhaled as he looked at the low ceiling, hand gripping his neck. "Yes."

His chin dipped and we stared at each other—something pulled between us; there wasn't a way out. This was written in blood and sealed by something worse.

"How?"

Two ghosts appeared in the corner of the room, near a locked wardrobe, silently observing. I didn't have the energy to wave them off but spent it anyway, turning them to dust with a snap as my vision shivered.

"You know how. You've been alive a thousand years."

"Seven hundred and eighty-four." My gaze narrowed as I sank into a barely cushioned chair, massaging my shaking hands. "Why did you bind her life?"

"To keep her from doing something stupid. I'm sure you can relate."

"More stupid than joining a tournament and facing a god at fifteen?"

"Eighteen." He looked up, the bright light exaggerating thin white scars on his cheek. "Still less stupid than fucking the king's wife."

"She enjoyed it." I stretched my arms, cracking my elbows and shoulders. "There wasn't a faster way to get exiled from this shit city."

"You could have left."

"Amazing. I never considered." A sour frown turned the corners of my mouth. "When Tyrlas announced the second champion, he put me in his debt *again*. The cuffs were a compromise on a prison sentence I'd served under his father. I was tired of negotiating something indefinite."

"Why were you in prison?" He raised his eyebrow and leaned against the wall.

"Taxes."

I hated how he looked at me . . . searching for something and loathing me all in the same blink. There was no way out. I couldn't say why; my mind wouldn't let the words form.

"You didn't conjure a Scribe of Nurem," he said into the silence.

"Huh?" Three ghosts moved to and fro near the window in shivering blue. My hands started to shake like my vision. I didn't have the energy to wave these off again. "I'm the Goddess of Death. Who else would I conjure?"

I rattled the cuffs as he fished around his pocket for the key and held it out. The silver gleamed bright as polished cutlery. He kicked off the wall and leaned over me—taunting.

"If it wasn't a scribe, who was it?"

"You think I'm lying?"

"Yes," Blackthorn muttered. Blond hair brushed his collar and the silver glinted between his fingers. "The Scribes of Nurem lost their fingertips."

I clapped slowly, cuffs clanging against each other and my other bracelets. Sarcasm hid the fatigue nipping at my bones. "Doesn't bode well that you were the smartest in the room, but fine, you're right."

"Who was it?"

"A priest who died in the palace ages ago. Pour me a glass of wine." He eyed me a moment before he stalked over to a table where a carafe sat beside a glass. I didn't have the energy to stand, and even without the cuffs, I wasn't sure I'd ever conjure a Scribe of Nurem—they were dead in a way that was indescribable.

He poured a glass, drained half, filled it a second time, then passed the carafe to me as I swallowed my admiration of the corded muscle in his neck . . . and the way his wide hands dwarfed it. Orion Blackthorn wasn't a teenager anymore.

I took a swig and he pulled a chair around, sitting with his legs spread as he pushed up the sleeves of his shirt.

"So how'd you do it?"

The cuff clanged against my bracelets as I swallowed a gulp of wine. "With a little magic, I can shove the screams from everyone who died in the city of Linvia the day it fell apart into a single apparition. Your king deserved a little healthy fear."

"He's afraid of nothing."

"He's an idiot." I took another swig. "We're all afraid of something. What are you afraid of?"

Blackthorn watched me over the rim of his cup. "You."

"You're not taking these cuffs off, then?"

"Absolutely not." He made a show of pocketing the key as he leaned back. "I've heard the stories, Godkiller, and I'm not taking chances."

"Yet, you'll walk next to me as I restore the power you fear?"

He turned to stone. "I don't have much of a choice, since you decided to swear on my and my sister's lives despite not caring if I live or die."

"I'd prefer you die if it's any consolation," I snapped, carafe hovering at my lips, waiting to see how his face contorted.

"Clearly," he muttered, "but I won't let that happen, nor will you shirk your oath on account of my sister."

"Fine. If it makes you feel like you're doing something, who am I to stop you?"

"Exactly." The knight finished his wine and rose to his feet, pausing at the door as his amber eyes swiveled. "Do you want it? Your godhood?"

"No." That was the truth; what came next wasn't entirely. "I do not want it, and Tyrlas doesn't deserve the power, but more than that, I want these cuffs off."

"It's power that could kill a king." He eyed me, hesitating in the doorway.

I didn't stand down. "I could kill him with the shell of what I am today. Humans are nothing to a god, and he should be thankful I've shown restraint."

"Even in iron?" He took a step back into the room. Apparently, he'd reconsidered. My heart beat faster as he posed the next more-prying question. "Why agree at all? You owe nothing to Tyrlas."

I looked at the ceiling. "Can't I say I'm bored? And Relia was a friend I owe a favor."

"No. That isn't it."

"Isn't it?" My gaze flicked to the window where the ghosts vanished as if they sensed I needed space. The Tyrlian ghosts were less nosy than some—likely trauma kept them at a distance.

"Fine." Some honesty was easier than none as I picked at my gloves. "Magic does not belong in Miria, and I'd happily destroy the godhood of Death." I leaned forward off the bed, carafe dangling between my fingers as my eyes narrowed on him. "Now, are you going to be a good boy and tell your king, or does this stay between us?"

His withering frown brought a smile to my face.

"Can magic even be destroyed?"

I shrugged. His loyalty might be an unintentional benefit of my ill-conceived blood bargain. "The pieces can be slivered apart with the bone of a god and put elsewhere, but no, a godhood can't be truly destroyed until it's whole again. Only whole can the same magic destroy it."

"You've done that to your family?"

It was done to me.

Doubt flickered behind his eyes, showing in the creases around his lips.

"I'm not the Godkiller for nothing."

Blackthorn cleared his throat as he returned to the door. "I'll see you in the morning."

As it closed, every resolve I'd pushed to my face shivered and cracked. I wanted to kiss him again, but I needed to kill that mortal part of me. Kissing mortals led to fucking them, and fucking them always led to something worse, something destabilizing.

I wasn't immune to love. I'd found love too many times and let it ransack my reason. Love led me to stand in the ashes of my mistakes, soaked in blood that never should have spilled.

The kiss was nothing more than Ephraim's revenge for making him watch me devour his wife in front of his court. However, by the way she moaned, I daresay ours was the most memorable kiss she'd ever had.

What Tyrlas didn't know was that of every god and king over centuries, he'd finally offered me the chance to end the Pantheon for good . . . if I were brave enough.

"Sit, Foriana," Koros commanded. I burst into the Pantheon dining room, straightening my silk slip of a gown with one hand while trying to pin my hair properly with the other.

Armine and Max scowled as I sank down in the chair to the left of Koros, directly across from Niany, our mother. She wore an even more pointed rendition of Armine's expression: like she'd been forced to eat lemon peels at sword point.

Only Fortune spared the smallest smile.

"I'm not late," I stated, pouring a too-full glass of wine. "You all were early, just to act disappointed when you forget I rule a kingdom."

"You weren't busy ruling anything." Armine breezed past my comment and straight into an accusation with an eye roll. "Who were you fucking tonight? Couldn't be your husba—"

"Rich coming from someone whose personality is so undesirable Father pawned you off on some fae who'd rather be dead."

My youngest sister gripped the table, nails digging into it like she wanted to launch herself at me. I wished she would. I was born fighting; she was born in a palace. Soldiers called me general and Your Majesty while they whispered behind her back.

"Enough!" Koros bellowed and pinched the bridge of his nose, dark eyes and haunted expression caught only on me. "I will not have this discord at my table. Not tonight."

"What's so important that you called me here?"

Koros rose to his feet and surveyed the four of us—the gods he called his children, while Niany remained seated, staring vacantly at the wall. We were never her children, not really; only Armine was born to her in the Pantheon. The rest of us were turned or found.

"Fae spies for King Ilverleigh were apprehended at the northeast border. I will be declaring war." Despite a second gulp of wine, I sobered, the rim of a royal chalice frozen at my lips as he stared at me. "Foriana, I expect your forces and those of the Northwest to rally behind Pantheon banners. Maxentius—you will go south and appeal to King Leveandread. Armine and Fortune, we've discussed my expectations."

"Stay out of the way?" Armine offered and Fortune elbowed her hard enough to get a 'hmph.'

Koros's gaze narrowed on the princess with the cratering force of the King of Gods. "No, Armine. I need you to sway Rivendeer's queen. We'll need her cavalry."

"And me?" Fortune asked as Armine stiffened and scratched the nervous rash on her neck.

"You, my dear, will remain in the Pantheon with the Masters. General Yarvin will need communication with the scribes."

Fortune bowed her head and I chewed on my lip, trying to find a way to throw back my father's order as if I had any authority to challenge it.

4

A peal of thunder shook me awake. Punishing rain fell in sheets; the sound of it shattered across the window with every gust of wind.

No servant or guard woke me, no bell tolled, and the only sight out the window was shades of gray. If dawn had come and gone, I had no idea as I pulled clothes out of my trunk and stuffed them into a leather bag.

The halls of the palace were empty under Tyrlian rule. It was a stark change from the drapes and tapestries of the prior kingdom whose dynasty dealt in excess. Tyrlas was the opposite with their single god and disdain for color.

My footsteps echoed as I made my way through the corridors to the northern gatehouse where two guards stood under the overhang, rocking on their feet. No Blackthorn—no king. I couldn't even see the end of the yard through the sheets of rain.

Cold, drenching unknown burrowed into my bones, reminding me how far I'd fallen. Dead is what I should have been, but here I stood.

A guard cleared his throat.

"Glad I'm not going out there," he had the nerve to say.

My hands balled into fists at the disrespect, and I opened my mouth to say something only to be cut off when *someone's* blatant cough echoed through the stone corridor over the drumming.

Sir Orion Blackthorn strode up, tweed coat pulled over his shoulders and buttoned beneath a black cloak trimmed in gold. Exposed by the coat collar was the signature vestment of a Tyrlian knight: Simple armor covered in a fine layer of thin ochre suede that wouldn't survive this onslaught.

"Where are the horses?" I asked, staring into the wet abyss, bracing for the next insult.

"Don't need them. We're starting in Verinium." He adjusted the straps of his bag. "Queen Relia was at the library the night before she died and Tyrlas requested her research be left out. I'm sure you figured as much."

"The library is a half-day's walk—"

"Is a walk not something a goddess is capable of?" Half of his lip turned up as I frowned, indignant.

"Is your king not capable of sparing horses or mules?" I snapped. "We are descending through mountains."

"Suppose not." Blackthorn raked a hand through his dark blond hair, which had started to curl at the ends. Water gushed from a nearby spout. "Is Your Godliness below walking downhill? It's a trade road, not a wild path."

"I am not below *anything*, but I'd prefer to be above the mud."

"Then make it stop raining," he murmured, gesturing out with his arm. "That's something gods do, right?"

"Funny. Does your single, all-powerful *new* god listen when you ask him?"

Blackthorn's stare hardened. "We should be going."

I smirked, kicking a rock into a puddle. "You first."

"No, I insist."

His wide hand pushed me forward. I dug my heels in with a noxious glare.

"You are the big, brave wolf. You ought to go first."

"As a chivalrous *knight*—ladies first."

This time he shoved me. I stumbled into the pouring rain with an undignified squeal as cold water inundated every scrap of fabric I'd layered on. In seconds, it turned my braid into a wet rope that hit my back with a slap.

"Fuck you," I growled, arms still out.

The knight walked out from under the shelter of the gate-house. He remained smug and poised as he barged past, shoulder slamming into mine. A deep garble of thunder swallowed my groan as our feet sank into mud with every step.

The first hour of the journey was the purest form of torture. Rain continued with no end in sight as we scrambled up rocks and slipped on boulders. I twisted my ankle twice and hoped Blackthorn had found a way to kill me that I'd never considered.

Eventually, the downpour tapered off to a drizzle just as I'd come to terms with being wet for the rest of my endless fucking life.

"You said this was a trade road. Where are the merchants?" I asked as we scrambled down a narrow trail where a torrent of water ran through the middle of a narrow wash. "Carts do not drive on roads like this unless you know something I do not, which I find hard to believe."

"The trade road probably washed out. This is a shortcut."

I frowned as he drew his sword. We were descending and the brush was getting thicker. A few steps later, he swung the blade through briars while I cursed.

It wasn't a shortcut. We emerged from the mountain brush and onto the bustling main road in the Valley of Oslin well after midday, just in time for the sun to poke through hanging gray clouds and remind me exactly how wet my clothes were.

With every step through throngs of people and shouting merchants, Blackthorn relaxed, but dread kept tickling the nape of my neck like paranoia. It twisted every muscle in my back as I gritted my teeth every time someone dared to look in our direction.

How long had it been since I'd left the Tyrlian Kingdom? Too long. Maybe thirty years—if I didn't include a few escapes to the eastern cliffs. Miacor was the only city I'd seen for a few decades and with every step away from it, excitement burgeoned.

However, the feeling didn't last long. I learned quickly that when the knight relaxed, he filled the air by talking. First, he prattled on about the dead wildflowers crunching underfoot, which led him to a story about cloud patterns and weather movements as if any of it mattered. My hand finally itched toward my dagger when he'd moved onto stories of his mother and the Tyrlian library.

That's when I stopped walking so abruptly one of the trade carts nearly ran me over.

"Something wrong?" Blackthorn piqued.

"Doesn't your jaw hurt?"

"From what?"

"Talking to yourself for the better part of two hours."

He shrugged and kept on. I picked up the pace so I wouldn't lose him in the converging crowd. Night fell as we approached the gates of Verinium.

"It could be a conversation if you'd participate."

"Frankly, I don't feel the need. You fill the air just fine."

"Well, I prefer it over listening to you breathe."

"What's wrong with the way I breathe?"

He walked even faster, taking longer strides, forcing me to jog. "You take these deep breaths and pretend you're not winded, but trying to hide it makes it worse—like you're gasping."

"Strange to call breathing gasping. I can stop if you like."

"Stop breathing?"

"Yes," I snapped, picking up my pace to walk ahead of him. "It would be my pleasure if you'd stop talking about the fucking clouds."

Shouting ahead of us redirected our attention as carts and travelers were corralled to separate sections of the black iron gates and red brick walls of Verinium.

The city was hardly a city by classification, only by importance. It hadn't belonged to a kingdom in centuries. Half of Verinium was a library. It boasted the largest record of Mirian history and without it, there would be no city.

Gold-plated spires towered over winding streets and made it clear the city belonged to knowledge. The decorative use of marble and gold was banned everywhere but the library to preserve its importance.

With every step closer to the heart of Verinium, ghosts appeared. Some remained in my periphery as a flash of blue, but many were bolder. As we came to the main square, I swatted several away.

Verinium wasn't dissimilar from most cities, but dead scholars were some of the more belligerent ghosts. One followed us, always in the corner of my eye, two fingers on his lips in prayer. He had too-long hair and the armor of a knight from several centuries past.

"Have you been to this library?" I asked Blackthorn. He grunted as he stumbled over a loose cobble in the main plaza, distracting me from one ghost as another reached for him.

"No. Never had much reason to go to any library outside of Tyrlas. I suppose you've spent time here."

"I've spent time everywhere." I sighed, ignoring the way two other ghosts stopped walking to stare at us as people walked through them. "I'll speak with the librarian."

Every step was more familiar as we walked into the library, below massive marble columns that held up a grand dome with mathematical precision one could mistake for magic. Twenty-three desks were spaced apart, each with a librarian. Behind them, obscured by bookshelves, were arches, stairs, and winding corridors.

The dome above us was adorned with a dramatic mural of The Founding—a fabled story of the day primordials handed their knowledge of the written word to the gods, who would later gift it to mortals.

A hundred years ago, I'd translated the ceiling as a favor. The banners on it were written in *Priminian*, the language of the primordials. Their language died with their influence, and only a handful of modern scholars recognized the curved characters and dotted lines.

Pristine white marble ran along the floor and ornate plaster walls. Every chair in the room was fitted with red velvet upholstery, stamped with the Verinium crest of an open book and two crossed sabers. Each librarian also carried a replica saber with a gold hilt, reminding patrons that librarians are defenders of the written word.

Blackthorn meant to approach the desk, but my outstretched hand stopped him. Our wet shoes squeaked on the marble to the alarm of several people around us.

"Welcome to Verinium." A librarian stared at me from her side of the desk, watery gray eyes unwavering.

"Good day. We come from the palace of Tyrlas seeking information on Queen Relia's whereabouts." I rolled my shoulders back, slipping into a former life. "Sir Blackthorn is a knight, and I am a liaison for the King; we requested the Queen's room be left untouched for our investigation."

Blackthorn handed over several papers with a raised eyebrow. The librarian shuffled them around, assessing each swoop of the Tyrlian crest before she handed them back.

"Very well." She eyed the stamp on Blackthorn's hilt. My Tyrlian papers were tucked in a leg pocket, but I hoped I wouldn't have to admit it. "She was in the royal room and, per your king's request, no one has cleaned it."

"Thank you, Dame Gloria." I smiled as she passed over a gold key. I took it quickly and her gaze caught my cuffs where bracelets knocked against the desk.

"I hope you find the culprit. Queen Relia was a beloved patron and staunch supporter of Verinium."

"I have faith."

I pocketed the key and practically ran to the royal room, forcing Blackthorn to keep pace while I wound through a corridor, into a twisted maze of makeshift walls of books and scrolls. The ceiling narrowed the closer we came to the true heart of the library.

The library was deceptive because it was self-contained. Verinium knights belonged to no one but the chief librarian.

With a thousand corners, basements, and cutouts, anyone patient enough could hide easily.

"Spend a lot of time in the library?" Blackthorn asked, cutting through the renewed squelching sound of our wet shoes.

"I suppose I did. Verinium was a neutral city and a refuge." I shrugged. "Plenty of books to pass the time."

He followed me up one white spiral staircase, then another and another until we were in the right narrow corridor where the stacks leaned precariously.

The royal study had been in the same room for two centuries. Only monarchs and their nearest advisors, with written permission, were allowed in. I was surprised the librarian hadn't pressed us further, but maybe she caught the streaks of blue in my eyes.

"You knew the librarian's name," Blackthorn said.

"I didn't realize you couldn't read."

"What?"

"She had a nameplate." I twisted around a narrow corner toward an angled set of stairs. "For someone in the royal guard, your observational skills are disappointing. If you were my guard, you'd already be assigned to the kitchens."

"Is that why you're still queen?" he snapped.

How wrong the histories always were, but it wasn't worth correcting a man—let alone a knight who needed to believe his life of service had been worth the sacrifice.

The door gave way to an achingly familiar room . . . I'd fallen back in time, and for a moment, I wasn't wearing a soaked-through tweed coat but a gown of fine Cascaadian silk, spun from the extinct silkworms of the western archipelago.

Phantom hands ran along my spine and stopped on my—

Blackthorn tapped my shoulder and I remembered who I was as he let out a low whistle.

5

THE ROYAL STUDY WAS two stories tall, with ladders on either side leading to a rounded balcony of ancient mahogany spindles topped by a brass rail. Windows on the far side overlooked the lobby several floors beneath. Shelves heavy with books and haphazard stacks filled every part of the room.

Tomes were spread open across a massive mahogany table in the center of the room as wide as the domed ceiling made of frosted glass where an artist had painted the spring fields of Oslin Valley with its rich green grass and spattering of tiny red etriol flowers.

Some of the books open on the table were recent leather-bound copies with printed text, but many were thrice the size and handwritten—books from another time, preserved and saved.

"What are we looking for?" Blackthorn asked, turning over a large page of handwritten text with his finger while I peeled off my soaked coat and draped it over a chair in front of the fireplace. "I can't read half of this shit."

"Tyrlas was right." My gaze snagged on a page decorated with sycamore leaves written in Olfain. "Relia was looking for it. She invited me to the palace because she thought she'd located my godhood and wanted to warn me before your king found out."

"Why would she do that?"

I lifted my eyes to look at Blackthorn, but they caught on the ghost of a young woman standing off in the corner. "She didn't want her husband to have another weapon. Given his stockpile of black powder and the loyalty of the last pack of shifters in Miria, he has plenty without the power of a god."

"Why did you agree to look for it?"

"Didn't I say I was bored?" I twisted my braid around my fingers as I looked at the books, dropping my voice. "I want the cuffs off and I want the godhood destroyed."

"I can't let you destroy it."

"Well"—my eyes snapped to him with deadly force—"good thing no one can stop me."

Blackthorn turned over another page. I eyed the ghost again; she tugged at a ringlet of hair and opened her mouth. She wanted to say something.

"How did you lose it?" he asked.

I laughed. The question was ridiculous, like I'd lost some scarf or an earring, but he watched me, jaw stiff and demanding as his presence dwarfed the room.

"Carefully." Memories slammed against my skull like a high tide in the northern straits. I picked at the hem of my sleeve, unraveling one thread after another as Fate had done to me. "The first time, it was extracted. The second time, I'd cut it out, and the third time . . . I'm not entirely sure what happened—"

"I didn't realize godhoods could split."

"I'm special." I tugged off my glove and reached toward the ghost. The two largest moons, Ich and Ore, were high enough in the sky that I could hold her form for a few minutes. Magic prickled through iron as I pinched my fingers and reached for a corner of the veil.

The knight's eyes widened when the blue, ethereal outline of the young librarian bent in a bow.

"Rise. We were friends of the late Queen Relia of Tyrlas. Do you know her?" I asked.

The girl stood elegantly. "Of course, Your Majesty. I heard you arrived. If you'll remember, I served you in this same room shortly before the events in Linvia—"

"Forgive me." I cleared my throat and tugged at the collar of my blouse as long-forgotten faces returned and guilt wound around my ribs. "I appreciate your help, and I am sorry for what befell you."

She shrugged and stepped closer to the table. "I died well before then." Recognition flickered back with relief.

"You spied for me."

She nodded. "This is my four hundred and eighth year. You were kind, so I've kept many notes for you, knowing you'd return."

"I will find a way to pay you, Ira." Her visage flickered. I hardly had the magic to hold her steady, let alone speak. "What do you know of the Queen? We don't have much longer. My strength isn't what you remember."

Ira moved toward the table and gestured at the books. "These are the books I showed the Tyrlian Queen. She said she wanted to find your godhood, to warn you, and the night she died, she swore she found the locations."

"Did she die here?" Blackthorn asked, but Ira shook her head. The Queen's death remained a mystery.

"She died outside the city. The ghosts of Verinium are gossips—"

"Or she crossed over," Blackthorn offered and a pang of guilt shot through me. That was a myth; no one crossed over anymore, but it wasn't polite to take away hope.

"Few souls cross so quickly." I gave Ira a hard look. "Is there anything else you learned?"

"Can I shuffle the papers, Your Majesty?" she asked, cocking her head as her hands hovered over the table. She flickered again.

"No," I said, lowering my hands to the edge of the table. "This is all I can do."

"Ah." She looked at me, hesitating, but whatever memory she thought of, she swallowed. "There are two handwritten books. I can't remember the names, but the Queen stuffed her notes in the cover. They have what you need."

"Thank you, Ira." There were a hundred books spread open on the table. Her suggestion was barely helpful, but my breathing quickened and my vision wobbled.

Suddenly, she vanished in a gust of wind as the veil slammed closed.

"How long would she have lasted without the cuffs?"

I hated explaining myself to mortals, but what choice did I have? "Fifteen minutes, depending on the moons. Tonight, they're in a stronger position. Ore is in the fourth quadrant with Ich, and Rea is below the horizon."

"And with your whole godhood?"

"Doesn't matter," I muttered, beginning to flip through the handwritten tomes, looking for a slip of paper with Relia's handwriting.

"Do you have spies everywhere?"

"No."

"You said she spied for you."

I slammed the book shut and glared at the man as he hulked over the table, uselessly thumbing pages and staring at illustrations.

"I am not the only being who can talk to ghosts. I grant them the same trust I grant mortals and they've spied for me too."

"Fine."

I picked up a book and shook it. Nothing fell out.

"Where are the souls of gods usually kept?"

"Most die with their godhood, or remain in their shrine if they weren't properly destroyed. Koros found creative ways to keep mortals from using the power to make weapons."

"So, it *is* possible?"

"Unlikely. Not impossible." I flipped open another book filled with handwritten Priminian notes. "Several weapons imbued with godhoods were gifted to demigods and eventually wielded by mortal kings. Most are lost. I have a list somewhere."

Blackthorn moved to the other side of the table and paged through a different book, squinting at a page written in a language even I didn't recognize.

"And you don't know where the pieces of yours are?"

"I have an idea."

"Will you know when you're close to one?"

I bit my lip. Of course, I'd spent the better part of three hundred years avoiding them—I wanted to be mortal. For as much as I complained, I didn't hate the cuffs: They allowed me to feel what godhood had taken away.

"Yes," I muttered. "Every god has a stupid tree that calls us. It sprouts in the wake of spilled blood, pieces of godhood, and where our bodies rest."

"And what tree did Fate prescribe to the Goddess of Death?"

I rolled my eyes.

No one had asked in so long. The forests of Miria were built on the blood of gods and primordials. Most wild land was a temple to one forgotten god or another, and the thickest forests in the heart of the realm were formed by wars between mortals, gods, and fae. There were also the wars against elves, vampires, and other lost creatures but they were gone by the formation of the Pantheon.

"A black willow, with gold-tipped leaves and bark the color of the darkest night. That's what the Queen was looking for." I flipped the book open to one of the bookmarks—a piece of green ribbon.

A crude drawing of my tree stared back as I laid it on the table.

"Can't be terribly hard to find a black tree. I've seen a few before—"

"Oh?" I snapped and he looked up. "I've gone to war against my father, a hundred kingdoms, and the fae. Black willows decorate all of Miria, Sir Blackthorn."

He flipped through more pages in a similar book, revealing a pine tree with red bark and silver needles. "Which of your relatives is this one?"

"Not all gods are related," I said—and it was true. Centuries ago, there were hundreds of us, thousands even. "That was a good friend of mine. Horatio. His blood healed, which made him valuable. If you turn the page, you'll see a map. He was slaughtered by his brothers and his body dragged along a portion of the Diadeus River before they buried him in a shallow grave. It's a shrine now."

"What the fuck?"

I shrugged. "Gods were ruthless. Fortunately, Death was hardest to kill."

He flipped to another page and then several more. I saw my tree and looked at the ceiling. I didn't want to know what they wrote about me. There were thousands of versions, written by a million scholars. Some true, some false, some missed everything that mattered, and a few were more accurate than I cared to admit.

Most of these books were banned centuries ago. There wasn't a way to turn a mortal into a god, not without the full will of Fate, primordial intervention, and the permission of Koros—the long-dead King of Gods . . . my father. Even if the stars aligned, magic had been so reduced in Miria that no mortal could survive what we had.

Blackthorn shook a book and a letter fell out with Relia's handwriting.

He plucked it from the table and held it to the light.

"Dearest Foriana," he started dramatically and eyed me, waiting for my protest. "You've found this letter because you haven't found me. I appreciate our friendship, and I leave one last request. The locations I've narrowed down are three and I hope you know better, as your heart beats for Miria with far better timing than my own."

Despite his irreverence for her last words, my heart beat at the back of my neck. Emotions compounded; grief tipped over in a field of a thousand regrets.

"There is a forest in the heart of Reen, a cave near Dover, and—"

"And Belfiante," I whispered, "where the mirror ponds sing to meet the sky and a black willow weeps on the eastern bank."

My gut twisted into knots because I never forgot. Fate knew I'd never go back to that memory if there wasn't a bargain tied around it. Fifty years wasn't enough. Six hundred years wasn't enough. Not even a thousand years would be enough to stand on that shore.

"So you do know?" He lowered the letter.

"I had an idea."

"There's a warning here about poisoned sap."

I nodded. "The poison disguises itself as your favorite food. For you, wouldn't it be scraps of meat?" I looked straight at him and closed the book with a puff of dust.

Blackthorn hadn't moved as I reached for my damp coat. "Did you know all of these?"

I shook my head. "I knew Belfiante and Reen. I'm surprised there's no mention of Linvia."

"Are there four pieces or three?"

"Good. You can count."

"How many?"

"I don't know. I've avoided them and the borders changed rapidly throughout the wars. What is Reen now might have been Dover or Linvia, but I trust Relia and her scouts."

"How did you truly know the Tyrlian Queen?"

I stared across the table at him. The low candlelight made his amber eyes glow with threads of gold—a reminder of the wolf he'd inherited.

"Are you not going to make a joke about how I'd taken her to bed?"

Blackthorn shrugged and turned over another page in a different tome. "I thought better of it."

"Relia was a princess in her own right with far more land than Tyrlas. I served the Tyrlian court and met her several times. When the tournament came around, at the king's request, she told me she wanted out, and so we tried."

"I can assure you there are more ways."

"Well aware." I drew my finger across an open book describing a potion for coercion. "I wanted my debts to the kingdom erased and the cuffs removed. Doing what Tyrlas asked—vetting a champion and collecting a reward—seemed easy enough until he announced I'd be a champion too."

"So you fucked his wife?"

I raised my brow and looked Blackthorn dead on to see if the man blushed. "His wife came on my hand, gasping my name on his throne, just before your knighting ceremony."

Blackthorn froze but didn't bend his gaze or drop his shoulders. Perhaps he wasn't the celibate knight Tyrlas and his god required.

"It got me out of the city, but unfortunately, Relia wasn't so lucky. We hardly kept in touch until she thought he was planning something."

"Now she's dead." Blackthorn snatched the letter and stuffed it in his pocket. "We should go before the inns fill up."

"Fine."

The spend of magic had me feeling every scrap of mortality that clung to me like dew, weighing down every bone and memory.

There was a blacksmith five hundred years ago, then Leander—my king—my true heart, and Henry, who had started to slip from my memory, but I imagined he was dead now . . . like the rest of them.

So many times, I had stood in this room with people I loved, trying and failing to find ways to hold on to them because I wasn't better alone.

6

[An old diary entry, written in Dovrian]

*[...] We buried my father today in the old sea-
side town. Fortune said it might help if I wrote
to myself. It hasn't. My baby sister bowed when
she saw me. If I'm a stranger to her—who will
I be in fifty years?*

BLACKTHORN ARRANGED AN INN for us that was nearly as bad as sleeping in the woods. The bed was lumpy, the sheets were stiff, and we slept on bunked beds like vagabonds . . . not sponsored representatives of a king.

Blackthorn snored above, while two other men slept unsoundly in the other set of beds. One jerked awake every ten minutes and the other kept tossing and the bed whined with every movement.

I wasn't surprised the knight chose the cheapest place to sleep. Lately, the Tyrlian people believed in modesty for every facet of life, except the clothes of the royal family and their knights. Even nobles dressed in gray or brown out of respect and humility for their single god.

It was a recent change that would change again; religions and morals ebbed and flowed with the changing streams of the hundred Mirian rivers.

Sometimes entire kingdoms became enamored with the idea of a single god. Sometimes they returned to a Pantheon of hundreds, and every so often, others would pluck a living prophet or an unfortunate martyr to reflect their beliefs.

The gods were long dead, with one exception, and I'd been forgotten with a few devout exceptions. They didn't know Death was a selfish coward who never should have been awarded her post.

Death wasn't supposed to take, nor was she supposed to stay among the living. Death was supposed to offer comfort and ease souls into the daunting black of the next realm, where they'd be returned to stardust.

The other side of the mortal veil was my responsibility. Soon after I received my godhood, I served for a short time, flitting between their afterlife, the Mirian Realm, and my father's Pantheon where I lived under his rule.

Koros told me that holding the keys to the afterlife was an honor, but it wasn't—not to me. It was a punishment. In only ten years, I lost track of how many mothers wept in my arms, lost children I held as they screamed, lovers who thought they had a future, and how many thousand soldiers begging on their hands and knees to be sent back.

The field between space and time, mocked by the trees of my godhood growing gnarled and twisted, was as horrific as it was beautiful. I gritted through at the Pantheon's insistence until the First War of Kingdoms tore apart Miria.

Four factions clashed in the Great Green Valley, and in the space of a few breaths—between pushing a child into the river and clasping my hands around those of an elderly woman—ten thousand soldiers flooded my field.

Ten thousand men weeping, begging, tearing at themselves, clawing at the ground, trying to find any reprieve—any way back—as regret and finality settled over them in the afterlife.

A better god would have fallen to their knees and wept with them. A better Death would have taken every hand she could hold and soothed every soul with the gentle song only death could sing.

However, I wasn't a better god. I swallowed the song, shoved through the crush of soldiers, and ran away, vanishing from the field to the steps of my father's palace. There, I fell to my knees and screamed before the throne of Koros until my voice turned raw and my husband, my prince, dragged me out.

The memory escaped when the cool metal of a sharp, flat blade pressed against my throat—I hoped whoever held it wasn't prepared to use it as I opened my eyes.

A man hovered. Another had ungracefully dragged Blackthorn from the top bunk with a grunt and a curse. I caught the glint of a sword to his throat, too, which ignited a small rush of anger behind my temple.

"Can I help you?"

The man's hand twitched, his blade pressing harder against my neck, but I didn't move.

"The Duke of Verinium requests you."

I peered around him, leveling a glare at Blackthorn, whose eyes visibly glowed. He was close to shifting, but it wouldn't help us. Two other men stood behind him, knives in hand.

"I politely decline," I said, kicking him back with the brunt force of my knee. He stumbled and I sat up, eyes straight on Blackthorn, warning him not to make it worse. We were outnumbered; a wolf would turn this room into a bloody mess and a larger problem.

"I've never heard of a Duke of Verinium, but we'll leave now and cause you no trouble."

"Too late," the man spat. "Devereux already knows you're here and the banner you serve."

"Does he now?" I rose to my feet and took a step closer to the man. He seemed to shrink. "Bold statement for a man I've never met."

"You're Foriana."

"Prove it," I warned, reaching for my sack. We weren't staying a minute longer. "Everyone knows Foriana is as dead as the rest of them."

His eyes narrowed and a corner of his lip quirked. "Is that why you were in the royal study?"

Fuck.

"We were looking for birth records," Blackthorn offered, voice gruff as he calmed the wolf and lied with little effort. "Hardly strange for those of high rank in their own kingdom. The lady here is the king's royal consort. She's practically a queen herself and you invite war by intruding."

The man seemed to consider the words for a moment. His elbow drew back.

I ran for the door. Blackthorn could do whatever the fuck he wanted, but I didn't stop running through the dark streets of Verinium until I couldn't hear the lumbering footsteps of Devereux's men.

Dodging down a shadowed alley, I pressed my back against a stone wall coated in frost as I caught my breath. Some gods were blessed with grace and speed when their godhood showed; I was blessed with neither.

Blackthorn skidded past, still in human form and—to my surprise—not tailed by anyone.

"Blackthorn," I hissed and stumbled out of the alley. "We need to go."

"Obviously," he grunted as I grabbed his arm and pulled us back into the shadows. "Are we close to a gate?"

"Do you have the map?"

His eyes flicked up incredulously. "The map? Do I have the fucking map? Did I walk around the four men who came to kill us just to grab the map, Raven?"

"I grabbed my bag." I shrugged. "We'll be fine. Just north through the woods, along the lake."

"Fine," he grumbled, but we didn't have time to be angry. We had an hour before sunrise.

If a self-appointed duke was looking for us, it was safe to assume he'd paid at least some of the library guards . . . if not most of them.

I led the way, far from the library campus, and eventually through a small gate along the city's red wall. Thankfully, today was dry, even if a winter chill clung to the wind.

We didn't stop or slow down until we hit forest cover an hour later. Then I realized we didn't have anything more than the clothes on our backs, nor did we agree on a plan.

Sure, I could starve as long as I wanted, but it would be miserable. Too many times I'd outlasted mortal men in prisons who didn't believe me, but I had no intention of proving myself now.

"When we stop for the night, I'll hunt for deer or something," Blackthorn said like he could read my thoughts.

"A whole deer?" I gawked. "We're two people."

"If you want to spear fish or catch squirrels with your bare hands, I won't stop you."

I bit my tongue. Of all the things I'd hate to try a second time, stabbing fish was at the top of the list, and cleaning a fish was second.

"Fine."

"We go north," he stated. "Are you sure there's a village?"

"Yes. We won't stop at any of the larger towns, but there are small ones along the lake which should be safe. That gives us only one night in the woods. You have the purse, right?"

He patted his breast pocket for confirmation. "Were you lying when you said you'd never heard of Devereux?"

I shrugged again. "I've never heard of a Duke of Verinium. Chief librarian—sure."

"He's the chief librarian, but he made himself duke shortly after to justify more guards around the city."

"Devereux isn't a family name, and chief librarian has always been an inherited title for the Verin family."

"Correct." He nodded and glanced at the canopy of gold and red above us where the sun shone through gaps—not enough to dry our still-damp clothes. "He also owns the largest poison guild in the southern parts, which might have contributed."

"And no one's taken care of him?"

"The Prince of Poison? No, Raven. No one's 'taken care' of him."

"I'll add him to my list."

I pondered the change in the beat of silence. Few men survived long in forced positions of power like that.

"We'll stay in the village tomorrow night and start for Dover once we have a map and dry clothes," he said.

A breeze sent small yellow leaves raining down; I batted them out of my hair. My heart stuttered at the thought of returning to Dover. I'd been many places in the last three hundred years, but I couldn't bring myself to return there.

The memories in Dover were insurmountable next to Linvia. Both were twined together in history, but in my memory, Dover was something perfect I never wanted to spoil, where Linvia was ruined a hundred times over.

"Fine."

We trudged for hours in silence. Or rather, something that resembled silence once I'd tuned out Blackthorn's much-too-long story about getting lost in the woods for four days while chasing a pig, then another about befriending a dog in a thunderstorm.

I had no idea. I was exhausted before the sun set. As we rounded a hill, a stupor came over me when the light caught his dark blond hair, making it look nearly as gold as his eyes in the same light.

It was a stupid, too-mortal thought.

"Can we stop for the day?"

"Here? Are you sure?" Blackthorn asked, looking around the late autumn woods. The road was traveled, but we only passed a handful of people and the loudest noise came from the occasional wild breeze. We'd be safe enough.

"I won't make it another hour," I admitted, feeling fatigue settle deep in the back of my neck. "I need to sleep. I don't care where."

His gaze stopped on my cuffs and I thought maybe he'd reach for the key, but his expression hardened.

"How close are we to the village?"

I looked through the trees ahead of us. "Using my god senses—at least half a day."

He frowned. "That isn't true, is it?"

"No. Unlike you, I looked at the maps last night."

He scoffed. "You reviewed them so you had something over me."

"I don't need to hold anything over you."

"Don't you?"

I glared. "If I take this glove off, I can still kill you."

"Can you?" His eyebrow lifted, amused rather than angry. "I don't believe you."

"Remove the cuffs and maybe you won't find out."

"I know that's a threat."

He brushed past me, and I followed him several paces off the road to a small clearing, hidden by brush. The ground sank under my hand, still damp from the last few days.

Beside a tree, I wrapped my coat around myself and wasted no time closing my eyes, hoping the knight would take the hint to stop telling stories as he lit a fire, but before he noticed, I'd drifted off.

7

[Written on another napkin]

*Vinliana ← witch erases memories
(lives alone, near bog)*

THE VILLAGE OF EMBER rested on the shore of a wide lake at the base of the Xerxes mountain range. From there, it would be three days to Dover.

"Have you been here before?" Blackthorn asked.

I shook my head, unable to hide a brimming smile as we walked through a deserted dirt street toward an inn that sagged on one side but provided a fair view of the still blue water. "Never."

And I was *excited.* There were so few places in Miria I'd describe as new—so every step in Ember was delightful. There were divots in the road I stumbled over and six gas lamps along the main street that had been shaped into squirrels. A plaque outside a shuttered building said, "a dead man walked here" next to a terrible drawing of some family crest.

Towns like this were so far removed from the games of kings and queens. They weren't weighed down by memory and notions, so I could pretend to be mortal again.

The shop below the single inn had everything from a bakery to a cobbler and whatever sat between. I plucked out a map, a thick, ill-sized sweater, and some soap. I wasn't sure what Blackthorn made out with, but he had a new leather sack large enough for his coat, bearing the Tyrlian crest, and some of the smaller pieces of his armor that now smelled like wet dog.

Upstairs, I had my own room with a fire and a clean bed shared with no one. To celebrate, I peeled off my clothes and left them where the innkeeper said, having graciously offered to have them laundered by morning.

I rinsed off with a towel and hot water before I pulled on the new sweater and sat in front of the fire bare-bottomed with a fresh bottle of wine and several hand-drawn maps of Miria that all happened to be shit.

In the first, Dover was too close to the sea. Linvia appeared six days away on foot, but I knew it was only three—I'd made the trek a thousand times. It could be done in two days on horseback, or six hours if I resurrected a dragon . . . which I hadn't done in five hundred years.

The second and third maps weren't any better. I'd find them a home in Dover as a placemat in some tavern.

A knock rang, but before I stood, Orion Blackthorn loomed in the doorway wide-eyed, wearing too-tight pants and no shirt so I saw every deep scar decorating his wide chest.

I remained in front of the fireplace, maps spread out, hair unbound, with a wine bottle between my crossed legs, granting the illusion of modesty.

He blushed but wasn't embarrassed enough to back away and close the door. Instead, he pulled a bottle from behind his back and winked. "I see we had the same idea."

"Get out of my room," I snapped.

His broad shoulders slackened. "What if we trade?"

"Trade what? You don't even have a fucking shirt on."

"For an hour of your time, I'll trade you a pair of pants?"

I eyed the pants he wore, nearly splitting the seams at the apex of his thighs. Wine obviously muddled my reason as my gaze snapped back to his. "And what would you wear?"

"I have an extra pair." He looked at me as his brow furrowed. "What were you thinking?"

"I wasn't."

The knight disappeared, only to reappear a second later with a clean pair of pants. He threw it at my head, nearly sending one of the maps into the fire as I scrambled to save it.

He laughed and did nothing to help, but the pants were a welcome relief despite being too big and sloughing off my hips if I didn't hold them up. Clearly, Blackthorn was a wolf shifter, built for wars and kings, while I was a dying goddess practically drained of everything that gave me power.

I knew what I looked like.

My skin had mottled and grayed around the cuffs. Black eyes sunk into my face with threads still glowing blue if a flash of magic surged. And my hair remained the same as it had always been: Black, tangled, and too long for the amount of attention I paid it.

"Haven't I suffered enough of your company?"

Blackthorn sat beside me, clutching his own bottle as we stared at the fireplace and relished in the heat. It was glorious after a day in the rain and a night spent sleeping on cold, greasy mud.

"We have two more months of this, Lady Raven." He'd washed, too, with some strong soap of fresh pine and mountain water. Against my will, I admired his chest and the rivulets of hair covering it, whirling around scars. "If you're suffering now, imagine what fresh hell awaits."

My gaze flicked up and sobered. "I've survived years imprisoned, at least fifteen hells, and as many end of days—I will survive a knight who can't stop talking. But I never said I wouldn't complain."

I took a swig and looked at the ceiling. The rasp of shuffling paper filled the silence.

"You do complain an awful lot."

"I have a lot to complain about."

Blackthorn's face pinched as he held one of the maps and turned it upside down. "Is that why you don't have any friends?"

"You wouldn't know if I have friends."

"Name one." He looked at me, amber eyes amused as my mind turned through names. "Benvie. He lives below my apartment, outside the city. He's a friend. Then I had another, Lord Henry, but I'm not sure if he's dead. It's been a while, but he's somewhere south. Vinliana in Av—"

"Friends ought to know if the other is dead, don't you think?"

Friend was an understatement, and it scratched my heart. If he were alive, Henry would choke on the word, just as he had the first time I said it nearly thirty years ago.

Although friends don't leave in the middle of the night after six years of sharing the same bed. So Blackthorn was right . . . he wasn't a friend.

"Prison and exile made it complicated," I snapped. "What does it matter?"

He took a swig and shrugged. "Making conversation. It was that or ask if you killed ten thousand mortals or twenty."

"I'd rather you make a plan."

He sighed loudly as I closed my eyes. I'd been avoiding this journey for too long, trying to be something I wasn't in order to punish myself.

"Right," he said, pointing to the map with a heavy finger. "Dover first, isn't it? Three days away puts it closest. Then Linvia. She said you had something in both of those?"

I didn't open my eyes to look. "Dover, then Linvia, through the fields of Reen, and then Avilla through to Belfiante. We can do it in three weeks."

"And get back in three?" The papers rustled again, and I cracked an eye to peer at his confused expression. "It's at least six days to Linvia and four through the fields of Reen."

"These maps are shit." I leaned forward and pushed a different map toward him, pointing at a dot labeled the capital of Tyrlas. "Miacor is not on a port and Dover isn't *in* the Xerxes mountains. No one in their right mind has ever drawn the boundaries like that."

"Not once?"

I shook my head and reached for the small pouch I'd left on the bed after I changed. From it, I pulled a hardly readable map and spread it out, pointing at a mountain range behind my scrawled notes. "Even when Dover and Linvia were twin cities under the Morav Dynasty, no part of Dover touched the Xerxes."

His chin tilted as he looked closer, running a hand through his hair that defied gravity, no longer soaked with rain.

"What map is that?" He pointed at a worn one folded up near me.

"Mine," I grumbled and folded it back before he started reading it. "It's where I keep my notes."

"Why do you have three dates in spring on it?"

I stuffed it away and exhaled. "Couldn't remember the day I was born. Took a few Masters to find."

"Oh."

"Lost records."

Blackthorn cleared his throat and looked at one of the shit maps again, pushing past the reminder of who I'd been. "Queen Relia said something was in the highest point of Dover? You said it doesn't have mountains?"

I shrugged. "Maybe in an old report. Dover did get confused with Linvia for a century. Or Relia's scouts misreported a willow tree."

"I thought you didn't know."

"I'm not sure *exactly* where it is, but I have ideas."

"Why Dover and not the Kingdom of Foria?"

A deep gargle of shame rose and burned in the back of my throat.

"Foria was captured," I said, taking a generous gulp of wine. "My guards rushed me out long before anyone so much as cut my arm."

"Then what does it take to split your godhood? "

The bottle hovered at my lips as I considered, then I slammed it on the floor with a thud, biting the inside of my cheek as anger surged. "What does it feel like to shift into a fucking dog?"

Blackthorn laughed instead of bristling; the contents of his bottle sloshed. "Fair enough. I will not pry, but if you must know, the first time feels like being torn apart, and by the fifth, it feels like becoming yourself."

"You don't need to find ways to relate to me. I'm fine."

"I'm not enjoying this either." He frowned. "My sister's life is tied to yours and you fucking terrify me. Sure, a mortal is nothing to the Goddess of Death, but ask me anything, Raven, and I will answer. Is it so bad to ask for even half the respect so I can sleep at night, knowing she won't die?"

My eyes narrowed and I drew my knees up. "Your secrets are weird things you've eaten and truths you won't tell your mother. My secrets are histories that had to be unwritten."

He rolled his eyes. "I just want to understand what I'm walking into." His gaze fixed on the fire, and an ember cracked and sparked. "I'm not immortal, Raven. Help me understand."

"No one understands."

"I don't believe you've tried."

"Or I've tried too many times."

"Well, I'm lucky to have people in my life who took time to understand me and I'm better for it." He tipped his head as I stared into the bottle.

"I've been understood before. *I've* withstood wars and explosions and murder plots and everything else; I've stood in the center of a burning palace and walked away—"

"You've lost a kingdom, lovers I'm sure, and your godhood. And you stood behind lines of mortal men who held your banners and died beneath them so you could win an argument with your father."

My lips thinned. "Let's not list all of my failures, but know I do not seek to be understood. I only want to get out of this with my godhood intact, just as you want to leave with your sister alive. I will not break a bargain."

"You said you wanted to destroy your godhood."

"Maybe." I raked my hand through my hair, catching on a knot that took both hands to rip apart. "After I've fulfilled the bargain with Tyrlas, you and your sister will be safe. I swear it."

"Will Tyrlas?"

"Do you care?"

He shrugged, fingers flexing around the neck of the bottle. "Would you kill Tyrlas? Surely a king is nothing to the Godkiller of Miria."

"His daughter would make a better queen. She doesn't seem eager to prove anything, nor to fall into a stupid war with Rivendeer."

"I suppose." He scooted back and leaned against the bed, closing his eyes. "She trained with the knights since her eleventh year. Tougher than most of them, but not cruel."

"For a Tyrlian knight, you're not doing much work to convince me your king deserves to live."

"Maybe so," he sighed and took another gulp. "I believe in the Kingdom of Tyrlas, the will of man, and whatever the fates and our god have in store. If that's up to the whim of Death, then who am I to argue? Certainly, it's not treason if you rank higher?"

"I rank as good as nothing."

"Not true." He slammed down the bottle and wagged a finger. "I see you, Raven. Or should I say *Your Majesty*? You've been called them all, haven't you? Earned them—or something like that."

The words settled around the room and I drank more wine, trying to swallow the clawing memories and wishing these damn cuffs would come off.

Twenty-six years had taken too much, including the protective pieces of immortality that kept us sane—safeguards to numb emotions and dull back memories so they didn't hit with a mortal punch.

I should have worked harder to chew my way out, but the iron tasted horrible, and growing back teeth was even worse.

"I said too much," Blackthorn acknowledged with a wink of shame as he rose to his feet.

I shouldn't have watched him leave, but I couldn't tear my eyes from the way his honed, scarred back dipped to his hips, nor could I look away from his broad shoulders where the hair across it blended into his own blond in a perfect symphony that I was certain would look more tantalizing under a sheen of sweat.

The door closed and I groaned.

If this went to plan, if what the Queen wrote was true and I restored the missing pieces of my godhood, there was only one way to destroy it all for good.

I wouldn't do it myself. Blackthorn could kill me the moment I became whole in Belfiante and save the world from the Pantheon once and for all. No Pantheon, no primordials, no gods, no scribes, no magic. It's that vision of New Miria that fueled The War of a Thousand Trees—and it was for New Miria I sunk a knife into my father's chest.

Blackthorn was the key to my salvation and Miria's; I would make sure of it.

King Tyrlas never should have struck a blood bargain with a god who'd negotiated with fae. We only agreed I would return to Tyrlas with my godhood restored: He never said I needed to be alive.

Year 608, The Pantheon
Raven is 58

BELOW THE CRISP WHITE stone of the Pantheon were worn gray halls and dungeons that once held the cages of wild beasts for my father's arena. Among them, a large circular stone room with flickering sconces on the pillars had been left for me.

The room was forgotten. Dusty shelves scaled the walls, filled with ancient tomes in Priminian and a hundred thousand jars, many with long dried-out vials of age-old potions we'd lost the names for.

I'd shoved the tables to the side to make room in the center for the body of a black pixie dragon. She'd escaped an elven farm in central Miria and died along the way, but Koros brought her here because of his curiosity.

Footsteps echoed in the hall and I exhaled, pinching my nose. I didn't need an interruption.

"I'm almost there," I ground out, not turning because I knew the stalwart gait as well as I knew my own. His had a certain cadence, a rhythmic stomp that either meant sex or war.

Malcolm stopped beside me, pressing his hard body against my back as strands of silver hair brushed my shoulder. "Your father wants you in the throne room, love."

"Why?"

"He's trying to prove to the Vitrosian general that you are capable of leading an offensive on your own."

Malcolm's arm wrapped around my waist, fingers digging into my hip, telling me exactly where he stood on the matter.

"There is nothing I need to prove to mortal men."

"We feel the same, but it is your duty to the realm."

Anger stroked in tendrils of fire against the palm of my hand. I thrust my arms out once more and my bruised black skin turned to ice, brimming with cold blue magic as death coalesced. It gathered and concentrated against the dull scales of the dragon's corpse, turning an oily black as it seeped in and evaporated into smoke.

The pulse of magic filled the room, sparking and spluttering in a haze of shadow as it plunged into the corpse of the dragon. Jars chimed as the ground shook and a flash of white-blue light swallowed the dark.

The rush of power felt like waking up, like moving the world and creating from nothing. I held onto it with an iron will until it drained my limbs and unraveled. I waited, testing myself, hovering along some edge until Malcolm screamed.

In an instant, my arms fell to my side as I cut the power. It stopped: the room, time, my ability to breathe.

The dragon's eyes opened, staring with an icy, vibrant blue matching mine—no longer entirely what she'd been before. Her toes curled as she stretched and came to life.

I approached the beast, awed and terrified. I was the Goddess of Death. I'd raised men before, and lesser beasts . . . but never a dragon.

"You did it, Foriana."

I nodded, gulping as she spread her wings, sending Malcolm stumbling behind me.

"Her name is Rathe…" I angled my head at Malcolm, unable to hide the delight in my voice and the curl of my lips. "Should the general of Vitrios like to meet her?"

8

THE JOURNEY FROM THE village of Ember to the city of Dover was three days through rolling hills and generous meadows straight to the east. It wasn't difficult, but it was boring. We took the high trail between kingdoms, a path exclusively used to transport grain and produce.

The most excitement happened on the first day when a runaway carriage careened into a river. Blackthorn threw his pack at me, raced down the hill, and helped the farmer drag the cart to shore before the current swept it away.

Together, they saved a cartful of hay. It was impressive, sure, but less impressive the third time I had to listen as the knight recounted it to several merchants we'd set up camp with on the second night.

We sat around a fire, roasting squirrels and quail as someone passed around a bland cheese with hard bread. It might have been a feast if anyone had brought wine and olive oil. Instead, everything tasted terribly dry and stuck to my teeth.

"We're heading to Dover," Blackthorn answered when asked by a weaver with a lopsided smile and a bandage on his neck. "I'm escorting the Lady Philomena here to her late-in-life match—the charming Duke of Kenterly—south of Vharos. It's quite the story."

"Isn't the Kenterly duke a century old?" another merchant chimed in, looking at me more like a fixture rather than a person. Blackthorn passed over a spit of squirrel that was certainly overcooked after twenty minutes over flame.

"Actually," I said, "he could be two centuries old, but the accounts he holds make it easy to call him a handsome thirty-eight."

The merchants chuckled, and I frowned at the squirrel before I took a desperate bite; I'd eaten far worse but had hoped these days were behind me.

"She's lucky," Blackthorn continued as bit into the squirrel. "The duke doesn't care she fucked half of the southern reach—"

I spluttered, spitting the squirrel at the knight's feet.

"It wasn't half," I wheezed, coughing to stifle a laugh. "It was a harmless tryst with a butcher, but you know how those southern gossips can be."

They looked between us, but the lie seemed to settle with a murmur of agreement as one of them started another story about the Duke of Kenterly whom I had never met.

This became our game—an escalation of storytelling to see who could make the most ridiculous situation sound believable.

Usually, I wouldn't trust a group of merchants and farmers to keep watch as I slept, but the skies were clear and I saw the way they looked at Blackthorn so I settled with my back against a tree.

Eyes closed, memories disguised themselves as dreams and dragged me into an abyss. Faces from my past in Dover and Linvia gripped my heart with talons like an osprey. Phantom touches were reminders of the loves I'd once had and the blood that ran because of them.

In my dream, I drowned in silk and the earthy sweetness of a Dovrian meadow. Hands wrapped around my neck, sweat-slicked and panicked as a heart beat beside mine.

"I love you."

My eyes flew open.

No ghosts, no merchants, no silk, only Blackthorn sleeping just out of reach. My hand cupped my cheek; I'd been crying and my throat whinged as I tried to breathe.

I needed these cuffs off—even a flicker of my magic would soften the punch of memory. I couldn't fucking do this. I couldn't walk into Dover feeling everything. I needed the numbness of my godhood or I would crumble.

Blackthorn's chest rose and fell slowly; his snore punctuated the rattle of wind as he lay on his back.

If I shifted just a little, I might be able to reach his sword and threaten him for the key. I inched closer, careful not to snap a twig as I stretched into the space beside him where his sword and belt rested, still slightly out of reach, but I'd stolen keys in worse conditions.

Grass crunched with every small movement, but he didn't flinch as my hand wrapped around his sheath and I held my breath.

Just as I meant to twist the hilt, he grunted. I froze and watched as he turned over, exposing his back where his pocket folded open. Maybe I didn't need a sword, just some sleight of hand.

I let go of the sword and sidled closer, just a bit at a time until my front nearly flush with his back—my side covered in dirt and dry grass.

Then I reached, fingers light despite the gloves, as I settled my hand in the slit of fabric just over his hip. Gentle, careful not to breathe, not to touch, until the tip of my finger hooked around the metal ring.

I drew back slowly, holding my breath as he remained still. And just as my hand nearly slipped free, a force pinned me onto my back, dagger pressed against my throat, and the warm weight of him caged me against the ground, knee wedged between my legs.

Blackthorn's eyes were wild, wide. Bits of yellow and gold flashed through amber as he panted, fisting the shoulder of my coat with the hand that wasn't holding his dagger steady.

His eyes caught the glint of the keys where they'd fallen in the grass, just a hairsbreadth out of my reach.

"What are you doing?" he growled, but he didn't release his grip. "You didn't think I'd wake?"

"*You* were snoring for the better half of an hour. I didn't think anything would wake you."

He loosened his hold on my shoulder but still didn't move. "It takes two hands to unlock the cuffs."

"I know."

"You have a third hand?"

"I planned to use my feet."

"Your feet?"

"Yes."

The dagger left my neck and he leaned back in the grass, pocketing the key. I sat up and brushed off the dirt and debris.

"When I trust you won't kill me, I'll let you try."

I frowned. "I won't kill you as long as I need you."

"And what is it you need me for?" he asked. "Certainly not for company since you don't hear a damn word I say."

"Nor is it because you make a good knight."

He raised an eyebrow and his lip quirked up. The stubble on his face and the way he'd dressed down since Ember made him look different—softer. "That leaves only one option to keep me around."

"And what is that?"

"You need a handsome knight at your side more than you care to admit."

"No."

Blackthorn sighed. "Well, if you can't admit *that,* then I'll assume you're still thinking of ways to kill me."

"There is a world of other reasons." I bundled my coat and tied it. He watched, biting his lip, waiting to say something, but without another quip, he lay back again and closed his eyes.

I tried to sleep, but the memories of Dover were crushing. I watched the sun rise through the sparse branches of the swaying trees and blinked away the frost on my lashes.

Eventually, Blackthorn woke up and threw my pack at me as clouds obscured the sun. Without a word, we started the last leg of our trek through the prairies into Dover.

The landscape flattened, and despite my attempts, memories floated back with every step. If I felt a twinge of sickness, the first time I saw "Dover" in Relia's handwriting, I choked on it now.

The city of Dover I knew had vanished and the grief had no bottom. The nobles died out long ago, their lines destroyed by a tyrant king after the Morav Dynasty collapsed in its four-hundredth year. The surrounding land hadn't changed. Every step on the road, lined by dry waist-high grass and dead wildflowers served as a reminder.

Gray clouds churned and the temperature dropped overnight. We were in a season somewhere between the first frost and the first snow as we ambled along the main road, winding between horses, merchants, and the massive carriages loaded to the brim with wares.

Though it didn't sit on the ocean, technically Dover was a port city and the largest shipbuilding power of the kingdoms. It sat near a large lake connecting a vast web of rivers across the kingdom.

Dovrian shipwrights invented river boats that could move against the river current and transport twice as many goods as ocean vessels. The discovery turned Dover into the heart of the Mirian realm and the main port for over three hundred commodities at one point.

The only mystery was how the Dovrian language—of all of them—was lost; maybe trade favored languages more easily spoken over the beautiful ones.

A thousand people moved toward Dover, some with carts, others with livestock, but I pressed forward, dodging shouting men and nearly tripping over goats until we passed through the gate into the grand merchant square closed in on three sides by large yellow brick buildings. My chest constricted as we shoved our way through the crowd toward the winding streets that still felt like home.

"I'm choosing the inn," I muttered to Blackthorn as I stopped to peer through the crowd. Strung between buildings were banners in a thousand colors. Loud, jovial music drifted through the air, and with it, wafted roasted hazelnuts. "How much coin do I get?"

"Don't worry." He patted his pocket as we both watched a woman in a bright orange dress spin around. "King's purse. Although if there's anything with gold leaf, let's find something worse."

I rolled my eyes and dragged him through the crowd. We emerged through the gate into a city fully awash in celebration.

It lodged in my throat. Once they'd done this for us, with banners of black and white, splashed by cerulean. They roasted the same hazelnuts on street corners, served fried carrots with goat gravy, and sang hymns in Dovrian. The hymns resonated through the city with such power that they earned Dover the nickname: *Rivrrin Vei*—the Singing City.

Color saturated every corner, food vendors shouted, and hundreds of people chanted the same song as an old man on a tavern stool strummed a guitar. I caught a few lines in Dovrian and smiled. Perhaps it wasn't lost entirely.

Blackthorn followed closely, scanning everyone as if assessing a threat. Odd, because he wasn't nearly this alert in Verinium after we'd been cornered. He almost had the same pinched face and angry frown I'd first seen in Tyrlas.

In plainclothes, we blended in well enough, but Blackthorn still had the Tyrlian crest emblazoned on his hilt. That alone wouldn't go over well any further north, and certainly not in Linvia.

For an hour, we wound through the streets, getting closer to the city center but finding nothing. Every inn we passed was full, with rate signs draped in fabric, banners, or whatever the keeper got their hands on.

The city was so overrun we went down alleys, two seedy merchant streets, and nearly ten neighborhood streets only to find every room in the damn city booked until one kind woman suggested an inn on the south side of the city, near the main square I'd been avoiding.

I'd take anything now that the sun was setting. My feet hurt, my hands were cold, and every part of me longed to experience a bed again after three days on the damn road.

The tavern we passed was engulfed in shouts and screeching chants of "Troculus!" as I rolled my eyes. Troculus is who they celebrated—the god of plenty—a name he'd actually given himself.

"Everything else was taken." The lesser god once bemoaned to Koros from the throne room floor.

The King of Gods, however, had no sympathy for the mortal turned god because Troculus had gotten everything he wanted thanks to several cocksure bargains. On more than one occasion, to keep him in line, Koros threatened him with marriage to me.

After he died, the Dovrian prince and I dedicated several years campaigning for Trocolus's temples to be replaced with shrines to Etta, the goddess of fields and grain and the forgotten daughter of the God of War.

Apparently, the effort failed. The people of Dover were less practical than I'd hoped. Panic and burgeoning memories clawed at the nape of my neck with every step toward the main square of the yellow-bricked city where a stage had been erected.

Every street but one was flooded with hordes of people dressed in orange and black—a combination Trocolus surely would have hated—but there was one quiet street. On it, an inn sat between a boarded-up building and a quilt shop.

Inside, bare wooden walls had sparse windows framed by dusty white curtains. The innkeeper eyed us as we walked in, flipping through his books with a scowl. Beside his desk was a long, narrow bar where a bartender pushed heady beers, dyed an aggressive shade of black, at revelers.

"We need two rooms," I said, trying not to sound as desperate as I was.

His scowl deepened. "It's sacrifice night, m'lady. One is the best I can do."

Sacrifice night. I racked my head trying to remember exactly what it entailed. Some were kingdom-wide, others were local, and some were funeral events to see one duke to the afterlife and welcome another to the palace.

Trocolus wasn't the kind to demand sacrifice—I couldn't say the same for myself or others; we all had phases.

"Fine," I gritted out, snatching the key from his rough hand in exchange for a few gold coins.

An invasive spirit pressed along my side in the space between Blackthorn and me. I waved them off with a flick of my wrist as the man behind the desk raised a brow.

"Top floor," he said, gaze roving up to Blackthorn. "Room five, and dinner's at seven. The bath is at the end of the hall. I recommend ladies bathe in the morning or, at the very least, not alone."

"Thank you for the advice."

Blackthorn stifled a laugh but said nothing as we walked up the creaking, narrow stairway to the top floor.

The door opened into a narrow room with a bed larger than I expected. The window overlooked the street where people were elbow to elbow, creating a raging sea.

"Know anything about Dovrian Sacrifice Night—or Troculus?" I asked as the door closed and Blackthorn set his bag on the floor next to mine.

His face scrunched, like he'd gotten a whiff of turned milk as he unbuckled his sword belt. "It's one of the human sacrifice ones."

"Ah."

Ages ago there were a few cities and several villages that used sacrifice to get my attention. It worked early on, but the method fell out of favor within a century because I made a point of discouraging it.

Trocolus never listened and hardly did anything for the patrons who decorated his temples. Long dead, it felt even more wasteful to waste a life in his name. Whatever prosperity the citizens of Dover found, it came from them and them alone.

Blackthorn ran his fingers through his hair and looked everywhere in the room but me as I adjusted my coat. Something about Dover was setting him on edge, and I had no interest in finding out.

"May I have some coins?" I asked.

He clutched his breast pocket. "What for? You plan on leaving me alone in a city I've never been to?"

"Yes." I took a step, which constituted crossing near a quarter of the room. "I need warm clothes and real maps so this journey doesn't take us half a century."

"Half a century? You think I have that left?" He dropped several coins into my open palm. "Flattering."

"Make no mistake, I would kill you long before we spent a year trekking across the realm."

"No doubt," he grumbled and turned to the door as I dusted red rouge over my lips.

"Where are you going?"

He looked over his shoulder. "Same as you. Keep the key. I plan to settle in at a tavern."

"We're leaving at first light, whether or not you can walk straight."

The knight said nothing and left. I rolled the gold coins in my hand. I had more than enough for what I needed.

Downstairs, the pub had filled up.

I elbowed my way through the busy street and moved opposite the crowd.

No one recognized me. I didn't expect it, but every step through the emptying streets felt more like waking up in a nightmare. The street names had changed, statues were gone, and the facades were erased and built over. Every monument I knew was bludgeoned to rubble like the palace but the bones of the city remained intact, only painted over.

Leander and I would spend our summer nights wandering this part of the city when we couldn't sleep and now it was a similar kind of deserted. Past storefronts, across uneven cobble-stones, the memories in this part of the city felt more comfort-ing and less choking.

Shopkeeps stood against their doors, looking for anyone to come in. First, I stopped at the mapmaker's shop, trading half a gold coin for several well-marked maps of the northern territo-ries. Then I found a clothing shop, collecting more layers and a better bag.

North of Tyrlas, snow was a guarantee. The thought alone made me shiver. I might have been the Goddess of Death, but I wasn't impervious to winter. Until I was restored, I'd feel every bite of the wind and pelt of ice so I found wool socks and an old coat lined with down feathers and fur.

But neither clothes nor maps were the reason I'd come this way.

Dover was home to generational seers—not just someone who heard a ghost or brushed against souls, but rare seers who learned the art of ascendance, spanning generations.

They commanded and could peer through the veil in a way I couldn't. It was learned magic, somehow similar to mine or Armine's; maybe stolen from one god or another and passed down, but it was magic I needed. Only they were capable of listening to the grating voice of Fate.

I was still bothered by what the Queen wrote of the highest point of Dover. I appreciated her efforts, but it was a detail I couldn't look past and a question I couldn't bring myself to ask aloud.

9

[*A crumpled strip of paper*]

You laughed when you saw me, Irrivina.
I could see you from the dais.
- L

IT TOOK THREE SEERS and too much red smoke before I found one who wasn't lying about their ascendancy. The seer's room was modest, void of crystals and other accoutrements, which never held magic properties, even in the days before—when magic lived as free as the summer breeze.

Her shop looked more like a noble's drawing room, with frescoed walls and thick, unwrinkled maroon curtains framing wide windows as the sun sank, casting the room in gradually darkening orange light.

Brass baubles sat on one display table, and red smoke only rose from a small stick of incense near the fireplace.

The seer watched me from across a modest kitchen table as an attendant poured two cups of a ruby-red tea matching the shade of her wild hair.

"To what do I owe the pleasure, Your Majesty?" She purred, and in the waning light, her narrow eyes turned black as she stared at my gloved hands. "The ghosts whisper your name through Dover."

"Raven," I spluttered—wanting to push out the past a little longer. "My name is Raven. I'm looking for something."

"I suspected." The woman smiled and waved off the attendant who closed the door and left us alone.

I observed the room a second time before I lowered my voice. "I'm seeking my godhood."

The seer stiffened, but her demure smile didn't falter. She leaned forward, a bracelet of onyx stone thunking against the table. "It will be weaker than you remember, and there will be costs for taking back what you were given, if I understand the warnings."

"Some of it was forcibly taken." I pushed down the memory with a deep breath. "I want it destroyed, but the godhood of Death needs to be whole if no one else should have it."

Her eyebrow arched. If I looked closer, wisps of ghosts and souls moved just behind her irises in wisps of blue—much like mine.

"Have you considered what your absence might leave Miria open to without the protection of gods?"

I shook my head and raked my hair from one shoulder to the other. "They will bear it or capitulate. Same as mortals did for primordials, fae, and gods. I am not a stewardess."

The answer hung in the air as she chewed on her dark red lip. "Why didn't you return?"

"Excuse me?"

The woman cleared her throat and looked past me as red magic overtook her irises. My mouth went dry. "You were trusted by Niany and the primordials with the crossing of souls and you abandoned them"—I straightened in the chair and considered running as she continued—"no boat, no way to cross but swim the channel of life that drains and destroys or *wait*. They call you reckless and a coward as they bide their time."

I deserved to be called worse.

"I never wanted to be responsible. Is that enough of an admission? Their souls are worthless to this realm."

"You would damn children to wander?"

"If that's the consequence of my actions, I cannot deny it." My hands balled into fists. I'd recognize Niany's cutting disappointment anywhere—I spoke to my mother now, not the seer. "Are you done interrogating me?"

The seer shrugged and leaned forward on her elbows. "You can leave if you want, but seers have been bound to hold you accountable. Or do you forget? Niany blessed our order to keep you in line as part of your bargain. We are not part of the Consortium."

I cursed at the ceiling. This was why I hadn't sought a single one out in centuries.

"What is the cost?" I reached into my pocket, knowing it was only a gesture. Niany would ask for sacrifice—that's how the Goddess of Life worked. Something about balance.

"Agree to return, cross the souls, and fix what you broke before the magic leaks back into this realm, unbidden."

My mouth opened and closed without a sound. By choice, I had never returned. Niany knew better than anyone else. "Why? It's been six hundred years; they should be used to it."

"They are as restless and tired as you, *Raven*. Only the monarch of death can give them relief. If you want your full power back, and that of the gods, you have to let the souls go."

"The gods should stay dead, and I will fix nothing," I muttered. "No one should have power when it only wrought destruction. Even you were relieved when Koros died."

"He was your father, Foriana."

"Just as you were my mother?" I scoffed and cracked my neck. "The blood of my *family* created forests where the trees whisper and spirits sing—I don't care. I've had everything and lost everything. I'm doomed to wander, just as they are, and I have no interest in continuing."

"Why? There are a million million souls in wait, unrested. Don't they deserve peace?"

"Do not guilt me as though I'm at peace." I glared. "The power of crossing them could restore gods who hadn't died properly. You are not so selfless."

"Perhaps power like that might revive Leander."

The room stopped and my voice dropped. "Do not say his name when you have not earned it."

"Isn't he the one you came to ask about?"

Of course, she knew.

Grief wrote itself across the lines of my face. Dover was a memory and the largest thread of it was tangled around him. "A friend believes a piece of my godhood lies in the highest point of Dover, which doesn't exist."

"Agree to release the souls you've abandoned and I'll tell you the truth."

"I've given you one bargain already, Niany," I warned. "I will not strike another to undo what I've worked so hard to create. You want me to tear the realm apart and—"

"Be forced to face them? The Pantheon whose judgment you deserve? I know what you're afraid of, and it makes you a coward."

I breathed slowly, measured . . . holding myself together. This was a terrible idea and now my mother stared me down from the prison in the afterlife I'd made just for her.

"I am not afraid of them, *Mother*. I am tired. So long as I keep this curse from anyone else, I do not care. I cannot take it anymore."

She lifted her chin, red hair spilling over her shoulder. "Is that why you have cuffs on your wrists?"

I held them up for her, ignoring the derision in her sigh. "Primordial iron because I did what I do best and pissed off a king."

"You are a goddess, Foriana. No mortal hand would be able to cuff you if you weren't so headstrong." I was a girl again, on wobbly knees in the center of an arena. "Funny, you think your godhood could ever be whole when you've let it split so many times. If Death was so easy to kill, don't you think someone would have done it by now?"

I leaned over the table, staring through the seer and straight at my mother.

"If I fall short, then may Niany rise and cut my head from my shoulders like she's always wanted."

"She will—gladly."

My mother armed herself with words—she'd never strike another way.

I sighed. "Once restored, I'll do what I can to cross them and seal the afterlife. If it wakes the gods, you will deal with them, and I will not. Instead, I will die knowing how damn close I came to eradicating all of you and wiping your undeserved power from this world and the next."

"Or you'll finally take the Pantheon as you always desired."

"If that's what you think, you have never known me."

"On the contrary, daughter, I know you better than you know yourself. The moment power rears again in your blood, you will not see the world the same. Koros did you a favor and you were ungrateful."

I looked at the ceiling and gritted out. "Where is it?"

When I looked down, the seer smiled as—I imagined—the voices in her head fell quiet. Even as a shadow of herself, the goddess's absence was distinct.

"Your godhood lies in the forgotten tombs of Linvia that had once been Dover," the woman said with the breathy cadence of reciting poetry. Her black eyes stared through me. "Your willow grows within the mountain in the northernmost cave, a day west from the end of the city road of Linvia. From the mont, you'll see the spires of Dover as they'd been once before."

My lungs constricted.

"That mountain is a full day north of Linvia. Maybe two."

"You knew the Morav Dynasty better than I. They wanted their dead to rest, away from robbers and thieves."

My voice skipped as I twisted my hands. "The Morav Dynasty shared little about death—" It was a privilege reserved for the family, and marriage was only one step toward becoming family. The final step, which opened up the trove of secrets, was a child . . . an heir.

"Do you need me to write it down?" she asked.

"No. How many pieces?"

The woman paused and closed her eyes. "Three. Two in mountains and one in a field. A fourth waits, but it will not make you whole."

"Reen, Linvia, and Belfiante," I whispered. "Where is the fourth?"

Her face pinched as she tried to look. "The Pantheon? But that is not clear to me. What is clear is that you retrieve it last."

"Right," I muttered, mind turning over, confused. "One more question. *Miryanai*—a god knife carved from Malcolm, the God of War. Where is it?"

"Buried with the artifacts of Foria. Your heart will find it first."

I frowned at the ambiguity and pulled at the frayed sleeve of my coat, unraveling a thread. "The artifacts of Foria were sold and scattered across the realm by pirates."

"I've told you what I see."

I opened my mouth to argue but thought better of it, rising to my feet. "Thank you."

Outside, the sun had set and the streets were quiet as all three moons lingered above. Every street closer to the inn was packed with more and more people until I elbowed my way through to the door of the inn.

Upstairs, the room above the street was a welcome relief as I dumped my maps and clothes on the floor. Blackthorn had been back too; a new map and another clothing box sat on the chair. He'd picked the lock, but I wouldn't let it bother me because the dreadful conversation with the seer confirmed my worst fear—*I was right.*

A sliver of my godhood was left behind when my heart cracked open: In all the places I avoided. I'd always be drawn back to Belfiante, but I feared the others just as much.

It would never be easy to fix the mess I made and end the reign of gods. I deserved the waiting punishment and looked forward to breaking my promise to Niany as I'd done many times before.

I was resourceful and cruel. Early on, I learned the Goddess of Death had as much power over life. When it came to the gods, I learned I could prevent the entire cycle and starve the world of their power while my father and the fae squabbled over the natural magic of Miria.

Niany was right; at first, I *had* wanted the Pantheon because I wanted to usurp Koros and lead a New Miria as the Queen of Gods. I never stopped wanting it, not until . . . Maybe I'd want it again when I restored my godhood, but that's where the knife came in.

The knife would end the gods once and for all.

I pulled my coat on and tied the waist. Dealing with the future was a useless endeavor when I hadn't dealt with the present, which included finding something to eat.

Nothing changed as I walked through the streets: I would restore my godhood and Orion Blackthorn would deliver my body to Tyrlas, alleviating the Mirian realm of the gods who didn't deserve the power they'd taken.

Cheers echoed through the winding streets and jolted me back. *Sacrifice Night.*

Celebrations weren't a favorite, but sometimes I couldn't resist the infectious energy, especially when I was hungry and ready for a drink.

Every street I turned down grew quieter until I found one quiet enough to sit alone, and unbothered by the Tyrlian knight, with hot food and a carafe of wine.

I'd planned the perfect night.

Instead, I turned a corner into commotion and shouting. Cursing my curiosity, I elbowed my way through, glad I did because I'd never smiled so wide.

Orion Blackthorn stood in the center of a crowd; his shirt torn open, a cut across his cheek and his dagger drawn, pointed at a large man with a twisted mustache. They circled each other, taunting—anger written across both faces in hard lines.

The man threw his knife to the pavement and Blackthorn did the same, then they lunged.

Blackthorn dodged several heavy fists and landed two swings of his own, but the other man kicked out Blackthorn's knee, sending him stumbling into the next blow, a hook straight to the space below his ribs.

A minute later, both men were bloodied and bruised, scrapping on the ground, trying to pin the other as sweat and blood clung to their skin. Another swing collided with Blackthorn's jaw, and I had enough.

I still needed him conscious tomorrow to make it to Linvia, so I removed my glove and lifted my hand.

Dover had plenty of willing ghosts, and the three moons shone so my meager magic would hold. I pinched the veil and willed a few of the standing spirits to show themselves only to the man. Three women took up the request. One must've died terribly; her head wavered on her neck, even in her spectral form.

The three stood at the edge of the crowd, glowing, transparent, frigid and disparate as they stared at Blackthorn's opponent. The man stiffened under him and his eyes widened.

Orion twisted to see nothing as the three women lifted their arms and smiled. The man's face turned white and he scrambled back, tears in his eyes, as the ghosts smiled hauntingly. Instead of being confused, Blackthorn stood, focusing on me. I took several steps into the crowd, putting my glove back on, hoping to disappear like the ghosts.

I didn't know where I wandered, but away seemed good enough. I escaped around a corner, stopping in front of a single lamppost where a man in an apron watched the crowd.

Before I dipped in, a hand caught the crook of my elbow and violently pulled me back.

"What the fuck was that about?" Orion Blackthorn spat, blood covering his teeth. More dribbled from his nose as a purple bruise formed around his eye.

"No 'thank you'? You're already going to be a sore sight when we leave in the morning. I made sure you can still walk."

"I've had worse." He blustered past me into the pub.

I groaned and followed, not entirely sure why I was putting up with his company. I could let him die and find someone else for what I needed—of that, I was certain.

He threw himself into a wooden booth; I sat across.

Wordlessly, the bartender set two glasses of some fortified wine in front of us. It was a common drink as the entire region of Dover was fickle when it came to grapes, but they were determined to grow them. If the harvest was bad; they'd just make the alcohol stronger and sweeter.

The first sip was sweet and bitter, but not entirely unpleasant, as the warmth of liquor calmed the frustration buzzing on my tongue.

Blackthorn looked atrocious sitting across from me with his torn, bloodied shirt and bruised face. Blood was crusted in a piece of hair that he raked away from his bloodshot eyes.

"What was that about?"

"An old friend. Please leave it."

"If that's how you treat friends, I'll be pleased to be your enemy."

The knight said nothing and dabbed the corner of a napkin into the wine and used it to wipe off some of the blood from his nose and the cut around his eye.

"Tell me about your day," he said through his teeth. He'd been testing my patience for days now. This was my chance.

"Thank you for asking." I smiled politely as though I were a lady having dinner with a lord. "I bought some clothes and some maps to replace the ones we'd lost. We'll need to go to Linvia straightaway. Dover is a dead end."

"How do you figure?" He frowned, and a moment later, a roasted chicken and two bowls of broth appeared.

"An old friend told me."

"I thought your friends were dead or drunk?"

My gaze flicked up as he ripped the chicken apart with both hands.

"I do see ghosts."

"Everywhere?" he asked with his mouth full before he gulped it down. "Seems quite frustrating."

"You have no idea."

Blackthorn took a steady sip of wine as I did the same. "Linvia? You're sure? There are smaller cities and villages that might be—"

"Linvia." I hardened; there weren't words for how little I wanted to go back. "As I've always said."

"Right, whatever," he grumbled and ripped off more chicken. "If you insist on going to the largest city in the north—when we've already been chased out of a smaller one—who am I to stop you?"

"Linvia is safe, so long as you get rid of your Tyrlian sword."

He glanced at his waist, but he'd left his sword in our room. "What's wrong with my sword? Sharper than anything around here."

"The northerners call him the tyrant king. His crest puts a bounty on your head."

"Oh, you care about my head now?"

"Believe what you want."

"I believe you care and just don't like the Tyrlian crest."

"Fine. Keep the sword and remove these cuffs. I'll protect the both of us."

He considered it for a moment, then stared at the mess on his plate. "No."

We ate in silence. Once I finished, I set a handful of coins on the table and rose to my feet.

"Leaving already?" Blackthorn asked with false remorse, wiping his hands on his pants.

I nodded. "I'm getting sleep before we get on the road at first light."

"Do gods *really* sleep?"

"We lie horizontally and stare at the ceiling, waiting for the next day."

"Remarkably similar to how I sleep."

"Of course it is."

I didn't wait for another response. He knew where to find me and, if he knew what was good for him, he wouldn't find himself in another fight.

Year 568, The Pantheon
Raven is 17

"WHAT DID YOU DO?" I asked, hearing the grating hysterics in my voice as I lay on the battlefield, knowing I should be dead. The King of Gods hovered over, his form blocking the sun as a smile curled over his features.

Arms of two soldiers dipped under mine, lifting me to unsteady feet as my head lolled. I coughed and blood spluttered. I was dying, my resolve slipping as black tunneled my vision. One of my lungs had been punctured.

"You proved yourself," Koros said. My world turned over like the axis of earth tilted or a moon collapsed. "Welcome to the Pantheon, Foriana."

"No."

The field was full of dead and dying soldiers. Their cries and screams rang through and rattled my head; it was the worst noise I'd ever heard

"I don't want it. Let me die. Please, Your Eminence, leave me here. I don't want it."

"Too late, little bird. It's written in the stars." His voice was cruel and patient and sorrowful in the same exhalation.

"Stars?" I thrashed against his soldiers and tried to escape, but then I forgot.

I woke up ravenous with the iron sting of blood in my mouth.

The curtains of the room were drawn and my skin was on fire. No, not fire. Brimming with power? It tingled and rolled through in waves. I rushed to the window and threw it open, hissing at the bright light.

It burned, but my eyes adjusted as I blinked. After minutes, or hours, I could open my eyes but I didn't recognize anything. The world outside the window was full of white marbled walls, painted frescoes, fountains, gold, and bushes trimmed without a leaf or flower out of place.

I died. This was it; this was the garden my father told us about in his stories of the primordials and their gardens for souls.

The room was nothing like our creaking house in the village, with its warped wooden walls and too-small door.

The walls here were gray stone with white rivulets. The ceilings and pillars were carved in detailed motifs of flowers that looked real enough to pluck. When I didn't smell blood, the air was punctuated with jasmine.

The door opened and the King of Gods strode in, dressed in gold finery. Nothing like the man who pried me off the battlefield.

"You have given my staff a great fright."

"Have I?" I remembered nothing. My head pounded and filled with fog; my voice scratchy as my body hummed.

Koros stopped beside my bed and looked at me as the curtain slipped from my fingers and darkened the room. His eyes were black, but they crackled with gold like the lightning legends said he contained.

"Your training will begin after you've been announced."

"Announced?"

"Yes. Announced as Princess Foriana of the Pantheon—Goddess of Death."

Death.

That was impossible.

We already had a God of Death.

His name was Ersos and I'd left flowers on his altar and whispered prayers in his name.

10

THE INN WAS QUIET as the celebration raged elsewhere. I spent the evening bathing, reading, and drinking more fortified wine in front of a large fireplace in the lobby until the first bawdy man came back.

I barely heard him stumble in over the thousand memories of Dover. Of the gardens we built, and a city that welcomed us with music and food, in a time where I thought we had forever to make Miria something better.

Wine couldn't drown out the worst of it. If I closed my eyes, I could feel Leander's hand slip in mine or the way he laughed when his fingers got stuck in my hair. All of him was forgotten to time because we never had enough.

I drained my glass and retreated to the bed we'd paid for, but sleep never came because my mother's words kept prodding me awake in concert with a group of restless ghosts. They padded around the room at the top of every hour, briefly filling the space with bright blue light while they paced from the window to the door.

I waved them off, only for them to reappear, unaware I'd excused them.

By the third appearance, I sprang up and approached the tallest, gloves off so he saw the trickle of magic if the flash in my eyes wasn't enough. If I used too much, maybe it would help me sleep.

"Can I help you?"

The ghost's eyes widened and the two men behind him did the same. They stared straight at me, realizing they weren't alone.

I rolled my eyes; I didn't have the fucking time.

"What's wrong?"

The first said nothing, and the second opened his mouth, but no words came out; even his breath hardly made a noise.

"Right, okay, anyone else?"

They looked at each other. Another tried to speak, but only silence spilled out as their lips formed shapes without sound. I relented; ghosts like these were tortured and too familiar.

"There is nothing I can or will do for you. Let me sleep or I will make your night worse than it already is."

Perhaps I shouldn't have threatened them, but before I could regret it, the door flew open and Blackthorn stumbled in with a curious look on his bruised face. The ghostly men dispersed in a puff of air.

"Ghosts?" Blackthorn asked, a corner of his lip quirked up, amused as he walked in and slung his bag and coat onto the floor.

"Yes."

"What did they say?"

"Nothing." I padded back to the bed, hoping to grab a few hours of rest, but I paused at the edge, fingers on the sheets as my voice dropped. "They were suicides. Tongues cut. I imagine that's why the inn isn't full."

"Gruesome."

"Mortals often are," I said, slipping under the covers with a yawn.

"Can you do anything for them?"

The knight's cheeks were pink, tinged from the cold and ale. His blond hair was still crusted with blood.

"No." I thought about the state of the afterlife—it very well might be worse than this. "I don't have the power to give them peace."

"And if I removed the cuffs?" He tapped the pocket of his pants where the key jingled. His eyes stuck on my blackened fingertips, reminding me to tug my gloves back on.

I eyed him. He wasn't serious, not without a string to pull, but he might have been drunk. "My touch would put them to eternal sleep, as it does to mortals."

He seemed to entertain the idea and took a step closer. "I thought you could do that with cuffs on?"

"Do you want to find out if I wear gloves for fun? I don't make promises I can't keep."

He shrugged. "Ladies' fashion never held much appeal for me. If anything, I find it detracting."

"Distracting?"

"No." His face scrunched, second-guessing his choice of word. "Detracting from the other stuff? All the metal, the fabric, and the ribbons get in the way of . . . Surely you know what I'm trying to say."

"Are you admitting you struggle to undress women?"

Blackthorn's cheeks flushed as he looked for a way out of my forwardness. I dragged the itchy sheets to my chin.

"I'll have you know," he said, letting out a breath as his fingers combed his hair back, "I have never struggled, but I still find it rather annoying. Now, move over."

I gawked. "You are *not* sleeping in this bed."

"I paid for it!"

"The king paid for it." I tugged the covers tighter as he fisted them from the other side, threatening to pull me with them.

"I need sleep to heal."

"Whose fault is that?" I glared, looking at the blood on his shirt and the bruise around his eye. "You'll sleep on the floor."

"Like a dog?"

I tugged the blanket again, but his grip didn't relent.

"You do stink like one of the tavern dogs that sleeps in barrels."

Blackthorn released his hold, nearly sending me tumbling off the side as the door slammed.

Wherever he went, I didn't care. Until he came back several minutes later with wet hair, smelling pointedly of cheap pine soap. He plopped down on the edge of the bed, but I didn't move.

"Better now, Your Majesty?" he asked gruffly. "I'd like an hour of sleep, which will not happen on the floor. I will not touch you if that's what you're so worried about. Even a king's dog can be a gentleman."

"It isn't that," I whispered, triple-checking my gloves were secure. Something nervous flitted in my chest, a warning, begging me to look away from how the moonlight hit his back and shadowed the scars across it.

"Please."

"Fine."

It wasn't worth the fight. I turned over and seethed about it until, on some fucking moon, I didn't wake up between nightmares. Instead, I woke up to morning light peeking through the curtains and the frost on the window.

A weight draped over my ribs that hadn't been there, and the heat of a broad chest pressed against my back. I stiffened as Blackthorn's hold on me tightened; his arm adjusted on my waist, lingering too long on the curve of my waist. Gods, I wanted to pretend he was anyone else. I wanted to lean into the heat and lose myself in the ecstasy of touch.

One more second. I squeezed my eyes shut. His chest rose and fell as my breath hitched. Fingers pressed into my hip, gently pulling me into him but that was too close. I bolted out of bed, gawking at the knight who blinked away sleep as realization struck.

Then he jumped as if a cockroach had fallen into the sheets.

"I-I didn't," he stammered. "It wasn't—"

"No, it *wasn't*," I said, crossing the small room to stuff my things into a bag and layer on the clothes I needed. "It's dawn."

We dragged ourselves together and left the inn for the deserted streets of the city still asleep at such an early morning hour. They were littered with the colorful evidence of celebration as the sun crept over rooftops and warmed the frost that had settled overnight.

Confetti of dried flower petals eddied like a flurry of snow as we stepped over cracked bottles and fake blood someone had spilled between some of the cobbles. The air was perfumed with old ale, dying leaves, and the impending sting of winter.

Though the skies were blue, the dropping temperature promised no relief as we started for Linvia. I shivered, pulling my new coat tighter, wishing I still had some wild magic, but I couldn't scrounge up anything through primordial iron. Death was the only thing stronger and would never warm my bones or light a fire. I was mortal in every sense but one.

Blackthorn cleared his throat. "How far is Linvia?"

"Can't read a map?"

I glanced over and no playfulness glittered in his amber eyes. A purple bruise decorated the side of his face and crossed over his nose, emphasizing his scars. Perhaps he was in more pain than he let on.

"Two days on this road."

Blackthorn looked around and grunted in acknowledgment. We were in the wide-reaching mountain valley of the Linvian range; part of it named for Dover and the other for Linvia.

Alongside the range, between river cities and sparse, short forests, were flat and arable swaths of farmland. Several months ago, the grass would have been lush, green, and speckled with a thousand wildflowers in every nameable color. With the advent of winter, it was dull, dry, and brown.

I'd lost track of the hours I spent in this meadow under the summer sun, watching the grasses bend and clouds flit across the sky, wondering if those quiet moments could stave off the claws of Fate.

In the distance, the jagged white tips of the Linvian Mountains blended into the blue sky. Dread pitted in my stomach. One of those peaks was the Morav crypt, and I knew what lay there. Would I be strong enough to follow through?

"We're not stopping in any river towns," Blackthorn added after a little while. Whoever he fought in Dover had somehow taken part of his voice. The smallest spike of pity pierced my chest as he continued, "We shouldn't be walking on the main road with Devereux looking for us."

"I'm not taking a detour."

"Of course you're not." He huffed, readjusting his bag. "And when we're in Linvia, you're getting a sword. A dagger won't cut it in the mountains."

"Or you could uncuff me."

He shrugged, face softening. "I thought you were still a shadow of your former self, so which is it?"

"Still a god."

"Well, the king told me I could remove them when I wanted."

"What are you waiting for? I could have left you behind at least twelve times now. And if it's a sex thing, all you have to do is ask."

He raised an eyebrow and coughed into the back of his hand. "It's not that."

"I've been in them for twenty-six years. I have served my sentence."

"If I take them off, there will be no putting them back on, right?"

"I wouldn't let you," I admitted, massaging my wrist.

The drag of iron had become familiar, almost comforting. From the day old King Tyrlas ordered them on and threw the key in some drawer, I felt true quiet. My skin stopped humming at every waking moment, the power below my lungs shrank, and every corner of me was new, exposed. The first time I felt pain in Tyrlas's prison, bound in iron, I cried at the sting because it was a relief to feel anything.

"What was your power like before the cuffs?"

I bit my lip. "I could pull ghosts up and hold them for an hour, not minutes and return them to solid or move them from one plane to another. I could override living souls with dead, pull back the veil for longer than a few minutes."

Blackthorn nodded. "And with all your power?"

I couldn't remember what it was to hold the full power of Death—I didn't want to.

I let out a breath. "There isn't much that could stop me. One touch now can kill a mortal, but restored, I could crush souls and bodies with hardly more than a thought. I could see what Death awaited them if I wanted. I—are you listening?"

Blackthorn patted his pockets; something appeared to be very wrong because he looked around frantically.

I considered the worst and my rage turned white. "What did you do?"

"Nothing," he said and ripped the bag off his shoulder to rifle through it. The sun rose higher in the sky and merchant carts and other traders started to dot the road as it warmed.

"What did you do?" I asked again. He closed the bag and threw it over his shoulder, cursing as he raked a hand through his hair.

"Someone stole my purse."

I stopped walking. "What? The whole thing? You still have the key?"

"Of course, I have the key." He shook it off and looked at my pocket. "You still have some coins from yesterday, don't you?"

"Not enough to get through the rest of this stupid—"

Blackthorn held his hands up to stop me. "I'll figure it out, don't worry."

I charged ahead, walking with purpose, forcing him to jog to keep up as my blood boiled—men were so fucking stupid.

"It was an honest mistake, Raven."

I whirled around and poked his chest, wishing I had enough death magic to bring him to his knees and show him the power of who he kept. Fortunately, my own sense of right kept the gloves on.

"No." I glared. "It was a *stupid* mistake, and *I* will fix it."

"You don't have to—"

I threw back my head and laughed, caustic and empty.

"I *will* have to. Because if I let you, you're going to put your name in a ring and try to fight it back. You will then lose and try to pick it off some noble and you will get arrested because you are a knight with no tact for criminality. Whatever you'd try in Tyrlas will not work in Linvia."

Blackthorn crossed his arms and took a step toward me, closing some of the space as a creaking cart moved past us. I'm sure someone watched, but it didn't matter. On the roads, in the daylight, life continued.

"And what, moon's willing, will Raven do?"

"What is necessary." I narrowed my eyes, clenching my fists. "What I've always done. Do you really think I've spent my whole life in palaces being catered to? For nearly every year in a palace, I've spent one in prison, and another scraping by in exile or sleeping next to robbers in the woods. I mean it when I say Linvia is not the place to test your ego, Sir Blackthorn."

"And what do you know of Linvia?"

My voice dropped, and I closed the space between us until my breath curled around his face and he couldn't miss a single damned word.

"I was the last queen of the Morav Dynasty."

"No, that's—"

I didn't hear anything else he spluttered because I stormed ahead, mind running through every possibility as I prayed he'd shut up about it. We were days away from the Tyrlian Kingdom, and I would *not* be commanded by a man.

11

WE SLEPT EASILY IN the woods at another camp with several merchants and farmers who were also en route to Linvia with their last rounds of wares before winter largely shut down trade through the rivers.

One man bartered in fur and another in tiny telescopes made of brass. Even after a conversation with him, I didn't understand why anyone would need a tiny telescope, but if he'd made enough for embroidered leather and fine jewels, I wasn't one to judge.

Blackthorn remained silent until the merchants snored several paces away, as we sat beside each other near the dying fire. I picked up an acorn and rolled it between my fingers.

"Tell me about Linvia."

How could I summarize a history I'd worked so hard to destroy? I let out a long breath and scraped a hand through my hair, getting almost nowhere—I desperately needed a brush.

"What should I expect, Your Majesty?" the knight asked, reminding me yet again of a rank and title I'd worked hard to forget.

I threw the acorn at his head, but he dodged it with no effort.

"I was only queen for a year—then it collapsed." A little honesty couldn't hurt. "I was a princess seven years before that. I married into the royal family shortly after Foria fell, in an attempt to get it back."

"You married?"

"I did." Blackthorn's face smoothed. Firelight sharpened the scars across it. I always thought scars were beautiful and turned away before my attention lingered too long. "We met before Foria fell, before the Morav's hold on Miria slipped."

"Was it a choice?"

I picked up another acorn and started to peel it as the fire crackled. "Koros always gave me a choice, and I always declined. I never intended to marry for power. I meant to find it other ways, but it was convenient that we were—"

"In love?"

I winced.

Maybe—no, *definitely*—but even love couldn't describe what Leander Morav had been to me or still was.

He loved me the way the moon loves the stars and the sun warms the prairies—with everything that made us . . . from beginning to the end, as though we both would live forever.

We'd named stars after each other in the oldest dialect of Dovrian and no one would remember the words if I spoke them aloud.

"Sure."

For a moment, I hoped Leander heard me. I'd never been able to call on his ghost, but I also couldn't accept that he left me alone when so much of this world still reminded me of him.

"I was married once too," Blackthorn offered up, to my surprise. He told a thousand stories, but this was the first that didn't make him sound insufferable. "Both of us were too young. I didn't know it was real."

"How do you mean?"

The knight shrugged, picking the skin off another acorn before he flicked the fruit into the fire. "Her family left Tyrlas within a few months. I never saw her again."

"I'm sorry."

"Don't be." He sighed, squinting at the fire as the acorn popped, sending up a small spray of sparks. "I wouldn't be a knight if she hadn't left."

"Do you wish she stayed?"

"Do you wish you were queen?"

I thought of saying something and couldn't. I tossed another acorn into the fire and waited for the *pop*.

The words caught. I thought of Leander, of Dover, and of the palace I'd never set foot in again. Two hundred and eighty-two years should have been enough, but some memories never receded.

Then, there was Linvia. I'd been back before, but not like this.

Orion Blackthorn said nothing else and we drifted off until the clop of horses and faint morning light woke us. We spent the rest of the day weaving around carts and dodging pointed looks on the busiest road in the realm.

The gods were long dead to mortals, but myths grew in their absence. Some stories said Niany still walked the realm and opened the first flower every spring. Logistically, it was impossible and most pollen gave her a headache.

Others believed Koros shook the mountains, or Fortune stood at the edge of betting halls, appearing only to those who needed encouragement to take a risk, but neither of them had that kind of time.

What did they say about me? Death was either the nurturer, the Godkiller, or the daughter who rebelled and overthrew her father for nothing. The histories were divided, and my involvement in writing them didn't help. Few mortals knew I was still alive—that truth was reserved only for nobles, monarchs, and a few select others.

The gods had been gone for so long mortals didn't know what the glowing threads in my eyes meant. And for the better half of the century, I made no effort to be known as anyone other than Raven.

Foriana was a legend. Her touch calmed the dying and the magic in her eyes cradled all souls who looked upon her. She swallowed the darkness and death from the land so it thrived—just as winter always turned to spring, so did Death pave the way for Life.

Or something like that. I'd never lived up to the legends of my own name so I shed it.

Two hours before sunset, we approached Linvia. The entire city had been swallowed in the shadow of the looming, snow-capped mountains.

Linvia wasn't walled because it was surrounded by steep, craggy mountains on three sides. On all surrounding hills, nar-row towers were constructed and outfitted with a warning light and a squad of archers in case a threat came from the fields.

Once we pushed our way through the crush of people around the main entrance, I went straight to my favorite part of the city.

It was farther in, along the river, but I'd never forgotten it. An old building had been turned into an inn with several beau-tiful rooms looking over a vibrant street with daily markets and some of the best jewelers in Miria.

The winding streets and grand gardens constructed around Linvia calmed me. They were as I remembered—clean and beautiful, even in the impending shadow of winter.

"Why 'Raven'?" Blackthorn suddenly asked as we turned a corner to the market district, angling for a sloping street leading to the riverfront. "Can you turn into one?"

"What?"

"That's why you named yourself Raven. I'd heard myths about the Pantheon gods and their—"

I laughed. "I cannot shift into a bird. Did you hear it in a temple?"

"Not sure." Blackthorn shrugged. "Maybe I'd heard it as a child—sometimes Death would disguise herself to reap stubborn souls."

"I do not disguise myself, especially not as a bird. If I'm taking any souls, I'm taking them as I am. Since you asked, when exactly do you shift into a wolf?"

He paused, considering the question. "I don't, not often anyway."

"Why?"

He shrugged. "Usually, I just stop myself somewhere halfway. It's not much use as a knight in the palace, but I'll shift to go for a run in the mountains and hunt when I need to."

"Have you hunted recently?"

"Why does it matter to you? I will shift when I need to. I have control."

Blackthorn fell silent again. I'd pried too far just as we crossed over the river bridge to the ancient keep. Vines climbed up a stone fortress, turning red and brown in the late fall chill. Well-dressed butlers stood at the doors, opening them on our approach.

Blackthorn leaned over and whispered. "We can't afford this."

"I can," I said, and it was enough to leave him sulking behind as I traded coins for two keys on the third floor. The rooms weren't grand, and the space was too haunted for many people to stay willingly, but that's why I appreciated it.

I wasn't alone here and the ghosts, as I remembered, were always chatty. Aside from one, but I'd earned a free month of stay when I removed her decades ago.

"Why was this so cheap?" Blackthorn asked, walking into my room unannounced. I'd left the door unlocked.

"It was a prison two hundred years ago." I glanced at the window seat where two young ghosts sat, staring over the river as ships passed. "It's filled with ghosts. Friendly now, but filled with them. Raven, a seer of Dover, always has a room here for what she did to clear the tortured souls."

"Right." He looked at the mud on his shoes, turning the key to his room between his fingers. "Shall we get dinner?"

"With what coin?" I snapped, and upon seeing his conflicted expression, I flipped him a gold piece. "I'll handle getting the rest back. You're on your own tonight."

"You expect me to leave you on *your* own?"

"In Linvia? Yes," I said plainly, but his face soured. "My plan is to get a dress—"

"Raven." Remorse tersened his voice. "You don't have to do that. There are—"

"I'm not doing *that.*" I laughed, and he seemed to lighten up for a split second. "I'm fixing a match and you're not coming with me."

"You're a queen?" he said incredulously.

"Haven't been for a while. If you plan to follow me, you're not setting a foot inside the ring. Understood?"

He nodded.

"Good."

I bundled my coat over my shoulder and whisked out of the keep with Blackthorn at my heels. Luckily, he'd forgone the sword and appeared almost like any other person despite being larger than every man we passed.

The shops along the riverfront were vivid displays of gemstone-colored silks and finely embroidered cotton. The best dressmakers in Linvia made their names on this street before they were invited to the merchant street in the shadow of the palace.

I shopped for something simple and thin enough to distract from my eyes. It'd been thirty years since I last set foot in Linvia, which meant the memory of me might not be entirely lost, even if the king I'd befriended was long dead.

A thin black satin dress caught my attention and I tried it on. It fell to my shins in a single sheath of watery fabric that fit well under my coat. It also gave away just enough with a simple neckline.

Before I paid, the seamstress frowned at the clunky lace-up boots I'd been wearing. She slammed a pair of impractical velvet heels on the counter.

"Those shoes look ridiculous," she chided, glancing at the door where Blackwood stood, rocking impatiently on his feet. "Wear these tonight—no cost. I'll send these boots to your address."

"Thank you," I said pleasantly and traded the shoes. I tried not to think about the crush of my toes, or how the cold pavement would freeze my feet.

Blackthorn stared at the ceiling until I set another bracelet on the counter and barked, "Let's go."

My legs were exposed for the first time in a week and they were freezing. Worse, Blackthorn was indignant behind me, unable to decide if he wanted to walk beside me, in front of me, or on the opposite side of the street as we made our way to the city center. I remembered the turns and curves of Linvia like the back of my hand, guiding us uphill where the streetlights were more sparse.

Blackthorn's agitation got worse with every step closer.

"Aren't you going to be chilly?" he finally asked, and I'm sure the question tore him up inside with the desperate clip at which he blurted it.

"I'll survive."

I turned down an alley on instinct. We needed to be where the shadows and hooded men were going, where gas lamps hung low overhead and flickered in near-empty storefronts. The last time I wandered here, I wasn't alone but with a noble who scoffed the same as Blackthorn.

In front of us, a smart-looking gentleman in a well-tailored coat pulled a hat over his face as he strode across the opposite street with his chin pointed at the ground—he was the guide I needed.

I picked up the pace, heels clipping on stone. The man's hand moved to adjust the hat and I caught a glimpse of a fine silver watch, which confirmed every suspicion. I watched him approach a wooden door with chipping red paint and slowed.

My next step never landed because Blackthorn grabbed my wrist and I whirred to face him, rage simmering.

"What the fuck, Raven?"

"I told you what I'm doing," I hissed, nearly stubbing his toe with the point of my shoe. "*You* can stand outside if it pleases you."

"I shouldn't be letting you go in there. Not alone. That's a—"

"Then stop me," I challenged him as a freezing drizzle started to fall, dotting the street and threatening to turn to ice.

He looked at the ground and then again at me, jaw tight, warm hand still around my wrist.

"I want to."

"I dare you."

His hold tightened. I straightened my shoulders and backed him into the alley with my hand on his chest, knowing well rage turned my eyes a shade of black with a flash of ice—in case he forgot who I was.

He gulped, but I didn't care.

"We need swords. You lost our money. I am getting it back and you will not help me."

Blackthorn straightened under my glare, matching the heat with his own pale power. "I could."

I loosened my hold, ignoring how his corded muscles twitched beneath the touch, but I didn't relinquish it completely. Would I trust him on this? *No.*

"I'm going in alone as a Countess of Rivendeer. You are wearing leather and cotton, like a lord's guard, not his son. And now it's raining and you'll start to smell like a dog, so pardon me for insisting I do this on my own."

The glare he shot me cut like a razor. "Enjoy your evening, m'lady."

My hand slid down his chest, and without another word, he stormed away.

He'd come back. Tyrlas would have his head if he returned to the palace without me, and his sister's would roll with it.

I strode in the opposite direction, toward the red door with a practiced smile. There were many things I'd missed about life in the cities and this was one.

12

A MAN WITH A perfectly round face sat on the other side of a beaten-up oak table in a small, unassuming room paneled in incongruous wood boards that seemed plucked from street trash to add character. The man watched me through a monocle, flashing a subtle smile as his palms flattened against a large book spread across the table, open to mostly blank pages.

"A vision has appeared tonight," he said, folding his hands. Loud cheers echoed through a narrow corridor to my right, "but I'm afraid you're in the wrong hall for dancing."

I stepped closer, heels clicking on the worn floorboards as I unclasped two of my gold bracelets. "I am a countess of Rivendeer. I am *very* aware of where I am." I held out my palm with the bracelets and the last of our coins. His gaze only narrowed on the other gold bracelets rushing through my cuff as I shook my wrist. "What, you want those too?"

I moved to unclasp another few when a deep voice came from behind.

"Triple the lady's gold from my own account, Stenton."

I turned to see who'd inserted themselves into my affairs. A tall, deeply suave man stared me down through green eyes as vibrant as the enchanted wild horses in the valleys of Foria. He held intrinsic power in his shoulders, reminding me of the natural magic the gods and fae had leeched from the world centuries ago. I wondered if his rounded ears were a deception.

"You are much too kind, sir—I have my own accounts."

As I unclasped a third bracelet with a click, the man caught my wrist. I held my breath at the press of his fingers against my glove.

"I'm sure you do but I insist, Lady—"

"Fortune," I provided. "Titles are complicated. And you are?"

"Adler," he said, looking over my shoulder at the bookkeeper to make sure his command was documented and the gold was accounted for. His gaze then caught mine again with a brush of familiarity I couldn't place. "Who are you betting on, Fortune?"

"A good question." I scrutinized the competitors' board behind Stenton's head. Picking the best odds would be too obvious, as would the worst. A name near the center caught my attention for the last match of the night. "All in on the Red Knight of Belem."

"He's lost his last three matches."

"Then he's due a win. The Blue Dragon can't win everything."

Adler cocked his head to the side with curiosity and a gaze that didn't leave mine. "You have a point. Double my sum on the Red Knight."

Stenton nodded warily and scribbled a note as he banked several more coins and I slipped my bracelet back on.

"Shall we?" Adler asked, sticking his arm out with enough charm to wake up a warm and inconvenient feeling.

I flashed a demure smile and accepted the chivalrous gesture. He turned and walked us through the dark, winding passages to the dim and dusty hall.

A too-attractive human always caught me off guard; perhaps it was a reflex after spending so many years on high alert around fae. The stark difference between him and Blackthorn was a welcome sight after being practically chained to the hulking shifter knight for over a week.

Where Blackthorn was broad, Adler was narrow and sharply defined. Where Adler's hair was a shade of brown so dark it might be mistaken for shadow, Blackthorn's blond shone a hundred different shades in the sunlight. Most notably, Adler was quiet and mysterious, where, by now Blackthorn certainly would have told an extraneous, much-too-personal story.

I needed this distraction. Adler guided me to his table just in front of the pit, hand on the small of my back, as blood and dirt ransacked my senses, awakening a basal part of me.

I loved fight pits and it had been over a year since I'd been to one. There was an animalistic thrill in them I couldn't find in more palatable sports, nor in street fights.

The pits were always buried in some inconspicuous building their Crown had abandoned. Then, the dirt inside was dug out, unless it was a pit the monarchy indulged in—those floors might be paved, but it was unlikely.

The floor in this pit wasn't; it had been carved into the earth and was clearly uneven, with deep pocks and divots throughout the makeshift ring, designated by a painted white line.

Centuries ago, fighting pits brimmed with impressive magic. Gods and demis stood across from one another to see who would walk away. The god pits, though, were larger—more like stadiums—and most often, the win went to whoever conjured fire first.

Mortals were pitted against each other the same as beasts: No defense outside of their limbs and teeth. I'd never admit this to anyone, but there were stints in exiles, I'd throw myself in a mortal ring because few things were more satisfying than fighting without the proxy of metal sticks.

Despite the rising heat as matches took place, I didn't take off my coat at the risk of revealing the cuffs. Instead, I unbuttoned it, moving the lapel aside to show how the satin clung to my frame and dipped to my breasts.

Adler made a show of watching.

I intended to prod him and see if he had magic. I needed to draw on my own as subtly as I could because there was a chance the man would feel my power the way I felt his, which was certainly a risk.

Magic came more easily tonight. All three moons hung in the third quadrant, and for the last time this year, they all waxed at the same time.

God power was a tide—in and out, a constant presence just under my skin as they battled each other for full control. I couldn't see any of them, but their power pressed and pulled in tendrils below my skin, grating and building throughout the night as blood spattered, noses broke, and men bit their way to glory.

During the next match, I leaned forward as a man's fist connected with the cheek of his opponent in a distinctive crack. Adler leaned with me; an aura of power pulsed around him.

His eyes were too ethereal, too strange to be mortal, but the fae had been gone from Miria for centuries, and even if one stayed behind, I doubted they'd be so bold. I should have been worried, maybe even fearful, but the idea of brushing arms with another immortal thrilled me so long as he didn't stop me.

Mortals no longer recognized the influence of magic. No one in the room would notice the briefest bite of sulfur in the air or hear the barest snap as magic filled the eyes of a fighter and froze him in place for the very last seconds of his fight.

The control required by subtlety might drain my reserve, but it would fill my purse.

Applause filled the room as the final fight began and the Red Knight entered, then the favored Blue Dragon, his face painted to mimic scales. I made the right choice. Though he prowled around the ring like he intended to level it, the Blue Dragon's movements were slow and a purple bruise stuck out over his ribs.

The Red Knight sauntered around the ring. He was a hulking man, slick with sweat and drenched in oil, with long red hair braided into leather pieces. It was a wonder more women didn't come to the pits. There was something feral and delicious in watching blood drip down illustrious abs and broad shoulders, tangling in the hair of men they dared to call beastly.

The men in the pits were more man than their husbands would ever be—I wondered if they couldn't face it.

Adler cleared his throat and I came back to myself, dropping the magic like a butter knife from sweat-slicked fingers. He didn't seem any less mortal, but I wasn't convinced as jeers filled the room. Something about him was different.

The Blue Dragon lunged, slugging the Red Knight in the nose. Blood splattered, painting the dirt crimson.

The Red Knight stumbled, bleeding profusely, but all the blow did was light a fire in his eyes that came out in a bellowing roar. He charged the Blue Dragon, shoving his force into a hit that landed against the Red Knight's bruised ribs, wringing out a sharp cry.

The Blue Dragon tried to twist back, to get any leverage by kicking out a knee, but the Red Knight met him strike for strike. Perhaps my magic wasn't needed.

Then the tide shifted.

The Blue Dragon stiffened, swallowing the pain like bad liquor as he grunted and grabbed the Red Knight's wrist in the next swing, shoving his elbow with renewed vigor to dislocate it.

Snap. I pressed the little magic I had and the briefest vision of the afterlife froze the Dragon for a small second. Not wasting it, the Red Knight maneuvered around, swept the Blue Dragon's knee from under him and landed the man on his back with a finite thud.

The bell rang. The Red Knight stood over his opponent, blood dripping from his nose onto his sweat-slicked chest while my mouth watered against my will.

Adler leaned forward, lips practically on the shell of my ear. "You were right, Fortune."

"I usually am."

It was over—we'd won.

I clapped as I stood, trying not to think about the blood and sweat stirring every part of my core in the basest way. Goddess, shade—whatever I was or wasn't—I remained capable of pleasure and easily distracted by the promise of skin now that I could taste it.

Adler's hand lingered on the small of my back. "Would the lady be interested in another game? You seem the type I'd like to have on my side."

"Yes." I smiled back, measured. I wanted to read what lay behind his rich green eyes but couldn't see anything beyond a warning I was ignoring. "I'd love to."

"Good."

His polish and cologne were stark opposites to the bloodied men in the ring being led out back; somehow the contrast made the pulsing heat worse, instead of easing it.

We wound back through the hall to the madness at the bookkeeper's desk. It took a few minutes of bargaining and waiting, but we collected our winnings and I stuffed the pockets of my coat full of enough gold for another week, maybe two.

I followed Adler down a street, through another nondescript door that opened with a password. Instead of blood, dirt, and sweat, my senses were accosted by cigar smoke, strong liquor, and cards, coins, and hands snapping on tables.

A woman in a red gown, dripping in glass beads, led us to a table where three men sat; they grinned at Adler as we approached. The men were odd together: One as young as twenty, another certainly in his seventies, and a third was somewhere in the middle, but he was nearly bald.

"I can see why you're late, my lord," the oldest said, making a show of staring at me. A tuft of white hair curled over his forehead smooth as a teenager's. "Quite a pretty thing to find at the pits. I am sorry you had to bear witness to the depravity, Lady—"

"Fortune," Adler provided. "Her name is Lady Fortune, and she'll be joining us for a round."

I smiled congenially, slipping into a seat only half wondering what I'd gotten myself into. "What are we playing, my lords?"

"Not going to ask for names?" the youngest man piqued from my right as Adler sat too close to me, his arm brushing mine. The heat was apparent, even through our layers. If I were any younger or more mortal, I would've blushed.

"I don't need to know names to take your coin."

The men laughed, and I smiled sweetly, but I did mean it. They were mostly drunk; it'd be easy to see their bluff. Adler was the only one I couldn't read. He kept looking at me, just as I kept looking at him, like we were supposed to know each other. Did I know him? That would be unlikely.

It had been almost thirty years since I'd set foot in Linvia. Everyone I knew had died, or moved on to a life I wasn't privy to—with the exception of a few old nobles who might still serve the palace.

13

I lost the first round because I forgot Linvians played their hand with an extra bear, where, in Tyrlas, they removed all five. Luckily, I only bet a quarter of my winnings.

In the second round, the youngest man made several mistakes and revealed too much of his hand and I noticed. It wasn't technically a sweep, but it was adjacent.

Adler started shuffling for a third round when two of the gentlemen excused themselves, leaving me nearly alone with Adler, a full glass of liquor, and several questions I prepared as currency.

I just needed to get rid of the last man—the youngest. It seemed straightforward until the hostess seated another at the far side of the table.

Dressed in a fine black gentleman's suit, the man had gone so far as to comb his hair, but there was no disguising the particular cut and brutality of Sir Orion Blackthorn as half his lip turned up. He dwarfed the chair and I wanted to know how the fuck he found a suit.

"The hostess said there was a vacancy." He took a swig from his glass. "Surely three isn't much of a game?"

"It is not," Adler said, green eyes, again, stuck on me.

"Always happy for the company. I'll deal you in." I leaned back and glared at the knight, absently tugging on my sleeves as I laid one of two bags of gold on the table. The knight's eyes widened.

"You let your lady bet all of your coins, my lord?" Blackthorn said to Adler, who smiled as I dealt the cards.

"Lady Fortune is not mine. She does as she pleases, but she is a formidable opponent and I hardly think that's all of her gold."

"You don't say," Blackthorn muttered, looking straight at me before he scanned the cards in his hands. "She hardly looks like she has teeth. I'll tell you that."

I wonder what would happen if I jumped across the table and strangled him? Instead, I politely folded my hand on my lap. "I don't lose in my old age."

"Old?" Adler gawked. "You're too hard on yourself. You cannot be a day over twenty-five."

Blackthorn scoffed and swirled the liquor in his glass before gulping it in one swig.

"Something funny?" I quipped, knowing full well how gaunt I looked. The fading rouge on my lips couldn't hide the circles around my eyes, nor the gray pallor of my face.

Blackthorn shook his head, a piece of slicked blonde hair sprang loose. "Shall we play?"

"Of course," Adler agreed and elbowed the friend still sitting beside him. Blackthorn contributed his own small bag of gold from moons know where.

The game began as a battle of wills, each hand escalating as the three men became increasingly frustrated with every round.

I nearly won the first hand, losing only to Adler's friend by the slightest misjudgment, but I made up for my losses in the second. By the third hand, Adler stared at me slack-jawed, while Blackthorn merely watched as if he couldn't bother to be surprised.

Adler cleared his throat and stood before the next round. "I ought to be leaving. Do you need an escort, Lady Fortune?"

"No. Thank you for the offer."

"Of course." He bowed as he buttoned his coat. "A pleasure to meet you. Will I see you again?"

I folded the cards to my chest, still unnerved by the mysterious power he held. "I'm only in town for another day."

"Is that so?"

Blackthorn rolled his eyes as Adler played it off.

"If the fates see fit," the man continued, "I'd be happy to lose to you any day of the week."

Adler took my hand and kissed it slowly, as if he savored it. Green eyes flicked up and cut me with their precision. If he saw the cuff on my wrist, it went unacknowledged—and I was grateful for it.

My hand fell from his grip as he returned to full height, attention searing the skin of my cheeks. "Lose you will."

"Truly, it would be no trouble to walk you home. An honor, even."

"I'm perfectly fine, Lord Adler,"—I set the cards on the table and eyed the pile of gold—"but thank you for your concern."

"Of course." He nodded genteelly, his expression turning somber before he faded into the crowd and haze of the room.

"One more hand?" I asked Blackthorn.

"No, you cheat."

I leaned back in the creaking chair and took a sip from Adler's glass, watching the knight over the rim. "I've been playing cards for seven hundred years and you think *I* cheat. I have no reason to cheat."

"You cheat."

"I just know how to play."

We weren't getting anywhere. I scooped the gold from the table, dumping most of the coins into my pockets before I shoved a small pile toward him.

"You're not walking through the streets like that." He scoffed as I stood to button my coat. It visibly sagged under the weight. "Your pockets look ridiculous."

"I'll be fine." I tied the coat snug and finished the liquor in a gulp; the burn would last to the inn. "We have enough to buy a guard if you're so worried. I'm sure there's one for hire around here."

"You're not buying a guard when I'm a *knight*."

"A knight? You're miraculously dressed as a lord. You're not swinging steel in a coat like that. And—need I remind you—*who* made this necessary to begin with?"

He scowled and dropped the remaining coins into his pocket; Blackthorn wanted to say something worse and I deserved it.

"Fine," he conceded.

Blackthorn led us through the run of tables and chairs back to the quiet streets of Linvia's capital where the rain had turned to a gentle flurry. Ice smoothed the gaps between cobblestones, but thankfully, it only pooled in the center of the street, reflecting the lamplights.

The river district was several blocks away through winding streets that took us uphill. It was silent aside from the clip of our steps as they echoed off buildings while I straddled the questions I wanted to ask and an apology I was too proud to grant, until I finally blurted out something.

"Where did you find the suit?"

Mild annoyance ticked in his jaw. "What are you willing to believe, Lady Fortune?"

"Anything."

"Fine. I traveled with them. Just as you traveled with your dress."

His gaze roved over the gown exposed by my coat, though it had loosened from the weight of gold. I pulled it tighter. As much as I enjoyed the admiration, I'd almost had the right amount of brown liquor to forget I wasn't mortal and Blackthorn's physique was far too similar to the fighters.

"You saw me buy it."

"I did. You never saw me buy this, so you have no choice but to believe it."

As we walked, we passed a cathedral with its door wide open. The inside flickered with candlelight, exaggerating the moving shadows of several late-night patrons who were honoring some god or another.

I peered in, embracing the rush of warmth. Rose petals covered the floor and several people knelt among them before an intricate altar draped in pearls and deep green holly. A woman in ivory robes stood before them, holding a delicate charcoal blade in hand.

"What is she doing?" Blackthorn whispered.

I shrugged and backed away, continuing our return as he caught up. "I think they were bloodletting," I said when we rounded a corner. "Certain sects will gift blood to Niany at her altars hoping to cure illness."

"Does it work?"

"Sometimes."

A memory came back of Niany laying her hand on the shoulders of patrons, dressed as a priestess with her face veiled. She cared for the most broken—I'd give her that—but her sympathy couldn't stretch to accommodate anyone else.

"So who was the man?"

"You'll have to be more specific."

He flashed a withering look; flurries clung to his lashes. "The one with the strange eyes, who kept looking at you and spoke for you. Seems like a type you'd know."

"Met him at the fighting pit. I haven't been to Linvia in thirty years so he's far too young to know."

"Or fae?" I didn't blink, surprised to hear the words from a mortal; generational bitterness had wiped fae from Miria's history. "Unless they really all have pointy ears."

"They do have pointy ears—and he isn't. I'd know."

Blackthorn looked at my wrist. "Even through those?"

"Yes." His arm brushed mine and tugged my coat tighter, trying to chase away several thoughts and counteract the breeze as I blew out a sigh. "I'm sorry for what I said earlier."

Blackthorn stopped walking, and I did too. We looked at each other, our breath fogging in the chilly air.

"Repeat that."

I looked at the sky with a groan, avoiding his smug expression. "I'm sorry."

"Huh." He huffed, a grin apparent in his tone. "Never thought the Goddess of Death could apologize, 'specially to me—a mere mortal."

"Don't get used to it," I snapped, chewing on my lip and picking up pace.

My mind was still stuck on Adler. I'd know if he were fae—I'd feel it. What if I couldn't? What if I'd lost more than I thought? What if there was magic I wouldn't get back?

If Blackthorn said anything, I didn't hear it until the road changed. We'd crossed a bridge and were no longer standing on gray cobbles but large slabs of stone.

The buildings in this section were a stark white that glowed against the sky, reflecting the light of the three waxing moons.

It wasn't right. I looked over my shoulder. We weren't where I expected to be. We were supposed to be further north, at the confluence of two rivers where the debaucherous old town was.

Tch. Tchhh. I looked around for any sign that the raven of my nightmares had returned. Nothing, just the grating sound of its memory echoing in my head, warning me.

Where we stood now was pristine and silent—

Oh.

"I made the wrong turn," I whispered, and Blackthorn whirled around, leaning closer to me than necessary. I couldn't make my feet move; I couldn't feel them. All of me turned numb as an aching, constant spectral scream crawled up and raised the hair on the back of my neck.

He grabbed my arm and tried to nudge me to look at him, but I wouldn't, not as tears welled against my will and icy magic needled my fingers, itching for something.

"Where are we?"

"Nowhere, just lost," I squeaked, shaking his grip off as I came back to myself and left the bridge before worse happened.

"Lost?" I darted up the street and he tried to keep up. "Raven? Weren't you queen here?"

The words cut. He didn't intend it, but the question seared against a centuries-old wound and turned remorse into rage, and grief into fear so deep it had no bottom. I kept walking, feet pounding against the pavement until they bruised and a large hand folded again over my forearm.

If I were a better god, I would have thrown him a thousand paces back with a shock of ice, wind, and power, but I was useless . . . and he was stronger. I relented, cowering under his concern, forgetting how unsettling the quiet in Linvia was next to the screaming.

Forgotten ruins haunted the heart of Linvia, and they were all I thought about as I stared at his chest.

"What was that?"

His white shirt had pearl buttons and his dinner jacket wasn't black but a deep navy velvet with sprinkles of dust and cat hair; he hadn't buttoned his coat.

"Raven?"

"The Scribes of Nurem died there." His hold lessened. I looked past him into the distance as though I could see the long-destroyed ghosts. Their memory skated over my arms. "Even in Tyrlas, you knew their fingertips were taken as an act of devotion. Everyone knows that, but they forget the day they died."

I tried to stay away from Linvia, but it always caught up to me—or perhaps it was the other way around.

Boundary lines moved, disasters buried streets, homes, and neighborhoods. Wars pillaged, destroyed, and built over the old like it was erasable. The destruction of the scribes would never be erased; it left a permanent mark on Linvia and cursed anyone who dared to raze it.

"What happened?" he asked again, prodding the truth I bit back.

"They were destroyed." I looked at Orion Blackthorn now. "You shouldn't have been able to cross the bridge."

His hand slid from my arm and went limp at his side. The space between his eyes pinched. "Why?"

"The temple is shielded from mortals," I said, gaze falling back to the street as truth tumbled out. "I was in Linvia the day it happened. The scribes were entombed where they stood because of a miscalculation . . . It's getting late."

Blackthorn's eyes grazed over me a second time; he didn't believe me—but I didn't care. It wasn't a lie.

I barreled ahead, following the curve of the river, trying not to feel the sobering night air against my skin. Every whisper of needling cold reminded me exactly how fucking mortal I'd become.

The minute we stood over the Nurem Tombs had drained my magic. I clung to the last vestiges by a thread of desperation and resorted to dragging on the few souls wandering the river boundary.

We reached the inn and I slammed the door, dropping my coat into a heap on the floor. If cold brought clarity, heat brought delusion so I lay in front of the fireplace, hoping it would warm my bones and drag me back to myself.

I let my guard down and closed my eyes only to be accosted by every sharp and twisted memory of the day I killed the Scribes of Nurem and sapped every scrap of their power until they were nothing more than husks.

Not ghosts, not bodies, not skeletons or dust, but stone statues trapped in their own curse as they screamed for the rest of their eternity. The screams echoed still. So many they became a constant, shrill cacophony of noise, trapped in a constant state of dying.

The last time I returned to Linvia, someone held me down and stroked the nightmares away like flyaway hair. I was alone now, with a musty fleece blanket pulled over my shoulders as my heart pounded and sweat beaded. It wouldn't pull tight enough to stave off the pang in my chest, but I needed it to work.

Mortals couldn't remember the way gods did. The godhood imbued a shield or a wall around memories to render the worst as hazy dreams. It was natural protection so we immortals could live with ourselves. My mistakes and the cuffs chipped it away; I was combusting.

A thousand years of regret and shame compounded one over another until I couldn't breathe. My memory slammed against my skull unimpeded. All the blood gurgled up, spilled in my name, and by my hands. It pooled up from the floor and wrapped around my limbs, trying to drag me down to the afterlife I belonged to—

My door flew open and the shadow of Blackthorn appeared, in just his pants with a sword in hand, panting. "Raven?"

I looked up, tightening my grip on the blanket. "Are we getting attacked?"

"You screamed."

"I didn't?"

He stepped into the room, closing the door with a soft *click*. My throat was sore and my eyes burned. Maybe I did; this is why I stayed in Tyrlas and avoided my past—there was too much. Always too much.

"You should lock your door."

"Why?"

"Why?" he repeated, sitting on a chair near the fireplace. I hadn't changed out of the silk dress. "Because anyone could come in here."

"Like you did?"

"You screamed."

"Maybe."

I pulled the blanket tighter around my shoulders and wilted on the ground again, too tired to fight, too tired to keep him away from my darkness. His presence was a distraction and quieted the memories as I stared at the burning embers.

"Do you have a lot of nightmares?"

"I didn't say it was a nightmare." I glared and cursed myself for acting more like a cornered cat than a person. As I exhaled, my voice softened. "They come when the memories are worse."

"And the memories are worse in Linvia than Dover?"

"My memories of Dover are pleasant. Linvia is different, yet I've come back a hundred times. I lived here for six years, five before that, and then twelve or fifteen years at some other point. Before the Morav Dynasty collapsed, I split time between Dover and Linvia because we were gifted the Dovrian palace, but it doesn't—"

"Gifted a palace?"

"I was princess for seven years."

"Not queen?" His chin dipped. "You were Queen of Foria before, surely you wouldn't lose the title?"

Something in the fire popped. I watched embers scurry out and turn to ash on the mantel. Not one memory swelled back, but the feeling of the loss knotted in the back of my throat.

"Peerage rules never accounted for immortality. I gave the title up with Foria." His face had softened and his stubbled chin rested on the hilt of his sword. "My father was eager to call me princess again."

"Princess of Gods?"

"Or the Pantheon. Didn't matter. Koros didn't care about the mortal royalty so long as the fae—"

"So, it *is* true."

"What?"

"Fae were in Miria."

"Of course they were?" I tugged the blanket again, my bracelets rattled against the iron cuffs. "Tyrlas did a number on your libraries. Those towers in the east end were built by fae not even five hundred years ago."

"I heard some stories. Thought they were myths."

"Myths are truths your kings couldn't hide," I muttered. "There were dragons once, too, and wild magic, but the gods and fae somehow destroyed it all."

"Fascinating."

"Not as much as you think."

Blackthorn slid off the chair to join me on the floor, shoving his sword to the side with a squeal as he brought his knees to his chest.

"Do you remember the night before our match?" he asked, catching me off guard.

I tried to recall. It would have been the champions' dinner, hosted by King Tyrlas at the palace in Miacor. Blackthorn looked different, fresh-faced and scrawny, while my power was just as abysmal.

"What about it?"

"Why did you enter the tournament?"

The reflection of fire in his eyes set the amber alight and dug out the scars across his cheek. I didn't want to answer, but there was no point in hiding.

"Tyrlas asked me to—wanted to test the mettle of his next captain." The answer wasn't anything. I combed a knot out of my hair, sighing when my fingers caught another. "Even in exile, Tyrlas called on me to advise him—not frequently. I settled in a southern village outside the wall and needed money to keep up with a few debts."

A smile pinched his eyes as his chin bobbed. "The more I learn about you, the more I'm convinced it wasn't you I faced. Can you pick up a sword?"

"Of course I can. I trained for that." I stretched my legs, resting back on gloved hands as the blanket slipped from my shoulder. "It isn't my fault mortal steel is barely strong enough to sting."

"So you admit it," he muttered. "It wasn't a fair fight. You threw it."

"I never lied. Tyrlas didn't give me a choice. I was trapped in Tyrlas because his father had arrested me a decade prior.

Ephraim freed me from prison but committed to keeping me cuffed until I "proved myself"—his words."

Blackthorn closed his eyes. "His Majesty said both champions would serve his knighthood after the match? You threw it for nothing."

I flicked a piece of lint off the blanket. There was no point in cloaking the truth like I did for everyone else; he'd be the last to know me.

"Tyrlas cornered me when I had no interest in serving him. Crossing him through Relia bought me peace and quiet for a few years, even in the cuffs and yet . . ."

I waved my hand, clanging a bracelet against the iron cuff.

"Do you remember dancing together?"

"Do you?" I asked carefully. The night was one moment in a series of cascading events. I remembered him from that but also from a few times after, standing beside Tyrlas and scowling as I left the room. It wasn't often I said yes to the King of Tyrlas.

"I remember." He looked at the floor, smiling. "I asked you twice. You really don't know?"

"Remind me. I've danced a thousand times."

"But only twice with me. You thought I was a squire."

"You were fifteen."

"Eighteen."

I blinked. Memories of the night unfolded as I willed them. I hated the moons and wherever they were in the sky, pulling and prodding at the power under my skin, tricking it into behaving like I'd ever been a god.

"You wore an ill-fitting suit and the ladies of the court couldn't stop pinching each other over it. Then the cannons went off because Tyrlas made up some breach of his wall. Or was that another time?"

"It wasn't made up. There was a breach."

"He staged it." Blackthorn's jaw flexed and I admired the shadows of his neck. "Tyrlas had done it to justify the cost of two tournament champions. He knew what he wanted the next day and it was the power of Death."

Blackthorn leaned against the chair. "Well, you wore a very expected black dress and tried to convince me you'd been captain before."

"No, never captain. General twice, and commander when the one I trusted died in battle."

"So the stories about the Pantheon wars were true, and The War of a Thousand Trees."

"I've lived a hundred lives, Sir Blackthorn. I do not need to lie."

I'd said too much and not enough. Exhaustion hit like a wave. Without saying anything, I stood too quickly; the blanket remained on the floor. I swayed and the room tipped over, spilling something. No.

Black pepper and bergamot.

My gloved hands on skin.

A steady hand on my back.

I blinked. Blackthorn looked down, features crossed with concern. Everything was hazy, surreal, and draining. Did I stand there, leaning into his chest, for seconds or minutes? He said something else, but the words broke apart and chimed on the stone floor.

Protest died in my throat as he swept me up and buried me in the bed.

"Memories," was the only word I coughed out before I faded into some dreamless oblivion.

14

Niany is dead. She's rotting next to Koros,
who you said I'd never kill.
Well, I've killed them all, Leander. When I
told you who I was, you should have believed me.

My life was a series of moments, eras, and lifetimes that never fit in a single book. I'd been a hundred versions of myself, and no matter what name I tried out, I was always Foriana. She was inescapable.

Too many memories were chapters, meticulously filed away. Sometimes they came back unwittingly. Other times I'd stumble across something familiar and it would shake a moment loose, sending more tumbling out with no wall to hold them back . . .

Memories were unpredictable but then there were the defining moments—always waiting just under the surface.

Never would I forget the punctuating, silent minutes after I'd imprisoned Niany or how I woke up in the Pantheon, cursed with my godhood, every sense overwhelmed by the taste of blood.

Then ... the day I lost my favorite sister—it wrote itself across my heart the same as Leander. Never in a hundred thousand lifetimes would I forget him; of gods and men, his mortality was a disservice to Miria.

Visions of him plagued me when I picked off a glove and snapped my fingers to see if Nurem had taken everything. A faint spark of blue ignited, sputtering out in seconds. It was better than nothing, but my brush against the tomb of Nurem would live in my bones a few more days like a head cold.

Blackthorn said nothing about last night as we walked through the streets toward a merchant aisle where a black-smith's shop sat near the heart of the city, shadowed by the palace.

Unfortunately, he was far from silent during the hour's walk. By the time we reached the forge, I was thrilled to have steel in my hand. I fantasized about waving it at him if he ever dared to waste another full hour of breath on the daunting origins of cederwray black tea and its influence on Vharosian smithing.

While Blackthorn chatted with the smallest blacksmith I'd ever seen, I stood off against the stone wall observing. They turned over several fine swords, many the same size as her, but I didn't care what he picked so long as it was sharp. Maybe I wouldn't need it; I hoped I wouldn't need it.

The first time I held a sword as the Goddess of Death was my second week at the Pantheon. I'd more or less recovered from the transition from mortal to god . . . but I hadn't recovered from the betrayal of my father's bargain and everything I had to prove.

Niany and Koros, king and queen, expected me to sit beside them while demigods in the arena below faced each other for a seat at Koros's table. By this time, Koros only held tournaments to give his court a conversation topic that wasn't gossip or politics.

After the fifth hour, my new sister, Fortune, and I were bored. She elbowed me and shoved a stolen sword in my hand.

"Go out there," she'd whispered.

It was a joke from one sister to another, but I was proud and eager to prove myself worthy of the godhood bestowed on me. Goddess of Death? I was seventeen.

I discarded Niany's gloves behind a pillar, then I stepped into the sand arena, barely able to hold up the guard's broadsword but smiling despite it. I never saw Koros's face, but neither his guards nor his coordinator stopped me.

In fact, the Pantheon general pushed my opponent into my eyeline and beckoned me to step forward.

Facing me was some lanky demigod from the southern reach. He flashed a toothy grin just before he said something rash about bedding princesses and licking cunts. It triggered a surge of magic that raged through my bruised and blackened hands, manifesting from featherlight blue wisps to dripping, toxic ichor that smoked when it met the sand.

That day, the gods discovered metal was a conduit for death . . . just as Koros's gift of light.

I never touched my opponent. The moment my sword met the edge of the demigod's blade, he fell over dead and his flesh gave way to ash. Shock and the deafening roar of the crowd froze me until the king's guard ushered me back to the royal bay.

I'd expected a lashing for acting out.

Instead, Koros beamed—even Niany couldn't hide her smile: The Pantheon was cruel, and I wasn't a god who would make it better.

An ember from the forge flew out. I remembered myself and tugged my gloves tighter.

That was seven hundred years ago. Now, I'd had a hundred swords and Orion Blackthorn stood on the other side of the fire, blinking profusely like I'd forgotten to answer a question.

"Raven?"

"Yes? Can I help you, or have you forgotten how to hold it?"

"I was asking which you like better for yourself."

He walked around, holding out the crafted handles of two sabers, each of his hands wrapped around the blade, protected by a thick piece of shining cloth.

Both were fine steel, with subtle differences I cared about once.

"That one." I pointed to the left one and his brow furrowed.

"You don't want to hold it?"

"No. It'll work."

The knight had the sense to say nothing. Just stared at me for a second too long before he returned to barter with the smith.

My attention turned to the street, watching people pass until Blackthorn handed me a belt with the sheathed saber.

"Now what?" I asked, begrudgingly, strapping on the belt. It was finely crafted with stamped leather and fine, polished steel.

He frowned. "You're not going to ask about mine?"

"No. I think we should go to the market near the palace. There's no reason to hunt on the mountain if we don't have to."

"Lead the way." He gestured, and the way he bit his lip made me wonder if he held back a jibe; perhaps he thought better now that he'd given me a weapon.

We wove in and out of crowds, wandering uphill toward the eastern side of the city, near the palace. I wasn't sure why I'd made the suggestion. There were plenty of other markets in Linvia and it wasn't even the closest. The market I suggested was a climb.

As a kingdom, Linvia was difficult terrain. The proximity of its capital city to the mountains made it near impossible to assail, but the price was hundreds of winding streets, and some of the steepest hills I'd ever had the pleasure to slip down, drunk, in the icy thralls of winter.

Linvia was known to have the strongest archers in Miria and a cavalry that dwarfed the other kingdoms by thousands. Their strong defense kept their boundaries largely the same through several centuries on turmoil. The city also boasted one of two still-functioning palaces from the Pantheon age.

The market in the shadow of the palace, wasn't what I remembered and it was hardly worth the trek uphill.

It only took up four streets and the majority of vendors pushed clothes and trinkets. One stand had a massive display of tea, but food stalls were nowhere to be seen. Rumors spread of an indoor market ages ago, but construction depended on funding and merchants were always good at making requests, but they lost interest when it came to paying for them.

I peered around and tugged on Blackthorn's sleeve. "Did we pass a food market? Or did I—"

A shout cut off my thoughts.

We spun, and a man approached, flanked by four city guards. He was older, well into his fifties, dressed in the fine regalia of northern nobility with deep plum velvet and heavy gold stitching along the seams of his coat.

My heart stammered. Words caught as several passersby stepped out of his way, clearing a path. Was this real?

"I heard a rumor," the man said, lowering his voice as he strode toward me. Several other heads swiveled. "A goddess had returned to Linvia."

The man reached for my hand and placed a reverent kiss as whispers skittered.

"Henry—Lord Baskin. You're . . . You're alive—and *here*."

With a laugh that resounded, he straightened his jacket and looked nowhere else. "I couldn't turn down His Majesty's personal offer of the Upper Vale when it became available."

"Congratulations."

I couldn't look away. His dark brown hair was peppered with gray and more painfully handsome than memory served. I wanted to scream an apology, to kiss him, to do the thousand things I should have done, but I stood still, feet glued to the cobbles.

"It's been what, thirty years?" he asked, chin dipping lower. "You haven't changed, Lady Raven. In fact, you ought to come to dinner tonight."

"I'd love to, but—"

"Nonsense, I won't hear of it. King Donovan extends his welcome. He's even prepared your rooms. We're long overdue for dinner, wouldn't you say?"

I finally spared a glance at Blackthorn, whose skeptical lips were pulled in a thin line, meaning he wouldn't say anything but disapproved as my focus returned to Henry. I didn't care.

"Twenty-six years." I brushed a lock of hair behind my ear. "You also know I'd never disappoint the Linvian King."

"Of course not." Henry flashed a lopsided smile. Age had refined him into something unforgettable. "Come with me."

Alive.

Henry was alive.

"Our things," Blackthorn interjected. I brushed off his concern—what were a few extra days when we had weeks?

"They're plenty safe, but if you're missing something, *Lord* Blackthorn, I'm sure His Majesty would be generous enough to send a porter."

"Of course." Blackthorn tilted his head toward the immense white palace up the hill in front of us. "Lead the way, Lord Baskin. It'd be a shame for us to get lost on our way to Linvia's subtle Palace of Niany."

"Built for Niany," I said. "The goddess never lived there, but she was honored by the designation and the classic style."

Henry smiled, some flicker of pride in his watery eyes. "Of course. You were there, weren't you?"

"Opening day. You remember my stories?" We started our ascent toward Palace Hill, flanked by guards. My thundering heart calmed as familiarity settled.

"You insult me to think I'd forget anything about you." He flashed a knowing look and bumped me with his shoulder.

Behind us, Blackthorn was both bothered and nervous, likely about being brought to a palace that didn't fly the banners of Tyrlas. However, despite some misunderstanding, Linvia and I were staunch allies thanks to the several atrocities I'd committed in their favor.

They wanted the Scribes of Nurem gone; I obliterated them from time and space. They wanted a Morav King? I delivered them one with a goddess queen. The consequential war and immediate fall of their dynasty was out of my hands.

More than that, prior to my arrest, I spent almost six years in the palace with a much younger Lord Baskin and the previous king. We had a scheme to unite Linvia and Dover under a new dynasty and extend protection to the last elven commune in the north.

But twenty-six years had passed. The old king was dead, the kingdoms remained independent, and I was sure the last living elves couldn't look at me without scowling. The looming palace was equally unchanged and far more than just a royal home—it had become an untouchable shrine to Niany.

Tall white spires jutted out from smooth stone walls in the palest blue. Bright winter days would render the palace invisible if it wasn't for the deep green winter magnolia vines littering the sides of it. The broad evergreen leaves hid the foundation and several doors to cellars below.

As we approached, the delicate blue and pure white frescoes became visible. Each panel—I think there were two hundred throughout—represented a story of the goddess I'd been forced to call mother. How many were true? Hard to say.

My face was painted thirty-eight times and I spent several restoration days trying to disguise my most prominent features until patrons interrupted me and one master escorted me away.

Hopefully most depictions of Foriana looked less like me and more like the goddess of her mythos.

Eighteen arbors couched in dead vines marked the entrance as we approached the main hall. In the surrounding gardens, men and women dressed in plainclothes trimmed hedgerows and dead-headed roses while a teenager with a drooping face muttered prayers while they scrubbed the marbled heart stones of the grand fountain.

As Niany's shrine, believers came from across the kingdom and beyond on pilgrimage where they would offer their labor. They'd partake in garden maintenance, banal restoration work, or whatever the shrine required. By repairing her shrine, Niany would repair a broken part of their life in return.

She was as good as dead now, but even alive, she hardly lifted a finger for anyone but the most broken. The Queen of the Pantheon mastered the art of reverence as the wife of Koros. She did just enough to keep her name venerated on the lips of devotees.

"I hope it's as you remember," Lord Baskin said as the great hall welcomed us with its glass walls and frosted details—airy and light, echoing what mortals imagined the Pantheon to be.

Of course, it was nothing like the Pantheon.

"Exactly as it's always been."

The Palace of Niany embodied magnificence. Unlike Tyrlas's palace of undecorated stone and the occasional plastered ceiling with a spray of gold leaf, every detail in Linvia's was a forethought, carefully constructed by a thousand artisan hands over centuries.

Blue and white frescoes followed us through the halls, trailing up to the ceilings where mosaic tiles in varied shades of cerulean and pearl sprung from pillars, obscuring the metal frames of large glass panels.

I stopped on the landing of a staircase lined in red carpet. The hair raised on my arms and every part of me turned rigid. Blackthorn nearly barreled me over, and even Henry paused at the next stair, waiting.

A large painting of my mother stared down that wasn't there before.

"Is everything all right?" Lord Henry asked. Time was jumbled, constructed by Fate. I knew that, but I could still be surprised.

"This is new." I tried to swallow as the lord's hand reached out only to snap back as he thought better. "I wasn't expecting to see . . . *her*."

"Ah." Henry had a new softness in his tone. "I understand. It was from—"

"Foria . . . Yes, I know."

I barged past him to the rooms—my apartment—at the end of the guest hall. The painting came from *my* palace. It was commissioned during my first days as Queen of Foria—well before Tyrlas, Morav, and everything else.

Her painting was commissioned with my father's, to hang in the throne room of the Crystal Palace as a reminder of my loyalty. Both were lost when a self-proclaimed pirate king bested me and Foria fell in the early hours of the morning by fire, ash, and steel.

I never thought I'd see them again—least of all in Linvia.

Maybe there were more Forian artifacts. If he had the paintings, perhaps King Donovan had my knife stuffed away somewhere in his archives.

Or maybe this was a terrible idea. Too much of my past lived within this storied palace. Foriana was the Goddess of Death, and her transgressions were written plainly on the walls, canvases, and parchment across every library and castle in the kingdom—Linvia was no exception.

My rooms sat behind a double door painted a pale shade of blue with two busts on either side of philosophers I'd never heard of. The sunken panels were trimmed with gold leaf and the handle wasn't so much a handle as a near-perfect casting of the winter magnolia's leathery petals.

Henry opened the door and cast a furtive scowl at Blackthorn.

"I'll leave you to it." The lord pressed the key into my palm, his hand lingering while I tried not to think about how easily it fit. "Attending maids will be up an hour before seven. Kahn will be your attendant, and he's been sent for." Henry leaned closer, lips nearly on my ear as his scent of steeped black tea and dust muddled my composure. "If you do not tell me who put those cuffs on you, I will get the king involved."

The thrum of his anger radiated as I drew back.

"Who else knows I'm here?"

"Only the king. Perhaps Adler, who told me he ran into a woman with magic fitting your description." Heat flushed my cheeks at the memory of the man's green eyes—of course he had ties to the palace, important ones if his gossip reached the king.

"Your identity will be as hidden as you require. Kahn is bringing the list of attendees. Merely say the word and you will be no more than Lady Raven."

"I am no more than Lady Raven."

Henry nodded, but a sadness haunted him. "Understood. And the man lumbering behind you? I've forgotten to ask, as you are quite the distraction."

"Lord Orion Blackthorn." Blackthorn stuck his large hand out to Henry, who took it with hesitation. "I'm from a small southern province in the Kingdom of Tyrlas."

"Tyrlas?"

"Yes, Tyrlas."

"He'll lie about it." Feeling the need, I added, "He helped me out of exile."

"Fascinating," Henry clucked, gaze raking over Blackthorn before it moved to my wrists where I tugged my sleeves down, more blatantly than intended as the bracelets and cuffs jangled. "I'll have to hear more over dinner."

Henry took his leave while Blackthorn stood in the doorway, tugging at his collar with one hand and readjusting his sword with the other.

"Are you coming in?"

"Couldn't flirt your way to a second room?" A possessive edge in his tone bristled my spine.

"There are two rooms in this apartment, you presumptuous oaf. And it's not flirting when I happen to know several of the nobles who occupy my mother's fucking shrine. I did say I had friends, didn't I?"

"That's a friend?"

I rolled my eyes and stalked into the main room. The knot in my throat threatened to turn into something worse. The only person I owed an explanation to was Henry. Orion Blackthorn was nothing to me but one half a bargain and a means to an end.

15

*Dearest Foriana, I'd apologize for my behavior
the previous night, but I regret nothing. If I
remember correctly, neither do you.
Goddess or not, isn't all cum the same?
Or should I try harder this evening?
-H*

BLACKTHORN'S DOUR EXPRESSION FADED as he took in
the opulence of the room; like the rest of the palace, not a
detail was missed.

White wood trim lined the floor and ceiling, accentuat-
ed with gold leaf. In the center, large pieces of overstuffed
furniture in varying shades of blue and white were complemented by hand-painted vines and flowers on the back in
scenes of spring across Miria along the seams.

Tasseled white curtains hung over large arched windows
and wide doors led to a balcony overlooking the garden below Niany's eighteen ponds. They shimmered in the midday
light; each represented a different one of her eighteen visions
for the future.

On either side of a large parlor stood decorated doors leading to identical bedrooms and baths. I hurried into mine and closed the door before the onslaught of remembering caught up.

The last time I slept here, Henry woke up beside me—and another before him—but every detail of the bed was crafted for Leander and I before we occupied the royal rooms.

Sleeping alone here could be the first thing that broke me and it wouldn't be the last. Did I agree to this too quickly? Why did I think I'd escaped Henry? All I wanted now was time back.

I padded to the wardrobe and rifled through a run of dresses I'd never seen. Dust settled on the necks and sleeves of jewel-toned gowns, all in my size. They'd been waiting, set aside for *me*. Henry ordered these when he thought I'd never leave.

Each gown was made of silk, dyed in shades of purple, mauve, and rich autumn blues because, *"I couldn't live forever in black."*

Henry would whisper that against my ear as he buttoned the stays so he'd know how to undo them—it was our little game for years—then time ripped it away. More accurately, I ripped myself away.

The palace lulled me to sleep until a fist pounded on the door hard enough to crack it open. I bolted up. The sliver of Blackthorn's outline hovered as bright light from the parlor spilled in.

"What?"

"The attendant is here. He's wondering how long you plan to stay?"

"Haven't decided."

"You know why we're here," Blackthorn said with an edge of warning as I stood and ripped my fingers through my matted hair. "Tyrlas's bargain is only good for two months and—"

"Yes. I know." I flung open the door and brushed past him to sit on a couch. A scrawny teenager stood rigid in the doorway, dressed in the dark blue uniform of the palace pages. A pin on his lapel indicated some rank I'd known but since forgotten. In his hand was a wrinkled sheet of parchment.

Kahn bowed. "Hello, Lady Raven."

"Raven is fine. Is that the invitation list?"

"Yes . . . *Raven.*" Trembling hands handed me a list.

"Thank you—and are you the one I ask about lunch?"

Kahn nodded brusquely. "We have creamed spinach soup today. I'll be back in a few minutes."

"Lovely."

He scurried off before I could ask for bread.

The list was thorough, scratched out in Henry's handwriting that never could decide if it wanted to be decorative or practical. He'd written down every name, the courts they were associated with, their kingdoms and titles; I recognized a handful of family names, but the first names were largely new.

I was further removed than I thought until—*Prince Adler Ilverleigh.* I knew him. He was fucking fae. He'd also been engaged to my sister and declared dead two centuries ago.

Fascinating.

Did he tell Henry about the cuffs? I considered what the men might say to each other, but there were few things Henry couldn't handle with the graciousness of a lord. Blackthorn continued to hover, looking at me expectantly.

"Do you recognize anyone on this list?" I asked, holding it out.

His gaze drifted over it, lips pursed. I waited for Orion Blackthorn's thoughtful analysis of seventeen names long enough to wonder if he only pretended to read.

"Not one of them is a Tyrlas supporter."

"Tyrlas's people aren't supporters." The knight glared, but I didn't back down. "He's my client, not my king."

"And your exiler, unless you've forgotten what bargain you struck and the papers you hold."

"There's far to the world than whatever Tyrlas has taught you to think."

His stubble was almost a beard, but I saw his jaw feather as his fist clenched. "Right now, King Tyrlas is holding my sister's life hostage. Forgive me for my concern."

"Worrying won't get you far."

"Yet, I will worry regardless when you're risking her." He pushed the list back and I crumpled it. "I do not want any more trouble. Devereux is already looking for you, and if Lord Baskin and the Linvian King know you're Foriana, who else is looking?"

"The northern kingdoms owe me. They will not turn."

An exasperated sigh escaped him as he sank into a wingback chair and gripped the sides of his head. "You're making this more dangerous."

"Did you ever think it was *safe* to retrieve the shards of a lost godhood?"

Blackthorn's head snapped up. His eyes were red and tired around the edges. "*More* dangerous—"

"I am the last standing god in this realm, Orion Blackthorn." Leaning forward, I held my chin steady. "I know my worth and it is priceless. Nothing will happen here."

"Well, I don't trust Lord Baskin."

"I do." I gripped my thighs, nails digging through gloves to keep me from saying anything worse.

"Why? He's a smarmy—"

"I loved him." Memories tumbled and turned my words into a too-small admission.

Blackthorn raised an eyebrow, and his lip quirked like he'd finally gotten somewhere. "How long?"

"Six years. He tried to get me out of Tyrlas. I trust him with my life, as he trusts me with his."

"Six years is a long time," Blackthorn said, leaning back, "but thirty years is much longer. Everyone changes."

"He hasn't. Not in twenty-six years." Fondness was a dam around my heart. "Henry is a lot of things, but I will put my life to his constancy."

"Let's hope it doesn't come to that." The knight didn't believe me. I didn't need him to. "I'm still worried about exposure in a fucking palace."

"Let me worry."

"You and all of your power?"

"That was low." I made a point to jangle the cuffs. "Still more power than a Tyrlian dog." The words came out too sharp, and I saw something soften in his eyes and feather in his jaw like he was torn between smiling derisively or the right kind of fear a mortal should show in the wake of a god.

"I suppose so, especially in the palace of a Tyrlian enemy where you could easily switch sides and arm a kingdom with the power to destroy Tyrlas. Perhaps you've baited me here and lied to all of us about your godhood just to play games because you have nothing worth living for."

My gut bottomed out as a sudden chill clipped the air and took any feeling with it. "Is that really what you want to say?"

"Is it true?" he rasped, a hand on the back of his neck where regret always sat.

"No." Anger sizzled in the word as I glanced at the door, then at the fire in his amber eyes. "I am not playing a game and I would not lie. This is a pleasant surprise that works in our favor."

"How?"

"Pretending you didn't just insult the fuck out of me, this is the Palace of Niany. The Linvian kingdom has a large collection of artifacts belonging to her and Koros from the looting of Foria. Several artifacts that might help me *restore* my godhood if I can find them. So, perhaps, you should be less worried about your pride and look a few steps ahead, *soldier.*"

"I've never worried about my pride."

"Sure," I scoffed. "That's why your hands have been in fists since Lord Baskin showed up. Now if you'll excuse me, I have dinner with the King of Linvia. I do not care what you do."

"Of course you don't," he huffed, rising to his feet. "I'm going for a walk. Maybe I'll find Henry and ask him how you prefer your squirrel so you don't spit it at my feet again."

"Ask him whatever you want. I have nothing to hide."

"Perhaps I will." Blackthorn swept out of the room, slamming the apartment door. It rattled the small piece of me that deigned to care, but I brushed it off when a lady's maid knocked on the door.

I followed her to the wardrobe, trying not to consider how long these dresses had waited for me. But as the maid twirled and plaited my hair, I couldn't help but feel the sadness in the gesture.

"Do you have a preference, my lady?" Another maid held out two dresses, one in rippling purple silk and the other embroidered with cerulean flowers.

"I trust your judgment so long as I have sleeves. I haven't been this far north in a very long time."

The maids worked fast—so fast, in fact, I was already dressed in a gown, face completely done, and drinking a glass of wine near the balcony, watching the garden below when Blackthorn sidled in.

If the door hadn't slammed and a table hadn't crashed, followed by a long string of curses, I might not have noticed.

He walked out minutes later, dressed in a formal jacket and a pair of matching pants in a rich blue velvet speckled with silver. He looked handsome, except for the way he tried to fasten the wrist cuffs with his teeth.

I watched, amused, taking another languid sip before I set the glass on the table and yanked his wrist from his mouth.

"May I?"

He nodded, wary but softer than they had been. He'd also tried to comb his hair, but an unruly piece kept falling in front of his eyes.

"I'm—I'm sorry for what I said."

"Maybe I deserved it." I buttoned the five buttons on his right sleeve with lingering precision before moving to his left. "I have not been forthcoming."

"You have not," he agreed and stuck out his hand to admire the button work as I released it.

"That won't change. I'm hardly honest with myself."

"I've noticed." His jaw feathered—torn between the hint of a smile and a pitying glance. "Shall we go?"

Without another word, I left, knowing Blackthorn would follow. I should have dreaded everything this dinner would dredge up, but I couldn't. It was all worth it to sit across from Henry one more time.

And finding out what, in Koros's name, a dead fae prince was doing in the Linvian palace.

16

I love you, irrivina.
Never forget that.
Today, I miss the light of your smile
and I wish I could erase your fear.
-L

THE FORMAL DINING ROOM of the Palace of Niany was illustrious. Painted floor to ceiling in the richest azure, it was meant to mimic the fleeting moment of blue dusk just before night devoured.

The pigment came from a rock beyond this realm, ground into a paste, then mixed with a pungent resin. How they acquired it was one of fifteen great secrets of Miria.

Gold stars painted by deft hands dotted the walls and built to a crescendo where pillars met the ceiling in dramatic arches. Gas lanterns with filigree cutouts hung aloft, casting shadows of bobbing starlight across the table. Each of the hundred lamps were painstakingly refilled and lit by servants.

If the regular folk of Linvia knew the cost of the lamps, they'd balk. Every hour of fuel cost a cobbler's yearly wage, and four hours would feed eight of the poorest villages for a month.

My pointed shoes clipped the smooth, onyx floor as I walked into the dimmed room, wearing Henry's favorite color—a deep plum tulle. The dress was embroidered with bits of silver and emerald flowers that only showed in the right light.

Maids powdered blush on my cheeks to make me look more alive—like primordial iron wasn't locked around my wrists, draining me.

The dining table was black oak, polished to a mirror shine with intricate scenes carved into the legs that were impossible to distinguish in the shadowy light. I'm sure they told some story of Niany.

I sat across from Prince Adler. Discomfort kept me pulling my gloves up and adjusting the billowy sleeves to keep the cuffs obscured. His ethereal fae eyes stared anyway—green as grass in a summer storm when the sun poked through churning clouds.

After a few minutes, King Donovan of Linvia strode in to a warm welcome. The man was a spitting image of his father at the same age; I'd have to remind myself he had none of the memories and this wasn't the same court.

Donovan was a short, proud man, well in his early forties, with an easy smile and cropped black hair framing his handsome, deep brown complexion. He wore an indigo suit, matching the simulated night sky around us.

"Welcome, friends." His joviality, familiar. "It's a pleasure to have you here tonight, as well as the company of Lady Raven—a dear friend of my late father's. May he rest in Life's embrace."

"He was a good man and dearly missed," I said solemnly to some mumble of agreement as the king took his seat and dinner began. I remembered Donovan as a child, hugging his father's leg.

"How did you know him?" asked a man dressed in ruby, massaging a white beard.

"Lord—"

"Varine."

"Ah, Lord Varine." I smiled, searching for the blandest words I could find. "I served his court for many years."

"Years? You hardly have that. I'd remember someone like you."

Adler cleared his throat and several eyes snapped to him as the table went silent. "Lord Varine, she's not dissimilar to my-self—she has a similar *longevity*."

"Fae?" Lord Varine grumbled, staring shamelessly now. I closed my eyes to roll them and when I looked at him again, the lord's heavy gaze fixed on the king. "I told you I had tolerance for a single fae, do not make me come around to a second when I still don't understand Prince Adler's presence." He looked pointedly at the prince. "No offense, Your Highness."

"None taken." Adler hid his amusement behind the rim of his wineglass as if this wasn't the first time.

"I'm not fae," I said, folding my hands on my lap. "If any-thing, I'm more wary of them than you, Lord Varine. The prince is correct. I am no mortal, rather a former handmaiden of the Pantheon who fell lifetimes ago and has since found homes across Miria."

"You think we still honor it?" a woman asked. Henry sat beside her with a smirk that never wavered. Time was a fucking illusion if you lived long enough.

"Of course we still honor it, Donna Liette." King Donovan cut off anything the woman meant to say next. "We sit within the walls of Niany's shrine. Our safety and peace was forged by the primordials whose power the gods inherited."

"Hadn't realized demigods walked among us." Adler's fae eyes pierced like a too-sharp dagger as he played with a large black ring on his finger. "Thought they'd all died by now."

My eyes narrowed. "There aren't many, but we've found a way. Luckily, the gods aren't as interested in our whereabouts."

"I remember you from years past, Lady Raven. And I never asked—can you turn into a raven? Demigods can change forms, I've heard," a small, round man at the end of the table asked.

I knew him; he invited me here before Henry.

"Afraid I'm not a shifter." Henry hid a laugh behind his hands and I'm sure Blackthorn had a similar expression. "That gift is reserved for mortals. The gods never granted me that magic."

"Let's not overwhelm the lady, Lord Ferthing. Lord Blackthorn," Henry interjected, steering the conversation away from me. "Tell us, what is the tyrant kingdom like these days? I've heard Tyrlas is a madman who believes in trade isolation when half the realm would spend double for Tyrlian glass if he'd let anyone through the gates."

Blackthorn took a sip of wine and relaxed at the question, launching into a riveting explanation of the state of the Tyrlian glass trade. He explained it in such careful detail, and with enough flourish that the room hung onto his monologue about taxes through the first course of water beets in duck fat. Only halfway through the second course of squash pasta and brown butter did Donovan shift course to sharing stories.

Lord Varine asked me about my palace memories, and I spoke fondly of the few I dredged up, emboldened by Henry's gaze as our wines were topped off.

One story had King Donovan spitting wine. There was a garden party some spring where his father had the bold idea, after a long wine dinner, to joust on foot in a makeshift tournament among the dinner guests because the ground was too wet for much else.

Instead of poles, they tied canes together and the night ended with several broken ribs and three naked men laughing until they cried in the middle of Niany's gardens.

Dessert came soon after that story, as Lord Ferthing shared another until King Donovan rose, ending the dinner. I stood to leave; Henry touched the small of my back and my blood pounded.

"Join me in the drawing room." His gaze flicked over my shoulder where Blackthorn animatedly waved off Donna Liette. "Your lord is more than welcome."

"Am I?" the knight asked sharply, looking over. "I appreciate the invitation, but I need rest." His gaze turned to King Donovan who stood near Adler, whispering something. "Thank you for everything, Your Majesty."

"Thank you, Lord Blackthorn. The pleasure is mine." The king nodded. "Keeping Lady Raven safe is no small feat, I'm sure. She means a great deal to Miria, as my father oft reminded me. I do hope to corner you about Tyrlian glass the next chance I have."

"It would be my pleasure." Blackthorn bowed and left, followed by the king and Prince Adler.

Henry took me in the opposite direction, to a room I remembered for billiards; these days, it was a room with several mismatched couches and shelves of old books. Forgotten paintings draped in sheets leaned against the books, while light from two oil sconces cast dancing shadows across a dusty rug.

"Is the king redecorating?" I peeked under a sheet. It was a landscape of the Linvian Mountains in spring. The hills were dotted with clumps of purple linthriope and red-stemmed elven claw.

"He is, but it's perfectly functional as a room," Henry sighed, stopping in the center at a lopsided table while I continued my tour. "What makes a room if it isn't the walls and a door?"

His chin dipped, making no secret of the way he watched my body, lighting a fire I'd never forgotten.

Age lines were written like a story across Henry's face, framing his eyes and his lips. They plucked something in my heart.

"You're a vision," he breathed and closed the distance, dragging me into his arms. "Every day, Raven, I have missed you."

"Stop." Emotion tugged as I pulled away, putting a chasm of space between us; it couldn't be this easy. "Tell me what I've missed, Lord Baskin."

"Tell me why you're here—be plain. You thought I was dead?"

"I wasn't sure." I swirled the little wine left in my glass and tried to steady my thoughts as I took his hand in mine and turned it over. "I'm traveling. And what about the last thirty years? You married?"

Whatever he said next would lance through my ribs. Leaving him was a choice I regretted, but it was a choice I'd make a thousand times over.

"Traveling? I'm sure that's all." His smile turned wistful. "I did marry, and my daughters are nearly twenty-four and twenty. Both in Linvia—my eldest married a lord, and the younger is a healer in the temple."

"That's lovely." I meant it.

"Just like their mother. You would have loved her: Luella. She was a beacon wherever we lived. Spent years as a librarian in Verinium, studying the history of the god trees—even wrote a book about them."

"Did she?" I made the mistake of looking at Henry. His brown eyes glittered.

There was so much I wanted to say . . . to touch, to hold onto. I wanted to take my fingers and trace the freckles on his back like constellations and watch the creases of his eyes deepen and move in the shadows of the moons. I wanted to thread my fingers through his and kiss the stubble on his jaw.

"I told her about your tree." He tugged a button on his shirt, exposing just a sliver of his chest. "Lue thought it was beautiful—but it wasn't her favorite."

"And what was her favorite?" I asked, throat constricting.

"Etta's, with her single silver magnolia tree hidden in the hills of Reen. The rarity intrigued her."

"It was the only place her blood spilled."

I looked at my glass and took a swig, hoping it could numb me, but not even a drop remained. This was why I didn't revisit mortals; the mixture of grief and pride was suffocating.

I loved Henry, and I was happy he lived, but it didn't erase the tender, selfish corners of my heart wishing he'd had a life with me.

"Was Etta killed by her brother?"

Henry came closer again, nearly nose to nose as I crawled through memories. "She was almost killed by her soul bound."

"Did you kill him?" Henry asked. I leaned against him. Reflexively, his arm reached around my waist, and I didn't stop him as his fingers dug into me.

"His brother killed him." I stepped back and dragged a chair over to the window. "Later, I killed his brother . . . then I killed Etta."

I meant to sit, but he pulled me to my feet, flush against his chest like we meant to dance. His lips brushed my ear.

"If I remember correctly, *lyra*—you sit on my lap, not the other way around."

I leaned in and kissed the stubbled space where his neck met his jaw because I couldn't take it anymore. His grip on me tightened. "Can't a god change her mind?"

In a flurry of skirts, he spun us and I landed on top of him as the chair screeched against stone. We scrambled to right ourselves and when I finally stopped laughing; I draped my legs over his. His arm snaked around my back, and I leaned into the touch.

There was peace in the proximity as we stared at the other, caught in a moment, chest to chest. His fingers played with the fabric of my gown, absently trailing up my thighs. I needed to apologize for so much, but what good would it do?

"You don't know how badly I wanted just this," he whispered into my hair and pressed a gentle kiss to my forehead. "I'll warn you, I'm not twenty-seven anymore."

"And I'm not seven hundred and fifty-eight."

I took his beautiful face in my hands, admiring the lines formed from laughter and sorrow—each a memory and proof he'd lived where I hadn't. I ran my thumb over the curve of his jaw; silver overshadowed brown.

"We should talk."

The will to do so died as his thumb ran along my lips and his parted.

"Or you could kiss me, Raven."

He was faster. Hands grabbed my neck and he kissed me—rash and desperate; the collision was the same as coming home.

We savored each other. His hands kneaded my hair, loosening pins as our tongues explored and my curls came undone, brushing over my shoulder. I lifted my skirt, straddling him and rocking my hips.

Nails dug into my thigh. He moaned against my mouth and I shuddered, wanting him like no time had passed . . . like love was something I'd only felt once as his breath caught with every roll.

Would he still whimper when my fingers undid his trousers? I'd thought about that noise too many times in my sleepless nights, and now the hardness of him was a vice, searing between us.

Fuck. I reached down, fingertips trailing the waist of his pants as his hands splayed across my back and pressed me closer. He moved against me and my mouth watered as I kissed him again.

The door flew open and I broke from his lips, but I didn't move my hands. My attention flicked over his shoulder to see Adler stride in, unfazed.

The fae prince lit the fireplace with a brush of his wrist and closed the door with another. I wouldn't move off Henry if that's what he waited for. Instead, I rocked my hips again, desperately wishing I could finish the lord as his hands dropped from my waist.

Adler's gaze sharpened with a salacious grin. "Only stop on my account if you mind a third. Would you like a drink, Lady Raven? Lord Henry?"

"A drink would be lovely." Henry pecked my nose as the moment passed and his breath returned.

With a sigh, I stood up, brushing my skirts back to order as I watched the prince. Henry joined me, hand trailing my waist as he kissed my neck and Adler filled three glasses from a decanter.

"You're not planning to poison it?"

"I'd never." Adler bristled and handed the first to Henry. He set the second on the table and then stalked toward me, third in hand.

With fae reflexes, his free hand darted and yanked my wrist up with precision and a snarl so quick my breath caught as my sleeve fell.

"Who did this to you?" Henry asked from behind Adler. The soft pretense in his voice dissolved while the prince held me there like he had any right. "If it was the man you traveled with, we will happily take care of him, *Your Majesty.*"

I tore out of Adler's grip and whirled around to Henry, poking his chest. "I handle myself, Henry. I'm fine and you did not need to send a fae—"

"*I,*" Adler pronounced as I took a step back in order to see both of them, "was not sent to find you. I happened across you because I hadn't felt an ounce of magic in years and I simply couldn't resist. Then, I saw the iron cuffs and you denied my offer to walk you back, which is when I went to Henry with my concerns because I thought he might share them."

I stared down the fae male who stood nearly two heads taller than I. "Why should *you* be concerned?"

"I have my reasons."

"Your father is the reason natural magic is extinct in Miria. Isn't he the reason you faked your death, or was my sister so unpleasant—"

"I believe *your* father also had a hand. You are not the only heir to undermine their sovereign."

I took a step forward, nearly flush with the prince's chest, as Henry watched, unsure if he should step in. "I am not an heir and my father is dead, while yours still sits his throne and you—"

"Do not pretend to know me."

"I do not pretend because I do not care to know you. If Henry hadn't warned you about my feelings toward your father's kingdom, then perhaps he doesn't trust you as much as you'd like to think."

Adler's eyes darkened. His chin tilted up, haughty and regal, reminding me of every damned entitled prince I've had to smile at in every life. "Perhaps Henry doesn't trust *you* as much as you'd like to think."

Henry cleared his throat and held his hand to Adler's chest, brown eyes only on me. "Raven, I trust you with my life. The day you were taken, I stole a horse and rode to the gates of that prison. I lived in Tyrlas for three fucking years, doing everything I could to get you back to Linvia."

I angled my body toward him, forgetting Adler entirely as my voice went numb. "I told you to live your life."

"I did." He took my hands in his, still the young man I'd loved. "But I wouldn't break the promise I made."

Emotion turned bitter in my throat. "It was a dumb promise."

Henry shook his head. "It wasn't dumb. You were still imprisoned when I was called back to Linvia. Along the way, I met Adler and—"

"I warned you about bargains."

Henry held up his hands as Adler smirked. "I knew what I was doing. Adler killed the Tyrlian King in exchange for a place in the Linvian court and Linvia's protection."

I looked at Adler, rage an undercurrent. "You could have simply asked Tyrlas to free me. He'd bend over for fae."

The prince shrugged. "I had the opportunity to kill a mortal king who thought he might hold a god."

Something warm stirred in me and I shifted on my feet as Henry spoke again. "Be angry with me, Raven. Not him."

"I'm not angry with anyone. Hand me my drink." I gestured at Adler who scowled as he handed me the glass. I took it and sat on a dusty couch, away from both men.

"Those cuffs need to come off," Adler said matter-of-factly while Henry grunted in agreement. I wasn't keen to tell either who held it. "They're destroying you."

"Why does the prince of the fae care?"

Adler sat across from me, and Henry dragged a chair over. "Several reasons. You are the Queen of Gods with Koros dead, are you not?"

"The Pantheon dissolved with him, without an heir. There is no power in the title. Even if there were, you over-estimate how willing I'd be to work with fae."

Henry squeezed my thigh and added, "I think I know why you're here."

I did not look at him. We'd spent too many nights discussing it, talking of dreams and plans . . . of how much I ached for mortality.

"I made a bargain for freedom with Tyrlas. I intend to make good on one half because it's time I stop running."

"Raven." Henry said my name like it might break. "I know what you're doing."

Slowly I looked at him. "You will not stop me, Lord Baskin. I'm also no longer interested in this conversation."

"Raven—"

"Tell King Donovan I need two horses tomorrow, at dawn. I seek something from the Morav crypt."

"Of course," Henry conceded. "They'll be ready."

I swallowed the contents of my glass and left before either man protested. The skirt of my gown brushed against the honed marble tile as I paced the corridor. I'd speak to Henry privately, but I couldn't face him tonight.

Heavy footsteps clipped the floor, chasing me. I dodged into a different corridor, but a strong hand grabbed my elbow. "Henry—"

It wasn't Henry. Adler stood, clutching me a second time, forcing my eyes to his.

"You don't want the cuffs removed because you want to feel mortal," he breathed, and I wasn't sure when I gave him permission to see me so clearly, or who gave him permission to look at me in a way that set my core on fire.

I stiffened. "Why do you think that?"

His gaze dropped to my lips. Something shifted in the air between us; he relinquished my arm but didn't move. Fae or not, I couldn't deny he was striking and deadly.

"Because I feel the same." He stared, then his voice dropped. "*Fuck.*"

He gripped my neck and his mouth met mine. My hands flew to his chest, but I didn't push him away. Instead, I gripped the lapels of his shirt and dragged him closer.

"*Navrosia,*" he said against my lips like a prayer. Fingers dug into my neck and I moaned into roughness, desiring to taste all of him if he'd let me.

I shoved him into the wall behind us and he matched my frenzy, grabbing my neck to deepen the kiss. I pressed my body against his rigid form, standing on the tips of my toes to get a better angle, to get deeper.

This kind of kiss burned from the inside out. Dormant magic wrapped around me and my palms ran over his corded muscles, wishing the immortal strength in his hands would find their way back to my neck and pin me to the wall.

I tore myself away and took a step back, panting, staring at his swollen lips as he looked at mine with a lopsided grin and a ripped shirt.

"Imagine what that could be like without the cuffs?" He grinned.

Coming back to myself, I straightened my dress. "Maybe I'll put them on you instead."

"You never have to ask to tie me up."

I knew better and began to walk back, shoes clipping on marble. This was dangerous until I heard Adler say my name in a low voice that bordered on a warning.

I turned.

"What?"

"King Ilverleigh intends to march on Miria in four months' time."

Ice skittered down my spine as he walked, disappearing around a corner. I wanted to chase after him and demand answers. Instead, I clutched my chest as the words rattled my conscience.

War.

Or, rather, a hostile takeover in the absence of the gods. The fae had been without Miria for five hundred years. What was the mortal realm to them?

No, I wouldn't care—I couldn't—and my mind was made up. Adler was right; I enjoyed the mortality. Being a human-turned-god meant knowing exactly what it was to feel and being cursed to know exactly what I'd given up. I wouldn't live like that again.

Except for the sound of Blackthorn snoring, the apartment was silent. It was a welcome quiet in a familiar room that somehow always marked the beginning of something . . . another war, another shift, or change.

But this would be different. This time I wouldn't stand over a thousand dead soldiers, or before my father with a knife in my hands. I'd lay among the dead, a god knife in my chest. My lungs would fill one last time beneath the gold-threaded branches of a black willow tree—never to rise again.

That was my vision of hope.

"DON'T."

Leander held my arm and stared, fingers indenting my gloves. We both knew what waited. I knew what I was capable of and only I lasted forever. Not love, not hate . . . only death and Koros were eternal.

"I have to try."

He stroked my hair and wrapped around me, arm slung over my waist as he pressed his back to mine. Our heartbeats match too easily, like time would never come for us.

But it would. And the next day I went to the temple of Nurem, alone.

The temple was empty. Rays of sun though narrow, slitted windows lit the smooth stone floor like bars of a cage as temples were *for the most devoted. The head priest approached and I dropped to my knees before him.*

"Can I save him?" I asked, premature grief was a bone caught in my throat.

The priest blinked. "We told you the prophecy and can tell you no more. You, Foriana, know exactly what is written in blood on the shores of Ore."

"Say it again," I whispered, too close to pleading, hands clasped.

"When all other gods have died, a king will stand when Death's darkness twines with the brightest light." He took a careful breath, watching my face as he recited. "From beneath the blackened willow, as she splits in two—new dawn will rise."

"Leander is the brightest light I know."

"His name was brought to Fate." The priest said nothing else, so I pressed; the marble bruised my knees.

"Please. If it isn't Leander, it could be no one else and you know it. You see all. You see the future in his eyes the same as I do."

"You will destroy yourself to see him rule?"

I nodded. "I'd rather die. Living without him is not a future I'm willing to accept."

A shrug shifted his robe and the ochre rope tied around his waist. "It is a future you will have to endure."

"I'll give it up for him. All of it. I'll have Koros kill me. The primordials will not intervene. They abandoned us."

"As you are, a piece of you will live on until you are made whole."

I ran a hand through my hair and looked up at the arching white ceilings of the temple. My lip quivered. "Tell them to give it to someone else. War waits and the Morav King will not run. I cannot make him. Take this curse and let me die at his side a mortal. I don't care."

"We do not hold that power. Only Death and Life were granted the gifts."

Niany.

"Could she—"

"She forged you and the gods of the Pantheon at Koros's will. He controlled only the earth and the dirt that we stand on, not the souls who inhabit it. Primordials saw you worthy with the passing of Ersos—just as they saw her."

"Then I will save him."

"You will save no one, Your Majesty."

The haunting cry of a raven echoed from the rafters as one landed on the pure white marble, talons clicking as ebony eyes quietly observed me. It was an omen I chose to ignore.

17

Instead of going to bed, I poured myself another glass of wine and pulled open the balcony doors to watch the flurries of snow twirl out from gray clouds. Old magic kept the palace balconies temperate as frost spread and crystallized on the lawn below.

I still tasted the fae prince—and Henry. They lingered on my dress, taunting me a hundred different ways in wafts of tea and smoke. I knew what Henry wanted, but Adler? The kiss should have bothered me, but he kissed me the same way Leander had and I clung to the memory.

I'd kissed fae before, and gods, elves, orcs, dwarves and every kind of mortal, but none had ever left me out of breath and followed it up with a sentence like: *King Ilverleigh intends to march on Miria.*

The last time the fae king invaded, Miria had the Pantheon . . . three hundred gods and a thousand demigods at their command. They were dead now, and the magic they sought to defend gone with them. Mortals stood no chance, and fae rule would be worse than the gods ever were.

Both were ruthless and void of feeling, but where the Pantheon wanted to remain idolized and removed, the fae wanted more: They wanted Miria for themselves, to drive the mortals into dust.

What would that war look like without an immortal defense? There wouldn't be a battle. Visions of blood-soaked grass and discarded bodies played out on the frozen lawn below until a door closed and the scuffle of feet startled me.

My heart lifted for the briefest second until I saw Blackthorn wandering out of his room. The knight hovered near the couch, hair tousled from sleep.

"Shouldn't you be in bed?"

"You're not my mother."

I returned to watching the garden below.

"May I join?"

By the time I waved a hand, he already stood in the door frame, broad shoulders taking up most of it.

"What if I said no?"

"You didn't."

"I might."

"Okay. Tell me to go back."

I didn't.

Silence stretched and calm settled as I took a sip and looked out. The unchanging shadow of the Linvian mountain loomed in the distance. I couldn't bring myself to loathe the beauty and the lush cover of pine trees that trailed off at the rocky crest; somewhere near its peak. That was the Morav crypt.

"You could stay here forever, couldn't you?"

I shook my head. "Tried. I was arrested by the Tyrlian King . . . though, I would've left anyway."

"Why?"

"Overstayed my welcome." I thought only about Henry's soft brown eyes. Kissing him brought back a swell of emotion. I thought I'd moved on. "Henry deserved more than I could give him."

That's why I didn't return: Henry wanted a legacy, and ours would've been a curse.

"How was the rest of your evening?"

"Fine," I answered, biting my lip because I had nothing to add. "Yours?"

Dinner slipped my mind. All I held onto was what Adler said . . . and the way Henry had kissed me.

"Fine. Are we leaving tomorrow?" He asked with a lilt, cocking his head.

"Donovan will have horses ready." In the distance, a deer lapped from a fountain that hadn't iced over. "We'll leave at dawn."

No amount of time would be enough to face Morav. From the moment we set foot in Dover, my dormant grief started to wake. I never went back for a reason.

"Earlier," Blackthorn started, "I said I was going to find Henry. I didn't find him, but Prince Adler found me." I stiffened as Blackthorn continued watching the same deer. "He said you're powerless in Linvia. He seemed worried—is it true?"

"A fae has no reason to worry about a god." I swirled my wine and watched the red settle before I looked at him. "I'm powerless in every corner of Linvia. There are no ghosts on this side of the river."

"None?"

I took a steady breath. In and out. I couldn't look at him, only at the mountain.

"I destroyed Linvia and its access to the afterlife when I trapped the Scribes of Nurem. The veil is impenetrable and I cannot draw power from it. Any soul caught that day will spend their immortality wailing from some void I created."

"You hear it now?"

"I'm used to it."

Blackthorn gawked and I rolled my neck, listening to the cacophony beyond. I wished I hadn't said anything, but there was something disarming in the way he stood, shoulders back like we were old friends. The flurries in his hair were distracting too.

"How did you do it?"

I looked at the ruby-red wine as if I'd find an answer that wasn't an admission.

"Two hundred and eighty-seven years ago, the Scribes of Nurem lied to me. I obliterated them when I lost control and turned a quarter of the city to ash. The temple withstood, but I was exiled from Linvia for a hundred years."

"By the bleeding fucking plains." His stare burned my neck but I didn't look up.

"I don't tolerate being lied to," I said.

"I thought scribes couldn't lie."

"The scribes were men like any other and died as easily. The only difference was the magic they hoarded, which is gone now."

Trapped, in fact.

The knight loosed a breath and looked out. The true destruction of Linvia was a secret. There were stories kept in temples, whispered by seers and old Masters, but no one remembered the day or how it happened at my hands.

Over the years, I let the detail fade into oblivion and become something of a legend too big to possibly be true as my magic waned and faded to nothing.

"You are in danger without your power."

"My life is still impossible to take."

"Aren't there worse things than death?"

"Nothing I'm afraid of anymore."

He sighed. "Adler was right, though, wasn't he? I've been thinking about it all night—the way they look at you."

"I need nothing, Sir Blackthorn," I said in a small voice rivaled by the breeze and shaken by a second mention of the fae.

You want to feel mortal. The prince wasn't wrong.

I blinked. Blackthorn now towered in front of me, blocking my view of the garden as his amber eyes dug in and excavated my defenses. I was powerless as he sank to his knees.

My heart hammered, but I didn't lower my wineglass. In fact, I didn't dare move or breathe as tension curled in my belly and warmth bloomed. He stared up, his face calm as the winter wind lifted his hair.

"Hand it to me." He gestured at the glass.

I let him take it. His eyes were tight and wary, but he seemed sure as he set it on the stone floor and tilted his chin.

"What are you doing?" My voice shook, more breathless than intended, but I couldn't think with the way my heart pounded.

He raised a brow, turning his attention to my wrist; he took it in his large hand with a gentleness that might have been mistaken for reverence.

From his other pocket, Blackthorn fished out the silver key, then twisted it in the iron lock until a distinct click shattered the silence. With both hands, he slid the first cuff from my wrist and set it on the ground. I tried to breathe, tried to ignore how easy a motion it was for the weight they bore.

He did the same for the other, but he didn't stand. Instead, he looked up, lips parted as bits of magic crawled up my arms for the first time in twenty-six years. I ran my gloved hands over my wrists, awed by the way it flared again—thrumming in my veins like a second heart.

As I flexed my hand, his own wrapped around my wrist and trailed my arm. Then his cold hands dropped to the bare skin on my thighs, between sheaths of fabric, and froze like he thought better.

"Touch me," I whispered through the haze of rearing magic and a bolt of feral desire.

Blackthorn's expression didn't change. Amber eyes remained on mine as his hands squeezed, nails digging into the ghostly flesh of my thigh with a bite of pain. My senses flared.

"Like that?"

What was I doing? His palms grazed, moving around to cup my ass where he squeezed again—harder this time; a moan escaped my lips.

I leaned back against the stone wall and stared at the swirling snow as he brushed aside the dress and I bit my lip, all but begging for connection. Cold struck my legs, but it was nothing as magic came in waves and the warmth of desire built. His fingers teased, running over the band of my underwear before sliding the lace to my ankles.

We should have stopped, but I closed my eyes. The pressure of his touch relented, then the heat of his tongue burned against the inside of my knee and trailed to the seam of my leg. In the brief, cold absence of his tongue, I shuddered.

Then he licked the tender area, and my knees started to shake. A moment later, the weight of his lips pressed the space between, punishing—unrelenting. I tried to breathe as my core tightened and my body convulsed. Broad hands held me in place, the stubble of his beard grounding friction as I came.

It was a blur of magic, of lust and pleasure. It was otherworldly, impossible. His hands raked up my gown and flurries fell around us. Slowly he rose, arms caging me against the wall as I looked through bleary eyes.

He was too careful not to press any part of himself against me except his lips.

And when he did—Orion Blackthorn kissed me like both our lives depended on it. Hands in my hair, grasping for purchase, holding my neck still as I raged at the taste of myself on his tongue.

Then, something snapped; I couldn't breathe. I couldn't stop. I fought myself, wanting every part of him in a way that overwhelmed my basest instincts, until my hands found his chest and pushed.

He stared at me wide-eyed, beautiful, with swollen lips and ruffled hair.

I forced myself to speak, voice splintered. "I need to sleep."

Every part of me was cold in the absence of him. I half expected Blackthorn to reach for the cuffs. Before he changed his mind, I slipped inside and crawled into bed more fearful than I'd been in a hundred years.

A word I'd forgotten pressed my temple. I tried to ignore it, but it woke me up every hour because it was too impossible—too big, too wrong for everything that lay ahead. The moment his tongue swept mine with the taste of my arousal, there wasn't any mistaking it for anything else.

Ancient, forgotten, impossible. Soul bound.

Impossible because Orion was mortal and forgotten. Impossible because gods only had one soul bound and I'd killed mine centuries ago before a single notch of our bond could click into place.

I'd taken every precaution to ensure I'd never be prey to the blind emotions and irrationality of a bond.

My oldest memories clawed back, scratching my heart and wringing my lungs as I buried my face in the pillow. I was ready to run back into his room and beg for release, but who would I be if I did? If I tore apart my soul just to feel him move against me?

What if he gave me the will to keep going?

What then? If I kept my promise, I'd have my father's power, and my own ambition. I could swallow all of Miria and force it into my vision of what a world should be . . . what we had envisioned all those years ago.

I'd only felt a pull like this shortly after I'd come into my godhood. The moment his eyes met mine, I saw the world and panicked. I'd seen what the loss of a soul bound could do to a god, so I'd killed him before Fate had his say.

Until tonight, I thought I'd made peace with my broken soul. So what was this?

Blackthorn *was* mortal.

Mortals couldn't be soul bound. In a hundred lifetimes, I'd rarely seen it happen among the gods, and certainly not to a member of the Pantheon, unless . . . unless he wasn't mortal, not truly.

But I'd killed every god. I knew magic anywhere, and I knew *him*.

Perhaps I didn't.

This was the gnashing teeth and claws of Fate coming for me.

I stared at the ceiling.

Maybe I should have realized it in the Tyrlian palace when the king made us kiss. And maybe I should have realized in the moments my mind quieted near him—I was naïve.

Renewed magic charged and flared in my veins, reminding me that I was never mortal; a mortal destiny was nothing but a dream.

Something fated had fallen into place, and there would be no ripping it out of my chest.

18

MORNING CAME TOO SOON.

Ice-white light filtered in through the curtains; the chill of winter was unmistakable, and a dusting of snow stuck to the flagstones. Why didn't I wait until after the thaw? How was this so pressing to Tyrlas that he couldn't wait for spring?

I dressed in insulated leathers, a fur vest, and stuffed my arms through one coat and then another, hoping it would be warm enough for two nights on a mountain—three if a storm came through.

The clouds hung low so I suspected a snowstorm wasn't an impossibility, but Henry promised two horses and, knowing him, he packed enough provisions to see us through a few nights.

As I flexed my wrists in a thicker pair of gloves, magic brushed against my skin—tired and familiar, flickering like a candle with the same small pinch of heat. I was still missing most of my godhood; if I stayed like this, it might be weeks before my power recovered.

A knock sounded on the door and my stomach sank as I strapped on my sword. Though imminent, I wasn't prepared to face Blackthorn in case he asked the right question.

Biting my lip, I turned and Henry stood in the doorway instead. Peppered hair gleamed in the morning light, and a smirk turned up one side of his face, sending my heart skittering.

"You look warm."

He eyed the fur underneath my coat and the knit hat I'd brought over my barely braided hair. He couldn't see the missing cuffs, but I'm sure he'd be pleased.

"Nearly sweating," I muttered and both of us stared at the other's lips. Desire and history were two tangled threads drawing us together. "Odd seeing you in the morning fully clothed."

He cleared his throat. "Horses are saddled and waiting. I'll lead you to the trailhead—it's tricky to find."

"Thank you."

I pushed past him into the common area, but not before he grabbed my arm and pulled me close enough to smell the weirwood of his cologne and feel the heat of his breath on my ear.

"Are you sure you have to do this?" His grip loosened, and his forehead pressed against mine. "I'll never forget when you said torture would be preferable, *lyra*."

My moon.

The Xerxian word unlocked something lost. I softened into his touch as he played with the end of my braid, brushing below my breast. "You know why."

"And if there was another way?"

"There isn't." My fingers danced along his jaw, tipping it up. A desperate kiss waited in the tension of unspoken words. "Who would I be if I didn't try?"

"Mortal."

"I'll never be mortal."

Sometimes love was a reason to leave.

"I know." He cupped my cheek and kissed my forehead. "I just don't want to accept it."

Blackthorn cleared his throat from the other side of the apartment and Henry's hand slid back.

Finally, I looked at the knight who stood by the windows and didn't break my gaze. The cuffs were clipped below his belt but he'd never put them back on me. I'd make sure of it.

"Lord Baskin is taking us to the stables," I said, pretending I wasn't affected.

Blackthorn's expression remained unreadable and quiet as we followed Henry through the palace to the stables across the north lawn. The sky remained gray and equally ambiguous, which was unfortunate because my cheeks froze after a few minutes.

When I was fully a god, temperature merely prickled my skin. I never truly felt the warmth of the summer sun or the sharp, achy cold of a winter freeze until pieces of me were slivered off or drained.

Whatever magic had swelled back last night wasn't enough to chase out some. I shivered as we mounted and rode out past the western gates, toward the forest edge.

Behind us, a layer of frost coated the sleeping city. Smoke curled away from chimneys and blended into the cloudy sky as we approached the daunting rise of the Linvian mountains—less daunting with every step as pine trees obscured it.

The trail began an hour out of the gates and the entrance was overgrown, shrouded by low-hanging pine branches. Henry turned his horse, nudging it as close to mine as it could go before we went separate ways: him back to the palace, and me to face my husband's grave.

This wasn't our goodbye, but it hovered like one. Henry had only known me with the smallest fraction of my godhood . . . when I returned, I wouldn't be the same.

"I don't want you to go," he whispered as an overdue apology soured on my tongue. "You're going to break your heart up there."

"Maybe I won't," I said, tightening my grip on the reins. "I'll come back."

"And I'll be waiting."

There was more I wanted to say. Blackthorn had already led his horse a few paces up the trail so I gave Henry a half-hearted wave and followed Orion Blackthorn into the wilderness.

Soul bound.

Henry wasn't bound to me in any way, and his gaze could break me apart. What would happen now that I knew who Blackthorn was to me? Even if he couldn't reciprocate, the distance didn't stop the ache or tension in my chest that I was now keenly aware of as I stared at the trail ahead.

I'd been here before at the base of the mountain, sometimes willing and sometimes unwilling, carried into the forest by the whispers of the dead, desperate to find something that didn't exist.

The last time I came unwillingly. I'd been drawn away from Henry by a nightmare during a lull in the spring rains. I wandered through the pines barefoot and overcome, looking for any sign Leander had moved on—that his soul wasn't destroyed.

Maybe the afterlife wasn't better but an empty field couldn't be worse than an eternal void.

Leander couldn't be nothing.

He'd been so much that two hundred years later, on a warm spring night, I fell to my knees and screamed his name so loud it shook the trees.

Henry found me covered in mud with needles in my hair and still decided he could love a god who'd chosen to fall. I didn't want to fall again. I needed this to be the end.

The trek up the mountain passed in a haze of memory, sore hips, and the soft crunch of hooves on a wide trail up the mountainside.

Eventually, night fell and we stopped. The city below was nothing more than a faint twinkle. We'd crested the first peak. Tomorrow, we'd journey along the ridge, into the range, so long as the meandering snow flurries didn't turn into a flash storm.

Orion Blackthorn sat on a log he'd rolled over and stared at the fire, holding a piece of bread out. "You've been quiet."

"Is that unusual?"

Six hundred things weighed heavily. Immortality wasn't worth whatever debts my father settled with it.

"Is it what I did last night?"

My eyes flicked up as my gut knotted. "I asked you to do it; it won't happen again."

"If that's how you feel," Blackthorn shrugged, shifting on the log as he peeled off a coat and laid it on the ground. "Though I'd rather enjoy it if you changed your mind."

"I won't. Change my mind, that is."

"Fine." He flashed an infuriating smile—more infuriating than the prince because it wasn't haughty but genuine and grating. "Can I tell you a story?"

"Can I say no?"

"Absolutely not." A log in the fire cracked and sputtered, sending up a spray of embers as he pulled his second coat tighter. The wind was picking up. "My father was a butcher. I grew up terrified, axe in hand, and somehow disgusted by blood. Terrible qualities for a butcher's son who wanted to be a knight."

My eyes narrowed. "I know you're a terrible knight. Why are you reminding me?"

He sighed and flicked a hardened edge of bread into the fire.

"Well, I had no interest in butchering. But somehow, as a child, I thought a person would actually deserve punishment more than the pigs. So I left home, forged a few documents, and lied my way into squiredom, working for a knight in one of Tyrlas's eastern provinces."

"So we both cheated in the tournament." I squinted at him. "Why are you telling me this?"

"Fifteen years. Only my sister came to Miacor." His gaze hardened and seemed to trap my attention. "The anger and pain and—"

"We are not the same," I said tightly, throwing up my guard. "I'm sorry you were abandoned by your family, but I wish I were. I'm like this because of my parents, not despite them."

He leaned forward, the shadow of his stubble more severe in the bare firelight. "Lord Baskin was worried the moment you said what you'd come here for. Why?"

"Because he cares for me, he'd rather not see me take back my godhood."

"You care for him too."

"Astute observation." I deadpanned, but there was no malice behind it. "We spent six years together. I *am* capable of feeling."

"I'm noticing."

His expression was painfully sincere and tugged at the lingering truth. "Henry only knew me after I'd given up everything and before I was put in those cuffs. All he knows of my godhood is my loathing for it."

"And the pieces of it are only in places from your past?"

"Obviously," I muttered. "If I thought I'd ever take it back I might've tried for somewhere further south."

"Are you suggesting we could be on a beach?"

"Maybe next time." I stood, holding my coat tightly against the whipping wind as it turned the flurries into pelting ice. "I'm going for a walk. If a bear eats me—let it."

"I will not do that," he said and laid down on the coat spread in front of the fire. "On second thought, wouldn't you live through it?"

"Yes." I cringed at the visual and reconsidered. "That was a Pantheon punishment for a few years. If I scream, save me."

"I'll consider it."

I angled past the horses and wandered a few paces, hoping to find at least one ghost with enough soul to warm my hands and maybe my feet. The magic had to be here, and without the iron, I could use it without spending mine.

Whatever I'd done to Linvia stopped at the city's edge, but the destruction to the dead and the magic within it was absolute. To think I'd done it with only a third of my godhood. I shivered, imagining what I'd do with more.

A whisper of a soul brushed my hand as a pointed breeze. There was nothing when I looked, but I plucked off my glove and reached; my fingertips were freezing and preemptively glowing an icy blue. I reached for the veil and drew a ghost forward with the wave of my hand.

The form of it slowly flickered into being. My heartbeat picked up as the cool liquid of death magic ran over my palm. This was the lightest of my magic—a soul tied to the land, left to wander.

True death magic started blue and then became black icy tar. In the early days, I waved it off with a single flick of a finger. Without the cuffs, it was easier, but dredging it up still felt like moving mud.

A ghost took shape: sharp nose, dark hair, and honed arms I'd begged for in my darkest hours.

King Leander Morav stood and my heart jumped into my throat.

"You," I breathed, knees shaking.

A hundred, three hundred years, I wandered this forest hoping he'd respond. Every part of me believed I'd sent his soul to the same damnation as every other clinging ghost in Linvia.

"*You're in Linvia?*" he asked in the old Dovrian dialect we used to speak. The language was dusty for me at best, but the song and dance between us still familiar. "*Why?*"

"*I thought I'd go for a walk.*"

I smiled through tears, hands glued to my side, afraid a single touch would break him into nothing—I'd seen a thousand ghosts dissolve the same.

"*Some things never change, princess.*" His gaze scraped over me. I already wanted longer than I had. "*You do know I forgive you, Foriana. I know what you tried to do and—*"

"*I don't forgive myself, Leander.*" My voice cracked. "*I need you. There is no one like you.*"

"*And no one is like you, Foriana.*" My eyes squeezed closed at the tenor of my name. A tear streaked down my cheek. I never thought I'd see his concern again. "*I told you a thousand times you could do it and you still doubt me. How long has it been?*"

"*Too long.*"

"*Too long?*" He seemed to freeze, but I admired every curve of his face. It was etched into my memory and sewn across my heart. Even the air smelled faintly like him: old books and his mother's herbal tea. "*And after too long, you still remember me?*"

"*I'd never forget you,*" I whispered and he stepped closer. "*Why didn't you respond? All these years—*" Another tear fell as I inhaled. I caught him stopping his hand in midair; neither of us could touch, and he knew.

"*I heard you but . . .*" My heart panged at the longing in his voice. "*I'm tied to this mountain, this tomb. You didn't walk far enough.*"

Far enough.

"*I couldn't face it.*" Shame wracked me. I'd never walked far enough. It seemed too simple now and I wanted to tear my hair out. "*Every time I tried, I thought about how my heart would break if you weren't here. I'm sorry, I couldn't bear it.*"

"*You don't have to be sorry.*"

"*It's all that's left of me.*"

I looked at the ground as a breeze passed through and more tears fell from my lashes.

"*You're not here for me.*" The sorrow was palpable. "*Your godhood? The one you didn't want then? I don't believe you want it now. Unless . . .*" He might have been corporeal, but he saw through me. "*You cannot.*"

"*You won't stop me.*" I took a staggered breath as I tried to dredge up the truth I'd guarded so deeply. "*I've lost my power, outlived everyone. A king wants a shade army and you know I can't do that again. It ruined me. But I did what we dreamed of . . . only one god lives—*"

"You can't face Malcolm alone, Foriana." My king straightened, rigid as a tree. He was the man I'd given up everything for but my life. *"Even if you get every ounce of power—"*

"I killed Malcolm first, then the Scribes of Nurem, and Koros last. They're all gone."

"You did it." His voice softened, as it always did when he needed me to hear. *"And the last?"*

"Why are you asking me?" I bit my lip and forced strength into my voice. *"It's been three hundred years and even then you knew the answer."*

Leander exhaled. His fingers tangled in his curls. *"You waited three hundred years to find me, princess?"*

"You were the memory that hurt the most."

The shade of him flickered and disappeared on the edge of the wind, leaving me behind.

"Raven?"

Blackthorn's heavy footsteps crunched around the corner and I saw his broad shoulders in the shadow of the fire. I turned back to where Leander stood but only ominous forest remained.

"Thank the fucking stars," the knight exclaimed. "Who were you talking to and what language was that?"

"A ghost," I whispered and tugged my glove back on. "It was old Dovrian, specifically a lost dialect of Rivish from before the Pantheon Wars."

The knight continued to think as I took a deep breath.

"Irrivina. Do I know that word?"

"Princess." I bristled at the way he butchered it. "Do not say it again. Not in front of me."

Before he tried again, I started back to the fire. Rage and grief pounded with every step as tears burned my eyes.

"Who was Malcolm?"

I stopped walking, squared my shoulders, and then I whirled around, shoving a gloved finger into his chest, hoping he'd feel the cut of every truth that came next.

"Malcolm was the first god I killed." Fire reflected in his eyes as I challenged him. "Don't think you'll ever be anything more than a roach under my boot."

Blackthorn held his hands up and I stalked to the fire, throwing myself to the ground in front of it. There was never enough fucking time.

Malcolm was also the first god I loved, but that was a different wound. I curled up beside the fire and closed my eyes. He was the last man I wanted to think about as Leander's visage haunted me.

Blackthorn sat with a crunch of leaves and cleared his throat. "Why is a crypt all the way up here?" I opened one eye to show my annoyance, but he couldn't see it. "If it's for a noble family, certainly—"

My voice tightened. "It's a tomb for the Morav Dynasty. They didn't want to see the bodies of their rulers desecrated so they hid them."

"The ghost you spoke with? Was he the prince you married?"

The words cut; Leander was more than that.

If we weren't alone on a freezing mountain, I would have taken my horse and run, but I had to answer.

"He died a king, not a prince."

"And you?"

"I lived."

"Just asking."

"Don't."

Leander Morav wasn't just another king or another man. He was the only mortal I'd ever met who saw a better world—a world that wasn't ravaged by war or fragmented by disagreement. His vision was of a realm united by shared ideals where mortals flourished.

He knew what Miria could have been and together we would have created it.

19

I couldn't decide which god to pray to,
so I prayed to them all for a week with my wife,
surrounded only by the sand and sea.
This war will end, I promise.
-L

SOMETHING WET NUDGED ME awake. I blinked. Swaying pine trees came into focus and flecks of snow whirled through them. I was warm and covered in fur; a massive paw curled around my leg. Fear sent me scrambling back before I leapt to my feet.

Judging from the way its amber eyes narrowed, I'd woken him too.

I wanted to be angry at Blackthorn for taking the liberty, but I was grateful because it snowed overnight and it only froze to my lashes.

The wolf stood and shook, sending snow flying like a spray of glitter in the early light before he padded into the trees. I stoked the fire and added more tinder to warm my hands.

Minutes later, Blackthorn returned with both horses on their leads. His hair was disheveled and his shirt lopsided under the layers he piled on, but he was in human form as he watched me from beside the fire.

"Morning," I quipped.

"How are you feeling?"

"Better."

The sun hung low on the horizon, casting a thin line of golden light over the mountain ridge behind us.

"I didn't want to shift," he said with an apologetic lilt, "but you were shivering and I want to respect your—"

"No apology needed."

"I'll ask next time."

"Your wolf won't fit in the tent I'm bringing next time." He smiled so maybe I wasn't as awful to him as I thought. "You don't have to apologize."

"It was a selfish choice, really. The way your teeth chatter is a nightmare."

Wind lifted the branches above with a whistle.

"Was I harsh to you last night?"

"No more than usual."

"Right, well . . ." I trailed off, looking for something better to say but not finding it. "Today will be worse. I haven't been to the crypt since Linvia fell, and I don't handle these sorts of things well."

"You avoid them?"

"When I can." I stretched to my feet, adjusting my coat. "Understand, that if I had wanted power, I would have sought it."

He nodded and handed over my reins as he mounted his horse.

The path up was rocky and narrow. We only rode for an hour before we dismounted and proceeded on foot, guiding the horses behind us. I leaned on intuition from three hundred years ago, but it wasn't hard when the path only went one direction.

Orion Blackthorn stayed silent, only occasionally pointing out a bird as it flew past or sharing some stupid story about being a young squire in Tyrlas's kingdom, which is neither a universal nor interesting experience. It was, however, better than every thought and memory traipsing through my head.

Three hundred years should have been plenty of time, but Leander's absence didn't leave a mark; it left a chasm.

After two hours, I saw the first sprig of a black willow. Dread and guilt coiled in my gut—so much guilt it turned into a mouthful of orange pith.

A few minutes later, there was another, and another cresting through the melting snow until they formed a winding black trail to the mouth of the cave.

My feet moved ahead, disconnected from my thoughts. I clasped my chest and tried to breathe, but I couldn't.

I'd never bled here. *He* did. Profusely—every drop of Leander's blood tainted by my godhood, leaving a tree in its wake.

He was alive when they brought him here.

No one wrote about it; no one told me.

My stomach churned. I stopped walking and swayed into the rock wall, clutching a clump of frozen moss to steady myself against the onslaught of realization.

Every time his family came to pay their respects, they had to reckon with the goddess who made it worse—the woman who had tried to save him and destroyed him instead.

None of them knew Leander was dead either way.

All they saw were my hands in his chest, pressed against the gaping wound, begging him to live like I had any power over life.

Guards dragged me off, screaming, covered in his blood, and loaded him on their horses before they escaped to the mountain.

The Morav Dynasty fell that day and never came back.

I should have ridden after them. I should have been in the crypt, holding his hand as the last breath left his lips. I should have known better, but revenge burned hotter and I thought he was gone. I *believed* he was gone.

My finger traced the letters of "Morav" chiseled into stone beside a nondescript entrance. If I hadn't known what to look for, we would have missed it.

With a deep breath, I pushed off the wall and stepped into the abject silence of the cave.

Blackthorn held out a torch. It cast shadows across jagged, natural stone, appearing like nothing more than a musty crevice until we turned a corner and descended carved stairs which opened into a series of rooms.

The last of the Morav line died out ninety-seven years ago. A film of dust coated everything and I doubted anyone had been here for decades.

Carved stone arched overhead, collecting at marbled pillars. Stone replicas of grand Dovrian oaks held the ceiling up. Underfoot, the floor was tiled with pieces of angled black marble shaped to fit between strips of gold granite. It was a perfect duplicate of the old, opulent throne room in Dover—an echo of the palace.

We continued down the corridor, past a run of busts carved into the walls. I remembered the construction: Leander beamed as he showed me the sculptor's rendition of his father's face and how wrong they'd gotten his grandmother's nose.

Leander cut off a question about his grandfather with a kiss like we had the world. Even then, I'd lived too long to know it couldn't be true, but I was young enough to wish it would be.

"Raven?" Blackthorn said gently. "You stopped walking."

I did. My eyes trained on the floor as my fingers itched and magic pooled in the back of my neck. This is where I needed to be, but I wasn't ready to face it. Gods, I'd never be.

"Is that his tomb?" Orion whispered.

My heart contracted. I pulled the gloves from my hands and approached the tomb at the end of the room. An ancient, gnarled willow with gold-tipped leaves stretched above it, chiming in a phantom breeze as I approached.

"King Leander Morav," I rasped, choking as I placed my hand on the stone coffin where his bones remained. "The last king of the Morav Dynasty."

The sculptor's work was impeccable.

Unbidden, my hands traced the details of his immortalized face in deep-hewn veins of blue against white marble. This slab had been excavated from the Dovrian meadow after a battle at his request. It was the same stone we stood on when we married on the eve of battle: the second time I became a princess.

The sculptor even caught the laughter in Leander's eyes, the pinch of his mouth, and the line above his brow that furrowed whenever his father walked into the room. Even his hands and their scars were frozen in time despite being lost to it.

Too much; this was too much.

My hands shook.

"Raven," Blackthorn said again.

I whipped around and gulped down three hundred years of sour regret.

"A part of it is here." My voice wasn't my own—it was too steady. It knew my humanity waned.

I was naïve to think my godhood could save a mortal. Only Niany had that power, and my attempt, my reach at more, had burned the man I loved from the inside out.

"You're sure?"

I nodded.

A faint pulse beat below the unnatural willow. I sank to my knees at the foot of the tomb and placed my hand in the dirt, near the trunk, feeling for the draw of raw power as I squeezed my eyes.

Maybe I didn't need it? Maybe I could walk away. Everything was long gone, so what would an ounce of magic be in a world that lost its use for it?

No, I needed it. I needed it to kill the last standing god and save the realm from our machinations; Miria was mine to protect and mine to give up.

The weeping branches swayed. The tree had rooted itself in Leander's tomb. Bits of his memory clung to the blood that formed it and they pressed against my eyelids.

Reminders of what I'd done, what I'd tried, and what I'd failed to do were so overt they squeezed the air out of my lungs.

I clawed at the hardened soil around the trunk, but it wasn't hard. It crumbled under my touch as if it had been waiting. Flashes of our life tormented me.

Digging took mere minutes before the cold, sharp edges of a buzzing, magicked shard chimed against my fingertips with a piercing, vibrating trill.

I plucked it from tangled roots, ripping part of me from the heart of a tree. The power connected with the wisps of my own, welcoming it like an old friend.

In my hands, the broken godhood was a sliver of glass and starlight. It hummed and warmed: We'd been separated for too long.

When I tore it out the first time, it was light and without form. Time and pressure forged it into a physical thing that couldn't be destroyed—not until it became whole. Destroying it now would only shatter it into more and more pieces.

Starlight mingled with the black and blue tips of my fingers as the vibration intensified. I wouldn't go back—we were made for each other, tied together by the will of some primordial and a god who thought he might be one.

With a sharp exhale, I hung my head and pressed the sharpest point into a space between my ribs, then I thrust it through my chest like a knife.

Blackthorn gasped.

I remembered nothing else but the way my body lurched. Fire crept through every vein, igniting the sleeping parts of me that had always belonged to the gods. Cold became less biting, the stone warmed, and every ounce of fatigue plaguing me was replaced with the silent hum and flutter of waiting magic and possibility.

For a moment, or an eternity, I was light and darkness floating along a river of ether as my soul and my godhood found themselves entangled again, forging a home in my veins.

Then I blinked.

I leaned against someone's wide chest and the warmth of him was too sharp, too poignant. I was here and I wasn't. Breathing came slow as a cave came into focus.

No—a crypt filled with bone and dust . . . and *my willow tree*.

Realization struck. I bolted up and a knight—no, *Orion Blackthorn*—stared at me with pinched brows and an open mouth searching for words.

"Raven?"

I backed into the wall. A sharp pang constricted my chest. This isn't what it felt like. Losing my godhood or giving it up was always empty and desperate, concave and broken. So much of my life was spent crawling away from this power that I'd never noticed the loss.

This was different.

This wasn't in the middle of battle, running on adrenaline. I wasn't clawing my way past grief in order to find revenge, nor was I bound in iron chains. I could *enjoy* it.

The ancient part of me woke up and I relished the change. The fire of the torch burned brighter with a myriad of colors, some I'd long forgotten the names of. The blue stone Leander was carved into had traces of agate, like the meadow grass it came from.

How did I live without this for so long? How would it feel to take it all back when this was a fraction of what I could hold?

"How do you feel?"

"Fine. I feel fine," I whispered as Blackthorn angled to repeat his question and I relaxed. I tasted the stone in the air, mineral and sour, and I tasted the acidity of his confusion.

"Good," he said, dusting himself off. "Now what?"

"We go back." My voice cracked; explosive and renewed. "Can we ride through the night?"

"Absolutely not."

He frowned. I took a step and stumbled forward, catching the wall. It was strange to be heavier and lighter simultaneously as I followed a cautious Blackthorn out of the crypt.

We started our descent and didn't stop until sunset when I nearly collapsed.

"I'm fine," I insisted again, straightening on the horse.

His brow furrowed. "We'll stop here."

Snow started to fall again and I tripped, catching myself on the back of my horse, who wasn't too thrilled but didn't spook.

"One more hour."

"No."

Blackthorn tied his horse and mine to a tree. I wanted to keep going, but I couldn't push my legs any further. Giving in, I slumped against a tree trunk as he pulled twigs together and set a fire for us.

Different and the same. A hundred and thirty years had passed since the last of my godhood departed. Emotions were suddenly further, more orderly, and more like my own.

I was in control again.

Blackthorn stared across the fire, waiting for me to say something.

Soul bound.

I remembered.

The word broke me once and certainly would again because I'd never tell him. How could I when I needed him to kill me? No one else was blood-bound to help me in Belfiante.

"Raven?"

"What?"

"You seem different."

"It's the godhood," I muttered, holding out my bare hand, nudging magic to see if I could force the flame any taller, but that magic was never the gods'. Instead, blue death magic pooled in my palm. "I've been without it for too long. It needs to reacquaint itself. Imagine your memories all unfolding and then being folded back, but the lines aren't quite the same as they were."

"Sounds unpleasant."

I shrugged. "Better than when I'd been granted the godhood. It was all at once—two weeks passed before I left the room."

Blackthorn looked at me and I admired the golden cords floating through his amber eyes, an echo of the blond threads of his hair.

"You were mortal though, how was it possible?"

"Mortals had a tolerance for magic and I was decidedly complicated. The greed of the gods and fae took away that tolerance. " Memories of my father and mother drifted through and I waved them off. "I was seventeen when my real father struck a bargain with Koros because I refused to marry. I was a young soldier in an old king's cavalry—"

"You?" He gawked. "Raven of Miria, a mortal soldier? You said you couldn't relate to me."

"I wanted out of my village—that's what I remembered. Hardly believed in the Pantheon at the time."

"How? You could fucking see them."

"Do you believe everything you see?"

"I suppose not."

"Exactly. Before I reported to the field, Koros stood at our front door with a bag of gold."

Blackthorn flicked a leaf into the fire and the flames leapt. "Your father sold you out?"

"My mortal father wanted me to marry and set an example for my sisters. The gold went to their dowries and none to me. Koros held his brother, the old God of Death—Ersos—in prison, waiting for me to go to battle because I needed to prove I was worthy."

"And you did?"

"Koros found me near death in the middle of a battlefield. I thought I'd died until I woke up in the palace as Princess Foriana of the Mirian Pantheon."

"I'm sorry."

"Sorry?" My eyes lifted to his and I wasn't sure what I felt. "Why?"

"You had no choice over who you'd be."

I shrugged. "More choice than you in Tyrlas. I was made and Koros never forced me into anything, even when it might have been easier. I was quite happy being a god for hundreds of years—"

"Until Leander?"

"No . . ." I trailed off as other memories crept up like a pit of snakes. "Before him."

"Another war?"

"Something like that." I hardened again, tugging a glove back on. "It's not worth talking about."

Blackthorn watched me turn away and lay on the forest floor before he slunk off and shifted into the wolf. Minutes later, the wolf curled up beside me, careful not to touch, but close enough as he rested his snout on the ground and closed his eyes.

Against my better judgment, I rolled over and let myself enjoy the warmth, far too tired to fight the corner of the bond I'd opened.

Year 1044, Outside of Dover
Raven is 494

"COME TO BED," I said from under a thin white sheet as shadows played across the canvas walls of the tent. The sun set hours ago and it was still terribly humid.

Leander hunched in his chair, outlined by lamplight as he poured over a map. His head cupped in his hands as his fingers flexed through his soft curls.

"What if we lose?" He strained. "I couldn't—"

"It's war."

"I'm not like you, Foriana."

His hand hit the desk with a thump and he turned around. His shirt was unbuttoned as he rearranged to sit with one knee by his chin, the other leg stretched to the floor.

"That's why I love you."

I threw off the sheet and padded toward him, taking the sharp edges of his jaw in my gloved hands. Tears lined his blue eyes and I wanted to wash away his fear and doubt, but it was a necessary lesson by the Crown.

"How do you stand this?" he asked, wrapping his hand over mine, pulling it to his chest where his heart beat.

"It helps when there's something worth fighting for." My gaze dropped to his lips. "Your father's instincts are right. Morav needs this to steady his rule—"

"What if I haven't done enough?"

"You've done what you can. There isn't any more you can do tonight."

Leander looked at the ground, squeezing my hands before his gaze caught mine. "Marry me, Foriana."

Doubt is what I should have felt because mortality was lost to me. Instead, my heart filled. He was different. Leander Morav was my equal, my everything in every way I'd ever needed a person, and I'd be damned to live without him.

He scraped me off the ground after Foria fell and held me through my darkest nights when Malcolm had forced himself back into my life. I couldn't find words for Leander; I didn't have them.

I wanted forever with him, and I'd find a way to forge our eternity.

"You know I'm yours," I said as fear washed from his expression.

We donned our cloaks and left the tent for the edge of the meadow where he'd kissed me the first time. It happened in the middle of a storm my father concocted; we'd found cover between marble boulders near the tree line.

"You can say no," he said again, tugging me up the same rocks as the light of two crescent moons barely lit the white stone, "but I will never love another as I love you."

The words crashed into my chest, stealing my breath. I wanted so desperately to be mortal and grow old, to face death and the empty afterlife hand in hand, but even for a god, some dreams were just that.

We faced each other as Leander pulled a worn crimson ribbon from his pocket. It was the color of Morav and he pressed it against my palm, attempting to tie it with one hand. When he secured the knot, it became Fate's tether, binding us together with a promise larger than ourselves.

He tipped up my chin, fearless and perfect. "You need to say yes, Foriana," he whispered, lips quirked up. The wind nudged a strand of hair across my eyes. "Or say no and I will never ask again, but you will never lose me."

"Yes," I said, emotion tangling around the words.

"Good." He squeezed my hand and smiled. "Now, which gods do we marry by?"

"Marry us by your gods, Leander. I have no love for mine."

His gaze fell on our clasped hands. "Then we'll be married by the wind, irrivina, because the only god I love is you."

20

As the godhood settled, I splintered. Memories worsened as the pulse of magic strengthened. The piece I'd given up when I tried to save Leander had sewn his memories into mine.

Why was I doing this? Did I think I'd be better? In seven hundred years I was never better and I wasn't sure I could be.

The descent passed in excruciating silence as I gritted my teeth and relived my mistakes. If Blackthorn was worried, he was damn good at showing it. My rage and remorse only grew every time I caught him watching me, and the hard lines around his mouth when he swallowed whatever question he meant to ask.

I nearly collapsed at the gates of the palace where King Donovan greeted us. The sun had fallen behind the mountain and the smallest moon, Rea, showed her face. It had started to snow in large white clumps.

"Welcome back, Lady Raven. Lord Blackthorn," said the king with a booming voice and jovial smile as he brushed his shoulders off. "I hope your journey went well."

"Indeed, it did, Your Majesty. Could Lord Baskin not greet us?" I dismounted and shoved the reins at a stable boy.

"He's handling an issue on the east side of the city. I thought I'd personally welcome you back and see if there is anything else I can offer our valued guest."

"Only discretion." I stepped closer to the king as Blackthorn helped the stable boy. "It will be to your financial advantage when my business with Tyrlas is sorted. I promise. We'll also be out of your hair in the morning after some rest."

"No repayment needed." The king assured as he clapped my shoulder. "Stay as long as you need, Lady Raven. My home is yours, as it was under my father and his before. We have a feast tomorrow night—a celebration of eight hundred years of Linvian cuisine."

"We'll consider." I forced a smile, hoping he couldn't see the way my lip quivered. "Have a good evening, Your Majesty."

"And you as well."

Inside the palace, I stumbled on the stairs, falling against the railing in a wave of overwhelm. My vision tunneled as I gripped the rail and tried to breathe through it.

I meant to stand straight, but Blackthorn swept me off the ground and my head lolled back. He clutched me to his chest and carried me up the last steps, past the watchful and distrusting eyes of my mother.

Had my willingness to fight died with the mortality I almost had?

I barely registered that Blackthorn laid me on the bed because I was in the midst of drowning. Drowning in memories, and sick with sudden power I'd been separated from for centuries. Pure power—blinding and raw—I didn't realize how much I'd tried to give Leander. Was it everything I had?

I forced myself to sit. Blackthorn remained at the door, frowning.

"You need to rest."

"No." I swung my legs over the edge. "I'm not sleeping in the same clothes I've spent three days traveling in. They're covered in dog hair."

He raised a brow. I ignored it and turned on the bedside lamp. Blackthorn rolled his eyes and threw open the wardrobe, pulling out a cotton nightdress before I had time to stand.

He held it out and I stared at the white fabric. I hated white.

"I can dress myself. I will be fine."

"I don't believe you." He set the gown on the edge of the bed. "I can get Henry to help if you'd prefer?"

Magic surged at the tips of my fingers. Gloves were the only thing holding it back as my voice scratched and the faintest impulse stared at his neck where his pulse beat. I felt wild and suddenly parched.

"Please leave."

"Dinner is on the table," he said cordially and backed out, closing the door. I didn't move until his footsteps faded, then I ran the bath with the hottest water I could wring from the faucet.

I shrugged out of the leather and fur until I stood naked, watching the water rise. Then I plucked the fabric from my fingers, discarding my gloves on the floor.

The nature of death was all-encompassing. I turned my hands over in the light. Small streaks of blue death, like lightning, showed beneath black, which had spread from the tips of each finger to my second knuckle.

Even without the cuffs, and with a piece of my godhood returned, the veil in Linvia was impenetrable. But I had more power than that. Death could always take.

I balled my hand into a fist and closed my eyes, imagining the crush of magic and power as it swelled back.

When I unfolded my fingers, blue-black ash fell out, drifting to the floor like toxic snow. Several flakes floated on the water's surface, disappearing as I submerged myself.

Tears welled and knotted in my throat because the water felt warm—it didn't *sting*. It wasn't turning my skin pink nor did sweat prickle my forehead; it was lukewarm and the same as the winter wind. Gods, the numbness came fast.

Adler was right—I wanted to be mortal because I wanted to feel. True gods never felt alive. Everything Koros did, Niany, Fortune—all of them—was in pursuit of something to give them purpose, feeling.

I only found purpose when my godhood was chipped away. So what did that make me? My mind wandered as I dried off and slipped into the gown with no intention of staying put.

I needed out of my head and I needed to get into the archives before we left or I might be forced to survive Belfiante.

Outside my room, Blackthorn wasn't anywhere I could see. Despite that, I carefully closed the apartment door, gripping the latch so it made a faint *click*.

Intuition carried me up a flight of stairs, down a hallway, past the ballroom balcony to the door where a hand-stitched crest of a crow and fig tree hung from the handle.

I knocked once, then again.

The door opened and Henry Baskin stared ahead with a flash of disbelief.

"Raven?"

"I did it." My voice cracked and my lip trembled as he ushered me into a room that was nothing how I remembered.

Clothes were draped over chairs; books were spread out and open across a wide mahogany table where empty cups gathered beside bottles, trinkets, and a pair of boots. His white furniture had been replaced with darker wood and heavier accents.

The only constant was the roaring fireplace near the balcony where a door was wide open, letting snow in as it accumulated outside.

Cold didn't bother me. I sank to the floor in front of the fireplace on a threadbare red rug as flakes whirled in. Henry draped a blanket over my shoulders and sat beside me. For a minute we were silent. His hand slid over my knee and squeezed. Memory and feeling slammed in as a tide.

"You miss her still?" I asked, pushing away his attention. I didn't want to talk about me.

"Every day." The sorrow in his voice opened a wound in my chest. "I'd wish it on no one . . . I was too young to see the pain you had, but I see it now. It was selfish of me to be jealous of the dead."

Henry looked so much older than when I left him, but still so much the same. I threaded my fingers between his and rested my head on his shoulder.

"I never thought you were selfish."

"I was." He let out a long breath. "Luella hoped to thank you."

"Why?" His arm wrapped around me and his stubble caught my hair.

"If not to find you, I'd never have gone south."

"I told you to stay."

"You weren't my queen, so I ignored your command." His head lifted as his voice dropped. "Besides, crossing the realm for you was as easy as deciding to breathe."

"I missed you too." The words stuck in my throat. They were true—too true and painful. "I'm remembering."

"Had you forgotten?"

His fingers danced along my foot and dragged up my calf, taking the hem of my dress with them. They lingered a few tantalizing seconds before he retracted and the dress fell back.

"I never forgot . . . but, of everyone alive, you *know* me."

"Is that why you came here?" His arm wrapped around my waist again, anchoring me while my thoughts circled between wanting distraction and comfort. "What happened?"

A gust of wind pushed another flurry of snow into the room. He shivered, pulling the blanket tighter.

"I went to his crypt and took back my power. The memories all came back."

"The scribes? And the war?"

"Leander." I brought my knees to my chest to cage my raw and grieving heart. "I saw his ghost on the mountain. He didn't die in the temple; he died in the crypt."

"What?" Henry moved to look at me. Lines of concern framed his lips, elongated by the firelight. "You looked a thousand times."

"I never went far enough."

That was the truth of it—the embarrassing admission after the tens of times he'd found me in the woods, begging for Leander's ghost on the hardest days. I had pinned too much on Henry when he was so young.

"*Lyra*." He wiped the tear from my eye with his thumb, cupping my face. "I'm sorry. I can't—"

"Kiss me," I demanded. It was that or I'd fall apart on this rug, but the same combination of grief and hunger reflected in his eyes—an echo of the past folded into a vision of the future. "*Please*."

"Kissing you isn't enough."

"Then fuck me, Henry."

I'd settle for feeling anything. I leaned back and pulled my dress up, running my fingers along the inside of my thigh to the seam of my underwear.

"Are you sure?" He gulped, voice straining as I dipped my finger behind the lace where wetness pooled. I didn't want to think. "You just—"

"I need you."

"Raven."

"Henry."

Memory dragged us back as the blanket fell from his shoulders. "There isn't a part of you I haven't missed."

The last thing I wanted was his softness. Any mortal could be soft, but I wanted Henry. I crossed the room and shoved books off his desk, scattering them across the floor before I bent over it, breasts against the wood and gaze on the balcony. Warm anticipation surged.

There was no command, no please.

A breath later, hands roved up the side of my nightgown, teasing it up to expose my ass. Henry pushed me into the desk, a steady hand between my shoulder blades as his other ran along the curve of my hips.

The hardness of him pressed into me and wiped my thoughts clean as he traced my bare skin, mapping the scars on my back. Instinct rocked my hips as he leaned over, lips to my ear. He caged me to the desk as his finger rounded my thigh and pushed the lace aside, teasing the pulsating part of me that warmed for him.

"It's this wetness they write poems about." He snapped the band. "Would you believe I was a poet once?"

"No." My answer came out breathy and wanting as he slid the lace down my legs and pushed me deeper into the desk.

The tip of his tongue ran along the jagged scar on my spine as he pulled the gown up, leaving me entirely exposed to him.

To Henry, my body was an instrument. I cherished every moment of borrowed time pinned against the desk with his lips on my neck. Then, he pushed his fingers into me with a sudden spike of pain and pleasure I'd gone too long without.

Our breath quickened as my walls clenched as pleasure built; a small gasp escaped as he pressed a third finger and arousal dripped down my leg.

"I'm not letting go," he said. His breath tickled the shell of my ear, multiplying the building crescendo. His hand slowed inside me and he ground his cock against my leg, taunting me. "Not until you come for me, *lyra*. Not until you've soaked these pants."

With my cheek against the desk, I almost whimpered as his fingers turned inside me and his knuckles pushed against my clit. Warmth spread. My thoughts and my body separated as he held me down.

Another thrust. Henry groaned and it undid me—liquified me. Tightened my core and wrung me dry with the sound of a splash as his hand stilled. He whispered, head against mine as I lay there, "You always listen so fucking well."

The pressure of his hand slipped away, the shape of him replaced briefly by cool air as he undid the buckle of his pants. They slid to the floor with a clink and anticipation tasted like wood varnish and the iron tang of blood from biting my lip.

I wanted him to fill me. I wanted the memory of getting fucked on the desk while watching the snow fall to supersede the others. His hard cock pressed against my ass and I whimpered unbidden as his hand roved over my body again with earned reverence.

Henry's other hand tangled in my hair, pushing it to one side as he kissed my shoulder.

"Sit up. I want to see you."

I rolled over, his hand steady on my back, running along my arm to keep me from falling. My nightgown fell back and his brown eyes consumed me.

How could anyone claim to only fall in love once? I'd admit to falling a hundred times because what was the point of living if not to love like this? Silent and adoring. His mouth parted and his thumb traced my waiting lips.

I drank him in, naked before me, cock waiting where the shadow of his hips cut to it. Gods, there were new scars I'd explore, new stories written across his skin, and bargain marks I wanted to know, but Henry licked his upper lip, grip tightening on my jaw, just before he jerked me forward and our lips collided.

We clawed at each other's hair. I needed every part of him the only visceral way I could have him. He groped my breasts, fisting the fabric of the gown for only a moment before tearing it in half with a sound that echoed through the room.

I wrapped my legs around his torso, clinging to him as he carried me across the room.

We landed in the shadows of the four-poster bed; him crouched over above me, cock between my legs like time had never passed.

I took his hair in my hands, pretending the silk was skin, pretending I knew what his hair felt like beneath my fingers as if there wasn't a barrier keeping him alive. He did the same, fanning out my tangled curls.

He kissed the scar on my neck where Koros resurrected me and I bucked beneath him, holding onto his shoulders like Fate might take him from me.

"I need you, Henry."

"I haven't forgotten how greedy your cunt is, Raven. Let me savor you."

His fingers trailed my ribs as he kissed and sucked, before they dipped between my thighs again and wrung another gasp. Henry drew them out slowly, measuring the beat of my breathing as I felt him smile against my chest.

Heat and pressure coalesced as he drew up and watched me again. I shivered with every motion of his hand until he stopped.

Then he dipped below, licking the wetness from me with a groan so deep the anticipation became suffocating, desperate.

"Henry, please."

"Please what, Raven?" Henry licked again, and this time with a wicked laugh as he came up, hand under my arms and his cock against my thigh, nudging the aching, needy spot I needed him to fill while I writhed. "Please what?"

"Please give me your cock. Fuck me like those days in the library: make me forget."

He shook his head with a coy smile as he stroked my hair and bucked his hips, teasing, pressing me with the head of his cock while desperation pulsed against my neck.

"Eyes on me, *lyra*. I won't let you forget what we are."

Henry gripped my hips and pushed into me with a long moan. Every tantalizing inch stretched and filled me as his lips parted and time stopped. I lifted my hips to take him deeper.

Fuck, to have him even one more time was an ecstasy I hadn't imagined as the heat built again in my belly with every plunge of his cock. He drove deeper and deeper until his body seized with a luscious groan, setting me on fire as he panted, grinning at me as his hips came to a stop.

"I'm sorry," he said shyly as he slipped out.

I reached for his face and stroked his cheek. "Don't be. I already ruined your pants."

"Twice, actually." Henry kissed my forehead as I rolled to my side and stared. I couldn't quite believe this—him. "I could—"

"This is perfect." I placed his palm on the curve of my waist.

His room still felt like home. With him, I could almost forget the magic buzzing under my skin . . . I could ignore the shift in the air. In his arms, I was me again. Or at least a version of myself I could live with—a version worthy of being loved.

"I want you to stay," he said. "Don't go to Belfiante."

"I have to." I drew back and stood against my will. "You know I have to finish this."

"And if you don't?"

"If I don't? Not an option."

Henry frowned as he sat up. In the moons' shadows and the dying firelight, he was the same man I met nearly thirty years ago and I wanted to curl into him and run my hands over his chest as he lied to me about his scars.

"Not even tonight?"

Remorse tasted like seawater as I rummaged through his drawers to find a pair of pants and a shirt that fit. He wasn't broad, but he was tall.

"It isn't a good idea." My voice cracked as I pulled on a pair of breeches and secured them with a tie. My gaze caught his from across the room. "I love you, Henry. I do, but if I stay the night, I won't leave."

"Would it be so bad?"

The strain in his voice made me want to stay, but reality clawed back with a gust of wind and snow.

"Yes."

I returned to the edge of the bed, his shirt bunched in my hands as he moved to sit beside me.

He helped me into the shirt, fingers brushing my nipples and lingering on buttons as if he had the power to change my mind. He wouldn't. We were leaving Linvia tomorrow, and I still hadn't sifted through the archives.

Henry kissed me slow and languid, savoring the last of what tonight needed to be until I had the sense to break away and leave.

No amount of magic or godhood would make it easier when we circled another goodbye.

21

THE DOOR CLOSED AND I stood in the corridor: back pressed against the tiled wall, hair sticking to grout as I stared at white trim and gold leaf. Tears brimmed because I'd been fucked before, but it was another thing entirely with someone who'd taken the time to love me.

Even with renewed power under my skin, the sense of loss crept closer and tangled with exhaustion as my adrenaline faded.

Before I gave in to sleep, there was one more thing I needed to do—I needed to find a knife before I found excuses to live, and if my parents' portraits were hung in the hallways of this palace, perhaps there was a crate with some forgotten bone of a god or something sharp and enchanted by the primordials.

I meant to turn down the hallway, but I stumbled over the form of a guard who'd fallen asleep beside a bust.

It wasn't a guard.

I coughed loudly and Orion Blackthorn lurched, scrubbing sleep from his expression as he straightened his cotton shirt.

"What are you doing here?" I said through my teeth as he scrambled to stand and match my scowl.

"You could barely walk. Forgive me for noticing you skipped dinner to wander around a palace full of strangers, unaccompanied—what are you wearing?"

I scoffed, straightening the too-large shirt.

"I don't need dinner and I am the *only* person in this realm with any magic. No harm will come to me."

"Is that why you've made use of it?"

"Mortal steel doesn't bruise a god or have you forgotten a woman let you win?"

"Insult me again, Raven, and maybe I'll ask you to prove it."

"Insult *me* again and I'll throw a stick and ask you to fetch it." His dagger swept the column of my throat. Cool steel kissed the scar that made me a god and I smiled. "Is that all you have?"

His eyes narrowed and his breath strained as he tried to break my skin, knuckles turning white as he braced the hilt and shoved. I yawned. He thrust again and finally dropped his hand. It wasn't sharp and I wasn't the wraith I'd been in Tyrlas' court but it did piss me off.

"You make me feel like I'm losing my mind," he spat.

"Perhaps you are."

"I'm only here to see you keep your bargain."

"Oh?" I laughed hard and cold. "Is that all?" He paled as I hauled myself to my toes. "You forget, *Lord* Blackthorn, I've led armies, started wars, and executed gods with nothing more than a knife. If you think you could make me do anything, you overestimate yourself and what a king's dog is good for."

Blackthorn leaned back.

"By all means," he snapped, stepping to the side. "Certainly Lord Baskin has more to offer than the knight whose life you swore on."

"I do not owe you for unlocking my chains if that is what you imply."

I meant to storm away, but the knight grabbed the crook of my elbow and pulled me into him. My hand caught his chest and his gaze bore down—lingering too long on my still-swollen lips.

The proximity was torture.

My body wanted every part of Orion. What stretched between us was different, desperate, and ancient—from somewhere deeper than I'd ever dared to reach—but I wouldn't be so weak again.

"Let me go." I pulled my arm and senses back, moving into the shadows. "I am not ready to sleep and you will not make me."

"Then do not complain when I wake you up." The knight grumbled something under his breath as he stalked away but I didn't catch it.

Soul bound.

Hadn't Fate done enough? Had I not been thoroughly crushed—was there anything left of me to take? I'd loved mortals before, so why tie my life to another when I'd served my punishment?

I considered what more I had to lose as I wandered to a hidden entrance in the back of the kitchen. Beneath several bags of flour was a trapdoor that led to the archives where Donovan might have hidden some remnants of the gods.

If he had my parents' portraits, there was a chance they were looted with my god-killing knife and other artifacts from Foria's Crystal Palace. There were many things I'd settle for, but I hoped to find *Miryanai.*

Few blades were capable of piercing the hearts of both god and fae, but mine was one of them. *Miryanai*—Dovrian for 'justice'—was fashioned from the bone of Malcolm, the God of War.

Most gods had enchanted weapons, but many were lost, destroyed, or forgotten to time and of them, few could truly kill immortals like me. I'd lost mine in the palace of Foria during an ill-fated return a century ago and I lost my father's shortly after.

I ate a crusty piece of bread from the counter and moved several bags of flour aside. Then, I pulled up a loose floorboard underneath a rug, revealing a passage that I dropped through. The hard landing on a stone floor in a pitch-black room ricocheted through my knees. I panicked as I took a step forward and cursed—I couldn't even see my nose.

Only after a second step, I remembered the hum of magic and tugged off a glove to rub my fingers. Faint blue magic pooled in my cupped palm, just enough to see the narrow shape of the corridor and the five archways ahead of me, each marked with a symbol.

All large cities in Miria had vast underground networks leading out to the city walls. It started during the Mirian Reconstruction over five hundred years ago. However, Linvia was one of the rare cities without walls so the palace wasn't built for escape so much as it was built to trap intruders.

The tunnels were discreetly labeled, and only two led to the stables or the edge of the woods. Otherwise, they were dead ends or, worse, led to the heart of the city—useful in times of peace but deadly in a siege.

A wasp, clinging to a maple branch denoted the archives. It loomed over the second arch. The forest exit was marked by a small, horizontal line, and the two city exits were marked by a hammer with a ribbon around the handle and a worker bee resting on a scythe.

Five architects built the tunnels before the palace was constructed. The king framed it as a contest and the best tunnel should have won the contract for the rest of the palace. However, the king broke his promise in favor of a renowned fae architect.

I remembered the scandal. Koros refused to get involved but ended up hiring all five mortal architects to redesign several sections of the Pantheon.

The stone floor sloped and the ceiling above opened up with intricate pillars carved from the granite shelf Linvia was built on. Few people knew the tunnels were impressive as the palace above.

There were rumors the last dragon in Miria was buried somewhere around here and another that Donovan's archives held the long-lost treasure of ancient King Diadeus—including his scepter that raised the dead.

It wasn't true, of course; I stood beside Diadeus when he "raised the dead." Niany contracted me for the event, hoping to quell a rebellion in the early days of the rising city, years before Dover was anything more than a fishing village. The show worked and cemented his legend in the history of Miria.

The corridor opened into a wide rotunda and the floor changed from smoothed granite to a glass mosaic of wasps and flowers—the mark of the second architect and his tunnels. From here, nine doors led down nine corridors, each marked by another door because eighteen was Niany's number, even if it was *inconvenient*.

Another rolling wave of magic struck as I stood in the center. Power burgeoned, expanding the blood in my veins until they'd nearly burst. I focused on my hand again and tried to shape the blue light into a flame, but all I managed was an orb hardly wider than my palm.

Miryanai would call me, and so would my father's knife. Fate wove both weapons into my history. Unfortunately, the hum of a thousand forgotten objects filled my head as I closed my eyes and tried to focus on one.

I just needed to pick a corridor. Then something made a noise, like the chime of glass followed by a sharp breath as my senses picked up and recalibrated.

A door closed with a creak, then footsteps on stone stairs. I stiffened, swiveling to see Adler stride through another door, torch in hand, throwing shadows around the rotunda.

"Shouldn't you be in bed?" he asked, amused as his gaze raked over my borrowed clothes. "You traversed a mountain in the early days of winter and restored a piece of your godhood—you ought to be in bloodlust or, at least, exhausted."

"There are more interesting things than sleep."

"Stealing from a king, perhaps?"

"It isn't stealing if I'm taking what's mine." I straightened. Fae knew better than to challenge gods.

Adler stared at my wrists. The corners of his eyes softened as he moved the torch to get a better look. He wore a dinner suit with a blue velvet jacket.

"You're looking for a knife carved from the bone of a god." The flames reflected in his green eyes as he studied my face for an answer. "I could help you, but I have a suspicion about what you plan to do with such a weapon and I won't aid you in dying."

"What if we died it together? We could take turns." I raised my brow as his own furrowed in mock consideration.

"It could be lovely, right? The quiet," he said, watching me with the wariness of a street cat. "The smell of blood on granite?"

"Seven hundred years is plenty," I crooned, lifting my chin as I took a half step closer. "Maybe I'd let you fuck me as we both bled out. Imagine it."

"Truthfully, I imagined the first time with less blood—and it would be a shame if there wasn't a second, or even a third time."

"You wouldn't last a second time."

"Do not make assumptions you're not willing to prove." Adler cocked his head. There was a charge in the way he looked at me. "You still haven't answered my question, Your Majesty. What are you looking for?"

"Raven," I corrected with a frown. "Of course I'm looking for the knife."

"What a coincidence. I know where such a knife might be. However, I need something from you."

I gave him a withering look. "A bargain?"

"No," he said, matching my ire. "Not a bargain. Just a kiss. An easy request, truly, and I'll show you Foria's collection. Donovan moved it since you were last here—needed to make room for more interesting relics."

This was a trick. It was the moment with Tyrlas all over again, even if it couldn't be. I stepped back.

"You cannot be my soul bound," I said plainly, because something inside me fell sideways. "That is what you're testing—a bond, to see if I'll notice?"

"I'm testing nothing." Adler stared, eyes pinched and jaw taut as he closed the distance with another step. "Can I not desire to kiss a goddess? Besides, I know you killed your soul bound and I've been very clear about my intent to live. Unlike you, I haven't seen everything in six hundred years."

"Give it another hundred."

"No kiss, no knife." His eyes glimmered. "But if a kiss is too intimate, I'll settle for seeing those pretty lips on my cock."

"You'll regret that too."

"A kiss is my price."

I tried to read between the lines, to see if there was any secret behind his eyes as I dropped my magic and pulled on my glove. I'd already been jolted once—I was tired of Fate getting the last laugh.

"Fine."

His hands cupped my neck and brought my aching lips to his. My senses were already off-kilter, but the way magic bloomed between us warmed my blood, and I wanted to taste his. There was something wild and rabid, something dangerous in knowing we could both deal in the pleasurable pain of immortality.

When we broke apart, the room shifted as though I were drunk.

"I don't even care that you taste like Henry and smell like the guard."

I nearly blanched as he called me out, but shame wasn't becoming of a god.

"I—"

"Have nothing to apologize for. I know you are not mine, even if I wish you were."

It was too quiet to hear words so loud. They echoed off the stone and through my head, but I knew a fae trick when I heard one. He was trying to shake me and I met his gaze with the same confidence.

"You promised me a knife."

"Of course." Adler bowed and walked up to the door marked fifth.

It opened into yet another corridor; the light from his torch bounded off black polished stone. The next door led us to an expansive room with more than enough artifacts to keep someone searching for a lifetime or three.

Rows of wooden crates were stacked five high on one side. Massive statues and broken busts, painting, portraits, and furniture from every corner of the realm in every shade of wood filled the middle, as far as the torchlight would reach.

There were piles and collections from nearly every corner of Mirian history.

"Incredible, isn't it?"

I went into one of the narrow aisles, forgetting the magic waking up inside me, forgetting the fae prince behind me, and seeing only the history of Miria laid out in the strangest way.

"Where is it?"

Adler's deep green eyes darted around as he scanned the aisles from his place beside a dusty old carriage. "Not entirely sure."

He held his arm out and waved his hand. A whisper of magic lit the lamps around the room with a *whoosh* and the entire room revealed itself. There must have been thirty aisles. An old wooden ship hull loomed in the shadows; the nymph carved into its bow observed treasure below.

"I only knew it was behind the fifth door in Rodrick's tunnels. As you can see, Donovan doubled his father's collection efforts and, it seems, single-handedly funded Miria's pirates."

I took a few steps farther, stopping at an old sink filled with spoons. He stopped too, playing with a piece of furniture because the creak echoed through the anxious silence.

"Years ago, Koros told us you were dead."

"Dead to Miria maybe." He shrugged and moved around me, farther into the aisle, as I picked up a spoon only to put it back.

"Koros broke a bargain, which ended the marriage agreement between me and your sister, Armine. Perhaps that's when he considered me dead."

My spine went straight at the mention of Armine—she was every bit as diabolical. As the Goddess of Love, she could read the threads of fate and souls with more clarity than any seer. Love and Fate were games to her until the day she died at the end of my father's blade after interfering in the wrong affair.

There was no silence quite like the silence at dinner that night.

Her tree was a red maple and I made a point of cutting down the few I'd ever seen. Sure, they always sprang back, but at least I tried.

"I only met her twice." Adler cut through a rash of sour memories as I moved down the aisle. "You and I, however, have met more times than that."

"Three?" I snarked as I turned toward him.

"Four." His jaw twitched and he raked his hand through unkempt hair, loose waves of dark hair falling over rounded ears. He stared at something in the distance. "Twice when you were Princess Foriana, at your father's side, then again as the Queen of Foria, and once in Linvia, when you stood beside Prince Leander Morav."

"You looked the same?"

"Younger, maybe." Adler fiddled with the sleeve of his jacket. "I can provide more details, but I believe you lumped all fae bastards into the same category when you were a princess. Stepped squarely on my cousin's foot when he was too bold and I'd heard several stories about you biting another."

"I will not apologize. None of you could see any farther than your father's spittle—"

"Neither could you," he warned, voice losing any pretense of kindness. "When you stood with the Moravian prince instead of the Pantheon, I tried to dance with you. There were rumors you were at odds with Koros and I intended to learn how deep it went."

"Was it summer?"

"Yes." His brow quirked up, smothering his sharpness with a rich smile. "I'd be more impressed if you hadn't guessed the most obvious season for a ball."

"Oh—" The memory trickled crashed against the back of my eyes with force enough to catch my breath. "Months before I was queen."

"It was, and you were married to a mortal—much to my surprise." As he continued, I expected derision that never came. "I left Linvia shortly after and remained in Verinium through the fall of Morav. When Koros died, I fled to the fae realm. Then I remembered why I hated it and returned to Dover and now, Linvia."

"Why?"

"To get away from my father . . . but I did hope to find you after Morav." Worry crept along my spine like a trickle of blood. I glanced past him. "Two hundred years of complications got in the way until I met Henry in Tyrlas. If Donovan hadn't needed us in Linvia, we would have—"

"You and Henry seem close."

"We have a shared interest." He looked straight at me, searching for something. "You and he are quite close I gather."

"You know more than I'll admit." I straightened, feeling naked in Henry's clothes as one mask slipped, then another. Fae couldn't lie but deception was their second language. "I don't know what you want, but I'll say it again, Your Highness. The Pantheon dissolved and I am heir to nothing."

"Why do you discredit yourself?"

"Why did you kiss me and tell me of your father's plans?"

"As I said earlier—because I wanted to."

"That isn't what I meant." A red flush crept up my neck as we crossed a gap to a different aisle. "Fae marching on Miria is the beginning of several great wars."

"Well, I did intend to tell you quite differently, but you were distracting."

Adler pushed several chairs and a broken bust to the side, toppling over ceramic trinkets as he clambered to open a dusty leather trunk.

"How did you mean to tell me?"

"Privately, in a room, where I could also tell you what your arousal smells like to my fae bastard senses, and would you believe there are notes of citrus?"

His grin was maddening. I almost hated that I couldn't remember him—perhaps we might have enjoyed each other's company at the right party.

"What I told you the other night—does it change anything? Henry nor Donovan knows. Only you."

"Why?" I stopped and the lid of the trunk slammed closed.

"You know, you only want me to say it again." Adler wrung his hands, taking several steps into a narrow aisle, searching through a field of statues with missing left arms. "I am not telling the hand of a king that war is imminent if I believe it's avoidable. You returned to restore your godhood and there is no reason to waste it."

"To die is not to waste it." The words fell with a thunk as his green eyes searched my face.

"And hand Miria over to fae?"

I looked past the statues where another hundred more trunks and gilded mirrors collected dust. I'd let down the afterlife, so I'd be no worse for letting Miria drown under fae rule.

"War is not avoidable," I said and flicked open the creaking door of a cracked cedar wardrobe. "If you want peace—kill your father, take the crown, and call off the approach yourself."

"That will not stop them. They've made up their minds." He shoved a hand through his dark hair again, leaving it standing up on one side. "However, they would negotiate with the Queen of Gods if she had both Linvia *and* Dover, as you did before. Achieve that and most kingdoms of Miria would fall in line; my father would compromise on the right terms."

"Compromise is not so simple."

He left the shadow of a statue to stand in front of me. There was nowhere else to look but his damn green eyes.

"A restored Pantheon and united Miria would be enough to hold the line and push back an invasion. The kingdoms would unite under a queen as they did for Koros."

"Around the Godkiller? Not in four months, with the gods as dead as the Pantheon."

"That isn't true, *Foriana*." Something hopeful glimmered in his eyes. And the way he said my true name awakened something. "Your little afterlife has more magic than you care to admit."

"The Pantheon will stay buried if you know what's good for Miria." Thoughts barreled into me, a run of memories and fears in the wake of rising gods. "What do you get from it?"

I stepped around him and paced down the aisle, continuing to search for anything that tugged on the tether of time and magic.

"A realm where my father has no power, and blood is not wasted." He opened another cabinet and peered inside before slamming it. "That is what I want."

"Truly? That can't be everything you want."

"Well, the cuffs are gone, which is one thing off of my list." He looked at me for a split second before turning his attention back and reaching into a crate. I didn't turn around; instead I watched him hunched over in his finery.

"And?"

"Listing everything I want would only earn me a much-deserved slap across the face," he said salaciously. "I am at your disposal, Lady Raven. No fae trickery, no bargain. As you know, fae cannot lie, and I would not seek to."

There was a flash of something white in the bin Adler rifled through. He bolted up, hands behind his back, as he stepped toward me. The weight of his presence scattered every rational thought.

He'd found the knife and now stood within striking distance. If I begged him, would he strike me where I stood? Surely, for everything I'd done to his kingdom, he could find enough hate t do it.

Instead, Adler leaned forward, nearly caging me against a statue as he moved his arm and held out the jeweled handle of a knife with a bone-white blade in his palm. It wasn't my *Miryanai* but my father's—*Everund*—and it would work the same.

"Is this it?"

I reached for the hilt, only for him to pull it back with a curt laugh.

"The Scribes of Nurem are dead, but you and I both know the blood of their prophecy lives on the shores of Ore until the winds of Fate are satisfied. Is it wise to ignore them?"

Adler held the knife back out. This time he let me take it.

"The prophecy was a lie."

"Was it?" He chuffed. I pocketed the blade and he kept going. "You do know the scribes were fae? Lying about a prophecy would have choked them where they stood. What is it they said? Something about a king when Death's darkness twines with the brightest light?"

My heart pounded. They weren't fae; they were demigod seers blessed by Fate—Koros insisted.

"They couldn't be fae. Koros would not have—"

"Lied?" Adler muttered. "Like the gods did about the prisoners they kept? The prophecy remains and you're well aware." A smirk played on his lips as his eyes fell to the knife. "It's your father's, isn't it?"

"Yes."

"Well, I hope your intentions change." His face hardened and he took a few steps back the way we'd come. "Your power returns, but this time Koros can't control you."

Adler lingered. Deadliness in the stark lines of his hands and slender frame complemented the unsettling refinement he stood with—handsome, powerful, and practiced.

"Fae inherit powers, don't they?" I took a step closer and tilted my chin to meet his gaze. "So what is your power, Prince of Fae? It's certainly not your charm."

"I thought the Goddess of Death might never ask." He grinned, watching my face as he held his hand between us. I watched with bated breath as he snapped and fire filled his out-turned palm. "It's all I have of my mother."

He rolled his fingers into a fist, turning the fire to smoke as I gawked. Without another word, he turned on his heel and strode out of the archive, taking the air with him.

Alone in the silence of a thousand years of artifacts, my world tipped over and I clung to the edge by my nails.

22

THE SCRIBES OF NUREM said it a thousand times. It was written on the sandy shores of the moon of Ore in their blood—*fae* blood . . . if I chose to believe Adler. I trusted neither him nor my father. I'd already tried to fulfill its portent and nothing came of it, why would today be any different?

I was Death and I would create nothing—not a king, not a pantheon, not a future, or an afterlife. I needed to be forgotten; I needed my father's knife to slip into my chest and let the world move on.

That's what I dreamed about until I woke up to Orion Blackthorn frantically shaking my shoulder.

"What's wrong?"

I squeezed my eyes closed and turned over, grabbing *Everund* from underneath my pillow. The smooth jeweled hilt was so fucking impractical.

"We need to go," he said with more urgency. From across the room, he hurled a bag and several pieces of clothing onto the bed followed by the thunk of boots that was only superseded by the knight's next words: "Linvia is under attack."

I bolted. No bell rang, but several shouts carried through the window.

"No, that's impossible. There hasn't been a—"

"It's very possible." He glared and tossed a sweater at my face. The sleeve wrapped around my neck. "We need to go."

"Where?"

"What do you mean *where*? In your mother's shrine that's your job. Mine is to keep you safe."

The sweater already itched as I pulled it on.

"Some job you're doing."

"Not for lack of trying," he grumbled, glancing at my hand as I tucked the god knife into the spare sheath under my breast pocket and strapped on my new sword. "What is that?"

"A knife."

I pushed past him toward the door, scratching the back of my hands where magic itched under the surface. Urgency burgeoned in Orion's brows and shoulders, contrary to the mild annoyance prickling my neck. We descended the service stairs into narrowing corridors until the shouting from the great hall changed my mind.

A good siege was quiet until it was too late. Especially on the side of the palace facing away from the city.

Blackthorn blustered behind as I turned a sharp corner, then the sting of steel striking steel rang louder than a bell. I sobered and tugged on his arm, jerking him the opposite way.

"We're going the wrong way."

I jogged down the corridor, through a passage marked with lines that led to the stables—or so I thought. The door was bolted shut.

More shouting, more steel. We were running out of time.

I sprinted for the other corridor; I knew we could get to. It went the wrong way, into the heart of the city, but running through a city had better odds than our backs to a wall. Magic prodded. I couldn't control it in close quarters like this. One mistake and I was sure I'd find myself alive in a coffin.

The city it was.

I drew my sword as we hurried on, turning through a twisty old passage toward the exit where early light from an alleyway spilled in. Were we betrayed? I barreled down narrow streets, kicking up freshly fallen snow and ice.

Quiet and still—to my dismay—the crunch of our footsteps echoed.

So did our attackers, and the clank of their armor. They gained as we raced, leaving tracks in our wake. Blackthorn dumped an empty cart as we skidded around a sharp corner and nearly fell downstairs.

We were still blocks away from the city's edge when a sword nicked the back of my arm, cutting my jacket but leaving no other mark. I whirled around in a flurry of rage. Blackthorn bent beside me and centuries of training swelled back as I unleashed.

Three armored soldiers clashed and I cursed, breath fogging as I swung to block and steel screeched. They wore black capes, like soldiers in Tyrlas with no sigil stamped into their breastplates. We parried, swing for swing, but we were outnumbered.

"*Run!*" I screamed at Orion.

He grunted and ignored me, landing a heavy blow through one attacker's neck. It didn't cut cleanly, but the spatter of blood angered another soldier who roared into a flurry, driving at us with twice the force and twice the rage.

More soldiers closed in. Four now.

"Run!" I bellowed, meaning it.

Blackthorn heaved; his swings slowed. Mine were weakening too, but a rush of magic like adrenaline plunged my blade through the breastplate of another soldier, sending him to his knees, gargling on his own blood.

Two were left. I could take two.

I swung again, and again, gaining no purchase; each swing heavier than the last.

Then Blackthorn cried out.

Fuck.

He should have run.

A soldier's sword stuck out of his side. My heart stuttered. It wasn't fatal. I could *see* it wasn't fatal, but rage swallowed every thought as his sword slipped from his grip and he staggered back.

I ripped my glove off with my teeth. Black fingertips shrouded in blue death magic froze the two soldiers in place as they stared. Blackthorn screamed as he pulled the sword from his side.

There wasn't time for me to feel the surge, to control it, or to relearn what it was to be a god.

I gripped my sword and stormed the knights, crying out as I struck each with the same precision lightning strikes a tower. Death ran through them in a bolt when our swords touched and both fell to the ground—dead—as my curse stopped their hearts and choked their souls.

The street remained empty except for the rotting bodies at my feet.

I shoved the glove back on, grabbed Blackthorn's sword, then his arm, and dragged us downstairs and through the street. I was desperate to get out of here as the sharp, acrid smell of smoke assaulted my nose and stung my eyes.

"Stop," Blackthorn coughed out and fell against the brick wall of a shop. I looked around, frantic. We were alone, the sound of rattling swords gone, but we were only a few fucking paces from a merchant street.

I shoved us into a narrow alleyway—it was all the time I could buy.

"We can't stop."

He clutched the spot below his ribs where blood spilled over his hands, squeezing his eyes shut. "Then go without me."

"No," I said and some truth came out. Not all of it . . . but enough. "I won't go alone."

"I'm not making it out."

"You *will* make it out."

Amber eyes flew open, fierce and serious. I needed him in a way he couldn't understand. The wound wasn't fatal. Not if we could get out before more knights found us. But with every ticking minute, more people spilled into the streets.

Nearby, a woman swept snow from her stoop while others started to open their carts and shake out tarps.

A girl across the way noticed us. She dropped her broom and walked straight into the alley. Fuck. Immortal power didn't come with immortal strength. I tried to push Blackthorn up, but *fuck!*

I couldn't move him . . . not before the girl blocked our way.

"Can I help you?" I snapped. Gold eyes sharpened as she looked down at Blackthorn. She couldn't have been much older than sixteen. Honey-blonde hair draped over the collar of an oversized mink coat in a thick braid.

An ancient mark I hadn't seen in years was carved into her hand: A circle, a star, and a line that represented the staff of life. It was a mark of the Wrythian line—ancient healers once blessed by the primordials. Something about it was too coincidental, and doubt perched on my shoulder.

"He needs a healer," she said.

Blackthorn shifted over with a groan, confirming the obvious.

"We need to leave. He's fine."

He wasn't, but I could figure it out. I looked over my shoulder again. Still clear.

The girl crossed her arms. "He is not fine."

I sighed. Maybe letting him die wouldn't be so bad. I'd be freed of Tyrlas and I could find someone else to kill me—I'm sure plenty would line up—but a single thought poked through every intention of escaping and I cursed Fate.

Soul bound.

"Fine."

I moved over and she crouched beside him, hands reaching for his coat where he clutched his chest.

"Let me see," she coaxed, her delicate fingers pulling at the fabric surrounding the wound.

Blackthorn obeyed, moving his bloodied hand. Crimson dripped onto the icy ground. It steamed when it made contact with the snow and my stomach hollowed. My options were limited if I didn't want him to die; he was losing too much blood.

"I can heal him," the girl said, standing up, "but you'll take me to Vharos."

"Vharos? That's east."

"I don't see any other healers." Her gaze followed mine to the street where commotion rattled a cart followed by shouting. "He's lost an awful lot of blood."

One good thing about sieges—if they weren't looking for *me*—the soldiers should be focused on the palace. Vharos wasn't that far east, only four days at most. Annoying but not impossible if I weren't in a hurry to get back to Tyrlas.

"We stop in Reen first."

"Great." She smiled, attention falling to Blackthorn. "Can you stand?"

Orion nodded, but it was barely convincing as he grunted and swayed into the wall, catching himself by the shoulder. We helped him then, taking several painstaking steps toward a house.

The house was modest, filled with simple furniture that had seen several generations. Shelves lined the far wall filled with colorful vials, jars boasting the full range of Linvian produce, and several finer pieces of ceramic kitchenware. In the hearth, a pot frothed, near ready to boil over, but the girl seemed unconcerned as we dumped Blackthorn on the ground in front of it.

She sliced his shirt with a knife and inspected the wound as I locked the door and pulled the curtains closed on the two street-facing windows.

"I'm Ophie by the way," she said, dabbing the wound with a clean towel. Blackthorn winced. "Can you pass me the thread on the table?"

On the worn table, the spool of thread was beside a stack of plates, shreds of fabric, and several jars of pickled vegetables. I handed it to her and bit my thumb as I paced while switching expertly between applying salve and suturing.

At the latest, we needed to leave tonight—unnoticed—which was easier said than done.

Could fae heal? Could I call on Adler and see? No. Of course not. He probably betrayed Donovan. What transpired wasn't clear, and I'm sure we wouldn't have answers until we were well away from Linvia.

Crouched over the knight, Ophie's round face pinched in concentration. If she were Wrythian, she might have healing magic, but as she worked, I didn't see any of the gold tendrils or feel the static charge. Sometimes the air would even taste metallic.

"He's already healing," she stated, confused, leaning back on her heels. "Is he a shifter?"

"He is." I pursed my lips. "So long as he gets rest, he'll heal quickly. Are you a Wrythian? I see the mark on your hand."

Ophie gave me a lost expression. "Wrythian? Haven't heard of it before. This is just a mark my family carries."

"You're sure?"

"Yes, and you? Are you human? You don't quite seem it."

"I don't know why you think that."

Blackthorn gasped as Ophie's deft, willowy fingers sewed the last bit of flesh together with a needle and thread before cutting it with her teeth. Then she assessed me.

"You don't have a scratch or a bruise."

"I'm wearing twelve layers."

"Just an observation." The girl shrugged as she stood to wash her hands in a basin. "Well, he's healing—I have two horses at the edge of the city; we'll mount and ride to Reen at nightfall?"

"Horses?" I muttered. "You've planned this?"

Blackthorn's face relaxed and his eyes opened. Something was wrong. My hand went to the hilt of the sword and drew it.

The girl's eyes widened, fearful as she eyed the bloodied blade and backed into the wall.

"What are you doing?" I bit out. The room chilled.

Ophie visibly trembled. I took another step, holding the point to her chest as tears welled in her eyes. My trust was a difficult thing to earn from strangers, and it was already on edge.

"Why Vharos?"

"The temple." She gulped, lifting her chin, unable to move back any further. "They have a temple and I don't want to stay in Linvia."

"*Why?*" I hardened. Blood streaked along the silver blade as I kept it steady. Her gaze stuck to the shimmering crimson.

"My father died last year in an accident. Please—I mean no harm."

"Why help us?" I nudged the sword. "Soldiers were chasing us."

"Not Linvia's."

"I will not be crossed again."

The truth was debatable, but I had a point to make.

"I—I have no intention." Ophie held up her hands and I pushed the blade just a fraction farther as she cried out. Fearful tears streaked down her cheeks. "I don't. I really don't. Please don't kill me. P-please. I've lived here my whole life. My father was an apothecary. I don't know anything but Linvia. I swear. I swear. I just want to fix people."

My grip loosened and I lowered the blade to the scarred wooden floor. Her chest heaved.

"We ride to Reen in three hours, not at nightfall. He'll be healed enough."

She nodded emphatically and I sheathed my sword.

Sometimes it scared me how easily I slipped into my old masks. It was easy in the palace. But on the streets, when a threat crawled up, I snapped into a soldier before I took another breath.

Reen.

I dragged my hand through my hair and paced. Somewhere in those fields lay another piece of my godhood, buried with a different shade of my past. It was the last sliver of godhood I gave up. It cracked and shattered on its own because of how rotten I'd become.

Ophie stomped upstairs to gather her things. Blackthorn sat against the wall, under a knit blanket, watching me.

"Are you sure we should stop in Reen?" His voice strained as he shifted. "We'd be better in the woods."

My mind raced. "Two nights in the elements is better than three. Unless you think you'll be healed enough to shift in a few hours."

Blackthorn shook his head. "You'll be lucky if I can swing a sword tomorrow."

"You can stay here with Ophie. I don't—"

"You could hardly walk after the tomb." I crossed my arms and looked everywhere but him. The softness in his voice grated my sandpaper heart. "I won't let you do it alone, Raven. No one should do that alone."

The stairs creaked as Ophie returned.

"I'm packed." She wrapped a scarf around her neck and slung a pack over her shoulder with a bow and quivers. Then she handed Blackthorn a large sweater and a clean shirt. "How are you feeling?"

"Could be worse."

Before I knew what I did, I knelt beside him and pulled off his coat and shirt one arm at a time. My hands brushed over the muscle of his arms that stood out even through the layers.

The shirt went on easily but the sweater was more difficult. I threaded his less affected arm through the sweater first, then his head. He winced with every breath, but we needed to move. Gingerly, I took his other arm and maneuvered it through the sleeve, holding my breath as he held his.

Our eyes met and the fissure in my chest split.

"Something wrong?" he asked. "You're staring."

"No." I swallowed what feeling I could. "Give me your arm again."

Silently, I helped him back into the coat and said nothing. He hissed as I moved too quickly and stretched the stitches, but the noise stirred something deep inside me. I wished it hadn't.

Maybe he could stop me.

Maybe the burn of his skin against mine and the sear of his kiss would be enough to hold me back and remind me what it was to feel.

Gods. I wanted to know what his hands felt like again, but I was afraid of hope. Fear swallowed me as I rose to my feet.

Hope would keep the knife from its place between my ribs. Hope would hesitate to keep my promise because *maybe* tomorrow would be different. Hope would let me forget—forget that I've been here before and all stories of power ended the same.

Hope made me want to live when I couldn't. I was Death, and Death couldn't stay. I knew that before, and I knew it now as Ophie helped me ease the knight to his feet, propping him against the wall.

I gathered a few other things from around the house—more salve, a loaf of bread, some twine, and a promising soft cheese.

Then someone pounded on the door with a broad fist. Rattling metal chimed behind it and Ophie's face paled. Blackthorn already hauled himself toward the stairs.

"The closet," Ophie whispered. "Under the stairs. Go—"

Blackthorn grunted. We dodged behind a lopsided door and held our breath as Ophie handled her visitors.

"Cozy," Blackthorn muttered. It wasn't; it was barely enough space for him, and certainly not enough for both of us, but something was too soothing about my chest against his.

"I'm hating it as much as you are," I said, fighting the parts of me that were too mortal and warming.

If I thought about it any longer, I was sure I felt his cock against my belly, and *by the dying hand of Ersos—*

"I'm sure you are."

The front door barged open, spilling light under the crack of the closet. Two sets of footsteps scuffed the floor with the weight and chime of armor. Male voices came through, muffled, as I tried to keep my breath steady and Blackthorn upright.

Ophie's high voice carried through the crack of it as Blackthorn stumbled and I steadied him.

"I haven't heard anything, Lord Ferthing. No one matching—"

Ferthing. Bastard. What was he doing out here if the palace was taken?

"Men are dead . . . Rotted by death—" I only caught pieces of what he said. "Nothing?"

"No," Ophie said clearly. "The candlemaker must've confused me and someone else."

Silence, then the sound of something turning over.

The only word that stood out was: "Blood."

Did men *have* to mumble?

"I've taken over my father's practice," Ophie said, clearing her throat. "I haven't had time to clean up. Now if you'll leave, I have a patient to attend on fortieth. He was struck by a cart yesterday and is in quite a dire state."

Blackthorn's chest rose and fell against mine, shaking a bit with each inhale.

"Fine."

Ferthing mumbled, clear enough I caught the frustration and bite of disbelief. Then feet shuffled and the door slammed. Ophie's house quieted, but we didn't dare move or breathe until she cracked the closet open.

"They're looking for you, aren't they?" Ophie stared at me as Blackthorn made his way past us and slumped in a chair. "And you killed *four* men?"

"We were attacked."

"You rotted them from the inside out? With magic?" A spark of fear ignited Ophie's gold eyes as her voice wavered. "The lord seemed to think it was the work of a demigod."

"Demigods can't do that; sounds more like paranoia." I looked out the window to make sure no other guards had passed by. "We should leave now. We'll get to Reen before nightfall."

"Are you sure?" Ophie looked over my shoulder at Blackthorn, biting her lip. "Can he walk?"

"How far?" Blackthorn asked.

"Half an hour to the stable." Ophie slung her pack back over her shoulder and retied her scarf. "It's near the southeast entrance."

"Fine."

All I needed to hear as I gestured at the girl. "Lead the way."

Blackthorn stood on his own, face less pale as he strapped on his sword with a wince. The streets of Linvia were crowded—few people seemed aware anything had happened, but sieges often had little impact on the lower portions of the city unless the attacker wanted a high body count and an angry populace.

Siege drama must have been localized to the palace and homes of nobles—assuming the goal was regime change.

The fall of Morav was different, of course.

Unseating a dynasty with centuries of power took a far more insidious and bloody effort. It didn't fall in a day, but over the course of years as alliances deteriorated. Then, several kingdoms had coordinated and surrounded both Dover and Linvia, chasing Leander and his nobles into the scribes' temple.

They set fires at every stable and did the same at the gates of Dover as they ransacked and cut their way to the king, overwhelming city forces by half. They found us in one of Linvia's alleys, begging the scribes for refuge.

Blackthorn was stronger than Lleander, but my heart hammered the same because memories were tied to every wall and stone in Linvia.

By the time we reached the stable, Blackthorn steadied enough to mount the horse.

Ophie rode alone, which meant the knight's chest pressed against my back; his arm tightened around my waist as he tried to withstand the ride. At first, I almost enjoyed the way it felt to be so close to him, his chest against my back and arm around my waist.

But every time his breath caught, my heart twisted. Reen promised to be just as painful and exposing as digging through the dirt of Leander's tomb.

If taking back my godhood were easy, I would have done it ages ago and stopped myself the same day I stopped Koros. How beautiful it would have been to die with the man who made me, but I've always been a coward.

I SHOULD HAVE RUN. I should have followed my guards through the painted tunnels of the Forian palace. At the least, I should have felt the vise grip of fear as its teeth closed around my throat and I watched my city burn, but what was a man and his army to a god with none?

Clink. Clink. Clink.

Steady as the dripping water of the ancient falls in the Nephrian swamps. Smoke rose across the narrow inlet, flames licked the spires of the university and there was nothing I could do. Pirates had outsmarted my father and me.

They swarmed the port, surrounded the city walls, and executed my nobles on a hunt in my own halls. I remained, trapped in the royal rooms of the Crystal Palace, gripping the railing as fire from cannons rained down on the shore in luminous streaks because I hadn't yet surrendered.

If I had Rathe, I would have taken the dragon to their ships. But even her amethyst fire would be no match against their forty galleons when I only had four. The rest of my fleet aided my father against the fae, along with half of everything else: foot soldiers, archers, cannons, and cavalry.

No one knew an enemy was approaching until it was too late. Leave was the very last order I gave.

Clink. Clink. Clink.

Few listened because as the footsteps grew louder, servants screamed. The rough stone of the railing scratched my fingertips. I stared at the ground where I'd discarded my gloves and considered what options remained.

"Queen Foriana."

A man's voice slithered up my spine in the language of the sea, weighed down by salt and wind, carried only by an overdone lilt at the end of every word.

I turned around with a genteel smile, swallowing fear before I answered in common tongue. "I thought I'd greet you. Maybe show you around, grant you a queen's welcome."

He glanced at my hands where blue death magic undulated through my veins in streaks of fraught blue starlight, then his gaze met mine. His eyes were pretty—a lost shade of rich blue only a shade lighter than his navy hair.

"A pleasure, though you should know I've taken your city."

The pirate king wore gold armor matching the hilt of his sword and the stamped metal decorating it. His soldiers wore nondescript leathers in shades of black and brown, scorched by the sun with streaks of white from dried salt. The only unifier among them were the fine, enchanted silver sabers glinting in each hand.

"I am aware, and I will not stop you."

"You won't?"

I willed the tears in my eyes to stay put as everything crumbled. The wind changed. Acrid smoke seeped in as the city died under my watch.

"Stop torturing my people and I will leave without issue."
"That is not how this works."
"Have you mistaken me for a different queen?"
His lips curled and another scream rang through the hall.

23

Reen was hardly a town now, rather a village in the center of rolling green hills, north of Linvia, on the other side of a small mountain range where rain and snow pummeled it. It was part of the agriculture Kingdom of Aven, known for its hills, wild, diverse forests, and wide-reaching meadows that turn to wetlands in spring.

The village had four inns, five taverns, and an indoor market teeming with produce, fish, and a realm-renowned vegetable cannery.

It was always a stop between Linvia and Foria, but never one I spent much time in aside from the weeks spent at war in the fields. Memories prickled the hair on my arms as we rode beneath a canopy of trees—many still flocked with colored leaves contrary to the frost and wind.

The forests of Reen weren't here because the primordials waved their arms and saw room for shelter as they had in Tyrlas and the Southern Reach. The trees around Reen were a testament to god blood spilled across too many wars.

In fact, the forests were more like graveyards—ghosts wandered the wooded expanse like everywhere else in Miria, clinging to the tree line in faded shades of blue. Some were lost and wandering, while others were caught in their cycles, reliving their deaths.

We arrived at the crooked welcome gate of Reen just as the bitter sunset cast blue shadows over the crust of ice where snow had melted and refrozen. The inn had two rooms and we'd make them work.

Ophie got hers and—

"I'm not sleeping on the floor," Blackthorn said before I offered it.

"You can have the bed."

I grabbed a pillow and a blanket, making space for myself by the fireplace. It seemed safer than sleeping next to him when the word *'soul bound'* rattled around my head every time he fucking breathed.

Blackthorn shrugged his coat off too fast and his features pinched as he clutched his side. A ghost standing in the corner, dressed in rags, exchanged a look with me but didn't move as the coat fell and the knight started working off the sweater.

"Stop moving so much," I chided, grabbing the edge of his sleeve. He tried to pry it back but gave up, stuck with it halfway off as I guided him to sit on the creaking bed.

"Does the Goddess of Death care about my comfort?"

He flashed a wry grin and I stared at the woven sleeve caught between my gloved fingers.

"Just keeping you alive—now sit and lift your arm." He grunted when I lifted it over his head, and again when I removed his undershirt, leaving his torso bare except for the bloodied bandage. But that wasn't what I stared at. Underneath the hair decorating his chest were a hundred other white scars, wisps of memories I wanted to know.

"Is it infected? You're staring."

His voice jolted me as I peeled back the gauze below his rib. An angry wound stared back, bright red and bruising purple. I groped around my bag for a tin of salve and he looked everywhere but the wound.

"Where did these scars come from?"

He shrugged as I opened the tin and dipped a gloved finger in the greasy black concoction. It reeked of mint and wine weed, but that was preferable to rotting flesh as I traced the edges of the wound.

"Learning to hunt in form isn't easy—I think that's plenty." Blackthorn grabbed my wrist before I applied a second layer. "Why are you helping me?"

I bit my tongue. The same ghost visibly shifted in the corner, making a point to look at the ceiling.

"I never said thank you for everything on the mountain."

"And the cuffs?"

"Removing them should not have been your choice."

"I'm glad it was."

"You won't be."

He released me and his hand slid to his lap. I wrapped a fresh bandage over his chest, gingerly laying it over his shoulder and then the tender space below his ribs.

Magic moved beneath my skin with the tugging gravity of ocean water.

"You should sleep. It's nearly three days to Vharos on horseback."

Blackthorn scooted back, reclining into the pillows while I sank down on the edge and stared at the fire.

"You said there's a piece of your godhood in Reen. Do you know where?"

"No." The bed shifted. "I have an idea and a thousand ghosts wander between here and Vharos. I'm sure if I ask one, they'll know."

He said nothing so I turned to look. A streak of moonlight elongated the scars etched across his cheek and darkened his beard.

Soul bound.

Touching him was a mistake. I wanted to kiss him now and return the reverence he'd shown me. Maybe he'd hook his arm around my waist and pull me close enough to hear the slow beating of his heart. I couldn't. What kind of curse was it to have my life threaded to a mortal? A bond between the souls of gods required a willing sacrifice of magic and he had none to give.

Until he died, if I opened it, the bond between us would writhe and stretch until it drove me mad. The best I could do was ignore it and not give Fate more power over me.

I turned to the window and envied him. If I closed my eyes, power crawled through my thoughts, desperate and cloying for any kind of grip. It was like being drunk and having total clarity all at once. Magic still reeled, needling under my skin—begging me to use it.

No one should have this aching power and no time to learn control, but the next piece of my godhood was imminent. I tugged the glove off to examine my fingers. The bruising black stopped at my second knuckle, but the drain of killing two soldiers wasn't any more draining than climbing a flight of stairs.

I conjured a small amount of magic between two fingers, rolling the cool depths of it between them like clay.

The light vanished when I closed my fingers, snuffing out with a hiss like a candle left in the rain. I lowered myself to the floor and tried again, hand held out, focusing on my open palm just as I'd been taught centuries before by Koros's hired tutors.

Always start simple, that's what mine said.

He was a master from Verinium who'd dedicated his life to learning magic despite not having any of his own. He had an uncanny ability to coax control from those with a gift.

"Imagine light or fire, then roll it between your fingers or palms until it becomes something round."

The first time, I tried to conjure light, but any light was consumed by blue because death sat closest to the surface, like an oil slick over an ocean.

A spectral giggle caught my attention. In the corner, three ghosts whispered among themselves, staring at Blackthorn as I shoved my hand into a new glove that wasn't doused in salve. Their whispered laughter was a relief after Linvia.

Sighing, I crossed the creaking floorboards and slipped on my coat before walking out into the welcoming night air.

Tonight, Ore was full and cast blue light across the frozen plain beyond the city's edge where old, crooked oak trees guarded the hills and cast long, spindly shadows. Ich and Rea both waned in their quadrant, hanging above the tree line for another hour.

I followed the main road, past closed shops and mismatched houses with candles in the window. Past another lopsided gate where the town turned over to hills and an expansive oak forest. In the near dead of winter, it was haunted as bare branches cast shadows over the frozen white tundra and creaked in the wind.

Somewhere north of here was the open plain where I faced my father in a battle we'd spent centuries avoiding.

Thousands died while we stood at a distance, watching the collision of our mortal armies, followed by our immortal cavalry and wyvern archers. Koros had ten kingdoms fighting for the Pantheon, while I'd coerced nine to stand against him, for a vision of New Miria.

The battle renamed the meadow from Etta's Plains to the Blood Hill Forest. Histories say there are more unique trees in this single sprawling forest along the Ettarian Road than anywhere else in Miria.

New scholars, however, claim the unique landscape and confluence of mountains created isolated soil conditions, but the old scholars know half the Pantheon fell in the field as my father slipped from power. It wasn't the last blow, but it did herald the end.

Ten years later, Koros would die at my hand.

Brisk wind whistled through the bare branches above and tickled my face. It was more sensation than discomfort. With my godhood returned, I'd feel less and less . . . short of sticking my hand in the fire or touching Blackthorn.

I stopped at the top of a hill where a gangly oak surveyed the plain below that trailed up to the edge of the Blood Hill Forest where thousands of trees retained their leaves.

Gripping the lowest branch, I pulled myself up, feet notched in the bark. I grabbed one branch after another, hauling myself higher and higher until I was satisfied with the view of the valley and the silence.

It was perfect. Until something rustled branches followed by the whirring like the grinding gears of a clock echoed between trees. Then there was a horrendous retching sound.

Silence.

I gripped the nearest branch, freezing in place—afraid to move.

More retching. My new senses picked up the acidic stench as I scanned the shadows and undisturbed snow. There was nothing out there but ghosts.

"Lady Raven?"

Fae bastard. It was Adler.

I exhaled and peered down. He was far below, spinning in a circle, wiping his mouth with his sleeve. The prince frenzied a few more seconds before I cleared my throat and all of his attention honed in on me like a target.

"Are you perching?" Adler asked. I only saw his shadows, striding toward the trunk and peering up. "Maybe I should believe the rumors of your second form."

"I was hoping to be left alone." I ignored the bait and shifted my attention to the valley. "How the fuck did you get here?"

There was a loud crunch and some scuffling as branches cracked and snapped. In a few beats, he found a space below and similarly perched.

"Some fae can bend space. Have you forgotten in your old age?"

"I have not forgotten. I did not know you were one of them."

"Surprised?"

"Surprised you had enough power to track me down? Yes."

"Don't get used to it. It's extremely unpleasant and I hope I don't have to do it again."

"Have to?"

I shifted; branches creaked.

"Seemed a courtesy to personally deliver an update—"

"And I should trust your word? For all I know, you gave up our location. You know Blackthorn is injured and this is the *second* time I've been driven from a city in two weeks—which isn't a record but comes a little too close."

"Injured badly?" he asked. The edge of concern in his voice was unexpected.

"We found a healer. He'll be fine."

"Good." The prince paused and chewed on a thought. Bark scratched and stuck to my coat as I tried to readjust. "It was Devereux from Verinium. His men infiltrated the palace by hiding in the gardens during dinner. Donovan was ill-prepared, but they succeeded only in sending a message."

"And Henry?"

"Don't you want the message?"

"Is Henry okay?"

"Henry is fine. They were looking for you. The Prince of Poison wants to bargain with the Goddess of Death and crush Tyrlas. If you ask me, it hardly ranks on my list of concerns for Miria when—you and I alone—could level a kingdom—"

"You folded space, draining your power, to tell me what I could easily guess?"

"And that Henry was safe." The thought lingered in the air like smoke on the stillest day as his gaze stayed on mine. "You know it drained my power?"

"I can feel it, or have you forgotten what gods are capable of?" I leaned against the trunk, letting my guard drift as I closed my eyes. Adler's presence felt like a hum or a crackle on the edge of the air, but now it was quiet. "You'll have to walk back or wait a few days."

Frustration scratched my arm. It was bad enough to be in Reen. Far worse that there might be an audience when I ripped my chest open whenever my godhood found me.

"His Majesty gave me permission to stay as long as you need me."

"I need no one." Doubt prickled the nape of my neck, reminding me: Even in exile, buried under memories, I always needed someone.

"Blackthorn is a good knight, but you forget I know what happened in Reen," Adler said no louder than the wind. I picked at a fraying thread on my coat. "I've also lived and relived my own kingdom's wars—I thought you might use a friend."

Friend. That word was a joke from the lips of fae.

"We are not friends. First, friends do not corner the other into a kiss."

"Can there not be kissing between friends? Touching is not so complicated as mortals make us believe." Adler paused, exhaling sharply. "I will not kiss you again unless you ask."

"I will not."

"Then I will not kiss you."

"We leave for Vharos in the morning." I wouldn't dwell any further on the way kissing him disarmed me. If I would break for anyone, it would be the knight who Fate had tied me to.

"Vharos? That's opposite Belfiante." A hopeful lilt tangled in his voice.

"The healer we picked up only agreed to help if we accompanied her to Vharos. I didn't have a choice."

"Well." He adjusted on the branch with a frigid *snap*. Something else hovered on the edge of his tone—a hesitation. "If you insist, I'll accompany you to Vharos."

"You're worried. Why?"

"Many reasons." I broke off a small piece of bark as the prince continued. "The Duke of Verinium had no business in Linvia. It was a bold violation of a treaty signed a hundred years ago."

"Men were born to make bold, dumb choices." A snow squall whipped through the gap between two hills. Ghosts stood between, acting unaffected as they continued to wander. "The duke wants power over Death like the rest of them. I'd guess he wants their forces and to expand Verinium into a kingdom of its own."

"Perhaps," Adler agreed, but seemed to elongate the word into a wider thought. "Verinium is nothing more than a city of books. He has no reason to—"

"He wants an audience with me to undercut Tyrlas and strengthen Rivendeer's defense. It's the weaker kingdom on their borders." My lips pursed. "After I take back this piece of my godhood, I'll meet him under the pretense that he'll stop. Unless there's something you know something I don't?"

"The duke is not from Miria, but one of the seafaring realms . . . Are you sure you killed all the gods?"

"Yes. I killed every one that mattered."

"How?"

Amazing how few people had ever asked.

"Koros kept a register of every god and demigod of his Pantheon. I spent years using ghosts and shadows to track them down, leaving Koros for last and targeting anyone with a claim. I'd also cut the gods off from the power of the afterlife, so if any did survive, they'd be powerless."

"So you might not be the last god? Fae can resurrect, can't gods? We know the story of Tevairn—my father collected a hundred books trying to find that power."

I shook my head, I was thorough.

"Tevairn was a story. Nothing resurrected without Niany because only she can make the bargain with Fate. But she is powerless without a primordial's blessing, and they're long gone too."

"You believe that?"

"Two hundred and fifty years ago, there were three hundred gods. One hundred and seventy died in the eighteen-year war between my father and I which ended in Reen. Following that, infighting took care of the remaining. But before I killed Koros, I outfitted several assassin guilds with god knives and a directive to kill any gods they found—I gave them a list of every living lesser and Demi I knew.

"I wanted Koros to be alone when I finally destroyed the Pantheon. He was powerless by then. A single bolt of lightning cost him a day of recovery."

"So it was true? You had all the power in the end?" Adler asked, tinged with surprise.

"The mortal afterlife was half the magic reserve in Miria. Koros realized too late."

A wind rattled the branches and I waited for the fae to say something . . . anything.

"Your godhood will be that much more powerful. I understand why you rejected—"

"My intentions have not changed." I cut him off, holding the truth to my heart like a candle. "I am done fighting. Miria can fall to fae. I don't care; mortals will find a way to live, as they always have, and I do not negotiate on behalf of this realm—not even to save it."

"Do you know what my father intends to do?"

"I don't care, Prince Adler. I've sat thrones and had —"

"With a fae prince beside you?"

The cold became a run of needles up my spine.

"Death will not save Miria, no matter who I stand with."

"I don't need you to save Miria." He scrubbed his face and looked sharply through the bare branches. "I just need you to stop my father and his armies."

"What do you know?"

"Plenty."

"You're worried."

"And you're too calm."

"No. Because I know if you die, he intends to find a way to use your afterlife and imprison—"

"So did Koros." Memories resurfaced, hazy but of a place I'd never escape. "Whatever bargain you have with your father—whatever he thinks he knows—I know better. I sat in the rooms of Koros's generals and the three hundred years your father has on me do not matter because I am the Goddess of Death and there will be none after."

"Raven."

His voice was a warning. I didn't doubt him, but I wouldn't wear armor again, nor stand beneath the banners and armaments of any realm, kingdom or ideal—even if it was my own.

I stared at the field, tugging off my glove to hold my hand out in the freezing wind. Colder magic bloomed and dripped from it, turning from an ice blue like the veins in my eyes to a dark, swirling black in the moonlight.

As I closed my fingers around it, the weightless magic became a handle I hadn't held so firmly in centuries. I pulled back the veil separating Reen from its past. The field before us turned a magnificent shade of blue as a hundred ghosts appeared, wandering in their battle armor.

Some were on their knees, some cried out, and others stood dumbfounded, waiting for a reprieve that would never come because they were stuck in the loop of their tragedy: trusting me.

"Those are the soldiers who died in the first battle of Reen when my father granted me command against the invading fae army more than six hundred years ago."

My vision shivered as feeling waned in my legs and I let go, allowing the veil to slip back over Reen again. It was a generous spend of magic.

Adler's voice turned dry and scratchy as if the memories clawed him too.

"I waited in the east at my father's side with our wyvern forces. Is this what you always see?"

"Only when I lose control too close to a battlefield. Places of destruction like this are . . . overwhelming, even with my full godhood."

"Three hundred fae died in that battle."

"And three hundred still wander: fae, god, and mortal. They'll spend eternity reliving the day they died because that's the price of killing gods." I exhaled with my teeth pressed together so he heard it over the wind as I pulled my glove back on. "Do not forget who you speak to."

The veil returned, but to me, several ghosts still remained in the distance. I didn't have the energy to push them all back. It was just as easy to look away.

Adler said nothing and I took it as my sign to leave.

As I ambled down, I underestimated how much showing him through the veil would affect me. I stumbled from the last branch to the ground, landing hard on my hands and knees, cursing as the impact ricocheted through my shoulders.

It wasn't weakness or fatigue; my head felt stuffed full of cotton. Like too much blood pumped through my veins and pressed against my ears. I scrambled up, brushing snow off my coat before I started back.

Adler walked behind, the crunch of his footsteps the only sure sign I wasn't alone. Unlike walking anywhere with Blackthorn, Adler remained silent until we returned to the inn where we stopped at the empty desk.

Adler's fae green eyes caught mine and he stepped closer, a lock of his dark hair sprang from behind his ear.

"I'm realizing how ill-prepared I am. I made sure I wore layers and two coats, but I only brought the change I had in my—"

"You sleep on the floor."

"And I'll be grateful for it."

He gave a grateful bow as I led the way to the modest room where Blackthorn remained fast asleep.

I threw several blankets at the prince, then I curled up in a pile of my own, trying to remember that tomorrow night we'd be sleeping in the snow, wishing we had any reprieve from the wind.

24

MORNING CAME TOO SOON. I slept on my shoulder wrong; it popped when I tried to stretch, aching like it had its own pulse as I tossed a log into the fireplace, renewing the light in the room.

I smiled, watching the flames roar to life, thankful I could feel the faint roll of heat as it was only a matter of time before it became a memory.

Blackthorn slept in the bed, face smooth and unbothered. His chest rose and fell. On the other side, below the window, the fae prince was curled up in a nest of blankets. Some sort of contentment settled in my chest despite the restlessness I felt.

A fist pounded the door, and I shuffled over. Ophie stood in the dark hallway, dressed and ready, looking up with bright eyes. Her green coat was pulled tight, bow and quiver slung over her back, and a yellow scarf wrapped around her face as she blinked.

"Where's your coat? You said first light?"

"Suppose I did," I muttered, and she was right. Glancing at the window, the cerulean light of dawn turned to tangerine. I hadn't packed. "Come in. Won't be long."

The door closed as I gathered one heap of clothes and dropped them on the bed at Blackthorn's feet, then I kicked Adler and sent him jumping up with a yelp.

Blackthorn sat up slowly. His hand clutched his middle where the bandage had fallen off. The skin around the wound was a faint pink instead of angry red, and the wound had mostly closed. He froze when he saw Adler at the window layering on his coats.

"What is he doing here?"

"Adler spent all of his magic to tell us the palace is fine."

Blackthorn pouted, staring at the fae prince who had turned to address the knight.

"How is your—"

"Palace?" Ophie quipped, interrupting Adler. "Magic? Is that what you were running from? The Linvian guard? Because you have—"

"No." I stepped between her and the prince. "We were guests at the palace when it was attacked by the Duke of Verinium."

"Those were librarians?" Blackthorn asked incredulously, massaging his chest as he tried to reach for his clothes, just out of reach.

"Are you fugitives?" Fear rose in Ophie's voice.

"No—"

"Who is the girl?" Adler bit out, glancing between the knight and I. "She hardly seems—"

"The girl," Ophie answered with venom, "is a trained healer from Linvia who's kept that man alive and was looking only for *company* to Vharos. Not trouble."

Adler's mouth formed an 'o' as he nodded, treating her more like an aggrieved horse than a teenage girl.

"Forgive me, lady—"

"Ophie. And you are?"

"Adler."

"No title?" She raised her eyebrow as he combed his hair back, but it was little use as dark curls sprung out again. His lopsided plain clothes didn't mask the prince's disposition. His shoulders were too straight and he spoke too clearly, with no hint of regional dialect.

"Titles don't matter on the road, Lady Ophie. If it's currency you're looking for, I'd prefer to part with gold over information."

"Of which you don't have much." I flashed him a withering look before turning my focus back to Blackthorn. "How do you feel?"

The knight stretched his arm, flexing the fingers on his injured side. "Fine. Bruised."

Adler conceded. "I'm returning once you are safely in Vharos. I know the King of Tyrlas, but I also know the Duke of Verinium, so consider this an offer of protection. And before you argue with me, Sir Blackthorn. You do need it. The duke fears me for several good reasons."

Ophie cleared her throat as she stared at me unblinking. "Why do *you* know these people?"

The men said nothing.

"We're working for King Donovan. Two of us have magic and will not let harm come to you—that's all you need to know." I swiveled to Blackthorn. "You do feel well enough to travel?"

He nodded, grabbing again at the clothes on the bed and catching the sleeve of a shirt with a wince. I wanted to help but hesitated. Before I made up my mind, Adler already had the sleeve in hand, helping the knight dress in a tender moment I'd never expect from a fae.

I swallowed the sinking feeling as we packed in silence.

Ophie rode with me while Blackthorn, comically, rode with Adler. Within the first hour, Ophie seemed happy to bicker with the prince as if the insults and crinkle of his face kept her warm. Before the sun crossed even half the sky, I wasn't sure any part remained of him she hadn't insulted.

Winter left the road deserted; we hadn't passed a single merchant or farmer. Ghosts weren't scarce, but they kept their distance, only stopping to watch us pass, most wearing the armor they'd died in.

"I've heard there are wolves out here," Ophie said, cutting through silence as snow and ice crushed under hooves. My hands were stiff, nearly frozen to the reins in the frigid air.

Blackthorn cleared his throat.

"They won't come close to us."

"Even the god-killing ones? With yellow eyes?"

"How do you know about direwolves?" Adler asked, lifting his chin. His cheeks had begun to turn white. "I haven't heard that story in ages, especially not in Linvia."

Ophie shrugged, shivering against my torso. Keeping her alive was already proving to be a challenge.

"My father told me stories about the gods. Said some creatures were enchanted to kill them for balance."

"And for balance, the gods killed them," I muttered, remembering the royal hunts I participated in when we had no better wars. "There are plenty of stories about direwolves razing towns in the old days. Does no one read anymore?"

"Why are you asking?" Adler tightened his scarf, which had started to ice over from his breath. "You'll be pressed to take down a sick deer with a bow that small."

Ophie shifted on her seat, drew the bow, and shot an arrow only a hair's breadth away from the prince's nose.

Adler's eyes had never been so wide as she shoved her bow back.

"You could have fucking killed me."

"I doubt that," Ophie hummed with a satisfied grin. "I've hunted plenty, just never seen a wolf."

"They won't bother us," Blackthorn finally ground out, teeth chattering. His lashes and beard were iced over. "Enchanted wolves don't fuck with shifters. The only thing to worry about is the snow vantross."

"Snow vantross?" I said, incredulous. Mortals believed anything. "A wolf shifter is worried about a snow vantross?"

"Are you not?" Blackthorn's cheeks were prickled white like Adler's. The bright sun did nothing but make it harder to see through the glare off the snow. "Vantross are terrifying. Have you never heard of one in all of your wisdom and reading, Raven?"

"They're real," Adler interjected. "The grass ones were a plague in the fae kingdom for a while."

"Ah!" Ophie exclaimed. "You *are* fae. That's why you're insufferable."

Adler scowled and looked at the sky like he was about to pray. "Mother fucking help me. I'm not insufferable because I am fae, I'm insufferable because you're driving me to the brink of my sanity."

"Good." Ophie tilted up her chin and nearly clocked mine with the jolt of her head. "Why are fae helping King Donovan?"

"I'm *one* fae, and why did a twelve-year-old agree to cross the frozen tundra with some obvious vagabonds?"

"I'm *eighteen*," Ophie seethed, and for the second time, I tightened my grip on her waist to keep her from jumping off the horse and lunging at the prince.

"Tell me, Sir Blackthorn," I said, cutting through their tension. "Why should I be terrified of a snow vantross? They haven't been a threat in centuries."

"Haven't been a threat? They're three times the size of a man, colder than anything you've ever felt, and they'll follow a lone traveler for hours, even days then steal their life force. One touch, one scratch from their talons, will turn a person to ice. And if there are multiple people in a party, they might possess one and lure the others to feed from them. My uncle died that way on an expedition in the Xerxes range."

"Sorry, about your uncle." Ophie's boldness softened.

Blackthorn shrugged. "Don't be. He was the one who didn't believe in them."

After a few more hours, if I wrung my hands together and closed my eyes, the whispering draw of power had quelled from a torrent to a lapping tide. It was a magnet in my skin, pulling every fraction in one direction. This morning, it was faint, but every stride and sway of the horse strengthened it. We were getting closer. I felt it as we finally made camp in the forest before sunfall.

Two of the moons were visible in the waning daylight, and Rea was expected to rise in another hour. Her gravity made my power wilder and more unpredictable than it already was but I welcomed it.

The prince ignited a stack of wood with leaping fire he'd conjured in his palm. Wide-eyed, Ophie watched it fill our small campsite with warmth and light in the dismal, lonely, iced-over woods. Even deer hadn't crossed our path, and the winter birds were silent aside from the occasional haunt of an owl.

We weren't in any forest.

We hadn't been for an hour or two. The same oaks surrounding Reen were mixed now with a hundred others. Some were saplings, some had rough bark, and some were pines still clutching their needles. We passed a lingering palm from the southern reach for Leo—the god of water. He didn't die here, but he stood with me as a general in The War of a Thousand Trees and nearly lost his arm in that spot.

Blackthorn studied a map, finger tracing our route as I helped Ophie put up a tent and stuff it with any layers we could spare. The temperature was dropping to bitter and it started to snow again—the freezing kind where flakes were more like pellets of ice that rolled across the crust of ice.

"I have a trick that might keep you warm," Adler offered, watching Ophie as she huddled by the fire with her hands held out. Her teeth chattered and the pink in her cheeks shone against splotches of white.

She eyed him warily, like a cat deciding whether to attack. "If it's the same kind of trick you used on the King of Aven like you bragged about, I'm not interested."

"That wasn't a trick." Adler frowned. "It was a charm."

"Doubtful."

Ophie lifted her chin and the fae prince looked mildly agitated. Adler ignored her and placed two branches on either side of her tent.

"What are you doing?"

"Keeping you mortals alive."

With a wave of his hand, an enchanted fire engulfed each branch, defying the wind. Ophie's derision melted with the flame as Adler added, "These will last all night. They will not bend in the wind or set anything on fire. You can bring them into the tent or leave them where they are."

"Th-thank you," she stammered and ducked into the tent as Adler walked back to the fire where Blackthorn and I sat.

"Can you magic more of that?" Blackthorn asked.

Adler laughed. "Only if you don't mind a few more days of my company. Magic has a cost and Miria is terribly draining." His verdant gaze fell on me. "I need to return and organize your meeting with Devereux whom Donovan is currently holding."

"Since when do you organize on my behalf?"

"What? Are you going to fly over and tell him yourself? You already said you'd speak with him."

"He's driven us from two cities. By the time we're in Vharos, killing him will be no issue."

"There's also the option where you don't kill him," Adler warned. "How you represent yourself is your choice."

"I'm only doing this to preempt any issues with Tyrlas. Tomorrow, I'll find the next piece of my godhood"—flashes of the ghosts I'd seen that night in Reen bombarded my memory—"so don't wait for me, stay on the road and I'll catch up."

Blackthorn folded the map. The paper crinkled as I stared at the snowy ground below my boots, a mix of pure white and frozen mud dredged up like cookie crumbs.

"Forgetting me won't work." Blackthorn's heavy, warm hand met my shoulder and I didn't shrink from the touch. "You won't do it alone."

"I'll keep my word if that's what you're worried about."

The knight bristled as I stood and spread my coat at the base of a tree, trying not to feel the bone-chilling cold, but even with my godhood, it bit at my skin like brushing pine needles.

Blackthorn and Adler remained awake, exchanging stories I didn't listen to because the whispers of memories and the ghosts in my mind were louder.

My heart ached where my godhood pummeled my ribs with every heartbeat. No one was meant to live this long, nor with so many torrid memories. How Adler did it was beyond my understanding, but he didn't make the choices I did.

Every version of Foriana I became, I regretted. I always thought I was capable of changing, but the truth was hard to swallow. Tomorrow would break me open a second time, and it came too soon.

Dawn crawled through the trees in brightening shades of gray as it continued to snow. I woke up, shaking powder from my hair and coat as I walked around the fire and pulled off a glove. Blackthorn had shifted into a wolf and slept soundly, curled around the fae prince.

I left them, wandering into the woods with my hand exposed. Blue magic swelled in my palm as I sifted through the ghosts lingering near the veil. Their souls brushed against my hand, along with flashes of memories. I steeled against the worst, biting the inside of my cheek until the iron tang of blood was all I tasted.

After ten tries, I found the officer and friend I needed. Blue tendrils turned black and dripped from my fingertips, drawing back the veil and forming the specter of Officer Riker who stood with me through the last Pantheon war.

Of course, he looked the same as the day he died. Mortal, no older than thirty, but he was sharp and proud, bearing the weight and responsibility of his title with more grace than most of my generals.

Riker bowed, a curt smile on his face. His white hair was braided as intricately as I remembered.

"General Foriana," he said in Olfain—a language of the northern coast, used in the upper rungs of the New Mirian military. *"It's an honor to serve, as always."*

"Honor isn't the word I'd use."

Riker shook his head and stepped closer, his phantom sword rattled in its sheath. *"I did not expect to see you again. Wasn't it you who said Reen could 'fuck itself on Koros's sword' and that you'd 'empty the fields like the Nurem scribes'?"*

I looked at my feet. *"Did I say that while you were dead or alive?"*

"Both." He smiled as if it were a hundred years ago, playing cards in my tent, trying not to think about dawn. The prophesied demigod we captured a few weeks earlier—hoping she was the chosen one—sat next to him. Her name was Dayvin. *"You really ought to take the long way to Avilla if you want to avoid the ghosts of the Bleeding Hills."*

"I want to see my willow."

Riker stared at me; the blue edges of his corporeal form shifted in the armor he'd died in. *"They won't be happy to see you."*

"Talking to yourself again?" Adler's voice carried through the trees. I groaned and tugged off my glove, ripping the veil open just enough for him to see I wasn't alone.

"Who the fuck is that?" Riker dropped his voice. *"I know a fae when I see one."*

Snow crunched as Adler walked around one of the trees, tipping his head with a grin.

"And I know the ghost of a New Mirian soldier when I see one," Adler replied in stilted Olfain, stepping closer to inspect Riker's ghost. "The brand on your neck was Foriana's mark in the Pantheon war."

Riker's gaze narrowed and I froze. That was a detail I hoped time had washed away and sanded over.

"Yes," I said in the common tongue, staring pointedly at Adler. "He was an officer of New Miria in the last battle against Koros. He knows where my godhood might be."

"Dayvin is buried there, too," Riker said in common with a thick accent, like the words were caught in the roof of his mouth as he looked between us. "It is a two-day walk. I'm Riker."

Warily, Riker stuck out his hand to Adler before snapping it back as he remembered his form.

"We have horses." My attention stopped on Adler who loomed over us, green eyes transfixed on the ghost. "Officer Riker will guide us. He's never let me down, dead or alive."

Riker perked up and gave a quick salute. *"It's an honor, General Foriana. I trust your company, so long as you do. It is dangerous out there."*

"We travel with a shifter. We're prepared . . . If you'll give us a moment, Officer, we need to ready the horses, then we'll meet you here."

Riker nodded graciously and crossed his arms to pace like he always did when he waited. I dropped my hold on the veil, pulling my glove back on with enough force that it caught my nail as I stalked back to camp, Adler at my heels.

"So the brands still hold in the afterlife?"

Adler said the wrong thing.

I stopped walking and whirled on him, shoving my finger into his chest, wishing it was a dagger as I backed him into a tree. He didn't relent.

"They took it willingly. Do *not* mention it again."

"Why?"

I dropped my hand and exhaled, pushing back my hair as tension swirled and crashed. "I shouldn't have to explain why loyalty in a war against the Pantheon was important."

"A brand over a fae alliance? That was your choice."

I barked a bitter fucking laugh as Adler straightened his coat—face too stiff and serious.

"I know your bargains. The moment we toppled the Pantheon, fae would sweep in and Miria would belong to *you*."

"I do not represent my father's kingdom," he said through his teeth.

"You have his crown and his name."

"And with it, it seems I've done more for Miria than the queen who destroyed what? Half of it? You can pin my father's crimes to my back if you want, but there is no one to blame for yours."

The prince stormed back where Blackthorn loaded the horses as Ophie packed her tent.

Ophie rode with Blackthorn for this stretch because he was warmest, leaving me to share the other horse with Adler, whose lips remained a thin line. Flurries fell in waves as I followed Riker's occasional guidance.

Every time I called him back, I couldn't help but look at the mark on his neck. It was a brand, burned there by magic to keep any ranking member of the New Mirian army from defecting. The magic tied their tongues and stole their voices the moment they betrayed New Miria.

It was my idea from the beginning because I was tired of getting betrayed by the hundred gods and demigods who promised me they'd never go back to Koros.

Some promised until I added a price.

I knew exactly how like my father I was, even when I denied it . . . and Adler's silence, in spite of our proximity, was a poignant reminder. I was no better than the men I despised.

25

[Letter written on charred parchment]

I never doubted you could kill me, Foriana,
I only doubted you'd be brave enough to try.

SICK IS WHAT I felt as we got closer, and riding with the fae prince made nothing better. The clouds vanished with the snow, leaving behind bitter cold and the odd purple-orange glow of midwinter sunset as we arrived at a field.

My legs were numb, but I'd be fine. I was more worried about Ophie, whose teeth still chattered like two pieces of porcelain determined to wear the other down. The horses were tired, too. Even with the breaks we'd taken in between, they needed a stable and better food than the meager oats we had.

"Vi liet tien sund averine, Sin Lie Foriana," Officer Riker said with a final bow because this was the field. I let the magic holding him up dissipate and dissolve his form on the piercing wind. *Good luck, General Foriana* was the base translation, but Olfain was a language of a million aphorisms—the exact translation was: *"What scares you won't kill you, General Foriana."*

When he vanished, I pulled the horse to a stop as every ounce of magic cracked open against my bones. Adler shifted, whispering something, but ghosts lingered in my periphery, dressed in haunted renditions of their armor—armor I'd commissioned centuries ago.

Adler's chest pressed against my back, protesting, but I dismounted, slipping away as he tried to grab my arm and called for Blackthorn to stop. I didn't listen. This was it—an empty field with a forest in the distance, littered with more ghosts than I could see, but I felt them.

I stared straight ahead, trying to breathe. If I turned in either direction, I'd see mismatched, waist-high trees in the otherwise barren field, poisoned by the blood of the long-dead gods. Bile burned the back of my throat.

In the distance stood a crumbling, makeshift vault of wood and marble, on the edge of the forest in brilliant shades of color against white, surrounded by a rusted iron fence. It was a graveyard filled with unmarked stones.

Ghosts surrounded it—more than there were in Reen, more than I'd seen before. Their grief and ire rippled against my skin, prickling my spine because they knew I was here. Their forms stopped moving, casting blue, still light through the distant trees as they hovered in stasis.

Blackthorn suddenly blocked my vision. He'd dismounted too.

"Is everything okay?" His presence closed around me; calm amber eyes searched mine. He brushed hair from my cheek, and for once, I felt nothing . . . not a shiver, not a pulse.

None of them could hurt me. Ghosts were only ever shadows. But that wasn't true, was it? Not when I was the villain in every story because I killed the heroes. Memories were the only swords they needed.

My chest tightened. Maybe if I didn't breathe it would go away? I needed them to go away.

I flattened my palm over my chest where *Everund* was buried in a pocket and wondered if it would work here. Maybe I could die before I faced them and never have to see Belfiante. Was ending the regime of Death worth this?

"Raven?" There was Blackthorn's voice again, an anchor in the concert of screams.

The dead were here—a thousand of them; all bodies I was responsible for, and somewhere among them was the piece of myself that rotted off. After what I'd done, I deserved nothing: not the armies, not the loyalty, not any of the life I'd been given because I'd wasted it.

"Are we stopping here?" Ophie asked aloud, breaking the layer of tension like ice.

I gulped down the sharp, cold air as Ophie pulled a map from her pocket and looked it over.

She remained seated on her horse, bundled in a blanket. "We're not far from Foriana's field," she said, and I shrank under the gaze of the two men who knew. "Once we cross, we'll be less than a day from Vharos. Did we go too far north?"

Her innocent eyes looked from me to Blackthorn and Adler, whose gaze hadn't left mine; his sharp fae features looked pained and twisted.

"Any idea why it's called that, Raven?" Adler asked pointedly as he slid off the horse into the snow.

I hugged myself like I could hold the broken pieces as I organized an answer.

"It was a battle, named for the goddess Foriana," Ophie chirped, and fury tightened my jaw. I could have shaken her as Blackthorn's brow raised.

"Let it go, Ophie," the knight warned. "We'll cross and set up camp—"

Adler's attention turned away from me as he took the horse's lead in hand and continued to walk.

"No, she's right," I injected, taking a decisive step back, nearly into Blackthorn. I regretted it immediately as a spectral arm burst from the snow, followed by an icy and desperate scream.

"*General!*" They cried out and I waved them off with a burst of magic that certainly wasn't enough to banish them all—not as I got closer. The veil was thin, but I wasn't strong enough.

"What else did you hear?" I asked, wincing at the building pressure in my temple. I didn't have to take the next step until I was ready; the only one making me do this was myself, and through every life, I was stubborn.

"Thousands of soldiers died in a New Mirian battle," she said, but her voice dropped. "They didn't know they'd been led to their death by the goddess when they faced Koros and his battalions."

Pressure continued to build as I looked up. The sky was the only place their memory didn't cling to. Blackthorn bristled.

"That is one story," he said, and I wished the defense meant something; he was afraid of me too.

"In the story I know, Foriana had no idea her father was ready to waste an army," I muttered, tugging at my sleeve. "She believed they were negotiating in earnest and the battle was a front . . . a formality."

"Hadn't heard that one," Ophie said, folding the map and stuffing it back in her pocket.

"It wasn't nearly as exciting." I wiped sweat from my brow. Blackthorn took immediate notice.

"Something wrong, Raven? We can take another route."

"No." If I faced Leander, there was no reason I couldn't face this. I barely knew the soldiers and I'd abandoned the afterlife. This couldn't be different, even if these soldiers knew my name.

"You keep going. I'll meet you at camp. It won't be long; I just need to do something."

My gaze swiveled past the knight to the vault behind him. Somewhere in that graveyard, the gold leaves of a willow tree shimmered in the last dredges of daylight before the moons took over.

I squeezed my eyes shut and said to myself in the barest whisper, "I don't want to do this."

The knight hadn't moved; he remained reaching distance before me.

"Don't do it, then."

I lifted my eyes and Blackthorn stared. What would happen if I listened? If I gave in to the warmth of him and lived just to know what it was to fall in love with him?

"I have to."

"Raven—"

No time.

I pushed past, unthinking. If anyone yelled, I didn't hear because with every surge forward; the dead became louder and louder as the veil between me and them collapsed.

The field echoed with weeping and begging. Cracking voices and piercing shouts shook the silence as I forced myself forward, trudging through knee-deep snow, toward the unwanted piece of myself in the forgotten graveyard.

I stumbled through the gate; my vision accosted by flashes of death blue. Anguished cries rang out, changing to screams of despair to desperate shouts of my own name. Every step was emptier than the last as my godhood kicked and scratched beneath my skin.

It knew where we were, it wanted to be reunited, and the power flared as I scanned the other trees for the symbol of my soul among my kin. There was an elm with heart-shaped leaves, a yellow maple, a cedar tree with ashen bark, a silver olive—too many to name.

The numbness of my godhood swept in like a wave, protecting me from myself as my heart tore open and guilt ravaged like a vulture, picking apart the space between my ribs where the worst of it lived.

General Foriana.

Foriana.

Tell them, Foriana.

General.

General.

Foriana.

Men bawled their last words in a symphony, aching for an answer to what their sacrifice had wrought, but the truth was nothing.

The truth was that the empire they died for fell that day.

This battle ended in a magnificent draw, the field littered with the bodies of soldiers and gods, who all dreamed of a better world but would never live to see one, while Koros and I still stood on our hills.

It was clear we brought our armies out to do what we never wanted to do to each other.

Of course, I'd kill Koros ten years later in his own bedroom, and my name was the last word he said.

This battle wasn't worth the thousand souls reaped and doomed to wander. He thought we'd restore the power of the Pantheon, but I knew better.

Shame.

General Foriana.

My son, my wife, my daughter—

Please help me.

General.

Sin Lie.

Sin Lie Foriana.

Foriana.

Too much, too much, too much.

Their hands grazed and groped. I slogged through a sea of hands like reeds, dragging me below. But there was no below, no reprieve of drowning. Only cold, hard ground, and the spectral arms of the dead who never rested.

I dared to look up. Through blurry eyes, I saw my willow—black as night, with a gnarled trunk. Gold-tipped leaves glinted in the rising light of the moons.

My knees met the ground and my whole body shuddered as I palmed the snow and dirt. Spectral bodies crushed me. I couldn't fucking do this.

Weeping didn't describe what happened next. Magic itched at my skin and I screamed into the void like it tore me in half as the spirits closed in.

One cold grip after another—each reaching for something they were owed but coming up with nothing because there was nothing left—I wailed again, pushing myself to unsteady feet, trapped in the agony of my making. One step, then another.

The ground around the willow was bare; no snow covered it, no ice. Only dirt and the litter of dead willow leaves like it had been waiting.

I sank to my knees again and pressed my hands to the ground; silence swelled. The dirt was warm as my godhood throbbed in my chest. Rippling magic thrummed through my blood in recognition.

My godhood splintered, unbidden, as I buried soldiers I'd worked with for decades of my life. I'd lost Foria, I'd lost Leander, and when this battle reared its head, I'd lost to my father at the cost of everything I had left.

Instead of taking back the power when it fell, I buried it with everyone else because I didn't deserve it. Now I saw the truth as my fingers sank into the dirt.

Power wasn't a thing to be earned or guarded by the righteous; power was granted haphazardly . . . and so rarely to those who deserved it.

The men of the Pantheon never apologized for their power, never tried to make themselves smaller or more deserving—so why should I?

They were dead and the power was mine; this wasn't defeat. This was taking back what I was owed.

I plunged my hands through the soil and roots. The ground opened, welcoming me between the graves of a thousand forgotten soldiers.

Sharp edges like glass found my fingertips, warm and alive as I took a deep breath, bracing for the onslaught.

With a sharp inhale, I shoved it into my chest as I had before, wishing the penetration would stop my heart like it would a mortal, but I knew better. The moment it slid between my ribs, I *became.*

Magic spread and tied itself around my bones, burgeoning into something new. The cold became less: less aching, less mortal doubt and then—*more*—pain tore through me.

Too long this shard remained in the soil near the souls I'd abandoned . . . and they knew. *They fucking knew.*

Tainted wasn't the right word, nor was grieving, but something in the middle, something horrible and overwhelming. Something that crushed every bit of my body and forced my cheek to the ground.

What was it to feel everything at once?

To die a thousand times in the span of a single second and be remade tendon by tendon?

I'd fallen from the highest point and every single bone broke on contact and reawakened me a second time and a third time, maybe more. I screamed and writhed, begging for long-dead gods.

Then there was silence.

Silence and the feeling of nothing as I blinked and breathed, reminding myself with every conscious movement, I was still alive and none of the dead could hurt me.

I was alone now. No blue, no screaming, no whispers of my name. I'd banished them all with some rippling magic. Every unsettled ghost gone—destroyed—or now a part of me. Power ebbed and ached in my bones, making itself at home again.

I tried to push myself up from where I lay prone on the ground. This wasn't all the magic I could hold, but it was more than I'd controlled in three hundred years; it was heavy.

Dread settled, and again, I was Foriana, the Goddess of Death—waiting, becoming what she never wanted because there was no other way to kill the gods.

Footsteps crunched from behind and I bolted to my feet, vision jerking with the sudden motion, but only Blackthorn stood there with a pensive expression.

"How do you feel?" The shock of his amber eyes in the moonlight caught something in my throat.

"Fine," I said, but the edges of the world blurred. Magic spiked like a rush of fever and I swayed. This piece was larger than what I'd left behind in Linvia.

"Fine?"

"Fine."

His brow furrowed, then pain rippled through, doubling me over onto the ground in a torrent of agony as every vein in my fucking body stretched to the point of bursting. It was an unrelenting, white-hot pain that tore me from this realm.

The pain was merciless, because death would never be easy—not for me. I writhed on the ground, holding on until it dragged me into black.

Cahh. A raven screamed, begging me to get up.

Dirt crusted under my fingernails and stuck to my cheek. My head pounded. A warm breeze tickled my face, timed to the gentle rustle of grass I didn't want to see. My mouth was dry and tasted like ash.

"Stand up."

Niany.

I groaned and her haughty laugh echoed.

"Have you changed your mind, daughter?"

With too much effort, I hauled myself to my feet. Power raged, weighing down my body just as it had centuries ago in my room of the Pantheon.

The Goddess of Life stared at me with a smile on her round face. Her gold hair caught the wind and rippled in rivulets, indistinguishable from the endless expanse of dried grass around us. A stream gurgled.

"What is this?"

"The afterlife you left in my care. This was the last piece you gave up, if I'm not mistaken."

"And it brought me here?" I blocked out the glaring sun with my hand, blinking profusely. Winter in Reen was a far cry from summer in the mortal afterlife.

"To my prison," she said venomously, pink lips holding the word hostage. "What a nice reminder of your responsibility, unless you'd forgotten what it was like those first weeks at the Pantheon."

"You have no power here."

"You're right. I'm nothing more than one of your little ghosts, but you remember all power has a price. Koros and I had to claw it back from the primordials to prove we were worthy. Why shouldn't you?"

I tilted my head, watching the form of Niany stare through me as I remembered the vivid dreams, the craving for blood, and the way my senses vanished to nothing. Then she stepped aside and a wall of power collided with my side, sending me flying through the air as it took the breath from my lungs and cracked my ribs.

I rolled over gasping as a sword dropped on the ground beside me. I scrambled for it, crawling toward the hilt before I stood to face my mother.

Though she didn't stand over me. Instead, it was a figure shrouded in white robes, black feathers poking up its neck, framing a sallow, sunken face like a collar. He stood twice my height and held another sword, gripped in a skeletal hand with nails so long they may well have been talons.

"My child," he started in Priminian. "I had higher hopes when I gifted you the godhood of Ersos."

"Strange to wait until now to express your disappointment." My head pounded.

"It is not. You seek what Koros was commanded to remove and promised you would never find again."

"Is this all I needed to do to wake you up? Were the wars not enough? The death of my father? The fae draining Miria? You'll wake for my fucking prophecy."

He crouched, brandishing the sword, but made no movement. "As it was in the days before Belfiante, you disrespect the power granted to you by the beings you ought to cower before."

"I do not cower."

"On the battlefield? In the arms of Koros, one breath away from death?"

"That wasn't me."

I held the blade out. It was impossibly light and elven, forged once in dragon's breath by a long-dead smith.

"You will not die."

"We'll see about that."

He lunged, sword coming down on me as I met his steel with my own. The collision sent sparks flying as Niany's hollow laugh echoed through the field, carried by the ghostly wind and wailing of the afterlife.

The primordial reared back and bludgeoned again, catching my shoulder. I cried out; he'd cut through the thin shirt I woke up in and the cut of the blade seared as it gashed my shoulder.

I dropped the blade and backed up, lifting both hands as I called on every ounce of magic I contained. This was my terrain. The ghosts and every ounce of power that breathed life into the trees and contained the Goddess of Life belonged to me.

The sky blackened and churned as magic gathered in my palms, dripping through my fingers like oil. He took another lumbering swing and I laughed, but then he discarded the sword and water gathered in his own palm.

"So you haven't forgotten how to play?"

I roared and magic streamed from my arms, pummeling him with the force of a gale wind in a sea storm. Blue and black ichor slammed and threw him back before he could strike.

"Raven?"

It was night again. I blinked. Silver moonlight trickled through the gaps between branches, slowly coming into focus. Ich, Ore, and Rea looked down, casting odd shadows through the frozen woods.

I was on fire, but nowhere burned worse than the muscle where my arm met my shoulder.

Adler crouched beside me, otherworldly green eyes searching mine. We were still in the cemetery. Did he leave camp? Where was Blackthorn? No.

"Raven?"

My name—like I'd forgotten it, but I hadn't.

I panicked and tried to move, but something much heavier than a human leg was draped over my middle; it wasn't only my magic but a physical thing. And I was warm, far too warm for the dead of winter, even when my blood hummed with the magic of gods.

It was a wolf on top of me.

Blackthorn.

I relaxed. The knight had shifted and now pinned me to the ground. If I touched the magic under my skin, I could blast him off. In fact, with the way it scorched, I could blow both of them to the trees. I didn't, and perhaps that was against my better judgment.

"Raven?" Adler asked a third time.

I finally responded with narrowed eyes and a rasping voice. "You left Ophie alone?"

"She's fine," he grumbled, rising to his feet—his cross expression seemingly permanent. "She has Blackthorn's sword and his wolf scared any animal within a half-day's walk. Forgive me if I heard you screaming and thought to do something about it."

He scowled in disbelief and the wolf huffed.

"I was quite fine." I rolled my eyes and groaned, trying to shove the wolf off, but he wouldn't budge. "Look, if jamming a shard of my godhood into my nearly human body were easy, wouldn't everyone be doing it?"

Adler soured further. "You know the answer."

"The truth didn't fit the point I was making." I pummeled the white, furry leg of the wolf, but his muscles only stiffened. "Let me go."

Adler's gaze flicked to the wolf's amber and then to me.

"You're not going to kill us?"

"No." I held up both gloved hands, feeling like a petulant child. "If neither of you mind, I'd like to get some sleep before dawn."

Blackthorn's leg finally moved, albeit hesitantly. I sat up. Something else bubbled up in my throat—a numbness. I expected to feel the bond more acutely, but my hunger for his touch seemed sated. I stood, dusting the dirt and snow off my pants.

"See? Not dead." I looked at Adler. In the glow of the ice, his eyes nearly glowed. He didn't believe me, but it didn't matter. I crossed my arms. "It comes in waves, I'm fine right now."

"Right now?"

"I have no desire for blood, if you have to know."

The wolf moved. Suddenly, the air charged as a large crack rang through the forest. In place of a wolf stood the naked form of Blackthorn. The muscles of his back rippled as he moved to dress, but not fast enough. I saw the fresh scar on his ribs and the sharp definition where his hips angled to his cock. The bond in the back of my neck wasn't sated, actually. It reared itself; numbness turned to warming desire as my mouth watered and considered what it would feel like to be so fucking full of him as he moaned.

Adler cleared his throat, dragging me back, but he'd joined me in admiration. Neither of us shied away as Blackthorn returned, shaking snow off his coat.

We left the cemetery of a thousand graves and a hundred dead gods. I'd silenced them and shivered, not from the bitter air—I hardly felt it—I shivered because of the memories and the pain left behind, and what I'd do with this new power expanding and becoming under my skin.

It had been three hundred years since I'd felt this, three hundred years fighting it, and now I couldn't remember why I'd given it up. Everything was so much smaller, so much quieter as I walked behind Blackthorn and Adler. I wasn't drowning.

Ophie's canvas tent glowed an inviting orange when we reached camp.

I sank against the smooth trunk of a silver-tipped maple and fastened my coat before I pretended to sleep. Memories and visions were louder, coming to me like a flash of a fever dream punctuated by the voice of my father.

Even when I tried to control it, to remember Fortune's face or the others, I only heard Koros giving commands, pounding his fist on the table, and telling me what it meant to be a princess of the Pantheon and rule at his side because *I* was divinely chosen.

He was so long dead, so far from returning that I'd started to doubt I had killed him. *I did.* I know I did. His blood ran over my hands. His body convulsed beneath me under the mural of his own bedroom in the Pantheon. If Fate and the primordials decided on a final laugh, it would be their last. The power pounding through my veins was overwhelming and it would eviscerate them.

Growling.

My entire body went rigid, humming with magic that clung to the hair on my arms like a second skin. My gaze darted around the campsite. Something was wrong. The light in Ophie's tent was gone and the massive wolf of Blackthorn's form crouched beside it, teeth bared and snarling.

I grabbed my sword and followed his attention as the outline of something shadowy and black kicked up snow. It lingered, moving slowly, almost like the nameless primordial from my dream. Shoulders, arms, then sinewy fingers like talons reached toward him as his jaw snapped.

Adler ran up behind the creature and ripped a sword—Blackthorn's sword—through the side of it, sending wisps of shadow flying. The creature spun in a mess of smoke and fury.

Ophie screamed and I ran, tearing my sword from its sheath.

The creature's sinewy fingers gripped Adler's throat and pinned him against a tree, lifting him up as he spluttered and groped for purchase. A shiny black beetle perched on the back of the creature's hand and glinted in the moonlight. The prince didn't turn to ice—it wasn't a valtross; it was something much worse, another scavenger if I had guessed.

I plunged the sword at an angle through its middle, barely missing Adler. The creature released his neck and the prince landed with a thud, gulping air. It wasn't over. I drew my sword and backed up. The creature didn't waver; its form didn't change. It towered over both of us.

A tar-black skull stared at me from beneath a charcoal shroud, taking one step closer . . . then another. I could try cutting off its head, or I could run and draw it away from camp.

Another step, I tightened my hold on the hilt and bolted.

Adler shouted my name between fits of coughing and a bark rang out. I didn't care; it couldn't kill me. But it *was* fast, nearly at my heels as I dodged trees and darted over a hill before I skidded into a ravine with steep rock walls on either side.

Gripping the sword, I spun around. There was nowhere else to go. *Fuck.*

The creature stopped running too, and stood, staring, cloaked in a rush of shadow and smoke. Empty eye sockets assessed me. What was it?

I took one step closer. Sword held out, shaking in my grip as magic built. I waited for it to move, but its hands remained limp at its side until its skeletal head cocked to the side and the jaw fell open.

From it, one shiny black beetle crawled out . . . then another and another. My heart beat once, twice, and before the third time, beetles spilled out like water from a bucket.

"What do you want?"

The beetles piled up at the foot of the creature. Crawling over each other, becoming a shimmering mound.

A hand reached out, grasping at air. More beetles fell from the sleeve, waiting for a command. The figure pointed, its fingertips clearly missing. I stopped breathing, and a thousand beetles charged.

All I saw was black. I dropped the sword and ripped the gloves from my hands. I swept my arms out and blue rushed forward in a wave of lightning as death struck like a wall.

The ravine filled with the chime of beetles collapsing on the frozen ground like rain as the shadow figure disappeared into nothing. I stood, hand on my heart, trying to catch my breath.

A fraction is what I was—still a piece of who I'd been, but all of it was returning. The thrumming power itched below my skin and I swayed. Not from fatigue, but realignment. My godhood wanted more.

I raised my arms again, closing my eyes, as power undulated and gathered first in my belly—icy and charged—before it slithered to my hands, coating them in blue-black tar.

If I wanted, I could tear open the veil here and unleash the ghosts of ancient beasts. With another push, I might throw a second wave of power. Perhaps I had enough to obliterate every ghost around us or maybe I could call on Riker to find whoever sent the effigy of a scribe to me in the dead of night.

Instead, I balled my hands and smothered the power because there was nothing I needed to prove.

I shoved my gloves back on, sheathed my sword, then I walked through the ravine. Beetles and ice crunched underfoot as I found my way to the edge and tried not to consider how every scavenger had a master.

"Raven?"

I looked up. A fully dressed Blackthorn peered down.

"Are you okay?"

"Physically, I'm grand," I said, using the stubby branch of a shrub tree to drag myself up in a fortunately fluid motion.

Blackthorn caught my arm and steadied me, regardless. Even through our layers, his touch burned. I ripped my arm back. "It's gone. Just some scavenger. Adler is lucky I don't miss."

26

The pantheon is past its time.
You cling to something meaningless and
I will not surrender until
the mortals are freed from you.

ORANGE LIGHT PEELED THROUGH the trees. My skull was raw, like the bone just above my temple had been branded. This felt more like the first time I received my godhood when I spent the first week laid up in my room of the Pantheon unable to move, swallowing the taste of blood.

"Can you ride?"

The words came distantly as I straightened against the maple tree. My blood felt thick, my heart beat too slow, and my thoughts muddied.

Blackthorn squeezed my shoulder. The smell of him was overwhelming and I looked at the sky, hoping something in it would kill me. Heightened senses were going to make this unbearable. He didn't smell like a dog now; he smelled like wet stone, wild pepper seeds, and fresh leather cured near a blacksmith's forge.

For gods, lust and love for a soul bound turned us into monsters. Our sense of touch was dulled so anything that reached past it was magnetizing and addictive. The longer I stood near Blackthorn, the more irrational and desperate I was to be touched by him.

"Can you ride?" He asked again, shoving my coat into my hands.

My stomach churned. I bent over and retched out the empty contents as Ophie exclaimed her disgust from a few paces off.

Adler had also stopped saddling the horses.

Blackthorn watched me, not knowing how much worse he made this. His beard had grown in the last few days and bits of it looked red in the sunlight, which I hadn't noticed before. *Fuck.*

"Better? We need to move . . . You'll ride with me."

"And if I hurt you?"

"Hurt me?"

Over his shoulder, Adler listened as he loaded the horse Ophie was loath to share with him.

"Mortal."

Adler raised his chin. "If he survived you last night, he can survive you today." The fae prince continued adjusting the saddle. "Unless you take those gloves off, right?"

"What's underneath the gloves?" Ophie asked. I combed my hair, which was exploding from the braid. It did nothing, and I was too sick to tame it.

"Poison," Blackthorn offered. I wondered what Ophie thought of us. She was perceptive.

Magic bolted through my spine like a lightning strike. I doubled over, slamming my eyes closed and digging my nails into my thigh until it passed.

I'd survived worse, but this was miserable.

Every step was too much. My head and body and eyes were all separate entities trying to run in different directions. I barely made it onto the horse.

Blackthorn grabbed me by the waist and practically threw me onto the saddle. His arm remained tight around my waist for the entirety of the ride, pressing me against his chest to keep me from slipping off as the waves came.

As much as I tried to resist, the steadiness of his back against mine and his even breathing soothed the thawing parts of me that were stretching to fit returning magic.

I didn't have the energy to call on Riker, so we were trusting Adler's sense of direction to get us to Vharos. The route followed a frozen creek through some of the forest. Snow shook off trees, and an occasional breeze rattled branches, which offered temporary reprieve from the straight-line winds in the open plains.

Ophie and Adler stayed silent for most of the ride because none of us quite knew what to say, and no amount of talking made the frigid air more bearable. My mind wandered as we crossed a wide-open, snowswept tundra.

There was nothing else to look at, but I shouldn't have watched the way Adler's hips moved in step with the horse, shifting his shoulders and back in alternating movements with every sway and trot as Blackthorn held me in place, wide hand gripping my waist.

Snow and bits of ice stuck and shimmered in Adler's dark hair, picked up by the scourging wind. In the stark daylight, his sharp cheeks reddened and showed a smattering of small freckles below his eyes.

I shouldn't have noticed the way he smiled and how it moved only his left ear—or how dimples pinched the corner of his mouth. Beneath his coat, he wore a thick quilted fabric in an array of patterns spanning too many shades of blue. A part of him reminded me so much of Leander; it was the way he held himself, in the way he smiled.

What would it be like to feel his hands again? His slender fingers, cold as the winter air, against the warmth of my skin? Would I even feel their bite? Could his kiss melt the ice around my heart the way Blackthorn's set mine on fire? Maybe Adler knew a winter forest was the best place to go down on a woman because every stroke of heat was that much sweeter with the kiss of cold between.

Blackthorn readjusted, dropping his splayed fingers to rest on my thigh. An unbidden rush of heat stabbed through me, rivaling the overwhelm of magic as dreams scratched my temple.

I wanted both of them.

Feral desire crushed and formed under pressure with every pace forward, like a diamond just below my navel. The thought was invasive and indulgent, but I couldn't stop. I imagined Blackthorn's hands around my neck and his lips on mine while Adler held my hips as the pressure of his cock pushed into me from behind.

It was a heaven that left me salivating. To be touched by one would bring me to life, but both would remind me I'm immortal.

But that was a dream—a desire left unspoken. I wouldn't give in to both if I couldn't bring myself to give in to one. I was a god with centuries of practice resisting so I swallowed the fantasy and stared ahead.

Soul bound.

I hated the word.

Fate was cruel to bind me to a mortal. Few gods were forced to suffer like this: to know their soul bound and never fulfill it was a special torture and all of them were dead now.

When we stumbled through the iron gates of Vharos, the sun had almost dipped behind the horizon. Unlike our other stops, the city was nearly deserted as the world turned a hazy shade of orange.

I dismounted immediately. I needed to stretch my legs and feel the steady ground beneath my feet as the magic continued to adjust and shift like the ocean.

We left the horses with a polite stable owner not far from the gate and continued into the narrowing streets of the city as iron gas lamps flickered on, drowning the moonlight as we passed storefronts and restaurants with fogged-up windows.

I was used to glances, but the constant staring from the sparse, bundled-up Vharosians was uncomfortable.

"Where are we going?" I asked Ophie, breaking the silence as a ghost rushed through me in a puff of air.

She shrugged; her bright red cheeks had flecks of white. "Haven't been here before."

I bit my lip, but it wasn't enough to mask my frustration. I needed a bath and a bed. Presently, there weren't any signs for an inn, yet Ophie walked with rapt confidence up a set of stairs to the next level of Vharos.

Blackthorn's voice dropped before I opened my mouth. "You said you were going to Vharos."

She crossed her arms indignantly, cocking her head to the side as Adler frowned. Ophie wasn't afraid of us.

"Four days and not one of you asked if I'd *been* to Vharos."

"I assumed—"

She shook her head. "I heard the healers of Vharos are—"

"Not the best in the realm." My eyes narrowed on her gold gaze and we all stopped on the staircase. I gripped the iced-over metal railing. "Most healers trek south to apprentice at the palaces of Ernmore."

"I'm not most people," Ophie stated. Her eyes hardened and she climbed a step closer to me. "I'd rather make a difference in a city where I can learn than not touch a patient for ten years. Have I explained myself?"

"Do you know anyone here?" Blackthorn asked, and the poignancy of his comment surprised me. Was he capable of observation?

Ophie stiffened. "I do not, but I will manage. If it pleases, Your Grace, I'd like to find a bed and a fireplace."

Her cutting glare met Blackthorn and the fae prince with vengeance.

"I'll find an inn." I sighed, starting up the stairs toward banked hills and terraced gardens that were far more charming in the spring.

If the men wanted to complain, they could, but I was tired, my hands shook, and the streets were caked in ice.

Vharos was built-in shelves and called the city of eighteen steps not because it had eighteen steps, but because it was composed of nearly eighteen shelves, each known by its largest building.

I was last in Vharos with Henry thirty years ago, but I knew my way around.

Henry.

Mortality was a thief. My chest constricted and I forced myself to breathe. I still wanted more time with him.

Swallowing the pity, I pushed ahead toward an inn along the city's edge that I knew by heart because we spent a few weeks there, escaping the all-encompassing nature of Linvia.

It was on the fourth shelf, in a neighborhood called the Canteen, which centered around a park and a glistening well filled with spring water. Presently, it was frozen over.

It was half named for the well and half named for the several barrel houses it was home to. They were explicitly built to age the rich dark beer Vharos was known for.

The front of the inn was no different from the surrounding barrel houses with their small sitting rooms and smaller kitchens. It was quaint and unassuming; the accommodations were hidden behind a heavy wooden door.

"We're staying here," I announced, moving to open it, but Adler interrupted.

"Sir Blackthorn, you and Ophie can go ahead. I need to speak to Raven before I leave."

"Are you sure you won't stay for dinner?" Ophie asked, stepping around Blackthorn and hugging a blanket tighter over her shoulders as flecks of snow whirled off the roof in a stiff breeze.

Adler shook his head; a dark lock fell in front of his eyes. "I need to return to Linvia, but I wish you the best, Ophie." His eyes flicked up to Blackthorn. "And I'll see you in Avilla, if all goes well."

With a heavy nod, Blackthorn pulled Ophie through the door and left me outside with the fae prince who immediately took a step closer.

All fae were beautiful.

I knew their languid voices, corded muscles, and exquisite symmetry meant to lure and trick. Rarely did I find beauty in their sameness, but Adler was different. There was beauty in his freckles, in the way he laughed, and in the way he managed to intrigue me.

He knew me when I didn't know him. I should have been terrified but there was something else . . .

"What does it feel like?" Adler asked. Errant flakes clung to his hair as they nested in mine. "Fae power is something we're born with. It can't be taken or traded, so the closest to powerless I've ever been is in Miria. Though it hasn't drained me of everything."

I pulled at the sleeve of my coat, trying to undo one of the seams.

"It feels like every part of me is being rewritten and insulated. But in waves? Sometimes I feel euphoric, then sick, and then like myself."

"And now?"

"Like myself."

"You're sure about Vharos?" Concern steeled his voice. "It will be a few days before I can get Devereux to Avilla. I'll be there too, should he need to be reminded of his place."

"Do you not think I can put a man in his place?"

Adler raised an eyebrow; a salacious grin turned up one corner of his lip. "I know you can put a man in their place. Even more, I'd love to know what you'd do to a fae man, but that isn't *my* place, even if you are wondering how I look naked."

"It is not your place," I warned, swallowing the bolt of desire.

"I know." He sighed, glaring at the swirling flakes drifting from the roof. "Did you notice the Wrythian mark on Ophie's hand?"

"First thing I asked her about. She knows nothing, and I didn't feel any magic."

"Neither did I." He scrubbed his chin. "Maybe it's dormant. If she did have that power, she'd be an incredible friend to have."

"Or enemy."

"Do you think the worst of everyone?"

"Only those who get too close."

Adler watched me, ignoring my answer. "How much time do you need before you can travel, and don't say tomorrow?"

"A few days," I muttered, hating the words when I wanted nothing more than to move. "This is the first time I've had this much magic in three hundred years. I won't face Devereux until I have it under control."

"And you'll do that in a few days?"

"More or less."

"Raven." His voice was a warning, low and careful, as he reassessed what I was capable of and took a step back.

"I want this over."

"I only believe you because Orion is here," he said and seemed surprised by his own words as his gaze held mine. "What? I trust him more than I trust you."

"You don't trust me?"

"If I believe even a quarter of the stories in the scriptures and histories, I never should have kissed you."

"You should believe most of those." The buzzing magic in my blood wanted him to do it again, here in the snow, under the lamplight, covered in three days of travel. "Foriana did even worse."

"I'm aware, but so far, I've not seen the ruthless version of you."

"Give it time," I muttered. "You've never seen the Goddess of Death before Koros removed her godhood."

"What?"

The levity left his eyes, and a seriousness ebbed into his throat that stopped me from thinking about his lips.

"He did that to you?"

"I shouldn't have said anything."

I tried to step back, but the rage in Adler's impossibly green eyes held me there on the step of the inn and wrenched the breath from my lungs.

"Is that what happened in Belfiante?"

"Yes," I said with hard-earned strength.

Centuries ago, the memories kept me awake at night, but now, with the godhood tangled in my veins—and distance between versions of me—I kept my voice even.

"Good thing you killed him."

"And I'd do it again."

Adler's shoulders rolled back, and calm eased over his features.

"You should go."

He nodded with a curt bow. "I'll see you in Avilla. You'll have a room at the Diadeus Chateau."

A clicking noise echoed as wind eddied the snow and vanished the prince to nothing.

Year 842, Foria
Raven is 292

VESTIOS FELL, NOT TO *fae but to a tyrant king of the Morav Dynasty in the 700's. It wouldn't stand, of course; Father feared the damage to the realm if too much port power was concentrated by one dynasty.*

Instead, the Pantheon decided I should wear the crown and renamed Vestios to Foria.

I arrived yesterday to a city that hardly noticed it was taken. Merchants stood in the streets shouting, trading goods and fruits across from the port, unaware blood was still on the floor before the throne. Dried, of course, but there none the less.

I noticed when an attendant eagerly showed me around the room, discussing details of a coronation I wasn't sure I wanted.

Niany's vestments were laid in my chamber instead of the gown I requested. I'd wear them because Koros would tell her if I didn't and I'd never hear the end of it, but they were ugly: white-trimmed robes with black and purple piping. The colors meant too much to the people of Vestios and the Pantheon, but they meant nothing to me.

White: Pantheon. Purple: the royal family, and black for death—I never had the choice of a color. This was Niany's reminder.

Armine was red, Fortune was yellow, and our brother, Maxentius, was green.

Everything in my new wardrobe was a mess of black and white. Koros knew better than to ask me to wear purple unless it was an amethyst collar or something more subtle.

For every reservation I held in my heart, the coronation went as well as I expected until I asked Haden if I'd be the Queen or Empress of Vestios—in their people's tradition.

He laughed and told me Koros renamed the kingdom "Foria" for his favorite daughter. I could choose whatever title I wanted.

But I wasn't Koros's favorite; I was the dangerous daughter he needed to make amends with, so here I stood.

Haden also asked if Malcolm should be crowned king, and it was my turn to laugh. If I could choose whatever I wanted, Malcolm would have nothing.

He could stay prince and consort and learn of his wife's position from court gossip like everyone else.

27

Inside the inn, a massive fireplace roared beneath a chandelier. The innkeeper handed me a key with hardly a nod. I wondered if the old lady recognized me from the weeks Henry and I spent here, but I doubted it.

Most of the inn was trimmed in polished shadow oak, which was common to Vharos—I'd once paid a very handsome amount to have a door carved from it for the Forian palace.

The rooms of the inn sprawled out behind the lobby into sections dug underneath the next shelf of earth.

Our room was an apartment suite in back. I smiled as I opened the door because this place was familiar, even if Blackthorn was draped over the couch and Ophie loudly sang from the bath in her own room.

The room was spacious. Several steps led from the door, down into a living area with a fireplace, two couches, and a table. The exterior-facing walls were carved out of limestone and known to seep water in the spring. All was reinforced with iron rods that held up the shops and terrace above.

Large faux windows painted with murals gave the illusion of a world outside, while fine gold fixtures hung from the ceiling, adding a sense of luxury. It wouldn't be difficult to hide here for a few days.

I desperately needed time between here and what happened next. Not only because I was adjusting to the new rush of power, but retrieving the last of my godhood would take everything . . .

because sometimes we bury our pain where we think we'll never have to look again—never have to face what we couldn't.

Behind the bars of the Tyrlian prison, chained to the wall, I thought I'd faced my pain, my grief, my guilt, and my regret for all my years of retribution. It was a footnote where Belfiante was the end and the beginning.

I'd avoided the gleaming shores of the mirror pond my entire life. They held anguish and guilt I'd never be ready to face—not in a million years or the lifetimes in between. Facing Belfiante was always the final price of death.

"The other room is yours," Blackthorn said.

"Thanks." I looked at the opposite door where the off-key words of some ballad came through. "Ophie is enjoying herself."

The knight planted his feet on the floor, resting his elbows on his knees. His hair was wet and he wore only a collared cotton shirt and clean pants; None of the dirty layers we'd arrived in.

"How long do we keep her?"

I hugged my pack to my chest. "I'll take her to the temple in a few days. I know one of their healers; she'll be glad to take her in."

"Not tomorrow? Have you grown attached?"

He smirked, and for the second time that night, I was desperate for touch as the ebb of magic expanded again and wrung out my mortality.

I shrugged off the pain of desire with a sharp exhale. "She deserves a little luxury, and I need rest. What's a day?"

Blackthorn raised his eyebrow. "It's taken us weeks to get here and we still have to return to Tyrlas."

"One week won't—"

"One week?"

"Five days." My gaze hardened. "I understand where you're coming from—truly, I do—but this magic needs to settle or I'll kill someone by accident."

"You say that and—"

"I have a plan."

"And I should trust you?"

"I haven't lied yet."

"Only withheld the truth," he snapped.

"Sometimes it's required." I couldn't deny it. "If you need me, find someone else."

As I slammed the door to the room, the nagging word came back with force.

Soul bound.

How long could I run away from it? Could I bury it? Or was there no point? As the godhood crowded out my mortality, the pull only grew louder.

I squeezed my eyes and tried to breathe. Tried to smell anything in the room that wasn't him, but the winter and pepper of him clung to the air, remaining in the tub even after he'd cleaned up.

Gods ignored the bond at their own peril.

I'd seen it before and it drove good men insane. Some gods became so driven with lust and desire that they killed their soul bound by accident—taking what they wanted.

Others tried to get as far as possible until death came, but most succumbed . . . whatever that looked like. We'd come too far; I'd gotten too close, and it was only a matter of time before I gave in.

Once I did, I hoped Fate was ready to learn exactly what I thought of his humor. Fate knew I killed the Scribes of Nurem. What would stop me from strangling him with his own blood-soaked threads if he'd tied me to another mortal and asked me to survive another death?

Nothing.

Once I had my godhood back, there would be nothing to stop me except myself and the stupid beating heart I was too keenly aware of. I tucked *Everund* under my pillow so I wouldn't forget my time was coming to a close.

I'd forgotten the way power vibrated. It was no wonder gods made mistakes when they were whole. Nothing, no feeling, was enough. As power settled, I only felt emptier.

A soft bed was a welcome relief, but I felt little as magic seeped and coated my skin. My other senses were heightened. I smelled the oil and perfume that had soaked into the sheets from several washes before. It didn't bother me half as much as the lingering scent of Blackthorn. I'd smelled him before, sweat and iron mixed with oak and pepper, but that was nothing.

It wasn't oak. He smelled like the edge of winter in a birch tree forest. Earthy, warm, with the faintest black pepper and suntanned leather. It stuck to everything he wore but it didn't matter.

I couldn't have him. I would deny, deny, *deny* this bond until it killed me because that was preferable to whatever fulfilling the bond would do to me—to Miria.

It was selfish to hope Fate had something in mind to erase his humanity, but I wanted no hand in their guilt. An endless life was a curse and I'd see it ended. Humans no longer needed gods—

"Can't you hear their screams?"

I shot up.

The voice in my head had come back and I growled. Ear-shattering cries rang. I didn't flinch. I'd heard it all before and cared even less now.

"What do you want, Niany?"

"Mother," she snapped.

I laughed.

"You still claim me as your daughter when I've betrayed everyone, killed my father, and banished you to the only world you can't escape from?"

"Daughter is a title like any other, Foriana."

"If that was true, it should not be so hard to shed. I am not yours."

A sourceless wind swept through the room and I rolled my eyes as a ghost appeared. Sharp edges, round face, and too young.

"I will take nothing," the ghost said, assuming my mother's voice and sharper posture as she paced toward my bed.

With a wave of my hand, I could send her back or absorb every bit of magic keeping her upright. Instead, I entertained the apparition.

"You made a promise," she warned.

"I've made many promises, but there will be no consequences for breaking mine to you."

She frowned. "That you're aware of. Was a run-in with a primordial not enough?"

"I'm not going back."

"Your afterlife is dying. Souls are trapped—"

I loosened my hold on the blanket. "And you agreed to take my place in a bargain for your life. Fix it yourself."

"I can't." She glared and hovered. Now I saw it; pox decorated the neck of the ghost. "You know I can't. My power is over the living. You granted me none of your power but the title."

"That's what made it a bargain. You get to watch me gain power, or would death be preferable? I'll happily arrange it, but I will not give the gods this world back or risk anything that might. Miria doesn't need the Pantheon, you'd done enough."

"Is that why they fight wars over lines and waste their own?"

"We did the same."

"We did not waste our own until *you* decided you had the power to."

I straightened my shoulders. Anger pulsed behind my brow.

"I *did* have the power. It was given to me by Koros, the Scribes of Nurem, and the primordials just as yours."

She ignored me. "Return and fix it."

"Or what?" I threw the covers off the bed and stood up, passing through the ghost. "You'll haunt me the rest of my life as you always have? You are nothing. Your gods and daughters and sons are dead. If I fix anything, it will be building a bridge with the bones of—"

"And your soul bound?"

My heart stopped. My breathing too. Of course, she knew.

"I felt it, Foriana. Your fate shakes the ground between worlds when there is no other noise."

I waved my hand. In an instant, the ghost was gone with the voice of my mother. She'd be happy enough her last words were a threat.

A few weeks ago, I'd be heaving. Tonight, the motion felt like nothing. The only reason my heart hammered in her absence was completely unrelated.

I never should have offered her the kindness of a bargain, but I was weaker then, and the way Koros wept over her body twisted a memory in me I held too close.

I'd saved them both for last. My hands only shook for my mother, and even then, I couldn't kill her.

Instead of the knife, my sword sank into her chest and I caught her soul just before it slipped the veil. That's when I shoved it away and buried her in an afterlife she didn't belong to: The Goddess of Life couldn't escape the mortal realm of death.

With a passing thought, I settled back in bed and tried not to think about how my skin crawled and the promise I'd made her. When I turned over, my attention snagged on the pile of Blackthorn's clothes. What it would be like to kiss him again.

Something had awakened and I couldn't force it back, but if I was strong enough, I could keep it at bay before it turned into something far worse.

28

*Dear Neander Ruse, I have reason to believe
you can forge a dagger out of any material.
I have a challenge for you.*

THE NEXT DAY IN Vharos, a winter storm rolled in. Snow and wind closed the temple, the museums, and most everything else.

The innkeep kept us fed and dropped off a stack of pamphlets and books in exchange for our pile of soiled clothes. He also mentioned the theater didn't close for anything, which presented an opportunity to sit in the dark with something aside from my racing thoughts.

Ophie sat on the couch reading a retelling of Maxentius, god of shadows and prince of the Pantheon. I slunk off to my room, spending the time we had to spare on the floor, propped against the bed, both palms out and gloves off.

The magic was viscerally cold at the tips of my fingers, like holding them against ice for too long. Without gloves, my fingers were black entirely to my palms as the magic settled.

I stared at my hand, guiding the vibrating power in my blood toward the center of my hand until it gathered there like liquid.

No one else could touch the mortal afterlife; it was mine and mine alone as it always was, but it was different. It was infinite now because I was careless.

I closed my eyes and gave into the hum of a million waiting souls.

Once the final piece was restored, blue would overtake my eyes and my hands would be entirely black. I'd become who I was before Koros and the God of War tricked me to Belfiante and tore my godhood from my chest—afraid of what I *could* do.

I tilted my palm and spilled magic to the other as it cooled. The magic had turned black and oily as I let it drip through my fingers onto the floor. It would seep into the carpet and fade to nothing in a few minutes.

I groaned and held my head as I stared at the pattern in the rug. I tried to breathe—to feel anything that wasn't magic stitching itself back into every thread of who I was.

The power I'd dig up in Belfiante would make me *world-ending*. All because I was a coward who couldn't handle the responsibility bestowed on me. It was never power I wanted. Fundamentally, I misunderstood power because if I couldn't save the ones I loved, then what was the point?

The knife needed to work.

A knock on the door sent me to my feet. Reflexively, I grabbed for my gloves, shoving them on as Blackthorn cracked open the door.

"You alright?" he asked, lips pressed together.

"Fine, why?"

I brushed the wrinkles from my skirt, pulling on my godly indifference that already felt like a second skin.

"I was practicing."

"Ophie wanted to get dinner before the show. I suggested the tavern across the way."

"Any warm food is fine with me. I'll get my coat."

The door closed and I exhaled, wishing any different future lay in front of me.

I couldn't take back the magic in my blood, or change course, but I could bundle up and enjoy a few hours of entertainment.

We trudged to the tavern through snow up to our knees, barely able to see our hands in the onslaught of white.

After too long, groping at buildings, we stumbled inside a damp tavern where we were greeted by a roaring fire, a handful of tables, and Vharosian oak barrels as far as the eye could see.

It was entirely empty and smelled like roasting grain and overcooked malt. The barrels nearest to us were in varying states of leaking black sludge onto the stone floor. Wordlessly, the barkeep set three glass steins on the table, each brimming with a rich, stout beer.

Ophie stared at it too long before she worked up the courage to take a sip.

When she did, her face contorted and she nearly spat it on the table. Blackthorn and I burst out laughing.

"You don't have to drink it."

I leaned back in the chair. The roasted bitterness of the beer was a welcome contrast to the jammy red wine I'd drank too much of in Linvia, and the too-sweet white I'd gotten used to in Tyrlas.

Ophie's face scrunched. "How do you stand it?"

Blackthorn shrugged, nearly halfway through his own.

"An acquired taste. Though they say beer is best in Vharos—also helps when you've tasted the worst of Tyrlas."

"And what's the worst of Tyrlas?"

"Swill." The knight grimaced. "Cheapest you can get at any of the taverns. It's any leftover beer poured into the same pitcher."

"That's revolting."

Ophie blanched as she stared at her beer, contemplating.

"Yes, but it *was* cheap. Can you imagine paying only a frir for a pint?"

"What's a frir?" Ophie asked, and suddenly we'd fallen into one of Blackthorn's conversations. I knew it was a trap as three steaming bowls of stew were set in front of us and Blackthorn grinned.

"A frir," Blackthorn started, leaning forward on the wobbly table, "is similar to the Linvian cron or a Forian bronze. It's the smallest currency we have in Tyrlas. And, quite ironically, the silver a frir is made with is worth more than the frir itself. It's quite a point of contention for our treasurer, but critically important."

Blackthorn continued on about currency and valuation while we devoured the hearty brewer's stew.

Ophie must have warmed up to the beer because she was nearly halfway through her stein as she placed her hands behind her head and changed the subject, attention back to me.

"You said you were a demigod?"

"I did."

She pursed her lips, and Blackthorn stiffened, watching me.

"That wasn't entirely true," Ophie chided, gold eyes searching mine. "I heard you talking in Reen. I wasn't dead, just in a tent."

"Tell anyone," I warned, bristling, "and I will make good on my—"

"I would never," she said, casting her attention into the depths of her glass. "I owe you my life for getting me out of Linvia. If I had stayed, I wasn't sure I would've lived."

"What do you mean?" Blackthorn asked.

Ophie looked at him, but I saw the sorrow, that kind of radiating pain as her finger traced the rim of the stein.

"I've been trying to break off an engagement for years, but he'd finally run out of patience. He killed my father as a warning."

"Has he hurt you?" Blackthorn asked. I leaned forward, elbow getting caught in a wet spot as her non-answer hung in the air.

Ophie cleared her throat, bleary eyes falling back to me as she pushed up the corners of her lips. "I couldn't marry someone I didn't love."

"No one should." I meant it. "We all deserve to be loved and I've run away from my fair share of marriages."

Her face lightened. "How old are you? The legends say Koros was—"

"Seven hundred and eighty-four. Koros died when he was almost twelve hundred."

"Killed by his daughter, right?"

"Exactly." I nodded, swallowing another gulp of beer like it could drown the memory. "According to him, I'm one of the lesser ones, which is exactly how I stayed alive. Have you ever heard of the goddess Vinliana?" She shook her head, and I smiled. "*Exactly.*"

"And now you run errands for a king?"

"We," Blackthorn interjected proudly. "We run errands for the king."

"And what is Vinliana the goddess of?"

"Wouldn't you like to know?"

Ophie crossed her arms with a laugh. "I would."

"Presently, she's the goddess of not missing a show. We need to go if we don't want to be late."

The theater wasn't a far walk, just a few turns from the square. However, the blizzard and lack of Vharosians in the streets made the trek far more difficult than it needed to be. We stumbled to our seats with only a few seconds to spare before the lights turned down.

So few people attended it became a show just for us and the five other audience members who'd braved the weather. I smiled the entire time. The play was one of my favorites: *One Night in Leven.*

It was an old play about the harvest goddess Etta and her doomed tryst with a half-mortal named Finneas, whom she'd promised eternal life, but only if he moved the smallest moon. None of it happened but it made a beautiful story.

When it was over, we spilled out of the theater into the streets. The snow had finally stopped, leaving Vharos covered in a pristine blanket of stark white powder that came well past my knees.

Blackthorn tried to make a snowball, but the snow was too cold and crumbled apart in the air before it hit anything. Ophie tried with more finesse. Her snowball held its form, but it sailed past the knight, colliding with a brick wall in a *splat*.

Banners and holly boughs hung over most doors, tied with blue ribbon. Gods, Solstice was in a few days. How?

Back in the room, Ophie buried herself in blankets, leaving only her head to poke out as she stared at the fire. Her blonde hair was unbound and stuck out wildly. Blackthorn sat on the couch and found a place on the floor.

It was hard not to admire the girl. She had the courage and patience of someone so much older, yet moments like this reminded me how young she was.

"Did you know Etta?" she asked.

"I did," I said carefully, veering around the truth like some intricate dance. There was nothing damning about Etta, but her past and mine were always intertwined—never friends, never enemies, but caught in the middle of always knowing the other. "She was exactly as kind as they say, which is terribly hard to believe because her father was the God of War."

Etta died quickly, unaware it happened at my hands with a knife fashioned from her father's bones.

"Is it hard to remember everything?"

I shrugged.

"I remember in pieces. Some memories and people stick out more; some blend together. I try to write down the important things. But I don't always know what's important. I also keep a timeline on me so I don't forget."

"Is that your map?" Blackthorn's voice carried over with a questioning lilt. "You haven't added anything to it."

"Do something worth writing about, and perhaps I will."

I fumbled around in my pockets and tugged out the small leather pouch from a hidden compartment under my blouse.

"It's a map?" Ophie asked, watching me unfold it.

"More than a map. It was a map I'd drawn a long time ago. I just wrote over it. Each point marks the important bits."

"Can you not read histories?"

"No," I chuffed, folding it back and tucking it away again. "Histories are complicated, even the ones from the Grand Masters of Miria. Some are more true than others, but they all tell a story. Even your school texts and healing books have stories."

Ophie's gaze rolled back to the fire. She tightened her grip on the blankets and I leaned against the couch, closing my eyes.

Tired didn't begin to describe the fatigue clawing up my back—a blend of magic, memories, and travel catching up as my body tried to remember how to carry it all.

"Did Finneas ever capture the moon?" Blackthorn piqued.

I opened my eyes. "Of course not. That's ridiculous."

"You're a goddess who just shoved a part of your godhood back into yourself after digging it from the frozen ground with your bare hands. Can't love capture a moon?"

I had no idea where the myth came from, but Ophie made a noise of agreement.

"Etta begged Koros to let Finneas trade his mortality in service to the Pantheon." The truth was far messier, and I remembered too much of it. "Koros obliged."

"And?"

"And?" I shrugged. "War came, Etta met her true soul bound on the opposing side, leaving her with a choice: Accept the pain of rejecting her soul bound and stay on the wrong side of the war, or abandon her bargain with Finneas and leave him with Koros."

Ophie's blanket fell from her shoulders as she clutched her heart. "What did she choose?"

"Wasn't much of a choice," I said, trying to be unaffected. "Soul bounds are fated, intense connections that overwhelm reason when they snap into place. Worse until they're accepted. She left Finneas with Koros."

"What?" Ophie's voice dropped in true surprise.

"It happened a hundred years after *One Night in Leven*."

"Did he have a soul bound?" Blackthorn asked, and I hated how the single word burned through me like a brand when it fell from his lips.

"Yes," I said almost immediately, swallowing the knot of emotion in my throat. "Finneas found her a while later. I don't remember her name, but Koros lost interest in Finneas's loyalty after Etta escaped the Pantheon."

"Is he still alive?"

Blackthorn's gaze burned my neck, but I ignored it.

"No. Killed in battle."

The very first battle where Koros and I faced each other in Reen—he was the King of Gods. I was a cavalry general for New Miria. Koros put Finneas on the front lines, knowing the power of my forces.

That day, I didn't care if I felled gods or men and my father knew it, despite what I believed. We hadn't respected each other for a very long time. Truthfully, I wasn't sure how Finneas died, just that he did. Riker died too—and Dayvin.

Blood was everywhere that day: on grass, on armor, on steel, and on stone as far as I could see. Too often, historians called it the Final Battle of New Miria because the losses were so staggering, but I debated the characterization.

Prepared for another question, but not sure I could answer it, I waited. Luckily, Ophie shrugged out of the blanket and went to bed.

As the door closed, Blackthorn's shoulders sagged and I curled into myself, wishing I felt either the heat from the fire or the cold in the room. Instead, magic reeled in my veins, thrashing against the remaining pieces of my mortality.

"Are you okay?" he asked as if I'd answer honestly.

"Can you define okay?"

"Raven."

The gentleness he'd shoved into my name melted some of my resolve. It slithered from my hands like a wet rope. I ached to hear my name from his lips, and it was even sweeter than I remembered as he slipped off the couch and joined me on the floor.

If I looked at him, I'd slip. But maybe it wouldn't be so bad? Maybe—

No.

"Are you okay?"

"I'm tired." My throat was thick with emotions too big to be held down by suffocating magic.

"You've been reliving the war."

"Oh? Which one?"

I scooted around to look at him. Amber eyes snagged on mine and it was a mistake. I should have kept my back to him but I held his gaze and wished I was closer.

Wish I could reach out and run my thumb against the shadow of his jaw—but he couldn't feel the pull, the fucking magnetism that overrode my thoughts. It wasn't fair to either of us.

"Is there anyone *alive* you talk to?"

"Yes."

I pushed the soft thoughts to the back of my head as his gaze on me narrowed.

"Don't say Henry."

"Why not?" I snapped. "He is a friend and he *is* alive."

Magic crackled through the room. I swallowed—that was my warning. Maybe Blackthorn couldn't feel the charge in the air, but I did . . . like a wool blanket in the winter that clicks and sparks.

Blackthorn's brow arched, but he didn't waver. "You haven't seen him for almost thirty years."

"Twenty-six is nothing to me."

"I don't believe that."

"Strange belief system, if that's part of it," I grumbled, picking at the hem of my sleeve. I wanted to disappear and I wanted to be touched in equal measure. "I have friends, but what would it matter to you if I named them?"

"I don't know," he admitted, running a hand through his hair and searching my face for something. He leaned forward, blond hair brushing his shoulder. "I just don't understand how you live with it."

"It's not my choice, just the lot I rolled. Many have it worse."

"Well, that isn't any way to live." The way his eyes bored into me felt like he'd flayed my skin and picked my bones. "All politics removed, if you were free from Tyrlas—"

"Impossible," I whispered, tightening my grip around my knees. "There is no world where politics are gone. Not for me."

"But if there were?"

"Am I living in a cave?" I snapped with no intention of doing that again.

"Raven." There it was, the warning with my name again. It calmed me in a way I couldn't bring myself to acknowledge. "What would you do? I'm sure it's not traversing the realm and doing whatever it is we've been doing."

I pursed my lips, stretching my knees out with a yawn. "Politics removed, I'd keep going as I always have. What makes you happy? What would you do if you weren't a knight?"

He relaxed at the question, amber eyes glimmering in the bare light of the room.

Soul bound.

"Me?" He looked into the distance as if it were playing out on the wall. "My sister raced horses for a while and I helped her care for them. We'd always talked about going to Foria, buying land, and breeding racehorses for the Forian games."

"The competition is steep."

One corner of his mouth turned up. "You asked what I'd do if I weren't a soldier; you never said it had to be realistic."

"Suppose not." I sighed and moved on. "What is your sister like? She must be important if you tied your life to hers."

He took a sharp breath, running his hand through the soft sweep of his hair. "A force of nature—younger than me. My father always had a chip against the king for one reason or another and Em inherited the same bitterness. I didn't worry about her until a nonsensical letter reached my barracks about two years after I was knighted. I left that night and found her in a city alley within an inch of her life. She'd been left for dead by the man who'd sworn—to *me*—he'd protect her.

"Well, he'd gotten over his head and it nearly cost *her*. I wouldn't have bound our lives, but I had no choice; it was all I could do to keep her alive. She was pissed about it—eventually landed her in prison."

"I'll get her out."

"How?" Blackthorn looked at me and his voice sharp and cutting. "How would you get her out when you couldn't free yourself?"

"Tyrlas should not have bargained with a god who spent centuries negotiating with fae." I stretched my leg across the couch. "I have a plan; I just need you to trust me."

He squeezed his neck. "I want to trust you. It's difficult when it's my sister."

"I understand."

"Do you?" He raised his eyebrow. "I've heard the stories of what you've done to your sisters and family."

My voice hollowed as the memories snagged and dissolved—like the godhood knew the guilt wasn't worth my time.

"They deserved the end they got."

"And you deserve to live?"

"I never said that."

"But here you are."

A brusque wave of power swelled, reminding me who I was and would be again.

"You think they could kill Death?"

"Of course not." Orion eyed me. "You avoided my question."

"Evasion is a talent of mine."

"What would you do if you were free?"

"Never considered it," I admitted, pinching at the fraying fabric of my sleeve like it might unravel the rest of who I was.

"Time changes too much, and I always get bored when it's calm for too long."

"Bored?"

"Bored."

"Is it that or because you know everything ends?"

The heat of his gaze burned through my chest with a truth I couldn't bring myself to say.

"Everything does end." I tried to steady my pounding heart. "And I'm the one who has to watch it all, so forgive me for being cynical."

He tilted his head. "Is that why you ran away when I kissed you in Linvia?"

I jerked up, opening my mouth to say something, but no words came out.

Blackthorn's expression remained steady and calm. "I've seen the way you look at me. It wasn't a mistake, and I'd crawl through fire to kiss you again, Raven."

Soul bound.

Seconds passed like minutes. His gaze dipped down to my lips, his own parted and inviting as he licked them.

"Please," was all I said.

I blinked and Orion's hands were on my jaw, my lips on his in a kiss that felt like coming home. Fuck, he was everything—spice and leather and pine soap, and by gods, he tasted like the salt of sweat.

His hands cupped my back as the kiss deepened and I rolled my hips against his, pushing him against the couch. Every sense of mine was on fire, desperate to feel him because I had no room to feel anything else.

He moaned and I lost myself. Fuck, I started clawing, groping the fabric of his shirt to feel him, to draw him closer.

I wanted to worship him—to drag my hands across his skin with the reverence of a praying god while I drove my name into his memory with my hips. But something icy dripped down my back, like a memory or a warning; I pulled back.

Orion was beautifully undone with swollen lips, panting in front of me. He held me tight as if we were back on the horse and not on the floor, fingers splayed across my spine.

"Something wrong?"

I pressed my gloved hand to his jaw and drew it along, feeling his strength in the smallest touch as I stared at his lips.

"Raven?"

My gaze flicked up and drowned in amber. No part of me was thinking straight, and now I had a choice.

"What I wanted was that." My hands dropped, lingering on his chest. "I shouldn't have gone to my room the other night."

His hands tightened on my back as mine slipped to his hips. "Why did you?"

"I was afraid it would feel like this."

"And what does this feel like?"

"Waking up," I whispered and pulled his lips to mine.

He kissed back, savoring me as much as I wanted to savor him. Fingers trailed up my back and into my hair, deepening the kiss I'd break soon.

I had to. He wouldn't burn the way I did. His lungs wouldn't char and crackle like mine would. His chest wouldn't break open to make room for mine.

But that's what *I* felt so I stopped.

He looked at me with a lopsided grin as distance writhed between us.

"We should sleep."

"We should sleep," he agreed as his hands slipped from my back, but the fire of desire raged in my center wanting too much more.

I left the room, knowing if I didn't, I'd regret the things I'd do. There was hope in his touch and hope was the most dangerous of all.

Year 1040, A Southern Kingdom
Raven is 490

MALCOLM GRABBED MY ARM as I tried to walk away, jerking me back. The stone corridor was empty and the scuffle of his boots echoed as he sneered. I shook him off, biting back a worse retort.

"I'm not going back to the Pantheon."

"What?" The god laughed, shaking his head so the silver curls of his hair fell over his shoulders. "You've had your fun with mortals, Foriana, but no amount of cum can turn you into one."

"I am not you."

Malcolm took a step closer. Even cleaned up, he still smelled like the iron and steel of war. "No, you're worse."

"I care about something, which is more than you can say."

"I care about the Pantheon, about your father, and about de-fending this place from the grimy fucking hands of the fae, while *you abdicate every one of your responsibilities. Name one you've kept."*

"It is not your place to remind me of my responsibilities."

"Isn't it? I am your husband." His eyes narrowed as he took another step closer, trying to cow me. "I am the only person who knows you, who can see you for exactly what you are. Pretend to be the hero. Rewrite the histories if it suits you, but they will all see you for the villain you are—the wretched Goddess of Death, covered in the blood of a million innocents. How do you sleep at night?"

"And the God of War isn't guilty?"

"I never said I wasn't, but it wasn't at my hand a whole field of soldiers was massacred. It wasn't my hand that raised armies of the dead and abandoned the afterlife. That was you."

His fingers caressed my bare shoulder and traced my arm—he wanted to see me wince.

I wouldn't; I had a hundred years of practice. I could stand before him and feel nothing. He could touch me however he wanted, but I'd long forgotten what it was to be loved by him, just as I'd forgotten what it was to be hurt by the same hands.

29

I tossed and turned in the too-soft bed and stared at the ceiling, wishing Blackthorn wasn't sleeping on the couch when I needed to escape.

I needed to stop thinking about how soft his hands might be around my neck, and the sting of heat when his lips met mine. How would it feel for him to move inside me? Would it break me into a thousand pieces? Would it give me hope I couldn't afford?

Hope was the enemy of rescuing this world from everything the gods had wrought.

I sucked in a breath and rolled over for the umpteenth time. It was early, but too late to get any restful sleep, so I shoved off the covers and resigned myself to getting ready.

Threaded blue and black eyes stared back at me in the mirror, glowing and iridescent as my godhood sparked to life. The space in my cheeks and under my eyes filled. For once I looked alive.

The new color made the scar across my neck more visible, more grotesque. I'd earned that one when Koros initiated me on the battlefield.

The other scar was in the center of my chest, opposite my heart, just above my breast. There, Koros cut me open with *Everund* on the shore of the mirror ponds as I screamed for death.

I wished he'd killed me, but I was too important to him, to Miria, and apparently to history now five hundred years had passed. The godhood beat and pulsed again, gaining strength as it deepened my immortal scars.

Who I'd been was slipping away. I was two people: Raven, the near-mortal, and Foriana, the immortal Goddess of Death. Two different lives, two different purposes with scars to mark the delineation.

When I opened the door, Ophie stood with the knight, bag in hand and with an excited smile on her face.

"Are you ready?" she asked, blissfully unaware that I avoided looking at Blackthorn despite the way he stared at me.

"Always."

This morning, the sun warmed the streets.

Melting snow created rippling streams and puddles as we made our way through terraces to the opposite edge of the city. The temple was nestled in an outcrop of buildings, surrounded by greenhouses tended by the healers.

The healers of Vharos weren't the best in Miria, not by a long shot, but their expertise in herbal medicine ranked higher than any other order in the Consortium.

I'd known a few healers who cut their teeth in the gray halls of the Vharosian cathedral. They learned how to care for the nearly three hundred plants—several that no longer existed anywhere but the greenhouses of Vharos.

The temple began as one stone-gray cathedral with arched windows and looming gargoyles but through the years, it spread to five adjacent buildings, creating a campus.

Memories flitted as we approached and I pulled my hood tighter.

We stopped at the top of the crumbling stone steps. I slammed the door knocker, which was the head of some single god the north believed in for a while. In the last two hundred years, due to several visions of Niany, they came back to the Pantheon.

The clang echoed even as the door groaned and gave way to a massive room with marbled floors and elaborately carved wooden pillars stretching to vaulted ceilings.

Hurried footsteps came from a hallway to the right. Several ghosts milled about but hardly looked up when we walked in.

"Welcome to the temple of Vharos," a healer said, stopping in front of us.

She was dressed in the fine white robes of Mirian healers and wore a deep vermilion stole over her shoulders, trimmed in gold—the highest honor a healer could receive. On her forehead rested a small gold circlet, identifying her as the Mother of her order.

I bowed, hood still drawn as I gestured behind me for Ophie and Blackthorn to do the same.

"Good morning, Mother. I am Lady Raven of Tyrlas and I've brought you an aspiring healer from Linvia who seeks to continue her training in your order."

The healer clicked as she looked us over. Ophie stepped beside me, arms straight at her side, breathing uneasy as the healer's dark brown eyes roamed.

Then they swung to me.

"Remove your hood in my temple."

I drew it back and the old woman stopped.

"Death has come at last," she whispered. Ophie flashed me a bewildered look.

A question caught in her expression but I wouldn't answer it here or now. Not even as the Mother dropped her chin in a curt bow.

"I am here on behalf of my friend, Ophie. She healed the knight behind us from a stab wound and her work left no scar behind. It was a jagged sword cut below the ribs—if you have room, she would be an asset to your order. You also know who I am, so you know my word is good."

The healer regarded us before she clapped her hands. Two lesser healers emerged from the same corridor both in green stoles. One hardly older than Ophie, and the other's age indiscernible through the burn scars across their cheek and kind smile.

"Sister Laila, Brother Kyn, will you be so kind as to take Lady Ophie on a tour while I have a private conversation with Lady Raven?"

Blackthorn looked between the two of us, unsure of whom he should follow.

The Mother took notice.

"Your knight may join Lady Ophie for the tour."

It wasn't an invitation but a command. The four walked down one corridor as the Mother led me to a small room with several bookcases and curtains that had been drawn for so long I couldn't tell what color they were.

Three rugs layered on top of one another muffled any noise. And, despite ample daylight, the room was dark, lit only by a few wax candles in the ceiling candelabra.

The Mother stared; her assessing eyes raked over me as she pursed her lips. "I was warned about you by the prior Mother of the Vharosian Order."

"Mother Neris? Sorry to hear of her passing."

"It was years ago."

"Is grief not eternal?" I asked with a smirk, leaning against a table and crossing my arms—for their title, healers were quite cut-throat.

"Only when felt so deeply the soul cracks." She eyed me, clutching prayer beads in her hand and wringing them. "It is not befitting to feel grief so strongly when we walk this closely with Death."

"I am grateful for your service," I said, intentionally leaving the statement vague. Some of their order hated the Goddess of Death for what she'd done and others believed she was righteous, gentle, and all-seeing. I've learned my lesson about assuming.

"Someone needs to help mortal souls meet The Black." The Mother cleared her throat and lowered her hands, beads chiming as they tangled. "There are many stories about you, whispered through my order and the others. Some say you're the warrioress, wife to the God of War. Others say your hands of shadow still reach and guide the lost through the river of the afterlife. Though many seers claim you abandoned your command to seek power in Miria and the Pantheon you emptied."

"Seers lost their credibility when the Scribes of Nurem died."

"An unfortunate incident," the Mother said. Her brow arched as she watched me, waiting for a crack.

I cocked my head and swallowed a flare of magic. "Why are you concerned to see me when your order and the Consortium have maintained temples in my name for centuries? Are you not honored?"

"Do not question my honor. Your name is only one commitment of our order," she agreed; tension crawled into her tone, setting my teeth on edge. "Few have the privilege to stare into the face of Death and speak for the mortal souls in your care."

"And what is it you wish to say to Death?" I bristled, kicking off the desk to stand at full height, which was, admittedly, shorter than the Mother.

She didn't back down; brown eyes bore into me. "Only that the Healer's Consortium of Miria does not want war and many leaders believe that is what happens if a new Pantheon rises."

"With all due respect, Mother, I have no interest in raising a pantheon. I am your ally among the gods and that has not changed—healers and Death will always walk in step."

"You believe we walk in step now?"

"What do you believe?"

"I believe war follows you, *Lady Raven*." She sighed and her gaze stuck to the scar on my neck. "A change of name does not erase the history you keep and your power is greater than it has ever been. Mother Neris and I had many conversations. I also met you when I wore my green stole. Your power has grown."

"That's no secret," I said, flipping my braid over my shoulder. "What do you want?"

"I already said my desire—no war. Miria has seen enough. If you choose that path, you may not find Consortium support when you seek it. I know how the last war ended. The pain and destruction is a memory shared through the Consortium, as sacred as our own base texts."

I stepped forward. "In the absence of Niany, the Consortium answers to me."

"The primordials gave mortals free will and the gods brought order. If you cannot maintain order, we will exercise free will." Her voice carried a warning. "For nearly four hundred years, you ceded your responsibility to Niany. Do not stand before me and try to apply the power you deny in the same breath. You cannot be everything."

"Niany was better equipped. And I am not trying to be everything."

"You did once."

"I did."

I conceded; many times I'd tried to usurp and thwart Koros to no avail. Power was an enticing thing, and revenge was worse.

"I am not that Foriana anymore. My word is true when I say I will not restore the Pantheon. I would sooner die than rule."

"We shall see."

The Mother's words settled in the room with the dull thud of disbelief while I stood there, unsure of what else I could say to convince her.

"Tell me about the healer you've brought."

"We were cornered in Linvia when the knight was struck. She had prepared anesthetic herbs and performed clean Nurem stitches effective enough we could travel before nightfall."

"What else?"

"She was recently orphaned. Her father owned an apothecary. Quite sharp and eager to learn. She studied at the Linvian temple when she found time."

The Mother shifted on her feet and gave me a sharp look. "And the mark on her hand? You noticed it?"

I nodded. "Wrythian. Nothing more than tradition now that magic is gone. We traveled with a fae. He agreed she has none."

"Perhaps it's dormant?" Her brow quirked. "We have had a few healers that are Wrythian descendants, but none bearing the mark. The Mother on the rim believes she might have found a way to unlock some of their magic, which would revolutionize how we work."

"Do not experiment on her," I warned.

The Mother shook her head. "They are spells and rituals. Not torture, I assure you. But we will happily have her in the temple."

"Thank you," I said sincerely and moved toward the door.

"Thank *you*," the Mother added, looking straight. "I hope to see you again in peaceful circumstances. I'd also like to show you the grounds when you have time. Neris had hoped to show you our work herself, but time comes for all of us."

"Indeed, it does." I sighed and rubbed my neck. "I'm doing everything in my power to maintain peace, please understand."

With another nod, I left the room to stand in the empty hall for several minutes, admiring the craftsmanship while I waited for Blackthorn and Ophie.

It was strange to think of all the times I'd been here. This temple was one of the longest-standing in the north and nearly as old as Koros. I couldn't parse any specific memories because they all felt the same.

As magic settled, the distance between the past and present stretched further and further. Soon, I'd only feel emotions strong enough to resonate through the haze and I feared the day.

Footsteps echoed as they came around the corner: Ophie beaming and Blackthorn stoic as the healers trailed behind. I expected him to be more enthused by the opportunity to gain useless information.

"Welcome back," I said.

Ophie nodded enthusiastically, dislodging a pin in her hair that sent a piece springing in front of her eyes. "I love it here. It's nothing like the Linvian temple—did you know about the herbs? Three hundred and forty-five. Fifty-*six* only exist here."

"The Mother is preparing your accommodations."

Ophie's eyes widened. "You did that?"

"No, *you* did." I stepped forward, and my heart shivered. "You demonstrated your knowledge when you saved Sir Blackthorn. The Consortium is lucky to have you."

Ophie was stunned but nodded, tears welling in her eyes. Awkwardly, Blackthorn stepped closer. Was he worse at goodbyes than I was?

"This is goodbye?" she asked. A sliver of my composure chipped as her voice wavered; I was unfortunately fond of the girl.

The Mother walked toward us, white robes and a green stole draped over her arms.

All of us bowed and the Mother glared. I wasn't supposed to, but I hated those rules because she'd worked much harder to get her title than I'd worked to lose mine.

"Lady Ophie." the Mother held the clothing out. "If you wish to join the Vharosian order and dedicate your life and time as an assistant to Foriana, the Goddess of Death, these robes are yours and you will be shown to your room."

Ophie reached out and ran her fingers along the fine white fabric as she glanced between us and finally looked at the Mother. I ignored that my name was still a part of their pledge. The Mother was right. I'd abandoned them.

"I join happily and of my own free will."

"*Rendia dae,* Ophie. Welcome."

Ophie took the robes in her arms and this was a goodbye. Maybe not for Blackthorn, but I needed it to be a goodbye from me.

He hugged her first, dwarfing her small frame, and then I took her in my arms and squeezed as she whispered thanks.

"Do good," I said with a sad smile and pulled away, "and don't forget your horses in their stall."

"I won't." She smiled. "Because you need them. Consider it a thank you for bringing me here."

"I can't."

"At least ride them to Avilla and leave them in a good stable. I'll get them as soon as I can."

The Mother and her healers whisked Ophie off and I stood alone with Blackthorn. We were two again, just as the journey had started, but nothing was quite the same. His face scrunched and his eyes watered—Orion Blackthorn was worse at saying goodbye.

30

[...] Another fight with a Verinium master:
Christopher Avirilin—I know you'll forget.

Foria was lost in a coup I should have seen.
They believe I was usurped, but I wasn't.
I was in denial.

BLACKTHORN CLEARED HIS THROAT; it echoed through the vaulted cathedral. We had no reason to stay, but I didn't want to move. I wanted to put Belfiante further from my mind.

Tomorrow, we'd leave Vharos for Avilla, which was be the last stop before Belfiante. It was suddenly too close, a hand wrapping around my neck with no intention of letting go no matter how loud I screamed and kicked.

"Raven?"

My resolve was slipping as my end crept closer. I was going to give in, but I wanted to delay until there was no going back. The way he kissed me, the way he touched me, how he *looked* at me . . . it all felt like hope.

Maybe he could give me the strength to leave this world behind as I'd always intended. Or maybe I was never as strong as I pretended to be—only a liar finally seeing through herself after seven hundred years.

"Let's go."

I whirled out of the room, snatching up my hood as we walked to the inn in silence.

About halfway back, there was a commotion in the street and his wide hand wrapped around the crook of my elbow, tugging me back.

I couldn't see around my hood and I didn't have time to think about it—

"*Seize them.*"

We didn't even bring our fucking swords.

I darted around a corner, hoping Blackthorn followed.

Footsteps gained as I skidded down another, turning too quickly, my hood snagged in the wind and fell back. I cursed as two unmarked guards stalked in our direction, armed with sabers. I reached for my magic, but it came up empty, hollow. My stomach dropped. Power squeezed from my lungs with the force of a gut punch. It stuttered in my chest and thrashed, but something held it down like a heavy thumb, and then there was nothing.

Nothing, empty, in several impressive seconds. I hadn't seen that spell in a very long time. Fortunately, it wouldn't last any longer than an hour.

How?

Blackthorn stumbled as swords surrounded us. Heaving back to back, we lifted our hands in surrender. The tip of a rapier poked the taut muscle of my neck by a coward who didn't want to get his feet bloody.

"We are travelers just passing through. We mean no harm," Blackthorn said between heavy breaths. "Let my wife go. We're here for our daughter's wedding."

I ignored the word. It was a lie and I came to play.

"We're here for ale," I added, eyes darting between the five guards surrounding us. Sweat beaded on my forehead. There wasn't a crest in sight—they didn't want to be known. "Certainly you agree that only the finest Vharosian beer will do for such a celebration?"

"Don't care," the guard with the rapier said, pressing the point deeper into my skin. Any harder and they'd realize I wasn't quite mortal; another poked Blackthorn and he gasped.

I was foolish to think they didn't notice my eyes.

"Kneel—both of you. We're taking you to the Queen."

No one refuted, but we were surrounded. I wouldn't get out of this without risking Blackthorn unless we managed to stall out the spell. Certainly, the knight could talk for an hour.

"Vharos doesn't have a queen."

"Kneel," a guard growled.

Blackthorn and I sank down, exchanging glances.

I'm sure he considered this could be a betrayal after seeing the way my magic worked, but they'd done something. I was almost mortal again.

Someone moved behind me. Iron cuffs clamped around my wrists. I rolled my eyes to hide the way I bit my lip and blinked away tears. The same old feelings crashed back but it was worse now; the emptiness and quiet more like an ocean than a puddle.

Of course they were primordial cuffs—the same Blackthorn had so gingerly removed and left behind in Linvia . . . unless I'd trusted him too much and he'd given them to someone else.

No.

The anguish and hurt rushed back, searing against my temple. I couldn't be chained again. I couldn't be powerless. I'd taken back the missing parts of me and I couldn't feel like this again.

Bitter wind bit my face as my stomach turned over. Was this his betrayal? Did it end here with my leash in the hand of another ruler?

True fear tickled my spine and I started to shake.

We were outnumbered, without power, and without weapons.

I stole a glance at Blackthorn, relieved he looked as forlorn as I. His hands were shackled in a matching set of cuffs that would keep him from shifting or healing. Left on a mortal too long, they would also kill him, but I hoped that wouldn't be important.

The guards prodded us to our feet, and we marched with them toward whatever large house their "Queen" waited in.

Vharos was hardly a province; it was more of a walled city surrounded by farmland. It had its fair share of dukes and earls, but never a king or queen, unless someone decided to expand and fold Vharos into a coastal kingdom. Alone, Vharos did not have the money or forces to defend the city, nor did they have the resources to conquer another.

As we marched uphill, at the tip of threats and steel, I considered the possibility that maybe I missed something, but we didn't stop until we stood in the oldest castle I'd ever seen. It loomed over the city from the highest level of the terrace.

Gray stone crumbled and much of it was hardly discernible as a castle. It was more like a pile of rocks that had been abandoned for centuries. We walked through the gate, over a moat, and into the center to a bare courtyard covered in more ice than snow.

Usually old was relative, but this place was ancient and I wondered why the "Queen" of Vharos had us standing in primordial ruins.

Before I considered the possibilities, guards dragged us into a stone corridor and pushed us down uneven stairs where rusted iron bars lined the walls. My stomach plummeted as they corralled us into a cell.

Iron and bitter cold overwhelmed my senses as magic quelled and stilted in my chest, straining because it wanted to be free. The charm was already wearing off, but the cuff's restriction would last as long as we wore them.

Blood stained the floor and walls, obliterating my expectations of a warm welcome.

Blackthorn might die here. The thought rattled me. Primordial iron would slow whatever inherent magic held his wolf. And once it consumed that, it would move to his mortality because the cuffs would drain any and all power.

Guards secured us to the wall with clinking chains, and the prospect of torture became infinitely more likely. I could handle it; fuck, if I closed my eyes, I might enjoy it, but the idea of them doing the same to Blackthorn grated my skin.

None of the living Tyrlian soldiers had seen war—it contributed to Tyrlas's fearlessness and explained his eagerness to prod the other kingdoms. He had no idea what the price are war was once he started one.

I took a deep breath as Blackthorn cursed at one of the guards. He'd be okay and we'd both get through this in one piece. Or I'd remain strung here, cursed to watch the light leave his eyes.

Unfortunately, the larger godly part of me wouldn't accept that reality because deep, deep down in the far reaches of my fucking soul: Orion Blackthorn was *mine.*

Any damage to him, even with the bond as thin as it was, would mutilate my soul . . . or so I'd heard from the gods who'd lived through it.

Blackthorn didn't have to know and I didn't have to say it, but the moment they lashed him with a whip, I *roared.*

Searing pain found me shortly after and everything in the frigid dungeon became a near-silent symphony of pain, blood, and gritting teeth as the guards took turns seeing how we bled. My steel skin was their challenge and they rose to it.

With my magic quelled, they could bruise and beat me, but no part of me would break. Not for their weapons. Until the glint of a white knife caught my eye. Before I knew it, the ivory blade sliced into my arm, sending up a spray of crimson blood as I screamed.

"I'd always wanted to know if gods bleed." The guard grabbed my hair and yanked me close enough to smell the stale liquor on his breath. "Good to know you're no different from any other bitch."

"You've never met a bitch like me."

Blackthorn shouted something; chains rattled.

And the lashes kept coming: snaps of whip, cuts from the blade just to make sure we understood we were at the mercy of this mysterious fucking queen and she knew exactly what I was.

They could carve me however they wanted, and I'd endure if it kept Orion Blackthorn alive. Maybe I'd get lucky and they'd kill me before I dared to look over at the mess they'd made of the knight—*my* knight.

I lost track of time. Pain blended in with everything else. Cursing and shouting and grunting transpired, but I didn't remember any words exchanged until I found myself at the brink of consciousness, trying to reassure myself Blackthorn was still alive because I *needed* him to be.

Blood that wasn't mine ran over worn stones. Where mine spilled, seedlings sprouted—ironic that any life could come from death.

"Harder," I demanded, voice steadier than I felt as I stared down the guard and swayed in the chains.

Blackthorn groaned in pain behind me. The guard drew the stark white blade across my arm again, cutting me open from elbow to wrist.

"Like that? Or bigger so my cock'll fit?"

I shook my head and kicked him square in the chest. He grunted and the knife fell, clattering as the guard's hands flew to my neck and squeezed. He strained every muscle trying to crush my windpipe as I insulted his mother.

Blackthorn yelled something I didn't hear, but the guard lost his grip before my consciousness wavered.

I rolled my neck with a sadistic smile. "You call that fore-play?"

The guard grunted and struck me with all the force he could find, sending my head spinning. I spat ruby blood at his feet, and saplings unfurled between the cracks in the stones.

"Good boy." My head lolled as I lifted it, vision shivering like my body in the freezing chamber, but I had plenty left as the guard sized me up. I'd survived months of this. Years even—what was one day?

"Just like that," I taunted. He picked the blade up from the floor. Then he shoved his fingers into my hair, fisting it as he forced my eyes level with his.

"You couldn't fucking handle me," he crooned and ripped open my buttoned blouse, exposing skin and scar. Hunger darkened his eyes and I wondered again if all men were the fucking same.

"You don't know what I can handle," I spat and tried to jab my knee into his gut but missed by a fraction.

The bone blade flashed as he cut into my chest, tracing lines across my ribs. Blood welled at the seams and I bit my lip to keep from screaming. He wanted pleasure but I'd give him none. The knife was agonizing. It scraped the bone and cauterized as it moved, splitting skin as if he meant to flay me.

Then he took the knife and cut down my sternum over my oldest scar. I bellowed and kicked him square in the chest. He reeled back, gasping to catch his breath.

Then something struck the side of my head and the world went black.

31

"You snore in your sleep," Blackthorn coughed. The useless statement echoed through the dungeon chamber as I blinked, coming back to consciousness.

"Only when I'm chained to the wall."

My voice was gravely from the screaming. It was also sore and bruised below my chin where I was sure the guard had choked me to no avail.

Good fucking gods, it was cold. I took back every complaint about my numbness. My skin burned everywhere the knife had carved. It started to knit together with a wisp of power, but it wasn't fast enough.

As I swayed in the chains, I tried to stretch my face. My lips cracked and bled; worse, moving my nose at all sent a bolt of blinding pain through me. By the dying fucking gods.

"He broke my nose."

It shouldn't have been possible, not in these cuffs and certainly not with the magic I'd reclaimed. I was twice the god Tyrlas had imprisoned.

"Looks fine to me." Blackthorn coughed again; his chains rattled. "The bruising complements the blood in your hair."

I glared through the swelling, but cursed at the consequent onslaught of pain.

He was pale and he wasn't healing. They'd cut open his shirt. Massive angry wounds decorated his chest and blood stuck to his hair as he leaned against the wall—chains preventing either of us from sitting.

The wound under his ribs was red again and clearly infected. Another gash ran the length of his thigh. Both were bleeding with no sign of abating. Gods, what did his back look like?

Rage struck first, then nausea. I swallowed the sick and let the rage stoke the fire—I needed it to get us out of here.

"Did they say anything?" His eyelids fluttered and I knew we were running out of time.

"No." Blackthorn's voice grated with exhaustion. "However, now would be a great time to use the godhood I've risked my life for—*twice* now."

"If I could, don't you think I would?"

"Well, you strike me as someone who likes to be tied up."

"Not like this."

I frowned; every movement was the same as washing my face with broken glass.

"So you admit it?"

He coughed again, a slight smile curled his lips, but then he spat blood on the floor. Gods, he was covered in it and getting paler with every passing second.

"Tyrlas could barely afford my cuffs. How would a fake queen afford a pair?"

"Fake queen? If the kingdom doesn't exist, isn't it as easy as declaring it? If I told you *I* was the queen and you believed it—"

"Stop."

"Stop talking?" Orion Blackthorn opened his eyes. I tried not to look anywhere else on his mutilated body. Rage and lust were opposite tendrils of warmth, too easily mistaken for the other. "Talking is keeping me awake and distracted from how close to falling off my leg is."

I groaned and rattled the chains to no avail. "We'll get out."

"I've been awake for the last two hours thinking exactly that."

"And?"

"And?" He chuffed, swaying forward only to be caught by the chains. "It's a dungeon, Raven, we're bound in primordial iron and I'm only standing because of this wall and the chains are—unless . . ."

He straightened and held up a shaking hand as he stared at the cuff carved with ancient primordial sigils.

"No," I snapped. "That does not fucking work."

Blackthorn flashed a grin, blood covering his teeth. "Why not? I've heard the stories. Just break your thumb, slip it off."

"Sure. And you have the strength?"

"Of course."

"Fine, I'll watch."

I crossed my arms indignantly, head pounding.

Blackthorn bit his lip and focused everything on trying to dislocate his thumb from the joint, using the cuff as leverage when he bludgeoned it against the wall with the little strength he had left.

His knees trembled and my heart twisted. He would have fallen without the chains. Time was slipping.

The knight roared and tried again, iron crashing into stone with vigor. His elbow twitched and hesitated before it gave out entirely on a third attempt.

"Told you." His eyes narrowed, and I'd lost too much blood to care. "What those men didn't say is that they were braced properly and complete sociopaths."

"Can you do it? Even without your magic, your emotional range is far from mortal."

"God bones." I held out my hand and shook the chain, ignoring his scowl. "Practically steel."

"Well, fuck us, then."

"Fuck us indeed."

Sharp footsteps clipped the stone. Not the boots of the guards or the rattle of their swords, but rather the whisper of fabric over stone and a far more delicate gait at odds with the blood spattered around us.

The Queen.

A young woman walked around the corner. She wore riding leathers and a billowing, deep crimson cape with the elegance of a gown.

Cropped brown hair sharpened the hard angles of her face as she stared, assessing the state of her prisoners and nothing else about the ruins. She then plucked leather riding gloves from her hand to scratch a rash creeping up her neck.

I recognized her. Why did I—

"General Nia," Blackthorn whispered, and some tendril of jealousy clamped around my throat. "What the fuck are you doing in Vharos?"

"*Queen* Nia."

"How?" Chains rattled, holding him back from taking another step as I tried to remember the woman standing in front of us.

"Tyrlas promoted me."

Tyrlas. General.

Nia had stood at the dais before we left. Her command assigned Blackthorn to me. I should have known Tyrlas would have us tailed. The king never trusted me and lied through his teeth about it.

My eyes narrowed. "What are you doing here?"

"After the commotion in Dover—and then in Linvia—Tyrlas was worried, so I offered to ride out and make sure his wraith and *my* knight were keeping their word. Imagine the surprise when I found out you were in Vharos, suspiciously close to port? Only two more days if you wanted to hop realms, isn't it?"

"You don't know where my godhood is."

"Do you? I have Relia's notes—no Vharos." Her lips pursed as she stepped toward the bars, a haughty smile pinching her eyes. "Have you even found *one*?"

"Yes," Blackthorn answered for me, forcing his voice steady. "We've found two, and if you take off the cuffs, I'm sure Lady Raven would show you. Where did you get these? Tyrlas told me I had his only set."

"Wouldn't you like to know?" Her gaze honed in on Blackthorn as she stepped to the left. "Tyrlas compensated in case you lost those. He expected you to take them off quite quickly."

Nia raised her hand and snapped. Several guards rushed downstairs, their armor and swords clattering.

"Take them off the goddess," she said as two soldiers approached the bars. A flicker of emotion crossed her face, gripping the back of her neck just before she hardened. "Leave them on Sir Blackthorn in case she tries anything."

Keys rattled. Two of the four guards stepped in.

One stopped beside me and the other held a knife to Blackthorn's throat, wiping my thoughts clean. The rage was brief because the moment the cuffs fell, magic whirred back in a blinding array of light.

I fucking hoped the way my skin glowed and burned would be enough to wipe the critical scowl from Tyrlas's new queen.

It calmed and she came back into focus, gaping. Even the guard had lowered his knife from Blackthorn's throat—though he promptly remembered his order.

"Excellent," she murmured, awed but not done. Her face contorted as she considered the warning she wanted to give. "He'll be pleased. And you do know you're bound to return?"

"Very aware." I bit out, trying to swallow the swell of magic as it raged and prickled against my skin. Suddenly, I felt too small to contain it.

Nia tilted her head, searching my face through the bars between us. She was mortal. She couldn't have known he was my soul bound. Nor could Tyrlas. There was no way to know without posing a very pointed question to an ascended seer.

"Good." The fresh queen glanced at Blackthorn as her hand slid to her hip. "I don't want to harm your sister, but I will if your charge doesn't keep her promise."

"Raven will keep her promise."

Blackthorn's face flushed. Death would find him if we stayed much longer.

"You have a lot of faith in someone whose legacy is betraying gods and mortals, Sir Blackthorn. I'd direct more of that to your god."

"Betrayal is not my entire legacy." It was difficult to speak as I burned. "I've been a queen myself but also worked in a kitchen for several years, Your Majesty. So I've done exactly two or three things that weren't shirking my duties, but ask yourself why some myths are more popular than others."

The Queen's gaze swung back. "Show me you can raise the dead."

"What?"

Her eyes narrowed and sinewy fingers braced the bars of the cell.

"You heard me, Lady Raven. Tyrlas wants to make sure you can do as he asked and that the legends hadn't overstated your power. Prove it and I'll release you."

"He understands nothing of my power." I gritted my teeth, dipping back to the corner of myself that once held the same title. "My only promise to Tyrlas was returning, restored. He's been warned about the stupid war he intends to start with Rivendeer."

"He *is* your king."

"I serve no king, Nia. Gods do not bend the knee for mortals, and it is below your station to make the assumption."

"Then stay here." She shrugged indifferently as she palmed the ornate hilt of her sword. "Watch him die."

Then, in a flash of steel from behind, the guard beside me brandished his sword and blood splattered across the floor, spurting across my vision in a gory display as my head whipped around and my mind reeled. Nia didn't flinch. She was lucky Orion Blackthorn remained standing, chest heaving, eyes bloodshot but alive with fresh blood splattered across his neck. The guard beside him slumped to the ground, throat gored as the other sheathed his weapon.

Grotesque gargling echoed through the narrow cell and I swallowed vomit as the guard's blood mingled with the gold-tipped willow leaves of mine.

"What the fuck?" Blackthorn wheezed.

Nia shrugged it off. "In one minute, he'll be dead. You'll bring him back and I'll release you both to finish what you started."

The guard choked; it was horrific.

Blackthorn only had an hour. I made my decision too quickly and fell to my knees in the pool of blood where I became the Goddess of Death in full, placing both hands on his convulsing chest.

Bits of the soldier's soul unraveled like cobwebs in a sight I hadn't had the strength to see in a hundred years. They drifted over him and I shoved them back with the burgeoning power bubbling in my knuckles. The splintered shards of him glittered in his blood and I tried to sew those back too.

Blood and soul were intrinsic to one another. Separating them was an abomination.

I didn't want to do it, but there was little harm in raising one shade to prove myself. There would be a larger battle later, and this would be the only false resurrection I'd grant Tyrlas.

No kingdom owned me—not anymore. Not after this.

I tugged my glove off and stuffed it in my pocket as all attention in the room turned to my blackened fingers.

Soul bound.

What an inconvenient fucking thought.

I throttled it and stared at the body of the soldier as my hands moved to his heart. Blue magic clung to my nails like a million tiny blue gnats.

If my mother were here, she would draw back the blood and breathe life into his lungs while she forced me to take the life of someone else to "restore balance."

But Niany wasn't here, and Death hovered, not bound by the same morality.

Death magic rolled into his chest like water, turning from weightless blue wisps into sticky black tar not unlike the blood drying on the stones. It was a shame mortals never knew how much magic they contained until death finally came. They were never as ordinary as they thought they were.

Seconds ticked by. I waited for his heart to stop and when it stilled; I plunged my hand through his ribs, took his warm heart in my palms, and closed my eyes as I shoved his soul through the veil.

His body would suffer enough. It was a kindness to release his soul to the moons and veil so he wouldn't bear witness to whatever Tyrlas might ask of his body. My power corrupted his blood in the absence of a soul, replacing red with black and life with death.

Magic turned over his heart and forced it to beat again, slow and constant in my grip. From there, I continued to cradle it, calling on wisps of blue magic to repair the parts of him that death had broken. The beautiful, icy light filled the room as I resurrected him.

The guard would be unstoppable in death; shades always were.

I leaned back on my heels, heart in hand while power knit him together, closing the wound on his neck and the one in his chest. The magic finished, tapering off like smoke and then his heart turned to ash in my palm.

"You will serve Tyrlas until Death comes again," I whispered. I always said it in case a piece of soul was left behind, needing comfort.

The guard's eyes snapped open, unblinking, ethereal and blue like the death magic that held him together and kept us both impossibly alive.

"I will serve Tyrlas until Death comes again," the shade repeated before clambering to uneven feet.

The shade knew Nia was the Tyrlian Queen and bowed to her. He left the cell and stood at her side, his vacant expression staring through anything that wasn't duty.

The Queen's jaw tightened as she watched, looking for a trick, but there was none. I had no reason to deceive, so I pulled my glove back and tried to steady my breathing. I hadn't overspent; my power simply wanted *more*—it wanted to reap.

Nia seemed pleased and turned her attention back to the cell where Blackthorn's breath labored.

With another wordless gesture, the cuffs came off. Blackthorn staggered forward, barely able to hold himself up. I lurched and caught him with my gloved hand and shoulder just before he toppled over.

Tyrlas's newest queen left without a parting word, guards at her side and shade at her back.

The undead guard would defend Tyrlas with everything he contained until *I* returned, then he'd serve *me*.

32

[The first line of a short letter in curt script.]

*[...] Etta died today. They buried her in Loras.
She'd be relieved to see you.*

TYRLAS TORTURED US TO prove he could.

The lacerations on my face and back started to knit the moment the cuffs dropped. The bruises on my arm turned through the gamut of colors, blaring now in shades of green and yellow. Even where the god knife cut me, I would heal in a few days, but it still burned.

Blackthorn lost too much blood and wasn't healing—not the way a shifter should. If I had any doubts about his mortality, his gaunt face, and shallowing breath erased them.

Nia delivered her message and Tyrlas got his shade.

"Where are we going?"

He coughed and my face fell. There was blood in his spittle. Fuck, he was more muscular than I remembered, and I didn't have the strength to match my endless life. Corded muscles twitched under my gloved hands and he looked at me through bleary lashes.

Purple bruises bloomed across his face and around the angry gash on his leg that continued to bleed. I wouldn't dare look at the whip marks on his back—they'd send me spiraling.

"We need to get up and . . ."

"And what?" He stared at me through blood-crusted blond hair. "Crawl through the streets like *this*? In broad daylight?"

I shook my head. "There was a well in the courtyard—"

"Raven." The way his voice held my name silenced every panicked thought. "It's frozen. You might not feel the cold, but I can't feel my toes."

I pushed his shoulder and looked him over.

His shirt was torn, his black coat crusted in blood. It wasn't obvious in passing. We just needed enough to hide it, to cover up. The knight's amber eyes glazed over.

"How bad do I look?" I asked and his brow furrowed as he scanned my body. "Like we got tortured. Your shirt is covered in blood, and so are your shoes."

"That's fine," I muttered and pulled my tweed coat over my shoulders, tightening it as much as I could to hide my torn white blouse steeped in blood where they'd carved me. "We can get to the temple."

"The temple?" He gaped as I helped him stuff one arm into his heavy coat and then the other. I'd never been so grateful for the color black. Aside from the damage to his face, he almost looked normal.

"The temple is closer."

"Still far."

"Then stay here," I snapped. "I'm leaving tomorrow and I'd prefer you healed enough to travel. Otherwise, I'm going on my own."

He looked at the old stone ceiling and cursed.

That was my answer.

I hooked an arm around his waist, helping him out of the dungeon and into the world above where clouds settled and snow flurried. We descended through Vharos back to the temple, shaking off the long stares and whispers as we passed.

Every step brought him closer to delirium; he was sweating and shivering. Would we make it? Doubt crept into my thoughts as we limped along. My power continued to whir back, but it built too fast. Nausea reared in the back of my throat.

When we finally blustered into the temple, Blackthorn slid to the floor as I caught my breath. Two young healers scurried for help.

They shuffled us into a room near the healer's residences. It wasn't a temple healing room, merely an empty room with a few chairs and a long table that was certainly a dining table.

Blackthorn crumpled into a chair with a cry while I paced from one side of the bare stone room to the other.

The Mother came in first, narrowed eyes critical, with Ophie and two more healers close behind in their green stoles and white robes. Ophie's gold eyes widened when she saw the blood on my shirt, but they nearly protruded when she saw Blackthorn.

"Again?" she croaked as the Mother walked around, eyes only on me.

"Lady Raven, I did not expect to see you so soon."

"We were cornered by Tyrlian guards and their new queen. She wanted to send a message."

The Mother nodded.

She didn't show a hint of concern. Of course, she didn't. Calm was required of healers, but of the Mother—she needed to be unbreaking.

"Sister Laila, please retrieve clean shirts for our guests. Brother Kyn, retrieve the birch salve and Vestian tonic from the stores; we're patching a shifter. Sister Ophie, you've healed this knight before, can you do it again?"

Ophie nodded and watched the floor as she walked forward to kneel in front of a too-pale Blackthorn, who'd already undone his coat and sunk further into the chair. His chest heaved as Ophie looked him over.

"They cut open my leg," he grunted, trying to adjust, but he grimaced with every movement. "And my scar."

"They also whipped him and chained both of us in primordial cuffs. His—"

"His healing is weakened," the Mother said for me, standing behind Ophie as she assessed the lacerations, gingerly pushing his ripped shirt aside. "We have new salves that will close those in a few days. I do have a tonic for shifters that should heal the surface wounds by morning. As for the deep, infected one, Sister Ophie, I want to see you repair them."

She set to work just as Kyn set down a rattling tray of tonics, salves, and several instruments. The Mother's lips were a thin line as Ophie yelled at Blackthorn to stop moving and he cursed when she poked the reopened gash from Linvia.

Thankfully, the weapons they used on him were mortal. If the guard had carved into him with the knife they used on me, he'd be poisoned. And not a pleasant poisoning that put victims to sleep. Something worse that seared like drinking a god's blood, which boiled most men from the inside out.

Where it cut me, the lacerations burned, but they *would* heal . . . eventually.

"Did anyone follow you?" the Mother asked as Blackthorn groaned in symphony with the sizzle of a cauterizing salve.

"No. We leave tomorrow."

"Tomorrow?" Ophie craned her neck as she cut open Blackthorn's pants where he hadn't stopped bleeding. "He'll open the stitches!"

"No, he won't," the Mother said and stared at the mark on Ophie's wrist as she pushed Blackthorn back in the chair and prepped to stitch him. "I want you to try something once you finish. A healer years ago, in this temple, had the same mark you do."

"It's nothing," Ophie muttered, trying to hide the mark as her attention shifted back to the knight. "It's a family heirloom."

"Then it doesn't hurt to try." The Mother kneeled beside Ophie as she worked. Several quiet minutes passed before Blackthorn exhaled; Ophie cut the last stitch. "Place your hand over the wound, close your eyes, and will it to close."

"I—"

"Do it."

The Mother's voice was gentle, despite the command. Kyn and Laila peered over.

A small spark of gold magic leapt from Ophie's palm as she pressed the wound on his thigh. She jumped, watching with trepidation. Blackthorn's eyes went wide, and so did mine. I hadn't seen that power in decades, not from a mortal—not since Miria's magic was drained.

Could the realm . . . heal?

Gold wisps trailed from Blackthorn's leg to his abdomen and wove into the stitches, drawing both wounds closed. Only the pink line of a scar remained, and the ridge of the suture.

"You'll still be sore, but the stitches should fall out in a few days," the Mother said. "I'll also send you with a tonic."

Ophie stood with both hands out, turning them over as if they were new to her.

Her gold eyes flashed to the Mother.

"H-how did I do that?"

"Old magic lives in some lines the same as seers. Some is also preserved in the older temples like this one. Few healers with that power still exist in our world and we look forward to seeing what else you're capable of." The Mother rose to her feet, looking at Blackthorn. "How do you feel?"

"Better." He stared at Ophie.

"Good." The Mother passed clean cotton shirts to both of us. "You'll be ready to travel tomorrow. Apply the salve every few hours."

"Thank you for your generosity," I said, turning my back and swapping my bloodied shirt for the clean one. "We ought to get back and not waste anymore of your time."

"It wasn't a waste, Lady Raven. Your knight is healed and we tested our new healer to great success." The mother smiled, but then her gaze focused on me and turned sharper. "Do not forget our conversation."

"I will not," I promised—or rather hoped—as Blackthorn stood.

"Thank you."

Ophie grinned and tackled both of us into a hug as we winced. "I owe the both of you so much."

I shoved away the grief bubbling in my throat. This was a second goodbye I never wanted to make. We left the temple a second time, returning to the inn just before the sun started to set.

I dumped our soiled clothes outside the door, hoping I wasn't too late to have them back by morning, while Blackthorn bathed. Afterward he collapsed on the couch in front of the roaring fireplace despite having a bed.

While he slept, I drew a steaming bath and inspected my own injuries.

The lacerations on my arm and across my chest remained red and raw. This pain burned like a memory. Every twinge of pain where my scar was reminded me of Belfiante. I shouldn't have been thankful for the pain; the bite was stronger than the heat, but not strong enough to erase the aching in my heart from the way Blackthorn screamed.

I'd been angry and useless and tortured before. I'd felt it all so deeply with Leander, but the tether with Blackthorn was different—taut and inescapable. Against reason, every time I looked at him, the pull grew tighter . . . I knew it would snap.

Tears lingered as I discarded my gloves at the side of the tub. He felt nothing and that protected him.

The thought nagged like a warning as water sluiced over the side of the tub. I paid no mind, sinking deeper as the gashes burned. Gods, it'd been too long since a god knife cut me. How did Tyrlas get that *and* the cuffs? Two, even. They'd cost a fortune he didn't have.

My thoughts reeled, drunk with pain. And of all the questions, one kept coming back: Why did Fate choose Blackthorn? Has my life not been punishing enough?

He was mortal. I'd know if he was a god—there's a certain hum to their presence, and his was silent.

Maybe I shouldn't have been so quick to accept Tyrlas's bargain. But what else did I miss? Blackthorn wouldn't take a shard to keep me alive and in debt to the Tyrlian throne, would he? Was that possible?

He couldn't be lying. A kiss between soul bound gods was dangerous. It would feel like something breaking apart for *both* of us. The crack in my chest would not have been a hiccup in Linvia but an earthquake.

Orion Blackthorn was mortal but I wanted every part of him for myself.

With a centering exhale, I drew magic to my fingertips and let it pulse through my forearms as I shoved aside the worry. I held the pulsing blue to my hand the way one holds a chunk of ice to their wrist . . . to see what they can withstand.

Instead of drawing away or biting my lip, I craved more.

Leander formed in my mind, a thousand memories compounding in a rush that took my breath away. Death seeped from my palms with the rush of air and I wanted him. Maybe with this power, I could put him back together and forget the way Blackthorn scratched my heart?

A ghost appeared. I felt it before I saw it, and I desperately hoped to see *him*. Instead, my heart caved when someone else stood, arms crossed on the other side of the room bathed in wispy, faint blue magic. A tall woman stood there with long, wavy hair that moved like tendrils in a phantom breeze.

"Fortune," I breathed and moved to get up, but she stopped me with a raised hand, squinting. Nothing about her form had changed. "You—"

"You've never called on me, yet you've called for that mortal a hundred times."

"That's a lie. Though he's a hundred times more worthy of life than any of the gods were. Why did you answer?"

She took a step closer.

Her skin was blue like a ghost, but the gods took a different, much lighter shade when they made it to their afterlife. Fortune's form flickered, shifting from blue to nearly opaque as though she stood in the room with me.

Her familiar round features stared through violet eyes with sparks of gold—a feature that made many think she was a true daughter of Koros. She wasn't.

Like me, Fortune was mortal, plucked from thousands and forced into the Pantheon. She was a commoner too, turned into an immortal princess through a bargain. The difference? *She* struck her bargain, where my mortal father negotiated mine.

"I felt you wake up," she said plainly, sitting on my bed with her arms crossed in disdain. "Finally trying to take back your power now that you've gotten rid of everyone else?"

"That isn't it. You know I don't want to rule. You've seen me fail a hundred times."

Hair fell over her exposed shoulder as she angled her head. "Oh, so you plan to kill yourself?"

I sat up, water sloshing to the sides; her gaze dropped to the lacerations on my chest. "Have you spoken to Niany?"

"*Mother?*" She chuffed the derisive correction. Niany was a bad mother to me and a worse mother to Fortune. "I still don't understand how you killed father and showed *her* mercy."

"He killed you." I stared, trying not to see the hole in her chest from the very dagger nestled in the nightstand. "Niany killed no one."

"Where were you that night, Foriana?" I looked at the ceiling as she came another step closer, ghostly skirts swishing on the floor as she leaned over and venom sank into my chest with every word. "You were out fucking around in some other kingdom, weren't you?"

"Why are you here?" I gritted my teeth, losing patience . . . even if she was right. "You've disappeared for almost a hundred years now."

"Oh, is that all?" She said flippantly and kneeled beside the tub. Her sinewy hands gripped the sides of it as she held herself at eye level. "I meant to stay away longer, but you needed some grounding and you were the one who called my soul back. Speaking of souls, the mortals need you to return to the afterlife."

"Mother already cornered me."

Her eyes narrowed, staring again at my wounds. "Your bargain with her was selfish."

"As is she? I don't see the problem. The afterlife gets a steward and her power is as useless as she was. She can't even conjure a fucking flower—I made sure of it."

Fortune's lips pursed, making them look even smaller and more dissatisfied. "You don't get it."

"Get what?"

"You're going to the mirror ponds to imbue your last bit of godhood and ask whoever your accomplice is to stab you with a god knife and absolve you of facing anything you did."

I glanced across the room. Fortune couldn't feel the dagger's presence. In my experience, the ghosts of gods couldn't feel anything but disdain for me.

"I'm right, aren't I?"

"You won't change my mind."

That was exactly my plan. It was the only way to destroy the Goddess of Death and the last god in the realm. If I left anything behind, there was a chance it would fall into the hands of someone else—someone worse.

"Sure," she muttered, "so you're not considering that there might be gods ready to return and serve you."

"What?"

"You're the Queen of Gods. The Pantheon is yours."

My lungs constricted. *No, no, absolutely not.* First Adler and now my sister? I stared at her, narrowing my gaze as though it were loaded with daggers.

"I've been queen before and I do not want it again. The Pantheon is over and the mortals deserve better than us."

Her fingers dipped into the water, but it didn't so much as ripple.

"You'd be better than Koros. The world could be whatever—"

"Miria has seen peace before, but it devolves. I will not be named in another war."

Memories swelled back, icing my voice. It wasn't all palaces and pomp; there was blood, and screaming, and a hundred thousand dead before I blinked—that is what it meant to rule.

In all my lifetimes, I'd never known something so fragile and ephemeral as peace. Even thirty years of peace was nothing but staving off something worse.

Fortune never understood.

"You only need a few of the loyal gods. The rest you could banish. And you know shards still exist. It wouldn't take much since you've killed the worst. You could appeal to the primordials and resurrect a few of us."

"Why bring this up now?"

"Because you've never been so close."

"I wanted Leander to lead. I *wanted* the mortals to rule."

Fortune shrugged and drew her hands back, leaning on her heels. "Then let them. Restore the Pantheon anyway and *watch*. You have a soul bound, don't you?"

"*Don't.*"

Silence, rage, and warning all twisted, amplifying the silent tension in the air.

"A human?" She asked, eyes boring into me. "And he was hurt as you are."

I hugged my knees together and looked at the ceiling, hoping it would fucking fall.

"You know," Fortune said, "there are a few stories about the gods and their human soul bounds."

"They die."

With a nonchalant shrug, she rose to her feet. "Some survive just fine. Some end up like your shades, and some turn into monsters. It's not unheard of."

"Those are stories."

"Funny coming from you. Everything about us is myth, Foriana." She clicked as she backed toward the bed and smoothed her skirt. "I remember the day you killed your first soul bound. Fate has a funny way of thwarting us."

Anger swelled and the water turned cold.

Fortune opened her mouth to say something else, but I cut her off with a wave of my arm, turning her into nothing.

I clambered out and wished on every dead god and the primordials below that I could at least have Henry one more time. Sleeping in his arms, feeling his breath on my neck, might chase away this blinding desire.

Fuck, I'd even settle for the damned fae prince. I just needed someone to *listen* who knew me or knew what was like to live for centuries.

Because what could I do? Queen of the Pantheon—of the Gods? Like Adler suggested? My father's throne? I didn't want to rule again. I wanted the gods as dead as the Scribes of Nurem.

Gods were a stain on the world and I was the only one who saw it and the only one brave enough to put a bone through every last immortal I could find.

This was my life's work, and I would not fail. The mortals might call me Godkiller, but liberator was a more fitting title . . . even if it was one I'd never see.

Year 1320, Miacor City, Tyrlas
Raven is 770

IT WAS TOO BRIGHT outside as I stepped out, covered head to toe in armor. My helm was secured with an extra two latches to make sure I wouldn't be exposed.

At the royal booth, Queen Relia, radiant as always, stood at the ledge, fussing with the vibrant floral sprays of wildflowers her attendants had combed from the mountain meadow just outside Miacor.

She smiled at me as though she knew I watched her.

Fixing a fight would've been far easier, but it was less fun. After twelve years trapped in this kingdom, I was willing to do anything for some peace and reprieve from court gossip.

Orion Blackthorn, the young soldier, swaggered out from the opposite gate to raucous applause. His helm was tucked under his arm, while his sword hung from the same hand so he could smile and wave at the crowd with the other.

I rolled my eyes and unsheathed my featherlight broadsword of Ernmore steel.

It was a shame this boy would be knighted instead of one of the more deserving knights who'd fallen yesterday and the day before.

A bell chimed—I wasted no time turning the spar into a story.

Blackthorn had barely fumbled his helmet on when I lunged. A roar tore from me and my sword came down on his shoulder.

He barely blocked it and stumbled back. The crowd gasped as he scrambled for footing. I'd pissed him off and he flew at me, a flurry of steel, but a damn green one.

I parried every cut, my blade finding his like it was a practiced dance. I'd had more exciting spars with children.

If I hadn't decided to lose, he'd be on the ground, but doing that wouldn't win me any leverage with the king. So, I stepped back and let him catch his breath as I circled. He readjusted his grip on the hilt, still choking it.

A stiff wrist wouldn't serve in war. Tyrlas was an idiot to throw the honor of knighthood at a lucky, overconfident teenager.

I lunged again, swinging at him hard from the right. He grunted when the flat side of my blade battered his armor with a loud thwack.

He heaved, adjusting his grip again while the crowd hollered. Amber eyes glared at me.

It was time to end this.

He came at me again, slashing the air, looking to land anything.

I blocked with my arm because he couldn't hurt me.

Clang. Clang. Whoosh.

A near miss. Blackthorn cried out, frustrated, and swung under my arm as he stumbled. His steel caught my elbow and I used the momentum to throw my sword dramatically and stagger back. Breathing hard like I'd been defeated.

He froze.

He fucking knew, and I lunged for him without a weapon.

The soldier swung back, blade meeting my throat. We both stopped and he lowered it to my chest, pushing me back several steps. I let my knee give out and fell on my back, hands held up as he stood over me and ripped off his helm.

The bell chimed and applause tore through the crowd.

Blackthorn's amber eyes tightened, confused as he lowered the sword from my chest and cursed.

I meant to sit, but his boot met my chest and drove me back into the sand, lips curled in a snarl as the king came down to the arena for his announcement.

My squire dragged me off the ground, pushing me next to the king and the newest knight of the Tyrlas just in time to hear an announcement I wasn't privy to.

"Danger encroaches," King Tyrlas bellowed. "For that, one champion will not do. Both of you have earned a rightful place in the knighthood, honor bound to Tyrlas with your life."

The king raised my hand and Blackthorn's as the crowd cheered. Neither of us had earned this, and that was apparent in the blond soldier's frown and my own wringing disappointment as escape vanished.

After I dried off, I dressed and stormed across the street where the brewery's lights still flickered in the bitter winter air. If I couldn't talk to someone who knew me, I'd talk to someone I'd never have to see again.

I sat at a table, sipping a dark beer until a man with evergreen eyes said something to me. His name was either Christopher or Felix. Truthfully, it didn't matter.

He had broad shoulders and a kind face not wholly dissimilar from Blackthorn on a good day. If I were any kind of betting woman, he was the brewmaster's son, and if I were also a betting woman, this would end with exactly what I needed to get my mind off the hundred things racing through it.

Soul bound.

No. Not here, not now.

The brewer smiled at me over his beer and I smiled back.

Eventually, he traded his seat at the bar for one next to me, where he told several long stories about Vharosian beer. We sampled some of his newer concoctions as I stretched out and listened, letting myself forget about time. There was something charming in his passion, like the world lit up around him as he showed me his heart.

The exposure left me dazed as the table filled with half-finished tasting glasses.

"I should go," I said eventually and stood up, wrapping my coat around my shoulders and pulling up the collar to defend against the wind. Gods, I was sore. Blood had dried my blouse to my chest and arms. Moving made it worse.

He stood, holding out a burly arm. "Let me walk you back, Lady Raven. It would be my pleasure."

I bit my lip, a debate raging, but I was weak-willed. "Sure."

Muscular arms mingled with the ambiance of hops and barley—another weakness. Worse, if the man was bearded and smiled with his teeth. I wasn't a complicated woman, aside from the immortal godhood and dominion over the afterlife.

Snow fell, casting a haze that made the inn look farther than just a few paces through a garden. I meant to step forward, but he grabbed the crook of my arm and pulled me into him, arm wrapping around my waist as our breath tangled, the aroma of the dark beer swirling between us like a spell.

I swallowed the rush of pain from the healing wounds his hand tightened around, unknowing.

"Are you sure about leaving?" he whispered, gaze dropping to my lips as his own parted. "I haven't told you how beautiful your eyes are. Or your hair. Or—"

My hands gripped the lapels of his coat and drew his lips to mine.

There was hunger in the kiss, and warmth where it should have been as he kissed back. We took our time in the lamplight, but when I pulled away, nothing had changed.

The brewer gaped as I wriggled from his grip.

"Have a lovely night," I said, leaving him standing in the street.

I wanted something to be different. I wanted to forget who I was, but I couldn't. The man kissed me and I thought of Blackthorn, then Adler, Henry, and even Leander in those minutes—never once the man I kissed.

Blackthorn was still asleep on the couch when I stumbled in. He hadn't bothered with a shirt and was spread out in only a pair of pants.

I edged closer for a better look; his chest rose and fell. The stitches had already started to shed and I was awed by Ophie's gift.

Five hundred years ago, gifts and magic like that were common among mortals. Now, I couldn't remember the last time I'd seen anyone heal with just a touch. Maybe during the last war in Reen? Maybe longer. After Horatio's death, many Wrythian and other healers went into hiding.

I wanted to lean over him. To watch the edge of my braid trail over the ridges of his chest and the dips of his hip where his pants ended. I wanted to see the surprise when he opened his eyes and saw me.

And, more than anything, I wanted him to pull me into a kiss—one hand on my neck and the other on my back—strong and rough, confident like a soldier as he kissed and fucked me on that couch until I forgot why I ever held back.

I couldn't. My heart was already shredded. He would eviscerate me.

But gods, Orion was beautiful, and in this damn quiet, I couldn't deny what he was to me. Even if I wanted to believe I was stronger than Fate.

Yet I remained standing in the room, staring at him, wishing I could run away. Wishing I could feel him move inside me without the fatal click of our bond.

It wasn't him I was afraid of, but me. I had no restraint when it came to the people I dared to love.

He readjusted on the couch but didn't wake up.

I watched, mouth watering like a starved animal, as his pants slid further down his hip and his hair splayed over a pillow. With Ophie gone, and Adler and Henry nowhere around, there was no distraction and my control was fraying.

Soul bound.

That hollow, echoey old phrase made a nagging home in the back of my head. It lived in me, taunting and waiting in those amber eyes.

"Raven?" His voice cracked, but he didn't move.

"Goodnight," I squeaked and took a few steps toward my door. "Just making sure you're alive."

Every part of me wanted to stay there, to become a part of him and to live in his fucking kiss.

He shifted. "Why are you looking at me like that?"

Soul bound.

The word crashed, an icicle falling on frozen stone, and I didn't hear anything else he said. He couldn't be mortal. Somewhere, I'd miscalculated.

I'd crawl through fire to kiss you again

No.

I turned around without another word and slammed the door, only catching a glimpse of him, disheveled, running a hand through his hair as he sat up.

I wondered if I knew it all those years ago in the arena and just couldn't see it because that's how impossible it was.

He knocked on my door but I ignored it. Daring only to breathe when I heard his footsteps taper off.

Then I crossed the room and drank wine from the pitcher until my chest warmed. Nothing I did next would be a good idea, but I did it anyway. I went into the common room. Blackthorn no longer lay on the couch. So I went to the bedroom door and several unrelenting questions turned over in the back of my head.

This was a terrible idea.

I pounded on it with the flat side of my fist and didn't wait for an invitation.

He stood on the other side of the bed, lips parted in surprise and fingers frozen on the button of the shirt he'd pulled on to my dismay.

What I would give to see those wide shoulders and corded muscles glistening under the light of the moon, even if I had to see what the scourge had done to him. My want would make him blush, but that wasn't why I stood in his doorway.

Or maybe it was.

His gaze fell to my sleeve where blood seeped through white. "You're hurt."

"Barely," I muttered, folding my arms as I pulled up the blouse so he wouldn't see worse. His eyes narrowed.

"Show me."

"No."

"No?" Amusement ticked the corner of his lips but I wasn't interested in it.

"Who are you, Orion Blackthorn?"

"You know who I am, Raven."

"And that is?" I teetered on my feet but only slightly as he surveyed me, crossing his arms. Amusement softened his expression.

"Born to a butcher and a fisherman's daughter from eastern Tyrlas. Why? Does title matter to a goddess?"

"Of course not."

"Does soul bound mean anything?"

I froze. The words. He said them.

He said them so carefully as though he knew it might break something. Then he added, "you've said that twice now."

"No, I haven't," I whispered.

Where did he hear it?

"Gods have soul bounds. I sat through the same play."

"Well, I killed mine before it meant anything."

He bit his lip and took a step closer. "Tell me about them."

"What did you hear?" I coiled, folding into myself as my knees locked.

"You shouted it in the field, and again tonight. The walls aren't soundproof and I don't know who you were talking to, but—"

"My sister."

"Fortune?"

"You knew?"

"Tyrlas might serve one god, but we know the ancient stories about the Pantheon." He sighed and sank onto the bed. "Koros and Niany had three daughters. One of blood, one of heart, and one by contract." I huffed, but he kept going. "Fortune was the soft priestess, Foriana was the Princess of Death, and Armine—"

"You don't know everything. I've been a queen and a princess and—"

"You asked what I knew."

"And I interrupted when you answered too honestly."

"Why did you ask about my family?"

"Curiosity." I shook my head. "This was a mistake."

Turning to leave, the grip of his hand on my arm stopped me just out of reach of the door while every sense flared. He spun me into him and I relented despite the pain. His deep amber eyes stared down, and I was stupid enough to ignore the sensible part of me that screamed.

My blouse had dried to the cuts again. I should have winced at the movement, but the pull between us was all-encompassing.

"You enjoyed kissing me. And the way I—"

"Stop." I squeezed my eyes shut , and my hands fell. I wasn't positive magic didn't flare and burn him the way it seared me.

His forehead pressed against mine and I ached. I hated every second his featherlight fingers ran over the wound on my arm.

"*Stop.*"

"Shit." He froze, face falling. "Did I hurt you? Let me—"

"No. You didn't. I just meant . . . you're making this harder—what I need to do." I admitted.

"Harder to return to Tyrlas like you promised?" Blackthorn's voice lowered. "Or harder to leave in the middle of the night when you finally get the chance?"

If there was air in the room, I couldn't find it.

My chest heaved. Maybe I tried to move, but he held steady and so did I against every rational choice.

"No."

"Raven?"

"What?"

"Is that it?" His voice graveled and my core heated.

"Orion."

He pulled back, hands slipping from me, and a cold breeze swept around me in his absence.

"You do know my name."

There were fifteen things I could have said. Instead, fear pulled without another word. I slammed the door and stared at the painted window on the opposite wall.

I'd killed my soul bound and maybe I'd do it again . . . or maybe I'd tell him the truth. *No.* Denying the truth was the only way to kill the gods—a shame it relied on my fickle heart.

The primordials and the gods could put aside their animosity, put a crown on my head, and I would still fucking run. Leander was the only man who'd ever given me hope. I called him my soul bound because no one else had ever held a candle to his beauty and compassion.

Blackthorn?

Gods. I wanted to fuse our souls together and lock us in a room until he found a way to bruise me, but *soul bound?*

What did he have that Leander didn't? What could I find of myself in another life lived and lost? I was nothing like the Foriana in the histories. I wasn't ruthless or tragic; I was tired.

34

Lord Ferthing, meet me for a drink after council tomorrow. I'd like to discuss the King's intentions and where I might help.

WHEN WE LEFT IN the morning, gray clouds churned above, threatening another round of snow as we pushed Ophie's horses through the road connecting Vharos and Avilla.

Blackthorn was mostly healed, and I was doing what I could to hide the slow-healing gashes from the knife. They'd mostly closed overnight, but the scabs still had sore red edges that burned and the salve stuck to my shirt.

Otherwise, the ride was easy. It was nearly silent across the plains, but as we progressed, the dips and valleys grew more and more dramatic, slowing our progress. Eventually night fell and we pulled off.

I dug through my bag and pulled out a pile of canvas and sticks.

"You brought the tent?" Blackthorn asked, and it was the first thing he said to me other than, "are you ready?"

"Of course I brought the tent."

I brushed past him and laid it out in the snow, thankful I hardly felt the bite of winter. It was no problem helping Ophie with it, but alone I wrestled with the sticks and canvas for several long minutes. Eventually, I looked pathetic enough for Blackthorn.

He came around a tree and took one corner of the canvas, propping up one side, then another, before shoving several stakes into the frozen ground before he stepped back. "How much traveling do we have left?"

My heart raced as I lifted my gaze. "We'll be in Avilla tomorrow, early afternoon if the weather holds. Adler said we'll have a room. Then one day in a village and three days to Belfiante."

The small fire Blackthorn started was mostly smoke as ice melted on the kindling, but fire was fire. He sat log prodding the fire, trying to get more wet sticks to catch.

"And we're meeting the Duke of Verinium in Avilla? Adler told me some stories about him the other night."

"What kind of stories?"

The knight shrugged. Orion's blond hair had grown out and now came past his ears when he pushed it back. Along his jaw, his stubble was turning into a handsome beard.

"Just some of their encounters. He sounds difficult. Are you sure you want to go through with the meeting? He's already cornered us twice and Ophie won't be able to heal me a third time."

"What did he do to Adler?"

"Poisoned him once." Blackthorn gave up on the fire as it continued to smolder. "Found out he was fae when Adler nearly killed him. Also said something about his cock."

"Did he?" That was less curious.

"I'm sure he'll tell you more."

I sank onto the floor of the tent, feet still on the frozen ground with my head poking out.

Blackthorn's voice lowered. "You're still healing. I see the blood on your shirt."

"If it gets him off my back, I'll do it—"

"And betray Tyrlas?"

My attention flicked up from the smoking twigs. "I'm not betraying Tyrlas. Your king doesn't know what chaos he invites. He sees himself beyond reproach and forgets he's mortal."

"You swore."

"I did," I said quickly and softened my voice. "Your sister will be safe, but I will not have a hand in another king's war. Have I not been clear about that?"

"And how do you plan to navigate the Duke of Verinium?"

"Easily." I shrugged with a non-answer. "How are you feeling?"

"Me? Fine. Did you know Ophie had that magic?"

Blackthorn prodded the fire again. This time a spray of orange embers went up with the smoke .

"I knew the mark on her hand. Five hundred years ago, several orders wouldn't accept healers without it. It's magic that's been gone for centuries."

"Is it strange," he asked, hand rubbing the back of his neck, "to see everything change?"

"No." I looked at the dirty snow melting on my boots. "I don't know anything different. Things were one way and then they weren't. Then every day is like that—"

"Again and again and again."

"And again, if you were counting." I smirked and my eyes met his. "Change is what I know."

"And death?"

"And death." The word hardly registered as I bundled up my coat and made a point of lying down.

"Do you mind if I shift tonight? It's warmer and ought to keep any robbers away."

"Just bark if you see a valtross or a scavenger." I yawned. "Better than being covered in wolf hair when I regain consciousness."

"Were you planning to be unconscious?"

"Hopefully close to it," I mumbled.

"Raven."

His voice carried my name with a different tone—something deep—almost mournful. I sat up, leaning out of the tent. Shadows from the meager light elongated his scars as he watched me, face in his palms.

"What?"

"I've been thinking about the guard who hurt you. I'm sorry, I can't remember his face."

"You have nothing to apologize for," I muttered, hugging my knees. The wounds still burned. "I'll kill them all so it won't matter."

"You don't remember either?"

Snow flurries blew into the tent with a fresh gust of wind as moved back into the tent. "I will."

The tent wasn't any warmer as I curled up, but it stopped the wind. Hopefully, I wouldn't wake up with frozen eyes.

Dreams came in flashes of memories that all melted into black ichor. Faces of dead gods stretched and twisted in and out of black sludge as death spilled from their mouths and noses. My mother's face crashed through with Fortune's voice, but I never heard what she said.

I woke up in the faint, tawny light as the morning sun peeked over the mountain. Blackthorn was quiet again. Had we run out of things to talk about? Or were the only conversations left the ones neither of us wanted to have?

It didn't matter. This leg of the ride was shorter and harder. Rolling hills turned sharp and rocky as we approached the mountain range where Avilla rested. The route tested every ounce of the horses' patience. It was paved with chopped gravel, made worse by ice and snow.

Eventually, we dismounted and walked beside them to get through the worst of it. Why didn't Tyrlas get this whim in the summer? Every leg of this trip would have gone faster under the warmth of the sun than in this unforgiving grip of winter.

Within a few hours, we came to Avilla—the city of labyrinths. It was gated, but unlike the stone walls of more southern cities,

Avilla was surrounded by copper fencing to display the wealth they'd made from mining.

Compared to the towers and castles that loomed over Linvia, Dover, and Vharos, the Avilla skyline was underwhelming in its sameness.

It wasn't an imposing city. Few buildings stretched much higher than the oxidized fence, but there was a reason. Legally, no building could be taller than the clock-tower at the heart of the university. It was a law passed eons ago.

We stabled the horses at the first stop, just outside the gates, and then continued, crossing over a bridge into the city, which at first appeared empty.

Below the bridge is what earned Avilla its second name: the city of labyrinths.

It was more like two or three cities stacked on top of each other. Where they couldn't build up, they dug *down*, creating a complex series of stairs, ladders, ramps, and bridges supported, in part, by ancient magic and several feats of engineering.

I'd spent time in Avilla, working with its masters on a few historical collections. Memories came back as Blackthorn dawdled behind, marveling as we passed through streets and alleys on our way to the chateau. Twice, in fact, I had to drag him forward by the elbow to keep us on track.

The clock-tower struck noon, and the deep peal echoed through everything. Adler hadn't exactly been forthcoming, nor had he bothered to send a letter, so I had no idea what time anything was scheduled for.

After an hour moving through the levels of Avilla, we reached the promised chateau behind the university. Its garden backed up to a private section of the copper city wall, built in the same red brick that graced every facade on campus.

Inside the grand oak doors, Blackthorn made a noise somewhere between disbelief and disdain when a man dressed in a sharp black suit bowed.

"Welcome to the Diadeus Chateau, Lady Raven and Lord Blackthorn. I am Sir Lavenry." The man stood straight, the white hair atop his head combed back without a piece out of place as he eyed our presence. "I'll show you to your rooms if you'll follow me."

He led us up a grand marble staircase to a corridor. Anything that wasn't marble was heavy-stained oak or gilded in peeling gold leaf.

"Make yourself at home," Sir Lavenry said amicably as he opened a door at the end of the corridor and the one across from it. "His Highness has reserved the entirety of the chateau for your stay. I am the proprietor, here to provide anything you need. Dinner begins promptly at eight."

"And who will be at dinner?" I asked, arching a brow.

"The two of you and the prince." He paused. "Was there anyone else you'd like to invite?"

I shook my head. Relief was cool against my skin, knowing we wouldn't dine with the duke. We hadn't met yet, but the idea of him made my skin crawl.

Sir Lavenry gestured to his right. "Lord Blackthorn, this is your suite, and Lady Raven yours is the other. Should you need anything, don't hesitate to call. His Highness should be here shortly."

My room was extravagant, with large arching windows reminiscent of the Linvian palace; a massive hearth sat opposite the windows, tall enough I could stand in the coals without bending over.

Near the door was a table with a full spread of lunch, from tiny sandwiches and steaming tea to a wine carafe and plates of cured meats and cheeses. I grabbed a squash sandwich and walked around the plush bed to inspect the adjoining bathroom.

It boasted a bathtub large enough for a small family with enough soap for a second. A deep purple gown laid across the bed with a new wool coat and a note set gingerly on top.

Welcome to Avilla, Lady Raven.

I hope you find my accommodations sufficient. Lord Henry insisted on this gown, but you'll also find my choice in the wardrobe. The Duke of Verinium agreed to meet at sunset, at the university library's attic—he's under the expectation he's meeting a queen.

I'll be your escort and look forward to seeing you both safe and well.

-Adler

I didn't want to claim the title, but if it kept Blackthorn alive, I'd take the chance.

I ran my fingers along the fine, heavy silk of the first gown. It was simple, in a deep plum and carefully tailored around the neck and waist. It wouldn't entirely cover the guard's cuts across my chest, nor my scars. But maybe the duke would respect a queen more if she were marked?

No part of me believed that Adler's dress would be anymore modest as I turned to the wardrobe. It was made of finely carved oak, depicting the scene of Miria's creation. The left side showed the first day when the primordials found it, and the other showed the first night when they created the moons. In the first lonely days, they created animals and plants and life, seeking to fill the realm with beautiful, fragile things until they found humans shivering on the ocean shore. From there, they took them in.

The wardrobe opened with a creak, and in it hung a black gown with a deep cut in front and back. A layer of tulle was embroidered with onyx beads.

I lifted a billowy sleeve; it fell back with a rattle. Something glinted below the skirt. I pushed it aside and stopped breathing.

It was my tiara—a gift from Niany from her own collection when I'd been granted the Kingdom of Foria. I took it in my hands and turned it over, not quite believing it.

Pure silver, decorated with small black diamonds in the shape of stars made up the bulk of it. Deep red garnets dripped like blood along the base, fading from the darkest shade on the bottom to the brightest shade of a near ruby at the top.

The piece was exquisite. I'd forgotten because it had been nearly three hundred years since I held it.

A knock rattled my thoughts. Blackthorn walked in before I'd taken off my coat. He eyed the gown on the bed and the one hanging in the wardrobe.

"Good to see His Royal Highness hadn't only left a present for me." Orion tugged at the fine purple silk he wore, which somehow fit him perfectly. Amber eyes flicked to the tiara clutched in my hands.

"Are you declaring yourself queen tonight?"

My lips pursed as I stared at the gown. "It's not a declaration. Just reminding the duke."

He searched my face for something. "Are you still a queen?"

I turned the tiara over in my hands. It glinted in the light and my chest was hollow as my voice.

"Yes, but not of Foria or Dover." I straightened my shoulders as Niany taught me. "Queen of Gods and the Mirian realm, if I seek my claim."

Blackthorn squinted. "But there is no Pantheon."

"No," I agreed and set the tiara on the bed beside the gown. "I'm trying to make sure there will never be."

"You don't strike me as someone who would back down if an opportunity arose."

If only the knight had known what a coward Foriana was.

"You don't know me."

He left the room and his absence left behind an ache in my heart. I ignored it and bathed quickly, washing off everything that felt like Raven as I scrubbed and twisted myself into Foriana for the first time in a hundred years.

Magic razed my skin as I let it build. I wasn't going to this meeting unprepared. Raising the shade was only a fraction of the power I held. If the duke threatened me, he'd learn there was plenty I could do as the Goddess of Death.

I slipped into the purple gown and thought of Henry while flurries fell outside. The coat covered my arms, but I couldn't hide the scar on my neck, nor the healing gashes on my chest. Maybe the tiara would be distracting enough.

Blackthorn stood in the corridor, and I couldn't ignore how handsome he looked in his suit. Adler had every measurement right and made him look regal. My gaze followed the purple jacket to the line of his pants and I cursed. Gods.

"You clean up well." I tried to fill the space, but the unsaid was suffocating.

His gaze narrowed on my chest where my skin was mutilated and red. It did look worse. "You told me it didn't hurt."

"I said it was healing."

"You never said it was this bad, Raven. I thought your skin was impenetrable."

"Not with the right knife." I looked at the floor.

"I have salve . . ." He trailed off, the tenderness in his voice was almost too much as his gaze stuck on the scars. "Will it help?"

"No. I'm—"

"You're in pain."

He was right in more ways than one. Every movement reminded me of the weeks after Koros tore me apart with a cut from the knife that was now tucked against my thigh. Worse, I didn't remember what the guard looked like. Delirium took that from me.

"It's healing," I repeated. "I'll be fine."

I blinked back to myself, burying the thousand thoughts as we descended the stairs into the foyer of the chateau where Lavenry stood looking at a clock. We only had a few minutes to cross the campus and the sun had already fallen behind the mountain, casting long shadows.

Click, whir, snap.

An extremely pale but finely dressed Prince Adler appeared from thin air, nearly on top of me, dressed in black and silver.

"Prince—"

Adler held up his hand and bent at the waist, eyes pinched closed in pain as he breathed deeply. It must not have worked because he dodged behind me and vomited into an unfortunate plant.

Straightening his jacket as he walked back, he nodded and took a glass of water offered by Lavenry.

"Good evening, Lady Raven and Lord Blackthorn." Adler coughed and proceeded to guzzle the water as color crept into his cheeks. "Welcome to the chateau. Apologies. I'm quite new to traveling like this. But both of you look considerably . . . alive."

"We are," Blackthorn said with a long sigh as Adler's rich green gaze stopped on my chest and stiffened. "A little torture in Vharos, but nothing we couldn't handle."

"Torture?" Adler's expression shadowed as he looked between us. "If the man who did that to you, Raven, is not dead, he fucking will be."

"We have more important things," I muttered and meant to push past him, but he stepped in front of me.

"No. Hurting either of you is unacceptable. Do not pretend with me when I—"

"Leave it."

"Raven." He reached forward, for me, absently touching where my scar was, and I flinched back. "I know how to choose my battles, Your Highness, and this does not involve you."

Adler's hand fell to his side as he straightened his suit with the other and cleared his throat. "I disagree, but if that's your command, I will respect it."

Year 1214, The Pantheon
Raven is 664

NIANY SCREAMED WHEN THE door locked behind her, and then again when her gaze fell on the slumped form of Koros, whose blood seeped into my white dress. He would watch me take her as I'd watched him do the same.

A white knife teetered on the edge of my fingers and my skin vibrated, reminding me exactly how far from human I'd become and the weapon grief had forged.

"They will not come for you, Mother. The Pantheon has fallen."

"No. Foriana, please," the Goddess of Life gasped as she faced Death. "That's impossible—"

"Armine, Fortune, Koros, Malcolm, Maxentius, Olvin, Virio, Venden, Etta—how many more should I name before you realize you're no better?"

Niany collapsed to her knees, jewelry chiming as she jolted forward, nose nearly to the ground. "Spare me."

"Why?"

Niany's head swung up. "You cannot rule the Pantheon alone. I'll be a steady hand, a—"

"There is no Pantheon."

Koros was still alive, though immobilized and bleeding. His chest rose and fell as his gaze stayed on his wife.

"You, daughter," Niany said as my gaze swung, "Are more ambitious than that."

"I am not. I am the Goddess of Death, and a woman who's spent the last hundred years slitting the throats of my kind because we do not deserve this power."

She ignored me and fell back on her knees, clasping her hands together as two emotions battled behind her eyes. "You were gracious once, Foriana."

"Then you sold me out to Malcolm."

"You loved him," she shot back, and it was true. I couldn't rewrite those memories if I tried. "You loved the Moravian King—"

"Do not speak of him."

"Or what, Foriana? You already know you can kill me."

35

We followed Adler through the winding walkways of Avilla's university. It was not the seat of the kingdom, but as the top university in all of Miria, Avilla had far more influence than the small kingdom it sat in.

Sulking skies obscured the last vestiges of sunset and night fell fast. A few sparse workers lit gas lamps as we walked, but the campus was otherwise deserted with Solstice encroaching.

I kept the hood of my coat clenched; I did not want to be noticed. Adler, with his height and entrancing green eyes, garnered enough attention as he walked beside Blackthorn.

Avilla was the perfect place to study. Six months of the year it was covered in snow, four months in a blend of ice and rain, and only two months—summer holiday—were tolerable, which made it easy to justify spending most of the year inside, flipping pages of books, many older than Miria itself.

I preferred the grandeur of Verinium or the sunlit libraries along the southern shores, but Avilla served a purpose.

As we neared the building, Adler matched my gait and leaned over, out of Blackthorn's earshot. "Didn't see my dress?"

"I did see your dress." The proximity and the rich scent of velvet and tobacco eddied through the air and fluttered something in my belly. "I thought I'd wear it for dinner so you can see how deep the scars go."

"You'd do that and tell me not to kill the man who carved you?"

"Yes."

"Dangerous choice, Your Majesty," he chided and I glanced over. The prince's eyes sparkled in the light; he was so opposite to Blackthorn, but every part of him was entrancing in a way I wished he wasn't.

"Why is that, Your Highness?"

"I have great difficulty resisting a woman in black and an opportunity for revenge."

"Well, consider dinner torture."

He opened a nondescript door of a red-brick library. "You've been torture since we met."

"Good."

Only a handful of ghosts bobbed along as we walked, following the fae prince up a narrow set of stairs. Blackthorn stood next to me again and the way he looked in the suit left my heart hammering when I needed to focus.

I hated stairwells. Few things were worse than climbing in a circle for a few flights, only to reach a straight hallway where a normal staircase would have been sufficient.

That was the beginning of my aggravation, which only continued when a set of double doors opened.

I drew back the hood and discarded my coat, handing it to Blackthorn just before I strode into the room, the heels of my shoes clicking against the worn wood floor of the narrow library, toward a man sitting at the very end of a long mahogany table.

The duke had dark hair, thin lips, a toothy grin, and the gall to keep his feet on the table, scuffing the mirror polish.

His outdated velvet cloak was obnoxiously embroidered and worn over a layer of gilded, impractical armor that would crumple at the mere sight of a weapon.

"A pleasure to see you again, Your Highness." Devereux clapped his hands together before standing to bow at Adler, who remained behind me, shoulder to shoulder with Blackthorn. "I thank you for arranging this meeting in such a charming corner of the realm."

Blackthorn and I exchanged glances as Adler cleared his throat and gestured at me. "Duke Evander Devereux, might I introduce you to the Queen of Gods, Her Majesty Foriana, and Lord Blackthorn."

Devereux sank into his chair while I remained standing at the table, ignoring the way Adler's use of that title itched the back of my neck.

"The pleasure is mine. To be in the company of a true goddess is a rare thing indeed—"

"So much a pleasure you can't bother to bow?"

He frowned, eyes flashing to Adler like the prince might save him.

Adler stepped forward, but I pushed him back, glaring at the duke as I plucked off my glove and tugged down the veil. Several ghosts appeared and the duke stared. His posture went rigid as his heart raced and the tenor of it vibrated along the edge of my magic.

Begrudgingly, the duke stood and gave a short bow, eyes remaining on a ghost whose head bobbled on her neck. She hovered at the edge of the room until he sank into the chair.

"We could have done this earlier, Your Grace, but you decided to reach out the hard way." I dropped the veil and pulled my glove back on. "I do not respond well to an attempted kidnapping when you could have asked me yourself."

"Throw myself in harm's way?" The duke laughed, ease coming back to his features with the ghost out of sight. "I'd heard *rumors,* but I had no proof. Tyrlas likes to walk with his cock out and lie to people about the size of it."

"What do you want?"

"I wanted to see what you could do and that was quite a nice trick." He rose to his feet, rounding the chair to lean his elbows on it. "Is it true the Goddess of Death can raise shade armies?"

"I will not do it for a king and that goes twice for a self-appointed duke."

"I'll have you know I am not self-appointed, but I'll double what Tyrlas offered. You know that's generous. Verinium has as much sway over Miria as half the kingdoms. Title isn't always representative of power. Which I'm sure you understand, *Foriana*."

Both men bristled behind me, coats shuffling as tension built in the room.

"Disrespect me one more time, *Your Grace*." I challenged, straightening my shoulders as Niany did in the presence of men. "You will call me Queen Foriana or Your Majesty. I will not tolerate less from someone who will never be my equal."

"Of course, *Your Majesty*," he muttered, watching the way magic swirled in my eyes.

"What do you want, Duke Devereux?" I asked again, hoping for a better answer.

"The fae prince and I have interests that temporarily align and I've heard of your disdain for Tyrlas."

"Temporary is a clause for war in kingdom negotiations."

"Not every time. I do not negotiate for a kingdom, as you know." He clasped his hands together. "And there are ways to find peace between competing interests."

"You want the Pantheon restored."

"If I can't have an army of shades, despite offering more money than Tyrlas, I want the protection of the Pantheon and a place in it. Mirian knowledge belongs there."

"You think I'd appeal to the primordials on your behalf? It's not possible, and if it was, you'd still be delusional."

"You did claim the title tonight, for this meeting." His brow furrowed as he wrung his hands. "That isn't for nothing."

"Perhaps it is. What do you gain from the Pantheon? It's never been friendly to mortals, nor to the overly ambitious."

"Ambitious? Your Majesty." He chuckled and danger limned his voice like a warning as a lock of white hair fell in front of his eyes. "I built an empire on shadows and toxins, and now I own the center of Mirian knowledge. I can write and rewrite history as needed, and I—"

"I understand the weight of Verinium's seat. You and your power are not special."

"Then work with me," Devereux said quickly, almost desperate as his voice dropped with his facade. "Verinium is under constant threat. Contrary to rumor, the dynasty was handed to me to keep it out of the hands of worse actors. Thus, I have a vested interest in its continuation. As does the rest of Miria."

"The Pantheon is not a guarantee of protection, even at full power."

"Then make it or risk the loss of Verinium." He leaned over the table now, fists mirrored in the finish. "I've thwarted twelve attempts to burn three separate wings and four break-ins to the restricted temple. Two of which were unfortunately successful in stealing primordial records."

"Who wants those books?"

"I do not know and hoped you might." The duke watched my reaction as his shoulders slumped. "My suspicion is Tyrlas or Rivendeer. They're interested in expansion, but there is something in Verinium I am not privy to that holds power even deeper than—"

"The primordials are not coming back, nor can they be restored." I hoped I was right as I racked my brain trying to think of everything Koros told me.

"Their magic exists," the duke said, searching my expression. "Nothing is ever truly gone."

"You do not know the primordials." The confidence in my voice didn't reflect how I felt. "The fae and the gods drained the realm with few exceptions. What aren't you telling me?"

He gripped the back of his neck and exhaled. "I need your protection because there is something wanted in Verinium and I fear its destruction and potentially yours."

"So you thought to kidnap me, warn me, and then ask for my protection?"

He shrugged. "I prefer some amount of leverage, and now I have given that up. So what is it, Queen Foriana? Can Verinium count on the protection of the Pantheon in whatever form you grant it?"

I stared at the table, hoping the answer would show itself as magic scratched my temple.

"Verinium has always had *my* protection. You, I am unsure of."

The duke nodded, understanding as he rooted around his pocket a moment. From it, Devereux pulled out an amulet of swirling blue stone set in delicate gold and placed it on the table with a clang.

The air charged. "This is the soul of my son, and I know you recognize it. So long as it remains in your possession, I remain in your service."

I reached for the amulet and closed my hand around it. It hummed as the soul mingled with death, separated only by the thin silk of my glove. My heart slivered. He believed he'd get his son back, but the reality was worse and one I'd never say aloud.

"This has your soul in it as well as his," I stated, lifting my eyes. "This is not a sacrifice given lightly."

"I do not give it lightly, Your Majesty."

I draped the amulet around my neck in a show of acceptance. I'd seen the most ruthless gods and men do the same and turn. I didn't want to care; I didn't want this to matter.

"Return to Verinium. I will have an answer in two weeks when I can see it for myself."

"Very well." Duke Devereux watched me as he rose to his feet. "I will be patient."

"Have a good evening in Avilla," I said carefully.

"You as well, Your Majesty." Devereux bowed as I walked for the door, barely waiting another moment because the amulet against my chest was an anchor tied to my feet and I needed out.

Once we were back at the chateau, I stormed upstairs before the weight of everything came over me in a crushing wave.

The tiara clattered on the nightstand with the amulet as I ran the water, cold as it would go. I cradled my head and exhaled hard because breathing was all I could do.

Foriana. Foriana. Foriana.

My mind reeled. Magic hammered my chest and wrapped around my lungs, dragging me down into something I never wanted to be.

Queen? No. Not again.

I gripped the sides of the vanity and stared at my reflection. Full blue eyes glared back and my knuckles turned purple; black hair fell around my face in a curtain of tangled curls.

The renewed power erased the traces of my humanity, of suffering, of the centuries I held. It wiped me clean—the shadows around my eyes, jaw, and cheeks were gone. I looked plump, alive, and so unlike the version of myself I'd been only weeks ago: a wraith.

Only my scars remained, and the damn cuts. I missed being powerless, being small, being forgotten to time—almost mortal.

I knew this would be hard, but the walls closed in and I was nearly *her* again. The goddess who failed, the Godkiller, the woman who lost everything she ever had, and turned her back as it burned because she couldn't bear to watch.

"Who are you?" I hissed at my reflection, but was it mine? My voice fell and grated in the silence.

"I can't do it. I can't do it. I *can't do it.*" I growled. Anger drowned the grief. "Is there nothing else? Is this what I am?"

"Why is there nothing else?" I leaned forward, rocking on my feet, wishing the mirror could tell the truth because the woman on the other side would never believe it if it did. "I could have been a thousand things, but I'm *this*. Again and again, and again. Fuck."

I leaned my forehead on the cool glass and closed my eyes as if I could wish away anything, but I couldn't—this was the cycle. I'd fall into oblivion only to be dragged back and forced to sit a throne I couldn't hold. It didn't matter what color magic turned my knuckles or threaded my veins.

Only half restored, I felt too empty, too disinterested and too much like the daughter Koros always wanted: unfeeling and unrelenting, because that was the power of the Pantheon and the cost of peace.

I drew away from the mirror, staring at my own eyes as I gripped my hair and pulled.

"I won't do it." I shouted, hoping the magic heard me, hoping the statement shook the afterlife I'd abandoned. The mortal souls could find peace on their fucking own because I was ending my cycle.

Godkiller.

"Fine, let me be remembered as that: Assign every atrocity to my name. Forget who made them possible. I'm the Godkiller, the abandoner, the evil queen, the walking Death and everything that should be feared and hated.

"May no one forget when I finally dissolve to dust." My fingers tightened on the vanity as water poured from the faucet. "I was the monster who killed their heroes and I will die in Belfiante knowing I'd never be anything else in history but a villain and coward who left souls to rot and her cities to drown."

I backed away from the mirror, shoulders tight with a rage like determination as I slipped out of the purple gown, pinned up my hair, and tied myself into the sheer black dress.

It displayed my wounds from Vharos and I couldn't be bothered to care. They were the only truth on my skin, and if men wanted to worry about a god, I wasn't one to stop them.

36

TOMORROW, WE'D LEAVE FOR the last stop, Belfiante, where there would be no return: Raven will die on the shore one way or another. I was running out of excuses.

I peered down one corridor and then another before I found the candlelit dining room by the wafting aromatics of a much-needed meal.

The dark wood-trimmed dining room was lit by several candelabras gathered in bunches around the table. Red damask wallpaper decorated the walls above the chair rail, interrupted only by a large fireplace and two wide sideboards. Blackthorn sat on one side of the comically long table with Adler across, leaving the head of the table unoccupied.

Both men watched me with a kind of rapt attention and hunger I might take advantage of with enough wine. At least until their attention fell to the space between my breasts, where my old scar was clearly carved open.

Maybe I shouldn't have worn Adler's dress, but it was the restriction I needed between the weight of the beading and the restrictive bodice.

"Your Majesty. *Meviandae Solstiecae*," Adler said with a smirk as he stood and bowed. Blackthorn did the same and I flushed before I sat, carefully angling my legs to keep from splitting the seam. "Good Solstice, unless you've forgotten. Thought a celebration was in order."

I kept my arms folded under the table. Adler's gaze was cutting.

"It's been years since anyone bowed at dinner for me."

"How long?" Blackthorn asked, leaning back as if he was comfortable in this room dressed like a lord with buttons and stiff black pants. Maybe he was.

"Since the fall of Morav, wasn't it?" Adler answered.

The knight poured three tall glasses of wine, emptying the bottle between them.

"Truly, I'm not a queen." I reached for the glass, ignoring the way both men glanced at the cut across my arm as the sleeve fell aside. "But I do feel like the change with the duke went well."

"Those cuts aren't healing, Raven. How deep did he fucking go?" Adler stared at my arm as I took my glass. "They cut you with the bone of a god."

"He didn't hit my bone if you're wondering." I waved away the concern and drank my wine. "And it is healing—slowly."

"She declined my salve," Blackthorn said with an edge in his voice. "She also denies that it hurts."

Adler opened his mouth to add something, but I cut him off.

"Can we talk about anything else?"

"Sure. You promised to protect Verinium over Tyrlas." Blackthorn looked at me as Sir Lavenry set soup before us. "And you took the offering of his and his son's souls."

"He isn't the first." I took a sip of hearty mushroom broth. "We'll see if he keeps his word. I don't know what protection the Pantheon could offer. Even if I took it back tonight, it would be years—"

"It would be the court of the realm," Adler provided, leaning back in the chair as he pushed away his empty bowl. "You would have myth and power on your side. You could trade kings and quell any kingdom that stretched too far."

"Like your father in his realm?"

"Or yours. Koros wasn't as removed as he'd like you to believe."

"My father was a liar and a tyrant," I snapped. "He was also calculating and deserved to be deposed as I was."

"Were you a bad queen?" Blackthorn asked and my attention swiveled. "From what I've seen—"

"At some point I preferred to watch the mortals run it to the ground. I got distracted."

"I don't believe you." Adler's gaze caught mine and I brushed it off.

"I wasn't asking what you believed—I stated what I believed because I've lived it."

The bowls were cleared as I shifted in my seat.

"Let's not talk about politics. It's Solstice. We'll have plenty of time to talk about the realm."

Adler raised an eyebrow. "Will we?"

"Yes."

I drained my glass and held it out for another. Blackthorn complied, filling it and then topping off his and Adler's as the main course arrived.

"I'm sorry. I want to talk about how someone carved you with a fucking god knife and I'm just supposed to ignore it." Adler didn't hide the way he stared at me.

"Yes, you *are*." I lifted my chin.

Blackthorn wiped his mouth with his sleeve before adding, "One of Nia's guards did it, can't remember which."

"The Tyrlian general?" Adler's face drained, and he gripped the fork so hard his knuckles turned white. "Dare I pay the younger Tyrlas a visit?"

"Do not." I reached for my own fork as roasted duck, boiled greens, and roasted white carrots were set in front of us. It was a traditional Solstice dinner among nobility. "General Nia—well, Queen now—had a god knife. Her guard nicked me with it. It's healing and I'd rather not talk about it."

"And where the fuck were you?" Adler pointed at Blackthorn, knife teetering from his fingers as his voice cooled.

Blackthorn watched Adler before he answered.

"In cuffs, chained to the wall, and beaten within an inch of my life. If it hadn't been for Raven's snoring, I might not have woken up."

I glared at him and stuck my fork in the duck. "We made it out alive. I did not put on this ridiculous gown to talk about the torture we gratefully survived."

Adler lifted his chin. "Why did you put on the gown?"

I couldn't win. Wax candles dripped on the table as Blackthorn cleared his throat.

"Right. What is your favorite place that no longer exists? And I don't want to hear anything horrific."

He looked at me sharply, amber gaze targeted.

"Lady Raven," Adler chided, and my belly warmed at the mention of my name. Maybe this was a bad idea. "You lived in the Pantheon. Surely it ranks among the top."

I shrugged, watching candles flicker as I considered my answer.

"The physical Pantheon? It wasn't destroyed. It's just in disrepair, but it was stunning. The main hall has floors made of opal tile as thick as my hand and gardens that stretch for miles all permanently in bloom. It's an impossible place."

"And the parties were incredible, I'm sure." Adler looked at me as his finger ran over his parted lips, making a show of biting his thumb to show off his pointed canines. If it bothered Blackthorn, he didn't show it and leaned into the table, a curious glint in his eyes.

I dabbed my mouth with a napkin as memories came back in flashes.

"After the fifth time you walk in on your father's orgy, the celebrations lose their luster."

"I can relate." Adler sighed. "Why do you think I came to this realm?"

"You crossed realms to escape your father's orgies?" Blackthorn laughed. "I think I'd have liked my father better if he'd gone to an orgy."

"Oh no, it does the opposite." Adler waved a hand, rings clinking. The motion cleared the plates with magic. Gods' magic was narrower and impractical—we couldn't do much outside of what we were given. "The King of Fae is worse because of his proclivities. In fact, it's caused more problems in court than fewer. You should be thankful you've never had to burn the image from your eyes of your father fucking two of your paramours at once."

"What?" Blackthorn's glass froze at his lips and I laughed, tension easing with wine and conversation.

"You too?" I tried not to remember a similar night at the Pantheon.

"Yes," Adler said. "Walked into the ballroom for a damn bottle of liquor and he was getting sucked off by the fae duchess I'd been courting, and fucked by a guard I'd fooled around with."

"That's possible?" Blackthorn tilted his head and looked at the wall like he was trying to picture it. "I've never—"

"Oh, you haven't lived," Adler said with a rakish smile. His foot kicked under my dress and ran down the inside of my calf. "She kneeled in front of my father who stood on his dais, cock in her mouth, while my guard fucked him from behind. Truly, it would have been the best of every world if it weren't my father."

"Awful."

Adler shrugged, sipping his wine.

"She seemed pleasured enough, so it wasn't all bad. What happened to you, Raven?"

"Nothing like that." I massaged my neck as I stared at the gold, tiled ceiling and the memory hung in the warped reflections of candlelight. "I was trying to enjoy myself in the gardens with some gods and demis when I turned to see my father across the garden, cock out, clawing over some elven nobles on a bench. It was my godhood centennial and Koros wasn't supposed to be in the Pantheon."

"Did you finish?" Adler asked and Blackthorn looked between us.

"Obviously not." I tried to push the memory out. Koros wasn't known for promiscuity, but he wasn't shy about it. "Is there dessert?"

"Of course—Lavenry!"

Within a minute, plates of rich chocolate cake appeared and I salivated. Gods, I hadn't had chocolate in so long. Even in the richest kingdoms, it was rare.

"You didn't answer the question, Adler," Blackthorn said between bites. The candlelight softened his features. "What is your favorite place that no longer exists?"

Adler considered the question, green eyes distant in a look I understood too well.

"A garden in the fae realm," he said thoughtfully. "Far south, the water was always warm, and the beaches were made of crushed pearls. We called it Olanoria, after my grandmother. Every summer when the three moons aligned, the shore turned the most beautiful shade of pink and there was always a celebration. Lights, dancing, magic even I couldn't explain—"

"It doesn't exist anymore?"

The prince shook his head.

"My younger brother destroyed it when he lost control of his power. It cratered a corner of the coast and my father never tried to rebuild it."

Blackthorn looked at Adler. "I'm sorry."

"My brother is alive, if you must know." Adler smirked, adding, "Though our mother died that day. Unrelated."

Blackthorn muttered, "Gods."

"It was hundreds of years ago, and Death is commonplace for us immortals, right, Raven?"

Something shifted in my gut like a changing tide as wine swirled. It'd been so long since anyone understood the way time stretched when it was endless.

"I am the goddess of it." My gaze shifted to Blackthorn. "Orion, what about you? Do you have a lost place?"

The empty plates disappeared with whatever magic Adler had. He was showing off as Blackthorn leaned back.

"Nothing like yours." Amber eyes shifted between us as he crossed his arms over his chest. "When I first arrived in Tyrlas, there was a temple I'd always walk to. Everything was covered in gold; it was beautiful. I didn't pray or anything, but I'd get a pastry from next door and sit there, in the very last row of chairs, eating it. it was the only escape from the squire's dorms."

"In the Fair neighborhood?"

"Near the gate," he nodded. "Burned in a fire. They rebuilt it, but the bakery never came back and the temple wasn't the same."

"They never are." Adler reflected, searching Blackthorn's face for something. "I'm sorry for your loss."

"Thank you," Blackthorn said as he opened another bottle of wine and filled our glasses. "It's not a pearl beach or an ancient palace for gods."

I turned to the fae prince who reclined in the chair with his eyes closed. "Do you know if the chateau still has the spoon collection in the library?"

"Maybe. Shall we ask for a tour?" He opened one eye. "Though it wouldn't be nearly as exciting as the Linvian palace. There's only one kitchen and if the spoons aren't there, the library is quite dull."

"Is there a ballroom?" Blackthorn asked. I cocked my head.

"A ballroom? Does a Tyrlian wolf want to dance?"

Curls of blond fell in front of his eyes as his gaze stopped on me, ignoring Adler. "Just thinking about how you don't remember dancing with me."

"She's quite good at that," Adler muttered and waved his arm again. Music filled the dining room. The prince must have planned to stay in Avilla a few days if he was showing off. "No need to make Lavenry clean another room when this one is perfectly suited. If she won't dance with you, Orion, I will."

The fae's verdant eyes darted around. The dining room was spacious, warm, and filled with wine. Perhaps I didn't want to leave, but maybe I should have—I was one glass away from giving into the very temptation I'd been choking on.

"How'd you do that?"

Adler flashed a tired half-smile as Blackthorn stood and swayed to the upbeat chime.

"Fae magic." Adler loosened a button just below the shadow of his stubble. "My magic is strained, but lighting a fire and turning on a victrola is quite easy—a wave of the arm and a specific memory of the action is enough. Can't gods do that?"

"We're not lazy."

"It isn't laziness," Adler drawled. "You gods only see magic as power. You're missing out on the other half of it. Pleasure and power are synonymous for a reason."

"Our magic is only what we're given." My gaze narrowed as I considered the action. "I suppose I could use a ghost to turn on the victrola or light the candles if I wanted—"

"You haven't?" Blackthorn asked. "That's the first thing I'd do."

"Oh?" Adler smirked. "And what is the second thing you'd do, Lord Blackthorn?"

The knight considered the question for a moment, watching a drip of wax pool on the table as he swirled the wine in his glass.

"I'd *love* to close a door while crossing a room."

"Like this?"

Adler winked, and the doors to the dining room slammed.

"See, *that's* magic."

"That's nothing." The fae opened his palm and fire danced in the center of it.

I leaned forward to admire it, reaching my hand over the flame. Adler didn't flinch back; rather he watched my scar as my hand got closer and closer to the heart of the flame. Enchanted fire was something I *could* feel; the heat licked through my gloves without burning them.

"Enjoying the heat, Your Majesty?" His gaze flicked up.

"Just nice to feel."

The flame reduced to smoke in his palm and I sat back.

Then, with a flick of his wrist, it sprang to life and bounded from Adler's hand to Orion's shirt, consuming it before the knight had registered what happened and leapt into the air. Ash gathered on Blackthorn's broad chest, embers floating off to nothing as he patted himself, checking for burns.

The low light caught his scars, and the shock on his face was beautiful as my gaze traced the curve of his chest to the dip above his waist and where his hips curved.

My mouth watered as Adler laughed, a wicked glimmer feathered his jaw as his gaze also raked over the knight.

"It was getting warm, anyway."

Unabashedly, the knight walked around the table where I sipped my wine to cool the rising heat of desire. But gods, I was hopeless and this was a mistake.

Orion held his arm out.

"A dance?"

Adler merely smiled and said, "Torture me."

What did it matter? I'd be dead in days. I took Blackthorn's hand and let him pull me to my feet in an effortless motion as the chiming rhythm of the victrola continued.

Orion gripped the small of my back where the dress dipped and he held me to his chest as we swayed.

He was so broad, everything about him made me feel small like his body could swallow me. How did I forget we'd danced before? Now it was so obvious, but how did I ignore the way his heart called to mine like they were tied together?

Was it silenced by the cuffs? Gods, his thumbs traced circles on my back as he hummed and already the ache between my thighs was unbearable.

Adler watched from the table and the thought stirred me. I was no stranger to the fluid world of gods or fae, but mortals were different, stranger, in their lines and rules as if to make up for being without a soul bound.

Blackthorn was entrancing, and I leaned into him, letting his warm skin against mine cloud my senses. *Soul bound.* I knew I was slipping. He spun me out and back to his chest, my hand landing flat on the corded muscles, scars, and hair that made him. I had no thought that wasn't kissing him.

There wasn't a way out. I'd whither if he denied me.

"This is the third," Orion said, voice gravelly and low as his chin dipped and my hand slid to his back as he pulled me closer, pressing my chest to his.

"Third time? For what?"

"Dancing together."

The words paused time and I measured my breathing. I wasn't thinking about Tyrlas or the night of the tournament or Belfiante. I only thought about the way he looked at me and how his hands and cock might fix the need that overwhelmed me.

Another hand wrapped around my hip and sidled against my back.

"I see I'm not the only one desperate to kiss you, Raven," Adler whispered in my ear and heat bloomed between my thighs. Pressed between both, I was alive.

Without reservation, I dragged Blackthorn to my lips and kissed him. His fingers gripped my neck and held me there in a sweet, aching kiss that tasted like chocolate and wine as I plunged my tongue deeper into his mouth because nothing would ever be enough.

Adler squeezed the curve of my hip and kissed my bare shoulder. Need and want were a fire that raged through my chest and stole my breath as I pulled away.

I took a step aside before Orion could run his fingers over my lips or Adler pull me back.

"I need more wine."

"This is your night, Your Majesty." Adler flashed a knowing look as I went to the table and filled my glass. "What do you want? And do not tell me nothing when I can smell your arousal from over here."

"You're too forward." I tried to hold up my veneer by clutching the glass in my hand while both men stared. Lust was a haze in the room. Orion combed his hair with his fingers, bottom lip between his teeth.

More wine would make this better—or worse. Presently, it made me want to take the knight's fingers in my mouth until he groaned.

I shook the thought off.

"I have everything I need. Perhaps I'll go to bed."

"Bed?" Blackthorn repeated, rounding the table. "You've said that before and I did not believe you then."

Adler smirked, prowling closer around the table. Both closed in on me. "I don't believe you either, Raven. Do you want to touch him? Or do you want him to touch you? Maybe you're imagining what it is to have both of us."

The prince stopped beside me and nipped my ear. Blackthorn stared wide-eyed, hiding his expression with the rim of his glass, saying nothing when I couldn't look away from the chisel of his chest and the run of hair across it where ash still stuck.

What was the danger to a dying god? I reached for Adler's hand and pressed it to my thigh, guiding his touch up the slit in my dress until his finger hooked on the lace of my underwear.

"You're wicked," Adler purred as his fingers dug into my hip with a promise I wanted to hear. "But he's the one who wants to fuck you."

"And you don't?"

"What I want doesn't matter." The prince moved away, standing beside Orion just out of reach. He leaned over to the knight. "Do you know what she desires, Sir Blackthorn?"

Orion cut him off with a kiss, gripping the fae's jaw.

Adler's shoulders jolted in surprise, then he deepened it, his hands on Orion's neck. I backed into the table, heat stirring and overwhelming my rational sense as Adler's jacket came off.

Gods, watching the way Orion's body moved on the prince was more than I could take.

When they parted, the table was all that held me up on shaking, desperate knees.

"I may be a knight of Tyrlas," Orion said, "but I've hardly been a man of my vow."

Adler's green eyes were wide as he wiped his mouth with his sleeve and straightened his shirt, nearly at a loss for words.

"I don't suppose you need my suggestions."

"Depends what you suggest?" Orion raised a brow. "Raven needs to be kissed and fucked, but she keeps denying it."

I gripped the edge of the table and held my breath as Adler walked toward me. His expression turned to stone and he leaned over, hands beside mine, trapping me, lips too close.

"Tell me how wet she is, Orion. I'm not touching her yet."

Adler didn't break my gaze as Orion came up behind him. I leaned back on the table, moving my knee a fraction, but it wouldn't move further without tearing the gown.

"The fae bastard can't do it himself?" I taunted.

Orion's hand dipped under Adler's arm and trailed up the inside of my thigh and the warmth of desire was all-consuming.

"This fae bastard is going to kiss you while the knight kneads your pretty cunt."

Adler grabbed my neck and kissed me, his tongue plunging; I kissed him back, hungrily. Blackthorn's heavy hands palmed the outside of my thighs and raked up my dress. One of them pushed me onto the table.

Orion's hand teased and slipped beneath the lace of my underwear. In a motion, he tugged them off just as Adler bit my lip and dragged a moan from me.

"*Navrosia*," he said against my lips with the same ferocity it had in the hall of the Linvian palace.

Fingers pressed against my core and Adler drew back. Catching his breath as Orion took his place between my legs. The knight pressed his thumb to the inside of my thigh, mimicking what it'd be for his rough hands to find their way into my wet cunt.

I tilted my head back. Desire clung to my skin like a film.

"How wet is she?" Adler breathed, then he climbed onto the table where he straddled me and started undoing the lacing of the gown.

Orion spread my legs with his hips, pushing fabric up my thighs, but not before there was a distinctive tear as he jerked my knees wider and brought my ass to the edge of the table. There, he pushed one finger into me, and another. It was sweet, slow pressure that left me imagining what it'd feel like to be filled with his cock.

"She's dripping on the table."

"Go deeper."

The prince purred and ripped apart the stays on the dress, exposing my breasts as he wrapped his legs around me and groped as Orion pressed further. I leaned back, losing myself in their touch. Denial was pointless when it felt like this.

"Add another finger; she can handle it."

Adler's nails skimmed the exposed part of my back and kissed the space between my shoulder blades. His hair brushed the nape of my neck as his fingers wrapped over my scar. Warmth came over as the hardness of the prince pressed against my back.

"I bet she looks fucking beautiful when she comes."

On the fucking stars and moons, I wanted to be fucked. Adler's grip on my throat and breasts tightened, careful not to touch my wounds as Orion took three fingers and stretched me.

"Wait," Adler said against my ear. He moved and Orion's momentum slowed. I leaned back against his chest as heat built in my core. My body started separating from pleasure with every pounding thrust of Orion's hand.

"Fuck."

Adler propped me up, hand tilted up my jaw as Orion's hungry gaze looked down.

"Tell me what her cum tastes like."

Adler groped me as Orion's face dipped between my legs, then something warm dripped on my shoulder. I looked up at the prince through the haze of lust as he tilted a taper candle, dripping wax on my shoulder.

The heat was tantalizing, mingled with the sting of pain and the pressure of his hands as they kneaded and Orion's lips sucked, teasing me to the edge of pleasure while the fae prince held me steady, in thrall with the sensation of the warm wax.

"Come for us, Foriana," Adler coaxed, and the command was the release I needed. The force of pleasure threw my head back and brought tears to my eyes as every muscle in my body tightened at their touch.

Orion stood as I blinked, slumping against Adler's chest while he continued to massage me.

"Perfect," Orion said, voice hazy as he leaned over the table, lips close to mine. Adler squeezed my breast and I arched my back. Instead of kissing me, the knight brought Adler's lips to his, eliciting a groan from the prince as need overwrote every one of my senses.

I flattened my palm on Orion's chest. He broke from Adler, tilting my chin to kiss me with the taste of *us* on his lips.

"The goddess isn't done," Adler rasped. I wasn't finished. He was right, and fuck, I wanted all of him. All of them.

The knight gripped my hips and pulled me off the table. My hand fell against Orion's hard chest and I wanted him to consume me, trap me against the wall and punish me with his cock.

Instead, Adler's strained voice dripped down my spine with a creeping authority as the knight held me steady.

"Take the dress off."

Blackthorn's hands slipped and I shimmied from the confines of the fabric.

"Fuck, you're stunning," Orion murmured as he remained in front me, gaze sticking to my scars before his eyes roved to mine. Desire burned in the amber with something undeniable. How was he mortal?

"A goddess," Adler agreed as his hands found my hips and his thumbs dug in, leaving indents before he turned me to face him. His green eyes flicked over my shoulder. "Hold her still."

Orion's body wrapped around me, pressing my back to his warm chest. Wide hands splayed over my belly and thigh as Adler peeled wax from my skin before his hand wrapped around my neck and we kissed.

Devoured.

Gods. It had to be more than a kiss as both of them explored me with their hands, lips, and stuttering breath. It was something from a dream when the Pantheon still meant something.

I reached for Adler's pants, tugging on the waist, but Adler touched my hand and shook his head as he unbuttoned his shirt.

"I don't need it."

"You don't want me?"

Orion's grip tightened on my ribs, cock pressed to my back as Adler's nails traced my breasts, my scars, and dipped between my legs where I ached to be touched again, and his lips grazed my ear.

"Do not presume to know what I want, Foriana. Just because tonight isn't the night I bury my cock in your cunt doesn't mean I don't want to feel every muscle of yours as you cum on my hand. That is what you want, isn't it?"

His hand jerked up, fingers arcing into my aching core as Orion kissed my neck. This is what it was to feel alive, to feel whole, and to—

"Let go, Foriana." Adler's voice was desperate, aching as I was. His fingers came in and out, pressure building up as he angled his head away from mine and kissed Orion, deep and probing over me as breathing came faster and my vision blurred.

His punishing hand pushed me off a cliff of ecstasy in a rush so destabilizing my legs shook as I soaked their pants and cried out, muffled then by Adler's kiss.

"Perfect," the prince said against my lips as my body came to. "I knew you'd ruin my pants from the moment we met, Your Majesty."

"Fae bastard." I heaved as the prince pulled away, licking my cum from his fingers. Orion was slower to release his hold on me, his fingers continued to run along my arm and trace the curve of my shoulders as I shivered against him watching the prince shrug out of his shirt.

"You are a dream, Foriana. A dream I'd never want to wake up from." With a salacious grin, Adler tossed his shirt at me as his lusty gaze roved to Orion. "We should do that again sometime, but I'm afraid I need to get some sleep while I still have a modicum of control."

I slipped on the prince's shirt and haphazardly buttoned it as he left the room without a parting touch or another word.

Alone again with Orion Blackthorn, I sobered. What was the point of holding back when his amber eyes held the world?

Regrettable words slipped out. "I really should sleep."

He gave me a half-smile. "Don't say you didn't enjoy that."

I looked at him, adjusting the shirt to cover my ass. "I'd never say that."

"Never? Since Linvia, all I've wanted to do is pleasure you again, but even when there's nothing holding you back, you waver. I want you, Raven, and you want me, but it's my mortality you're afraid of."

A truth bobbed at the back of my throat as I looked at the door. "It isn't all I'm afraid of."

"Isn't it?"

Silently, we left the dining room. Upstairs, I stopped at the door and Orion lingered, moonlight sharpening the scars on his face as my gaze stopped on his chest for the umpteenth time.

Even from here, I smelled myself on him and I wanted whatever this was. Only I stood in the way and the question I would ask of him. That's what I was afraid of, but I wanted him to believe I was fearless.

I closed the distance and kissed him, caging him against the wall as my lips worked. Slow, languid, and intentional, while his hands caressed my neck, pressing me to his chest like I was precious.

The hardness of him left me wanting as the kiss deepened. I unbuckled his pants, taking his length in my hand. Desire curled when his breath clipped as our gazes collided.

He drew back, leaning against the wall and I waited for him to stop me, to pull away, to make an excuse, but none came. Orion bit his lip. I tightened my grip, moving my hand along the thick shaft of his beautiful cock as his breath came faster.

"Raven," he moaned. Cum pearled on the tip. I wanted to lick it off as he shuddered, but one taste would drive me fucking mad. His legs shook; gods, I needed him to come for me. I needed his breath to hitch. Up and down, I tightened my grip until he came in a magnificent, trembling gasp.

Then I withdrew my hand and kissed him again, greedy to have any part of him for another passing moment.

"I'll see you in the morning" is all I said and went to my room, leaving the knight in the hallway with his cock out.

I was one more kiss, one more night, one more stolen fucking glance away from entirely unraveling and unlocking the bond as much as I could alone.

As I adjusted the pillow, my hand bumped the hilt of the knife and sent it clattering to the floor. It fell in a stream of moonlight as if Fate reminded me what waited.

But Fate also knew I was a coward.

The tether between Orion and I pulled taut as I turned over. Nagging hope crept up the back of my neck and softened my hardest thoughts. Letting go and giving in would undo everything I've sworn my life to end, but wouldn't it be beautiful to live in the destruction if it felt like him?

37

I woke up alone, but the graze of their lips on my back and thighs still burned. My body ached for them again, and I'd have given so much more to wake up between the knight and the prince.

It wasn't about sex—we hadn't crossed that line—but there was comfort between them I hadn't felt in years. Maybe centuries. Or maybe it was just the proximity of Blackthorn, my soul bound, whom I couldn't go any further with. Or could I? Was there any point in restraint?

The ride to Belfiante would be long. We'd traverse a treacherous mountain pass into the heart of the northern-most range of Miria, stopping in only one more town before being relegated to the elements.

Then we'd reach the mirror ponds.

My heart cratered as I tucked my father's knife deep in the pockets of my second coat. I wouldn't lose it. Only my father's dagger would collapse the Pantheon.

A soft knock rang on my door.

"Come in," I said, unsurprised to see the fae prince open the door and close it.

Adler was always striking, but the soft morning light and the tiredness in his eyes, combined with the casual look of his untucked shirt and black pants, made me want to feel his chest against mine again and so much more he wouldn't let me have.

"Last night was fun." He smirked, but it dissolved into a more pensive expression, showing the lines at the corner of his eyes and the sharpness of his freckled cheeks.

"We ought to do it again," I said lightly, but there was a heaviness in the air I recognized as something too near a goodbye. "Thank you for the chateau. It was nice to have a night without . . . everything."

"Of course, Lady Raven. I wasn't about to let you sleep in a shack."

"How did you find the tiara?" I plucked it from the nightstand beside the amulet.

Adler's eyes fixed on me. "It was in a box near the dagger you took. I went looking after I returned from Vharos, thinking a queen might like to wear her crown."

"Ah."

"You haven't changed your mind." His gaze flicked up, deep green and searching, as I lowered the tiara. "Having a soul bound doesn't change anything?"

The room froze. He stared at me for a long second before saying anything else.

"It's Blackthorn." He sighed and didn't move as my hands fell to my side. "I suspected it in Reen, but I saw it last night."

"Is that why you didn't—"

"No. That was . . ." Eyes hardened on mine as his expression tightened. "I told you the first night I'd take anything you'd let me have and consider myself lucky. Last night was restraint.

Trust me, I wanted nothing more than to bend you over and fuck that delicious cunt of yours until you forgot who you were." He moved a step closer. "But if I did, you wouldn't be going to Belfiante."

"I have to."

"I know." He gritted like it was painful to admit. "And that's why you stopped yourself with Orion."

"What are you saying?"

"Nothing that matters," the fae muttered, and there was a sudden coldness in his expression. "Whatever you leave behind here, I'll make sure it is returned to Linvia under Henry's care, but I hope you change your mind about dying."

"It's the—"

"It is not the only way, Queen Foriana. You are choosing to run."

"And you aren't? Prince Adler of Ilverleigh—heir to his father's throne? Where are you for your people?"

He crossed the room and stopped, toes touching mine as I lifted my chin and matched his ire. I wasn't afraid of the fae.

"Do not presume to know what I do for my people. Every choice I make is for them and a world where my father cannot cause another war. Who are your choices for?"

"The mortals should rule themselves."

A hollow laugh fell from his lips. "The Pantheon you shirk is all that stands between them and my father's rule. Your choice is the selfish one."

Adler was right. The words struck through me and settled in my lungs acrid like smoke. I wasn't the hero; I was selfish in every way Koros wasn't, but none of that made me better.

"What would you do if I decided to live?"

His thumb ran over my lip and then he kissed me like his life depended on it. His other hand tangled in my hair and pulled until I moaned, kissing him back, clawing at his shirt.

He flipped me around, caged my back to his chest as he kissed my neck and stuffed his hand down my pants. I gasped as his touch turned hot. "Magic can be for pleasure too," he whispered in my ear as I fumbled to unbutton while his other hand tugged my hair. "I'll do it."

Deliriously, he spun me around and pushed me against the wall as his fingers undid my pants and his body trapped me, lips achingly close but not touching.

"If you live, Raven, I'll give you this cock whenever you ask."

He rode against me and I felt his hardness through his pants, but the delicious pressure of it was soon replaced by the punishing heat of his fingers plunging into me with enough force to take my breath away.

"Harder," I rasped, and he delivered.

Lips on mine, he pulled my hair and wrung out every gasping breath of pleasure I had in me. He didn't stop even when my legs shook because he knew what it was to make a god come.

With a final plunge and burst of heat, I cried out and convulsed around him as my head fell back and his hold on me relented.

"Fuck," he said, heaving. "I didn't think I'd get to do that twice."

As I caught my breath, Adler stared and licked his hand with an exaggerated moan. There were many things I wanted and all of them were bad ideas as I straightened myself and buttoned my pants.

"Consider yourself lucky, Prince Adler," I said, trying to stand as if I was unaffected. Like I could live never knowing how it felt to take his cock.

"I always do," he said with a small smile. His eyes were soft and focused on me. "I'll consider this goodbye, then?"

"One more thing?"

He turned around with an infuriating, coy expression. "I'm not fucking you, Your Majesty."

I frowned, letting the words pass before I said something with a far different intonation. "We have Ophie's horses, but we'll leave them in Baneswood. Can you write the Vharos temple and let them know where they are?" I pulled another letter from my coat pocket, along with the small leather envelope that contained my map. I tried to mask the emotion building in my throat as I held them out. "Send this with it. It's for Ophie."

Adler took the letter but watched me. "What is it?"

"A private letter," I snapped, but his face pinched with a vulnerability I'd seen a thousand times in Henry's eyes and guilt prickled my skin. "It's just something I owed her. She'll know what it is."

"I'll make sure she gets it."

Adler's hand hovered over the doorknob; his shoulders stiffened as he turned around. Was he trying to make this last as painfully long as possible?

"What did they make you do? The scar on your chest is from Koros. Your torturer cut over it." Something flashed in his eyes—a warning.

I inhaled. There was no point in evading the question. "Nia forced me to raise a shade for Tyrlas. The knife was a test to see if they could hurt me."

"Right . . ." Adler's tone trailed off. "I'll still see to it the next time I see King Tyrlas. What they'd done to you and Orion is uncalled for and a clear violation of Mirian law."

I shook my head and played with the end of my braid, trying to swallow the memories of how broken Blackthorn looked and the rage burning inside me. "Leave it. They will not be a threat again."

He raised a brow and I rolled my eyes. There was no point in arguing with a fae over this. I rearranged my scarf to hide the healing scar. "Goodbye, Prince Adler."

"I'll await you in another life."

The prince left the room and his absence hung thick as I tied my coat and stuffed my bag.

Downstairs, Blackthorn waited with an extra sword strapped around his waist; morning light filtered in through several of the wide stained-glass windows.

Bathed in the orange light, the knight looked almost like a god and the thoughts swirling through my head and desire for Adler fell sideways.

"Ready?" Orion asked and I nodded, moving past his looming form toward the door before I had to say another goodbye.

Campus was quiet in the early hours and the sharp clip of our footsteps on the frozen stone echoed off the buildings.

"Do you mind if we make a stop before we get the horses?"

"Where?"

"An old friend I owe a visit. Baneswood is only a five-hour ride."

"Lead the way, Your Majesty." Blackthorn smirked, stoking heat and memories of last night against my will.

"Raven is my name to you."

"Surely there's a better name to use when you just had my cock in your hand."

Last night made things worse. Every part of me wanted to hear the way he moaned again and blow apart the distance I'd put between us because I was afraid of pain only I could feel. Adler was right—I stopped myself.

Giving in would be easier and maybe I deserved a last bit of light as my days wound down. Maybe hope was the strength I needed to get to Belfiante and follow through. I'd come too far to give up.

No one else could cut the connection to the afterlife and give the mortals back their autonomy.

The end of the Pantheon was all I could think about as I led us through the streets of Avilla, down a staircase into the below.

The bottom rungs of the city were shielded from the wind, which meant it was busiest in the winter.

We pushed through throngs of people in the narrow merchant aisle. I hoped the hulking knight wouldn't lose me, but the width of the street was nearly the width of his shoulders.

Rounding a corner where sun-bleached banners hung above and people lessened, I stopped at an unassuming door and knocked twice with the broadside of my fist.

"Oh, fuck right off." A sinewy woman with white-streaked black hair crossed her arms in the doorway. "What god below did I piss off to send this bitch to my doorstep?"

"Bitch? Look at yourself, Vin." I shrugged, pushing my way into the familiar, cluttered apothecary as Vinliana grabbed me into a choking hug.

"You said I wouldn't see you again because you hate good-byes." She relinquished me to step back and massage my neck. "That was thirty fucking years ago, so I will call you a bitch so long as you've earned it."

I glanced around at the trinkets, running my fingers through the dust-covered counter as her wild blue eyes snapped over my shoulder. "Is he yours?"

"Yes," I said too fast, ignoring the tightness in my chest as Blackthorn maneuvered his way into the terribly narrow shop aisle. "Sir Blackthorn."

"Oh?" Her hand flew to her chest and Vin's voice dropped. "A knight? How delightful. Sir Blackthorn, please lock the door. Now, what brings you here, Foriana? You're not just stopping by Avilla. Three hundred years and that isn't anything like you."

"Three hundred?" Blackthorn gaped, stock-still, afraid to knock anything over.

"Witch," Vinliana answered with a proud smile. "Not many of us, but we're some of the last long-lived mortals, shifter."

Blackthorn nodded, still a bit dumbfounded.

"I came to give you some of my memories and ask a few questions."

"Right, questions first. Do I need paper to write them down?"

"Do you?"

Vin shrugged and moved around to a desk piled high with trinkets and newspapers and a thousand other fliers, pieces of mail, and Ore knows what. She came back with a pad of paper and a quill she'd plucked from behind her ear.

"I don't need the answer to this one immediately, but if you find anything, I need a letter sent to the temple of Vharos addressed to a girl named Ophie." The witch nodded, waiting on the question as I figured out how to phrase it. "What did the primordials leave behind in the library of Verinium?"

"Ersos is buried there—the original God of Death, granted by Vistra. You should remember that? Koros always worried his body could be used to . . . bring back the primordials. Wait, did you know that? I have a memory here of you and him standing in the tomb." I cocked my head to the side as her lips pursed. "Oh. You're wondering if you . . . Yes, they could use you the same to open the gate."

"Attacks against Verinium are increasing and someone is poking around primordial texts. Is there enough magic in his tomb to stop an attack from the fae or wake the primordials?"

"Now, or when the Pantheon was in power?"

"Now."

"Koros only floated the threat when Ilverleigh overplayed his hand. In those days, he also had you and Niany, but you needn't worry; your own power is—"

"I know what I am."

Vin looked at me, expression softened. "They could be looking for anything. There's a book down there about raising dragons and another about killing Death. Worry less about Verinium. The threats aren't new, and you're the only god left."

"You know that?"

"I know what you tell me, For. Next question. Clearly, you're traveling and I'm sure you have important things to do." She wiggled her eyebrows at me and I ignored it.

"Did Koros show you how he killed Ersos?"

"He did." Vin paused and the tension in the room turned into something tangible. "You want to know in case you're killed?"

We'd spent many nights together drinking across the taverns of Avilla, accidentally falling into a friendship spanning centuries because who else did we have? She knew as much as Henry and Leander, but there were parts of me she'd seen that they couldn't.

"Well, Koros kept his brother imprisoned until the ink dried on your father's bargain. Once he bled you on the battlefield and carved the sigils of Death into your arm, Ersos was killed by Niany. The godhood went immediately to you."

"There were minutes when it didn't have a vessel."

She nodded. "Yes, that is correct."

"And?"

"And there was a large rush of magic in those seconds that tore the veil open. A handful of the dead stepped through, but it was brief. You, however, are not like your uncle. Ersos believed himself to be a priest, honored by the godhood when the primordial mother of death had given it to him. You were not quite so honored and fucked the balance, Foriana."

I frowned, unsure what I was expected. Seven hundred years stood between my dominion of the dead and Ersos'.

"Primordial magic was about balance until the fae and Koros made it about power. No one knows what happens now."

"It was always about power."

Vin held up her hand. "It was not. I have the memories of the primordial mother stored well away from here in my grandmother's trunk. You and I know they left because of what the Pantheon became, and their downfall was written in scribe blood on Ore, just as your prophecy is, which still hasn't washed away."

Blackthorn stared and I turned my attention back to the witch, breezing past it. "The Scribes of Nurem lied," I said simply, shaking off the way Adler looked at me when he suggested they might have been fae.

"That would be a first." Vin clicked as she moved around the room and gathered several empty vials. "Koros wasn't the only one who picked you. The primordial mother somehow thought your sorry ass would be a better custodian for souls than Ersos. An interesting choice for someone known, now as the Godkiller—*Sit*."

I sat on a vacant stool as she came around the side of me with her box of vials.

"It won't take long." She placed a hand on my forehead. "Lean to the left—a little more. Good."

Vin lifted a vial to my ear as she whispered her Priminian incantation. My mouth filled with the peppery taste of memory as an opalescent film spilled out. I couldn't see it, but I'd watched her do it several times at Koros' request.

I tried to push as many recent memories to the forefront as I could. In a few minutes, she managed to fill eight vials and the spend only left me lightheaded.

Vinliana could entirely remove memories if she chose, but more often than not, she merely copied them for her records, which she'd submit anonymously to the history Masters in Verinium, Avilla, and Cascaade City. It was easier than writing down what happened—as the gods weren't known for their unerring objectivity.

"Thank you." I fixed my hair and moved closer to Blackthorn, near the door. Outside, snow began to dust the streets as the sky darkened.

"Anytime," Vin smiled as she stopped the last vial with a cork. "Hopefully, I'll see you sooner than another thirty years. Where are you off to? Some grand adventure—I hope—if you're all the way in Avilla."

I looked at my feet, unable to find a way to lie. "We're going to Belfiante."

Vinliana stopped, and my heart sank when hurt flashed through her eyes and weighed down her voice. "You said you'd never go back."

"Thank you for your help, Vin."

"Foriana." Her stern tone caught as I nudged Blackthorn toward the door. "Are you—"

"It's my choice, Vin. You'll . . . You'll see it in the memories."

The witch sprang across the room and crushed me into another hug, cupping my head into her shoulder as I squeezed my eyes, trying not to think of goodbye. When she watched the memory back, there wouldn't be any doubt in her mind.

38

[...] It's been a while since I've tried this, but I want the record. Whatever the histories are, whatever the masters write at the direction of the pantheon: Princess Foriana was torn open on the shores of Belfiante and the pain did not make her better.

WE ARRIVED IN THE town of Baneswood an hour after sunset, but it was impossible to tell by the gray skies and random snowfall. I'd only been here twice. Once by accident . . . and once with Malcolm and Koros, unaware of what awaited me in Belfiante.

Baneswood was the last populated town at the base of the Belfiante Mountains. There were small outcrops along the mountain paths and passes, but they were few and far between.

If I remembered, there were a few hot springs maintained by the Belfiante order and several old crumbling castle keeps, but those were everywhere across Miria—not unique to the range. There was also a town so isolated no one was sure if the residents were fae or mortal—including the residents.

We stabled the horses and crossed one side of Baneswood to the other on foot in under an hour. The town was known for being quiet, but tonight the air was charged with singing and shouting. People swarmed the streets as snow fell and banners waved. Holly sprigs hung over every door in bundles, tied with blue ribbon and handwritten salutations.

"Happy Solstice," I said aloud as Blackthorn nodded.

Solstice was one of those celebrations, dragged through time and space as if every mortal and immortal was duty-bound to celebrate the darkest night. Regardless of faith, Mirians believed no shadow existed on its own, that light would always come, and the sun would always rise again, even when it felt impossible.

I never forgot solstice. Not in prison, not south, and not in the Pantheon, where the weather never changed because Koros wouldn't allow it.

Solstice also meant we had three weeks to return to Tyrlas, and on every moon, I hoped Blackthorn's sister accepted the rescue. Henry made me a promise, but it wasn't him I worried about.

The inn near the center of the town had one small room left with a single, mercifully large bed. But now we crossed a line and I didn't know it mattered. Maybe I'd let the bond take me? What was the point in denying myself when we'd come this far? When I was already frayed and worn?

Orion Blackthorn stood at the window, watching the streets below where children threw snow at each other—and holly berries. I admired the breadth of his back and the muscles of his neck.

I tried not to think about the way his hands felt, or the warmth of his kiss alone, and again with Adler's, but it was useless. The room already smelled like the knight in every corner, and my god senses wouldn't let me escape it.

"Happy Solstice," he said.

"We've been traveling for weeks now."

"And you haven't killed me."

"I've come close." I sighed, sloughing my sword belt off onto the floor, before I tucked the bone knife under the mattress while he wasn't looking. "However, if you start talking about Mercian frogs ever again, I will make good on my promise."

"So you were listening?"

"No."

Blackthorn turned, watching me stand up. His eyes narrowed, but he didn't say anything as I cleared my throat.

"You brought it up every morning we spent crossing Reen."

"You have no regard for a good fact," he said, shaking his head. "Care to walk? I won't mention frogs."

"I smell like a horse."

"So do I, but I'm starving and what is Solstice without a pork pie?"

"Too right," I sighed and pulled my coat back on. Cold was dulled, but I still felt it here. I also felt the soreness from yet another day of riding and healing.

Though Blackthorn left his swords behind, I watched him strap a dagger to his belt. Perhaps I should have done the same, but it was hard to worry in a town like Baneswood, especially on Solstice night. No kingdom would waste its money sending a mercenary this far north in the dead of winter.

Large snowflakes fell between the lights strung over the streets. A few storefronts remained open and inviting as we wandered while people sang songs, repeating choruses and stories passed down for centuries about light, darkness, and the hope in the middle.

A vendor near the center square traded our coins for a hot pork pie. The flaky, buttery crust melted in my mouth and the inside was a decadent pork stew with rosemary. This was a hallmark of Solstice in the north—the other was a cookie that split as it baked, filled with a warm custard.

We hadn't found them yet, but I would.

Blackthorn hummed some song about snow and an obstinate candle as we walked aimlessly. Ghosts milled about, almost equal to the number of people moving to and fro.

We passed a makeshift altar of candles in front of a brimming tavern. Blackthorn asked, "How did you meet the witch?"

"I'd asked her to erase a memory." I sucked in a breath of the sharp winter air. I'd rather be in the tavern. "Vin took me out for a drink instead and let me cry on her bed. I probably shouldn't have trusted her, but I was desperate."

Too honest again . . . but did it matter?

"What did you want to erase?"

I pulled my hood further down. "Belfiante."

"I'm sorry."

"You don't know what happened."

Blackthorn shrugged, shifting his coat as we rounded a corner and came to stop. "I don't need to. I'd hate to run out of things to talk about on the way up the mountain and I'm not sure how much more I could hate a dead god."

"You never run out of things to talk about."

"I can always recycle the stories you weren't listening to. Xerxes's frogs for one—"

"Hey." I bumped him with my shoulder. "I'll listen if it's interesting."

"You will not."

I let myself smile and admired the way the snow looked as it fell. Then I spared a glance at him and the breath in my throat hitched. Snow clung to his hair. Under the lamplight, it almost looked gold.

"My mother let us give cookies to the gods on Solstice," Blackthorn said as we walked toward the empty main square. One table was pushed against the fountain, quickly getting covered in snow as it picked up. "One year, my sister cried the whole way there and back because our father had eaten a cookie she'd made just for Etta."

"Etta? The Goddess of Harvest? I thought you all had one god."

He laughed. "My sister is irrational, and autumn is her favorite season. She was six and wanted to skip spring and summer so she thought she'd ask one of the other gods."

I kicked a rock and watched it leave a trail in the snow as we approached the gods' cookie table. "She was onto something."

"Do you not like spring or summer?"

"Do you?"

"I asked you first."

I poked him as we approached the table. Quickly, I grabbed a cookie and shoved it in my mouth. The custard center was chewy and frozen, but still delicious.

"Summer is my favorite," Blackthorn said just before doing the same. "It's warm, everything is alive, and people are pleasant until midafternoon, unlike winter where everyone wakes up as sad as when they fell asleep."

Three other people joined us around the table, eating cookies and giggling at passing jokes. It was a tradition among the adults because the cookies needed to be gone by morning or it meant the gods had forgotten a child's wish.

"Summer has too many bugs." I plucked one more cookie from the pile before I stepped back. Two other locals hummed in agreement with me, much to Blackthorn's disdain. "And spring is too unpredictable."

"And wet," interjected a woman bundled in raccoon fur, eating two sugared cookies like a sandwich.

"So you prefer cold and dark?"

"That isn't what I said."

"It is."

The knight stuffed two more cookies in his pocket before holding out his arm for me. Snow fell faster now, and I hardly saw the end of the street as we walked in comfortable quiet, taking our time.

Solstice never changed; it was a little respite in the middle of the dark until Blackthorn stopped walking and dragged me with him.

The snow was thick now and his hair was soaked through. I was sure mine wasn't better. But his fingers tilted up my chin and his lips met mine, warm and patient.

It was a kiss unlike what we'd shared before. It was easy and calm as my hood fell back and his hand moved to the back of my neck. It wasn't the kiss of desperate lovers, but precious ones.

When we finally parted, he stared at me dazed and my heart lurched. Warning tickled my back like melting ice.

"I want you, Raven. I want to show you how badly I need you, without all of this—as if we were nothing more than two people." His hands took mine. I blinked away snow, and pressure built behind my eyes. "What does it take? I don't have a few hundred years, only—"

"Stop," I rasped. "I want you, but it's . . . Can we go back?"

I tore myself away and started toward the inn.

"You've loved mortals before—"

That was the wrong thing to say. *Love.*

I whipped around, standing on the step, which put us nearly at eye level. Memories surged and froze my heart to protect it as magic whirred and pulsed.

"Yes. I have—and you do not understand where it got me, Orion. I am not a woman, not a mortal, but a god. What are you?"

I stalked to our room and curled up by the fire, wondering why I couldn't let myself have him if I was just going to die. Everyone could survive losing me, but the same couldn't be said when I was the one who lost. My words to Tyrlas were true: Miria wouldn't survive me a second time without a Pantheon.

Orion Blackthorn did me the service of waiting somewhere else while the words settled in the back of my head and dispersed into something that hurt less. He didn't open the door until my hair was nearly dry.

"I'm sorry," I whispered and his brief silence met it.

"What was it something I said?"

"Sure."

"Right."

There wasn't a better way to say the whole universe conspired against me and I was tired of denying it, because days from now I'd asked him to kill me.

"Raven?" His voice was gentle as he sat beside me, his even presence filling the room in a way that was difficult to bear when he should have been angry.

This was the very feeling and exposure I denied myself. I never kissed my soul bound the first time because I knew it was the first latch—I'd been warned.

Now, I was too confident in my denial: Looking at him felt like my life falling apart and coming together all at once. A piece of my soul laced through his in a way that couldn't be undone.

Every kiss, every touch, every time our eyes met caught my breath and rivaled the godhood in my chest because this was a different kind of magic.

"I'm sorry for what I said," he started, wringing his hands. "After last night—"

"I want a hundred more nights like last night and a thousand more with you, but all of this changes when I'm restored and I do not want to hurt you."

I angled toward him, taking his hands in mine, soul aching for this moment to mean something as I wrestled with reason. I would be the monster who asked him to put my father's knife between my ribs and twist.

"You cannot hurt me."

"I've hurt many people and let down entire kingdoms. I'd blow apart the realm if something happened to anyone I care about."

"Like you'd done for Leander?"

"Worse," I whispered and stared at our clasped hands wishing I could feel his skin on mine without the barrier of silk. "I had half of my godhood when I killed the Scribes of Nurem." Before he said anything, I wasn't ready to deny; more words tumbled out. "I have something I wanted to give you."

The words and thought choked me, but I couldn't tell the truth, not the whole one—not tonight. That would hurt more than anything else.

I crossed the room and took the white dagger from the mattress. It hummed, emitting a small amount of heat, but not enough to scorch. Then I sat by the fire again and did my best to smile through the truth.

"This is my father's knife," I said. He stared at it, awed, running his hand over the opalescent blade soaked and powered with the blood of a hundred gods. "It's made from the bones of Ersos. Its name is *Everund* and I want you to have it."

Orion's eyes lifted to mine, hand frozen on the jeweled handle. "Why are you giving this to me? This looks like the knife they used to hurt you in the dungeon."

"I want you to have it."

I nudged the blade toward him. Warily, he wrapped his fingers around the hilt and the room quieted.

"There's magic in it," he breathed, amber eyes wide as he inspected the pure, unscathed bone-white of it, and the silver hilt forged by a long-dead Forian jeweler just for Koros—the King of Gods.

"Useless magic, unless the gods return." Grief knotted in the back of my throat. "This was the blade my father used to kill my sister and I used to kill him. The bone blade retains a whisper of their magic until it's destroyed by dragon fire."

It was inlaid with rubies, peridots, and onyx stones to remind him of the daughters he'd once loved equally. In the shifter's hands, it looked more like a toy than a weapon that ended the Pantheon.

Orion stared, holding it back out to me. "I cannot accept this."

I pushed it back, biting my lip. "I have no use for it. Please. It's a thank you for your friendship."

"Friendship?" He tilted his chin, and there was an edge of warning in his voice I hadn't heard before. "Do you beg your friends to come for you?"

I blinked. "Friendship was the wrong word."

"And the right one?"

"One you'll regret."

If he asked why, I didn't hear. I scrambled to my feet and dove into the bed, leaving him at the fireplace holding the knife and his worry.

Friendship was the word I could swallow: *Soul bound* was the one we'd both regret.

Year 660, The Pantheon
Raven is 110

"WE SHOULD BE GOING," Malcolm said from across the room.

I didn't turn as I adjusted the bracelets on my wrist, trying to keep my composure cool as I stared at the black magic crawling up my arms like they'd been dipped in a cauldron of ink or bruised beyond recognition. Nearly one hundred years and it still felt new—inhuman.

"Foriana," he said gently. The patter of his slippered feet on the smooth stone came closer, then he stopped and dragged the knuckle of his finger down my open back, along the exposed ridge of my spine. I shivered. "We need to go or your father will be cross."

"He's not my father," I muttered, and even as the words left my lips, they didn't feel true. Koros used and betrayed me just as my own father had. They were no different, and with so much *distance between who I am now and who I was, I'd long forgotten the man who sired me.*

I turned to Malcolm—my husband and the god of war. He was beautiful, a born god with all the features separating us from man. Far different from the perfection of fae, he retained his scars from battles won and lost.

Malcolm rubbed my cheek with his thumb and kissed my forehead. "You're too hard on yourself, Princess."

His nose was a little jolted to the side. Busted by a fist that sailed into it years ago when he and Maxentius got into a fight. His mid-length, nearly white hair had been curled at the leisure of his attendants.

A pang of jealousy brushed against my ribs because I'm sure he let them touch more than his hair.

I lifted my hand and began to pull off my glove, but Malcolm caught my wrist.

"Foriana."

My voice wavered as my gaze lifted. "Let me touch your hair, Mal. Please."

He sighed, his grip loosened as he slipped the silk glove off, exposing my bruised arm nearly to my elbow. It wasn't beautiful. Mottled blue and purple swirled into black like a cadaver left too long in the sun.

With his hand still clasped around my wrist, my fingertips met the silvery strands. His hair felt like silk and the curls sprang back when I tugged. I rolled one between my thumb and forefinger, feeling each strand as he breathed.

The magic of death was impossible, uncontrollable. That's why Ersos long gave up on this world, but I wouldn't.

Seconds passed—maybe a minute—as I indulged in every part of Malcolm I could: the rise and fall of his breath through the vest he wore, the leather earring hanging from his ear, and the shape of his hip through his thin satin pants.

Then he stepped back, swaying on his feet as he fought to catch his breath.

39

After Belfiante, I killed my soul bound, sabotaged every marriage after, and tried to obliterate my closest friendships because life was easier alone until Leander showed me what it meant to be loved.

Even in the darkest trenches of my memory, I never stopped longing to be loved, but fear hardened my heart. Did Henry soften it again? Was one kiss, one touch, and three long weeks enough to break me? I woke up knowing I wanted Orion Blackthorn to love me.

His arm was draped over my chest, our legs tangled between each other, and I couldn't bring myself to push him away. My thoughts quieted because he was here. Could he love me like Leander? Maybe he could fuck me like Malcolm?

I wouldn't live to find out. My chest caved as his breath curled against the nape of my neck. The journey to Belfiante started the moment my feet hit the floor.

Soul bound.

Orion would never know because I wouldn't tell him. How horrible would it be to live knowing a part of you died?

"Raven?" Blackthorn's voice was gravelly with sleep as his hold on me tightened. "You're enjoying this."

"I am not." I tried to wriggle away and ended up turning over, where my eyes caught his in the palest morning light and my chest twinged.

I wanted him to kiss me, but the dread of what awaited set in, and I got up instead. Within the hour, we'd already crossed through Baneswood. The table of cookies was nothing more than crumbs—no child's prayer would go unanswered.

"Do you know where we're going?" Blackthorn finally asked as the sun tipped over the scarce mountain tree line after a few quiet hours. Even with my godhood, two coats, and two pairs of wool socks, I shivered against the biting, frigid air.

Without a word, I waved my arm and the spectral outline of a ghostly woman appeared to him that I'd been watching this entire time.

A map was useless in these mountains.

"Who is that?"

"I think her name is Mina." The middle-aged woman dressed in an old style of embroidered cotton robes scrambled down a winding path between two rock walls. "She was a guide a century ago and died somewhere near the mirror ponds."

"When did you have time to speak to her?"

I shrugged. "Asked around last night while you were talking to the stable boy."

"You trust her?"

The ghost's head whipped around, her braid nearly smacking her face as she leveled a glare at the knight.

"With my life." I smiled, and Mina returned to leading as I dropped the veil and pulled out a map, holding it toward Blackthorn. "I'm also watching this map. Three days by my estimation. Four if it snows."

"And getting back?"

"I'll worry about our return."

The higher we climbed, the sharper the wind became until we descended into the first mountain valley around a frozen lake. We stopped only briefly to catch our breath and find relief.

We kept going until the sun dipped well below the outline of the mountain as we reached the third lake. An old, crumbling keep stood watch over it, which seemed as good a place to stop as any.

I dismissed Mina as the sky turned a deep shade of blue and stars crowded out the single moon climbing over the horizon.

The keep's wooden structures and fixtures were long gone, but the stone walls were enough to hold in some warmth from the fire Blackthorn started. My godhood still hadn't entirely settled and continued to churn like a tide. Moments I'd be dizzy, others warm, but most of this journey was exhaustion.

I curled up on the floor, in a space that was nearly free of snow, and fatigue carried me to inconstant sleep until a loud screech echoed through the valley and I snapped awake.

Few things lived in these mountains except for goats, deer, and some shy mountain wolves. Once the dragons fell, nothing in Miria was the same, and that applied doubly to the mountains.

Was Blackthorn missing? I looked over the fire and he wasn't there. Footsteps trailed out of the keep, which seemed odd.

Warily, I took a sword and ducked outside, adhering to the shadows. My boots crunched and my breath fogged—those were the only noises in the eerie quiet of night. I scanned the empty tundra. Wolf tracks went toward the pine forest in the distance. What if he were hurt? No, he couldn't be. I needed him.

Something moved. I spun, sword outstretched and knees bent, poised to use it, praying it wasn't another scavenger.

Nothing but moon shadows and snow.

Crunch.

I twisted again, peering at the lake. *Nothing.* I sniffed the air and caught the faint smell of Blackthorn, then something else, something more like carrion or something dead. Something—

The wind blew out of me as I flew through the air, the cracking sound of my ribs echoed like a strike. I landed face down in the snow, gasping and clawing at ice as I scrambled to my feet. The sword had flown out of my hand.

I pushed up; ice cut my knees. The cuts on my chest and arm tore open again and every wheezing inhale came with acute pain. I couldn't see anything around as I reached for my glove.

Crunch. Another step.

I turned slowly, wide-eyed. A massive black mountain direwolf stared, growling. Its eyes glowed yellow. Of course, it was enchanted.

Not enchanted with power—enchanted to harm and protect the little magic resting below.

It lunged. I scrambled back, tripping over a hunk of ice, fumbling backward on my hands in true, honest fear.

I ran the moment I could, but the heavy, pounding steps of the direwolf gained faster than I could sprint. I tripped again on the uneven ground and cursed, skidding across ice as the beast closed in, jaw snapping as spittle struck my face and it growled.

Once more, blinding pain seared through me as teeth crunched through bone before I found my legs. All feeling drained as I screamed and flailed against the beast, crying and trying to pry out what was left of my arm from its jaws, but its grip was unflinching.

Pain was white and death was blue.

I tried to purge the magic I could, to force it into the wolf, but it didn't budge until I howled, making one final push that forced the magic black. Finally, it let go with a snarl and I fell to the ground gasping for relief as the surrounding snow turned red and steamed where I tried to push myself up. A small sapling poked through the crust of ice and I cursed.

Another growl thundered and my gut sank as a flurry of white soared into the direwolf.

A yelp, a scream, and then the sound of gnashing teeth followed crying out and whimpering I couldn't track as pain raged. I couldn't breathe, couldn't move.

By the fucking moons did I wish I wore the cuffs because I would've been unconscious by now, but the god part of me insisted on healing, which was as bad as reliving every heated moment of pain.

There was a sudden silence as I tried to roll over, but a set of familiar arms carried me back to the keep. Blackthorn cursed over and over again as I stared at the fire, unable to speak because everything was pain and my arm was entirely mangled.

I knew what it looked like. I didn't need to look. The skin was shredded and my bones were crushed in two places. I was in bad fucking shape. He stroked my hair behind my ear as I tried to find an angle to breathe that wasn't miserable.

The only good news was my arm remained attached, barely bleeding and I could move my fingers as long as I screamed. Even for a god, a broken bone took time to heal and in an hour, the pain would turn to agony as my bones fixed themselves.

"Sit up." Fear cracked in his voice and I barely registered how gently he touched me. "I need to set it so it heals."

"You can't," I croaked. I tried to push myself up and my head swam, stuffed with pain like cotton, as my stomach churned. *My gloves.*

My elbow twitched and the throbbing pain rolled through me again, hot and white. I couldn't keep it in. I retched near the fire, emptying everything we'd eaten as I strained to catch my breath. Sweat beaded on my forehead; I wasn't moving.

Blackthorn's arm wound around my middle, hauling me to his chest. Orion moved my hair again and kissed my neck too tenderly. I squeezed my eyes and moaned as he tried again to adjust me on his lap.

"You're safe, Raven. I just need you to stay awake. Please."

"I told you to let me get eaten."

"And I said I wouldn't allow it." The pain turned to delirium. My ribs healed first, swelling against my lungs. "Lean back and let me help. Please, I've done this before."

Tendons and muscles clawed their way back together, raw skin tried to heal around the bite of the wolf, but the enchantment blocked it.

I leaned into him, forehead resting in the crook of his neck as he took my arm in his hand. I tried not to scream as the shattered bone ground against itself.

I'd felt pain before, but it had been years since I stayed conscious through pain like this.

"I have to splint it."

My response was a choking sound as I readjusted on his lap, trying to brace myself and not move my arm, but then his fingers pinched the tip of my glove and I stiffened, drawing back my arm with a yelp as a fresh fucking wave of pain came.

"Raven, it's torn apart. You need to take it off."

Something squeezed my chest and I couldn't breathe. It wasn't pain, but something deeper. "I can't. I can't let you—"

"Why?"

"I'll kill you."

"You won't."

"You don't know that." I sobbed now as he shifted my arm. The idea of coming this far just to watch him die gutted me—his beautiful face rotted from the inside out because that's what my touch did.

"I do."

"You fucking don't." I gathered my strength and pushed back from his broad chest with my shoulder. I couldn't see. "Hand me the splint. I'll—"

"No." His arm was a vise as it tightened on my waist. "Your glove was already torn. You—"

"No—no, no, no." It was, and I panicked. Blinking away wetness and delirium as my good hand flew to his jaw, holding him in place to give myself a slipping memory. The onslaught of grief numbed the pain for a small second. "Stay with me."

"I'm not going anywhere," he whispered, placing his hand over mine before sliding both to my lap. "I don't feel anything."

The knot in my throat choked me as I shook my head. "You will—"

"I don't."

Orion reached for my hand again and I winced as I snatched it back, biting down a cry.

"*Raven.*" He frowned; it stilted his voice. "I will risk this for you."

He took my mangled arm again and I didn't fight—I watched his life end here. Death for me was an inevitability, but this moment would break me.

Orion tugged my glove off in a sweeping motion, taking all the frayed silk dried with it.

I yelped, but my tolerance for the pain was expanding with every ticking moment so I took in every detail of his face. I could handle pain; I wasn't fucking ready for loss.

He cradled my arm, touching my black and blue fingers with his as I held my breath. An eternity stretched through seconds as he placed the splint and straightened my arm, shifting bones like blades. Tears welled in my eyes . . . from shock.

When he tied the last strip of his torn shirt around my arm, I gave up. His final moments wouldn't be me fighting this—fighting him.

"I-I wanted to love you," I whispered. "I wanted—"

"How long do I have?" he murmured against my hair. Any moment now his voice would falter and his heart would stop. If it was enough, he'd even turn to ash.

"A minute," I choked. "Maybe less."

"It's been five."

"You're bad at counting."

Another beat . . . and another as wind whistled through the gaping stones.

"Raven, I feel fine."

"That's impossible."

I pushed off of him, cradling my now stable, ungloved arm. I stared and waited, squinting as if anything might change.

Orion's amber eyes glimmered in the firelight. The scars on his face remained. There wasn't a single part of him I didn't find beautiful, but that meant nothing. It was only an ill-timed thread of fate. It had to be.

Every heartbeat, every touch of him was mortal through and through. Shifters were only a degree stronger than humans, but they all rotted out the same when they touched my hand. I'd seen it too many times.

I had no control. My touch sickens fae and gods alike. With the power I had now, it could kill them too—even Malcolm and Koros winced.

Soul bound.

No. No it couldn't be. I tugged my other glove off with my teeth and lifted my mottled hand to his cheek, eyes swollen with tears as my exposed fingers grazed the stubble of his face and trailed the curve of his jaw.

Orion Blackthorn remained, watching carefully as I palmed his chest. When his eyes didn't so much as waver, my hand dropped. There was no flash of magic, no grimace at the sour taste of death. Nothing but his steady amber gaze and steadier heartbeat.

"How?"

"Not a single idea." He breathed, running a hand through his blond hair. "You need to sleep. Do you mind if I—"

"No." I swallowed hard, falling back on my knees. Too much raced through my head and mixed with the abject pain of healing. I wanted to touch his face all night and I didn't look away as his body stretched and transformed into the white wolf. Nor did I flinch as he padded toward me and lay down. I was grateful and shocked as I curled into his warm fur and wept.

In seven hundred years, I'd only ever touched another's face to release them to the Black.

40

I woke up panicked, thrashing as the sun came through the gaping cracks in the wall. My arm remained broken and I winced as I sat up. The fire roared and Blackthorn sat across from it, hands held together—eyes on me—alive.

Orion Blackthorn touched my hand and he was *alive*.

Sometimes relief and worry could be the same thing. Was this what I'd destroyed all those years ago?

"You look like you've seen a ghost."

The sky was already orange and there wasn't a cloud in sight. We needed to get moving, but I wanted to stay here just a little fucking longer.

"Why did you leave?"

Orion stared at the licking flames. "It had been weeks since I hunted—a small drawback of being a wolf I didn't want to bother you with."

"I know shifters hunt," I grumbled. "You could have told me."

"I'll tell you next time."

"Good."

"How's your arm?"

"Better." I pulled my sleeve up and held up my arm, turning it over as much as I could within the splint. The bite marks remained, but the bones were sore and mending. "The bone will heal in a few days."

"And your fingers?"

"They work." I demonstrated, opening and closing them over my palm, but his eyes didn't leave mine. "And you haven't rotted."

"I haven't."

"Even the fae and gods rot if I touch them. Only elves didn't."

"Perhaps I'm an elf."

"You wouldn't survive a spar with an elven child."

"Have some respect, Lady Raven. I'm a knight of the Tyrlian court." Orion rose to his feet and secured his sword. How was he so unaffected?

My heart sank as I followed his lead and waved my arm around, dragging down the veil. "Mina!" I shouted and the visage of our guide appeared. "Tren da'leer, ren Mina."

She flashed a smile and led us from the keep across the frozen lake. The wolf was dead, its body heaped a ways off from where my spray of blood still coated the snow. A willow began to sprout where the largest puddle was.

Blackthorn leaned over. "What did you say?"

"'Lead the way, Lady Mina,' in Priminian."

"Ah. Is she a lady?"

"I don't know. I'd rather not insult her by assuming less."

The spectral woman turned around at the mention of her name but quickly returned to guiding us up the next mountain pass. Thankfully, the threat of snow seemed nonexistent.

We journeyed in largely comfortable silence just as we'd done yesterday, but today, every step emboldened the pain in my arm as the bone rebuilt, grinding like a hundred shards and slivers as it rearranged below my skin, under the fabric of another set of gloves.

The deeper we ascended into the heart of the range, the higher the snow was until we trudged through powder well above my knees.

"Have you been to a hot spring?" Blackthorn asked suddenly as the pass began angling down. We navigated a craggy maze between two high walls where mountains met.

"I'm seven hundred and eighty-four, of course I've been to a hot spring. Why?"

"The caves are coming up—once we're through the next valley—I've heard the springs have healing properties." The knight glanced at my arm, which I'd been stiffly holding out in front of me for an hour now, hoping it would stop throbbing. "Perhaps it'd be worth it."

"How do you know about those?"

"Vharos. Read it in a pamphlet."

There wasn't much to consider. The caves would be warmer than the open air. I tugged at the veil so Blackthorn saw the blue-hued form of Mira.

"Do you know where the Belfiante cave springs are?" I asked in Priminian.

Her face lit up as she nodded enthusiastically. *"Of course."*

"Can we get there before sunset?" The sun above had already neared the peak of the mountains. We had only a few hours of daylight left.

"If you don't mind walking faster."

"I'll see what I can do. Lead us."

"I'll take you to my favorite one. It will help your arm."

I started walking faster; Blackthorn sped up his pace to match mine and leaned too close, his sword knocking my calf.

"What did she say?"

"She's taking us to her favorite spring, but we have to walk faster."

When a ghost wanted to walk faster, I knew better than to agree.

Their spectral form wasn't restrained the way our physical forms were. Mina didn't have to scramble up rocks and scrape her knees, or worry about slipping on ice. She also didn't feel the cold, nor did she have to kick through powder with every damn step.

After an hour, the aching in my legs became so visceral I nearly forgot about my arm. By the time we crossed the next basin and started through the ridge, I'd lost most of the feeling in my body.

And I pushed through until Mina finally led us through a narrow crevice, descending into the heart of the mountain. Rock sheets twisted above reminiscent of cathedral ceilings, but we weren't quite in a cave.

The air changed as we turned a corner. It was iron and pine and—beef? I was delirious.

Mina took a final left, then we stumbled into a wide space lit with gas lamps, but there wasn't a building in sight. Orion and I stopped in the orange glow. Terror crept into my gut and settled like a rock as my other hand wrapped around the hilt of my sword.

"Mina, what is this?"

She paused at what appeared to be a single heavy wooden door half the size of the knight. The ghost was about to knock when she remembered herself; her shoulders sagged as she gave me a forlorn smile.

"This is the order of Belfiante. They keep the springs and they will keep you safe."

"Of course," I whispered in the common tongue and Blackthorn looked at me, eyes wide. "The Order of Belfiante is buried in the caves. They're the keepers of the springs and the cattle of the basins."

"Have you been here before?"

"No!" I laughed, excitement bubbling up over the flash of fear. "Isn't it incredible?"

I knocked on the door. Gasps rang through interior with a hush. A moment later, it opened with the smallest crack.

Gold eyes and long lashes peeked through. Whoever it was wore the thick blue robes of a Mirian priestess with a yellow rope. Their order was beholden to Fortune. "Has Death found us again?" she whispered, followed by another chorus of hushing from within.

"My friend and I mean no harm." I bowed my head and remained prostrate for several seconds, ignoring the way Orion shifted behind me. "We are passing through. An old friend led us here."

"You haven't come to reap?"

Though I saw only a sliver of her face, the priestess was young—barely an adult. Terrified eyes blinked at me.

"I have not come for anything but shelter."

Another, much older, priestess shoved the girl aside and opened the door wide, stepping around her into the cold. The smell of beef and vegetables wafted from within, and my stomach grumbled.

"Your Majesty, Foriana." The priestess bowed; graying brown hair fell over her shoulder. Her face relaxed as she straightened and glimpsed my splinted arm. "Ignore the frightened youths. For many, this is their first winter in the caves. We haven't heard a knock in weeks and they're scaring themselves with stories of witches, minotaurs, and other frightening things."

"I understand, sister. May they not lose their fear; it keeps us humble."

"It does, it does," she agreed. Her gaze raked over Blackthorn, whose hand had drifted to his hilt and gaze remained on the ground. "You've returned to Belfiante as the prophecy says? The

Scribes of Nurem might be gone, but their blood remains. We hear it sing when Ore is full."

"Not for much longer," I said and discomfort grated my throat. The way she said it made it sound inevitable and I wouldn't accept it. Their prophecy was wrong and tomorrow would be the day Death died for Miria and nothing took her place.

"Thank the gods and moons." The priestess crossed herself, shoulder to shoulder, and kissed her thumb. "Bria will take you to the spring. Stay as long as you need. We are blessed to be visited by Death, no matter how brief."

Magic was extinct in Miria, with the exception of small pockets like this that brushed the core of the earth and remained undisturbed by mortals and immortals alike.

Fortune, my sister, made it her mission to protect them. In any given mountain range, there was some order of priests or priestesses, all part of the larger Healer's Consortium, keeping livestock and protecting the hearts where the last slivers of magic lived—too small to do any more than sustain the life on these mountains. The orders took it upon themselves to protect it.

A minute passed in silence and then another until the priestess named Bria stepped out, her eyes trained on the ground and several blankets stacked in her arms.

She was the same girl who'd cracked open the door and looked oddly like Ophie—same height, same blonde hair braided back and round face with gold eyes—but with every opposite mannerism.

"Follow me," she mumbled.

We did as instructed and followed her through a descending corridor of icy, gray rock, past several more lampposts until she gestured at a similar too-small wooden door.

"This is the *Everund* spring."

Orion and I exchanged a glance at the name of my father's dagger. Bria shoved the pile of towels, kindling, and blankets into my arms with little warning.

"You'll follow the walls. It isn't far back."

"Thank you," I said, but she'd already disappeared.

Both of us had to crouch to get through the short wooden door, but the cave opened up immediately.

The room glowed a faint shade of orange, not from lamps but from pieces of iridescent salt placed around, shedding warm light of their own. It wasn't bright, but it was enough to see each other and the other end of the room where the spring was.

"I don't think a wolf will attack you here," Orion said, approaching the water's edge. His voice broke the silence, competing with the steady drip of water.

Around the corner, a roaring fireplace cast shadows across the opposite rock wall. Beside it was a pile of logs, soup, and bread only paces from the pool of steaming water.

I dropped the blankets and stood beside him. He looked up and I followed his gaze to the churning gray sky above as dusk turned to night.

"Explains the fire." Snowflakes eddied around, falling faster and faster as a storm descended. The flakes melted in the rising steam before they touched the surface of the water. "Should we eat or—"

Blackthorn's shirt was already half off and I forgot about everything at stake, the pain in my arm, and the question I had to ask.

I could enjoy this . . . A last day to add to the other lasts and goodbyes of the past weeks. If I didn't want to, there was no part of him I had to leave unturned, untouched, unkissed.

"Raven?"

I blinked and pushed my lips into a smile as I peeled off my layers with the only hand that worked. It was painstaking when I reached my base layers.

Wordlessly, Blackthorn grabbed the hem of my shirt and peeled it off. Then he unbuttoned my pants and slid them past my hips, thighs, and knees, lingering a moment too long before he jumped into the water with a splash. I hesitated.

The faint sensation of cold prickled my skin. The last piece to discard was my gloves. I yanked them tighter before slipping into the water. There, I closed my eyes, sinking until my toes touched the bottom. I held my arms out, floating for just a moment in the warmth and stillness.

Every muscle in my body screamed after two days of hiking, but feeling this still felt like a gift before I gave up everything. I tilted my head back and smiled, drifting snowflakes tickling my face.

The contrast was mesmerizing as they swirled only to melt in the rising heat.

"You look like a goddess," Blackthorn said, reminding me he was there. His voice strained, as if he were holding back.

"Funny."

I spun in the water, prying my braid apart. Curls spread like seaweed on the surface and I finally ventured to look at him. In the low light and sheen of spring water, he could have been mistaken for Leo, the god of the sea.

Sadness crawled through my thoughts as I admired him. He should remember me like this—before the godhood took it all away and more, before I begged him to lodge the knife in my chest. I wanted Orion to remember me naked, with snow in my hair, floating in a hot spring, waiting for him. Not splayed out and broken on the eternal shore of Belfiante.

"Touch me," he said, floating near the wall. His gaze remained on mine, lips parted. I swam closer and took his chin in my fingertips as his lips thinned with a knowing frown. Large hands covered mine, teasing the fabric of my gloves. "Not like that, Raven."

"I could still hurt you," I whispered, recoiling.

"I don't care."

He took my hand in his and plucked the silk from my fingertips, gingerly pulling it off to expose the bruised black of my hands. When both were discarded to float on the water, he pressed my bare fingers to his chin as I held my breath.

"See?" he said. "I'm fine."

My breath caught as I massaged the stubble of his jaw. It was rough against my own fingers, not snagging on fabric. I traced the column of his neck and the ridge along his shoulder where muscle met bone, then I ran my fingers over the scars and through the hair on his chest as I choked up.

He pressed his hand over mine and threaded his fingers between them . I couldn't breathe. All my life I'd been without this touch. Never could I touch Leander like this—or Henry, or Malcolm.

The price was too steep. Thick emotion welled into something hard in my chest, but before it coalesced, I pulled his lips to mine and kissed him with every intention I'd held onto. I was too dead to care about the bond.

It wouldn't snap into place because it needed magic from both of us both and he had nothing to give. I'd die with my heart full if it felt like this.

Orion's hands tangled in my hair as he lifted me in the water and kissed my neck. I shivered at the exposure, nails gripping his shoulder, uninhibited.

My head rolled back and snow gathered on my lashes as he kissed the space above my breasts where my cuts remained, then again as he took my nipple in his mouth with a throaty groan.

Orion's hips rolled and the hardness of him pressed against my thigh and—*snap*. My eyes flew open and need superseded every pain ricocheting through my body. Every moment, every glance, every traded touch came crashing down.

I needed him in every way.

Soul bound. With my legs wrapped around his waist, he felt endless and impossible; this was the prison I'd denied.

We thrashed in the water and I clawed to feel every part of him in my hands because never had I touched a man so intimately. Then I felt his cock between my legs and took it in my palm, ready to worship him like the god I wished he was. But he stopped and tilted my chin.

"You're sure? Because I won't—"

I squeezed him as I pressed his head to my cunt where I ached for him in a way that shook every belief I'd ever held.

"I won't stop either."

In a whirl of water and skin, my back was against the wall of the cave, his hands held my hips in place, and I held him, relishing in something I'd spent my life waiting to feel.

He kissed me fiercely, keeping his promise. There was no teasing, no play. He brought his cock to my cunt and pushed in slowly, filling me with him. I'd had a sex a thousand times, but this was more.

I didn't look away. I didn't close my eyes, even as my vision blurred with every thrust. Water churned and his pace quickened, forehead pressed to mine as we breathed in tandem, racing a release that burned me from within as the tether between our souls became unbreakable.

Every thrust brought me closer to an ecstasy I'd never dreamed of, and when it finally struck, my entire body convulsed and I was floating. A final snap locked into place as he spilled into me and time stopped with my lips on his.

"Gods," he breathed. "Fuck."

I clenched around him, grinding my hips just to hear him moan again. That was my intention anyway, but his cock felt like nothing else and I rode him until my nails bruised his skin.

My mind cleared and I forgot that anything existed outside of us. For a moment, it was only me, clenched around the soul bound man Fate had tied me to.

Soul bound.

My heart clenched and he drew back, stroking hair behind my ear as his amber gaze pinned me.

If we were two gods, he'd be able to walk through my thoughts as I could walk through his. And if we fully accepted it with a mutual sacrifice of magic, binding us in life and death, we'd share the other's magic. We'd be two souls entwined, instead of me reaching for him every second his skin wasn't on mine.

"We should eat," he said. Did he sense something shifted?

"We should."

Orion helped me out of the pool and into a blanket before the crackling fire as snow continued to drift, heavier than when we'd arrived. Without desire filling every corner of my brain, the throbbing pain in my arm returned, but it was nothing next to the twisting pain in my chest as reality ebbed back.

Maybe I should tell him. If anything, just to hear the words on his lips.

Soul bound.

We ate in comfortable silence and my thoughts trailed. What if I didn't die tomorrow and I took all of my power?

With it, I could swallow all of Miria and force it into my vision of what a world could be—what Leander and I had dreamed of. Maybe Orion Blackthorn could stop me?

No.

I knew Queen Foriana and she would be no better than her father. I'd come too far, gotten too close, done too much: I ended tomorrow.

Wanting to be loved didn't supersede anything. I'd loved enough for lifetimes . . . It would be selfish to stay and love him too.

Spring water dripped and the fire crackled as we set down empty bowls. I crossed the cave and dressed slowly, twisting one button and then another.

I secured my pants as his voice echoed through the chamber: "What happened in Belfiante?"

"What happened in Belfiante?" I repeated, freezing in place, back to him still but running out of room to evade his questions. "Koros and Malcolm dulled their best weapon on the mirror pond shores because only she could destroy them."

My hands fell to my sides and I still didn't turn. "My husband held me down while my father cut out half my godhood with *Everund.*"

He swallowed. "Half?"

Half is what I was now. Half is all I was for five hundred years because whole was too much for them to fathom; Koros was my creator and my destroyer.

I walked toward Orion, stopping before I was within his reach.

"What did you do?"

"I served my king and father," I said, stiff and mechanical as I'd said in court and to anyone who fucking asked. "I did what was expected of me."

"What soldier hasn't done awful things for their Crown?" he said softly, but it was too soft. Mortals couldn't fathom the kind of destruction gods wrought . . . not anymore.

I sank to the ground and curled in on myself. "You saw it in Linvia—my gift—it works like lightning and spreads the same. My gift was like Koros's and Niany's. It was granted by the primordials and not made for a realm this weak. Miria, around 700, faced the first offensive in a war with a fae court and my father wanted to send a message."

I stopped talking because I hadn't said it out loud in decades. This was worse than Nurem and one of the truths that kept me in libraries, scrubbing evidence and removing myself from the narrative of Miria.

"What happened?"

The knight moved closer, leaning forward, but still not close enough to touch. No matter what I said next, he'd stay. Orion looked at me with the tenderness that made men irrational. Tenderness I always fell in love with, and tenderness that carried me to destruction. If I were stone, their love was flint.

"My first marriage was to Malcolm, the God of War, and I loved him. I trusted him, and he wanted me on the battlefield at his side so I agreed.

"Koros and Malcolm spent the week cornering the fae reserve into one of the southern swamps with our wyvern cavalry. The day came. Malcolm removed my gloves and told me to lead the charge, knowing a strike of my steel against theirs would kill anyone who dared to spar. What I didn't realize was that eight hundred men between our armies stood in ankle-high water and he'd chosen to test my power.

"I brought my sword down on a fae general and blue light struck the water. Both armies fell, rotting to ash in the water and reeds. The only survivors were those who moved fast enough as I reeled it back, but it was too late.

"I was mortified. Koros and Malcolm were mortified. They thought I'd plow through the front line, not end the battle in one fucking swing.

"A week later, we traveled to Belfiante. Malcolm promised it was a visit to honor the primordials. Instead, he and Koros tore me apart, heart and soul."

Blackthorn's voice was a low rumble—too calm. "He was your husband and he stood by?"

"The godhood dulls emotion to make room for reason. Three hundred years later, I killed him with my sister's blade and fashioned my own knife from his bones."

"Good," Blackthorn breathed as he searched my face for something.

Remembering was suffocating. Time and revenge couldn't fix a pain like that.

Blackthorn's lips found mine, but his kiss was too soft, too tender for everything I held back. This time, I couldn't swallow it. I coughed and spluttered on the tears and the swelling grief for a truth I couldn't hold any longer.

"We don't have to—"

I shook my head and leaned away, drawing my knees to my chest, careful not to look at him. If that truth didn't phase him, this one would.

"I'm not returning to Tyrlas."

"What?" His voice rose with every word. "And break your promise? Get my sister killed? You *swore.*"

I shook my head, loose strands of hair sticking to my face. "No."

"No?"

I inhaled; the air was sharp, and it stung. "I'm destroying the godhood tomorrow because it's the only way to save Miria. The gods cannot rule this realm any longer."

"My sister?"

Orion was so fucking mortal. "She's out of Tyrlas. Henry organized it with the Linvian guard."

"You're doing this just to rip your godhood out again?"

"I told you I wanted it destroyed." My gaze lifted. The pain in my wrist was nothing like the lance in my heart. "I'm so tired, Orion."

"Raven?"

The knot in my throat stuck, I stared at the wall.

"I need you to do something for me tomorrow—for Queen Relia and the realm."

His amber eyes narrowed, searching my face for anything else. "What?"

"The knife I gave you. I need you to use it on me the moment I take back my godhood."

"No, Raven. Why?"

"Why? I just told you." I tilted my chin. "The moment I'm restored, I'm a danger to the realm. Kill me, Orion, on that beach, the moment I'm whole, and save Miria from *me*. Bring my body to Tyrlas."

"No." His voice wavered, but I only heard the edge of anger. "Ask anyone else not me."

"No one else followed me here, and I trust you to do what's right."

"You said you loved me last night."

I stiffened and something slipped in my gut.

"I said I wanted to. But this—*this* has to be done. I cannot be responsible for anything else, and I'm too much of a coward to do it myself."

I glared, not at him, rather the reflection of myself in his eyes.

"You think you can thwart a prophecy?"

"Of course I do!" Something cracked behind my heart as rage swelled. "A million fucking times I thought I fulfilled it, so why would I keep living, keep trying, just to fail? I'm already in a thousand pieces. I want the prophecy to die with me and for this realm to forget my name." My voice shrank to a whisper as I wilted. "No one should have this power. It ends on the shore—"

"Of Belfiante, where the mirror ponds sing."

I nodded, words stuck to the roof of my mouth. His arms wrapped around me, hand smoothing my hair as he crushed me against his chest and let me shake.

"Miria doesn't need me. I will destroy it."

"Maybe *I* need you."

I shook my head, biting my lip because I couldn't hear those words. "You don't need me." I clutched his hand. "You hardly know me and I will not fucking go back to the Pantheon or Tyrlas or any of it. Promise me you won't let me go back."

"Raven," Orion said, desperate, pleading, and with everything I was cutting short. "Give me a few more hours and I'll make any promise you want."

"I won't change my mind."

"Maybe I will." Orion's voice tightened as his hands held mine. The knight squeezed his eyes. "You gave me the knife, knowing what you'd ask."

"Yes."

"Henry, Adler, Vinliana, know what you plan to do."

"*Yes.*" My voice cracked. "They know."

"And not me?"

"I wasn't ready."

"Then don't let this be an end."

I shook my head as tears ran down my cheeks.

My hands found his face and I drew his lips to mine, savoring the taste of him and the slow simmering burn between us that was the start of something I'd never wanted.

Orion Blackthorn was everything I couldn't have. I wanted him to be mine. I wanted to lay claim to the canyon of scars on his body and worship the curves of his hips and the valley between his shoulder blades, but who would I be if I gave in again?

Orion kissed me back, hands in my hair and reaching for every part of me, matching the desperation of my touch. If this was how he said goodbye, I'd let him say it a hundred more times.

41

[...] In the event of my death, there are twelve copies of this document to be distributed to each of the addressed. This apartment and its contents belong to Verinium and the following masters:

THE NEXT MORNING, WE woke up tangled in each other under a mess of blankets. Between the bond and the truth, so much had shifted and moved. All of it crashed to the floor of my rib cage and choked me as we dressed silently.

Today was the day I died.

I strapped on a sword. Orion's hand slid around my waist as he pulled me into a kiss that was too easy, too simple, and too dastardly mortal.

"Do not let me run," I whispered. "I have to take the godhood back. I need the piece, and I need you to—"

"Trust me." Orion gripped the fabric of my coat, tightening and loosening his hold as he avoided my eyes. "I know what you need me to do."

"You'll save Miria."

"I want to save you."

I couldn't be saved. I was the Godkiller and I would end the reign of gods in Miria just as I had promised. The Scribes of Nurem and their prophecy could go fuck themselves.

Over and over again, I repeated their words in my head like a song as we followed Mina through the final stretch of snowy mountain.

A king will stand when Death's darkness twines with the brightest light—from beneath the blackened willow, as she splits in two—new dawn will rise.

No king will stand and I would not split in two; I would die whole and no other would assume this power. And if I stepped onto that shore and Adler stood there with his light, I would kill him without a second thought.

The gods ended with me, and the primordials wouldn't intervene.

New dawn will rise.

The Pantheon ended here. The thought clung to the edge of every memory as we trekked out of the sinewy, snow-covered crags. I dismissed Mina after two hours because my heart knew. The shore called me through the dawning silence of snow and ice until we crested a final peak overlooking a sweeping basin in the heart of the range.

The hollowness swelled back as the mirror ponds of Belfiante came into view.

Blackthorn stopped walking, mouth agape. We stood on the ridge of a meadow stuck in a permanent state of spring. The surrounding mountains were white-capped and frigid, but as we ventured down, the air warmed.

Flowers in a thousand colors and grasses in every shade of green greeted us, filling the basin with life. In the center, three perfectly round ponds shimmered. A faint hum of an ancient song clung to the edge of the air.

"Is this it?" Blackthorn asked.

"What do you think?" I answered, bumping him with my shoulder.

"The ponds look more like ponds, not mirrors."

"Careful, you'll offend them."

"What? Really?"

"No."

I took a deep, gaping breath of spring air, but it wasn't relieving. Dread coiled in my stomach.

It was a beautiful place to die, on the shore surrounded by obsidian sand. Malcolm was right when he whispered those very words to me on this ridge five hundred years ago.

I always wanted an end. And here it was, coated in warmed earth and the wafting sweetness of wildflowers.

I took one step toward the inevitable and then another, through the colorful meadow, peeling off my layers as we descended until I was left in only my blouse and pants.

The ponds were perfect circles of still water and black shorelines, but only one shoreline was shaded by a sagging black willow. I expected to feel a wave of dread, the pull of grief, or at least the slow drain of sadness, but none came. I felt only calm and serene as I faced my tree.

Of all of them, this was the largest.

The trunk was gnarled and leaned over the clear water of the Belfiante pond as if it could admire the amethyst floor below and the reflection of the bright blue sky. Only Ore watched over us; Ich and Rea had fallen below the horizon as if they couldn't bear to witness.

I knelt in the sand before my willow and thought of nothing but the buzz and hum of the rare magic left behind by the primordials, unblemished by the hands of gods. It lived here, and it was an honor to witness it.

Blackthorn stood off, knife in hand, gleaming; he stared with unbroken intensity. I wouldn't apologize for what I asked as my focus returned.

I willed my hands to dig through the coarse sand, but my arm still throbbed where the bone hadn't fully mended. One scoop, then another, and the third was agony. I resorted to hopelessly scooping it out with one hand, but the sand kept falling back in, delaying as frustration stung my eyes.

"Raven?"

My name, but it never was. The pull of the shard was a vibration on my skin already changing me—dulling me.

I looked up at Orion. "I can't do it."

Where were the memories? Where was the onslaught of pain that came from the others? Why was it so fucking quiet?

I squeezed my eyes and wanted the noise, the distraction, the tearing apart because then I'd know if I was alive, but this silence, this quiet—I was dead already.

Blackthorn crouched in front of me and started digging.

"Stop!" My hand met his before my eyes did.

"I'm helping you," he choked, forcing it through tight lips as his blond hair fell in front of amber eyes and stuck to his cheek. "For Miria."

I shoved him back. "It will kill you and I need you alive."

"Will it? You said the same thing about your hands."

I ignored him and clawed at the ground with my one good hand, but I was near collapsing as the magic in my veins expanded and pulled. Desperation held me together.

"Fine," I whispered, falling back on my knees, arms limp as I prepared to watch him burn. If he died here, it might snuff enough hope from me to shove the knife into my chest.

Orion clawed at the dirt, tearing up the roots. Eyes glazed over, and my will to do anything emptied.

Then came the light.

He held it in his hands—the final shard. A relic of the primordials and the piece of me I'd long been separated from.

It sang because it knew it was home.

"Take it," he said, pushing it toward me, but the call of power was louder.

Clarity struck as my heart dipped. I no longer cared about the man who held it for a moment. The power was more than everything; it would make me invincible. Promise rolled off it.

"No."

"Raven." Orion shook it, voice raw as he begged me to take it. "Raven, please." The whisper was lighter than the fragile thing he held. "You told me."

It was a trap.

Everything I had ever been was contained in that tiny, fragile piece of starlight. It was everything I'd lost, I'd worked for, everything that broke me, and there it was, blinking in his hands.

The magic cried out to be touched just like I had. Begging just as I did.

"I don't want it." I sobbed. The breeze sharpened on my wet cheeks and he shoved it into my hands. Everything changed the moment I touched it. I looked at him—stared at him.

"We could run."

Orion shook his head and his voice cracked. "You'd never forgive me."

The shard flickered, illuminating every perfect line of the face I wasn't ready to leave.

My *soul bound*.

"Take it." Orion folded my fingers over the jagged piece and I didn't resist. He was mortal and I was the Goddess of Death—not Raven but Foriana, and her touch destroyed. What would the world become if I continued?

Power raised the hair on my skin and crept down my throat like bitter poison. Magic surged as I remembered all of Miria would bend to my will if I desired. And if I desired, I could remake it all as a testament to everything Leander thought it could be.

I stretched my neck and the memories of agony dripped away. My arm, my chest, my heart.

"Look at me."

The pressure of the shard in our hands cut both of us, drawing blood. Words failed as the magic built within me. I was a boat taking on water until my recognition failed.

I was inevitable.

"You came to end the gods, Raven. I'll do what you ask for Miria, but know that I love you now and I'll love you until the end of my days."

I tried to rip my hands back, but Orion was stronger than my own weak will.

Power rolled between us, charging the air and clouding the judgment I'd spent centuries building. My body wanted the power. It was stolen from me, but *I* didn't want the power. Or did I? *I* was afraid of what my body longed for, but who was I without it when we were born together?

"Orion."

His name on my lips was a prayer and a plea as the magic sang. My gaze dropped to the knife he held in his other hand.

"If you don't kill me, I'll take your life too."

"I know." The magic raged against the stillness of the mirror ponds. "To die at the hands of a goddess is more than I deserve."

"Don't miss."

I took the shard in both hands, just as I had done before, and shoved it into my chest with all the force I could muster.

Blinding white exploded, washing everything clean.

Light and dark collided together, becoming one of the same and opposite as I fell through time and space, water and sky. Pain became inextricable from the hum of ecstasy as I tumbled. My blood vibrated as my bones stretched and broke and knit back together in the span of a breath and the lifetime of a blink.

The magic was visceral, all-encompassing. Loud and quiet—impossible.

Years and seconds passed between the moment I became and when my eyes opened. I returned to myself slowly, remembering, but there was so much more. I was so much more.

This magic was bigger, wider, warmer, and different. I was aware now that I held a fraction of the primordials within me. I was endless and contained in the same finite form. How did I stand this all at once some seven centuries ago?

I was the beginning and the end, but I'd created nothing and ended nothing because still, I waited for the burn of the knife—unless this was death.

My fingers curled and uncurled in the sand.

Black and red.

Iron and spring air prickled my tongue as something raged where silence should have been.

I blinked. The sky above was pristine and blue as the grass swayed. I was back in the mortal afterlife. It couldn't be the gods—their afterlife was an endless palace above the clouds. I was far from it.

Blinking profusely, I sat up and before me stood Leander Morav, holding my shoulders steady as he crouched on one knee, the mirror ponds glimmering behind him.

My love, my king. This was a dream I'd had a thousand times. Could I make it real? Why did he look so worried, so pressed for time, if we finally had it all?

I reached for Leander's perfect brown face, cupping his strong chin in my hand and believing, for a moment, I'd brought him back in full with this power, to show the scribes who they lied about.

It was always him.

His hand folded over mine and his voice fell; an ache tugged at the edge of it—the emotion sour and abrasive.

"*Irrivina.* It is not your time."

"No." I remained still. My time? Memory scratched back. "The knife."

"It turned to ash at your touch, For." Leander's voice was so sad, so even. No part of him looked like a ghost, only the man I'd lost. Was this losing him again? "You will not die today."

I blinked again. Another word floated in front of me.

"Orion."

"You have a choice," Leander said, wiping a tear from my cheek with the pad of his thumb.

My eyes narrowed. "I hurt him."

"You killed him."

Air squeezed from my lungs. It was too heavy; I couldn't breathe.

"I can't. That's how I—"

Leander shook his beautiful head and the emptiness in my chest where the bond had been became a chasm . . . endless.

"He and I are not the same," Leander said with urgency. "You knew, even when you denied it. Either you leave Belfiante alone, or you walk away with him, but you do not die on this shore."

I fell back from Leander and looked at my hands.

They were black entirely and covered in red. Blood dripped into the black sand underneath me, trailing back to the willow where Blackthorn lay in a heap and a scream tore out of my throat from the depths of who I was.

I did this.

My legs wouldn't work so I crawled, clawing at sand and dirt, heaving my body across to do what I promised I'd never do again because I couldn't face being alone.

I destroyed Orion Blackthorn and stifled the scream in my throat with my fist. The vein in his neck was torn out, his amber eyes wide open, staring at the perfect sky as crimson seeped and coated every part of him, crusting in his hair, on his clothes, on his skin. It glittered with the last vestiges of who he'd been.

I didn't care about the prophecy or Miria. I didn't care about myself when I touched his face and a strangled cry escaped my mouth at the lifelessness in it. He was covered in the ash of the knife I'd vanquished with nothing more than a fucking touch.

Orion was different, but I wasn't.

I plunged my hand into my chest, screaming through the unimaginable as I broke open my ribs and cracked a piece of my godhood. A fissure skated through every part of me, living and dead.

It seared and hissed—angry to be separated so soon—but it wasn't separation, was it? Not when Fate, in all his claws and teeth, had tied us together in iron yarn.

My chest heaved as I hovered over Orion's broken body.

The blue wisps of his mortal soul evaded me in the magic of Belfiante, but he wasn't gone. He couldn't be gone. I wouldn't accept that even as I hesitated, starlight in my palm, tears in my eyes, and a rock in the back of my throat I'd have to swallow for what I was about to do.

There weren't any gods left to ask for forgiveness. The primordials long ceded their power. Only Fate remained, and he could go fuck himself.

I swung my arms and shoved the shard into Orion's chest with a strangled cry.

His body jolted, light erupted through, striking the pond in a blinding burst. The ground shook, but his eyes didn't blink, his chest didn't rise. The faint bond stretching between us twitched but didn't move, didn't become whole or taut.

When I reached past the veil, I was greeted with nothing, not a single ghost waiting to reach me. Was I too late?

I couldn't be too late.

"Please," I begged, touching his chest as my tears fell, mixing with the ash and blood. I choked out, "I'm sorry."

Sorry.

Words I never wanted to fucking say. Words that meant I knew better and did something, anyway.

"Come back," I whimpered.

Then a gasp, a cough, a spluttered breath as his neck healed and magic glittered. Blood pumped through his veins, starting his heart again and forevermore.

Orion blinked eyes wide. Blue veins now shimmered in his amber as my heart filled again and the chasm closed. Was this an end or a beginning?

"What did you do?"

I cupped his cheeks, not believing it worked as I stared at him, awed.

"I couldn't let you die."

Orion jerked away from me, crawling back in the sand.

"Raven, what did you do?"

I fell back on my heels because I was too weak to do anything else. Why wasn't he grateful? *Raven?*

"I saved you. I saved you with a piece of—"

"Your godhood." Orion breathed, eyes distant until they sharpened on me a hairsbreadth later. His hands groped his arms, then his neck and thighs, like taking inventory. "I'm like you."

"I—" Words wouldn't come. "I needed to save you and I—"

"Why?" The knight's voice was hoarse as tears strained the words. "Why did you save me—"

"I wasn't thinking," I choked and sifted through thoughts, but it was more difficult than tying sand together. "I won't die. I-I couldn't die, but you did and I couldn't lose you, not after . . ."

He staggered back, hands raking through his hair.

"I'm your *soul bound*."

He said it plainly—starkly—staring at me as the words hung in the inherent stillness of the mirror pond's ancient magic.

I said nothing as he scratched his chest, leaving finger trails in the drying blood where his shirt was torn open.

"That's why you couldn't let me die. That's why you wouldn't fuck me in Linvia. Why you ran when I kissed you—"

"It's more than that."

"It's not, though. Everything else around the bond strengthens it until—it started in Tyrlas."

"Stop," I pleaded. "Stop. *Yes.* You're my soul bound and I wanted to stop it, but I realized too late."

"I was mortal."

Was.

My voice lowered as every part of me relented. "Fates made you for me and me for you," I said the words I'd never allowed myself as the prophecy crawled into my memory. "The scribes knew it was never Leander."

"Written on the moons of Nurem?" He gaped.

I nodded and looked over my shoulder, wondering if I'd ever see Leander again.

"It said Death's darkness and brightest light. There was no light."

I shook my head vacantly; he was wrong. "You were too dead to see it."

A surge of power settled below my lungs and eased the doubt wrapped around my heart. He was afraid, but I shouldn't be. This power was earned, this choice was mine, and I stood on shaky legs.

If I didn't die here, then I would live. Fate made a mistake: It gave me a second chance I never wanted, and the power scratching under my skin *wanted*.

With every ounce of power once shorn from me, I would be the villain Niany knew. I would be the danger Koros had woven into my veins and tried to control.

I would be everything Malcolm never wanted in his bride, and I would do all of it in my own name, for the memory of Leander—the great Mirian King who never was.

The throne I never wanted sat vacant, and if Fate denied me the only future I longed for, he could fight me tooth and claw for peace because he would know none: I was the Goddess of Death and I was tired of running.

"I'm not only the Goddess of Death," I said into the stillness as I closed my fist. "I'm Queen of Gods, and Miria is *mine*."

Decided, I stood at the lapping shore of the mirror ponds, beneath the shade of the willow, and lifted my arm. Magic and power twined together and whispered to the bones of a creature below as I'd done centuries past in an old dusty room below the Pantheon.

Orion moved toward me on shaking knees as power settled in his bones, just as it did in mine. His expression was cautious as he approached and his voice took on the same fearful tenor I hadn't heard since we last stood in Tyrlas's throne room.

"You didn't want it. You said never again—the Pantheon would not stand."

"I wasn't restored." My gaze snapped to Orion's as power pulsed through and the pond rippled. This was the Foriana

Raven feared. "If this is what Fate wants, then this is what he gets. This is the new dawn of Miria."

"Or the destruction of it."

I lowered my hand. All motion came to a halt as the blood-ied knight took a last step and stopped an arm's length away.

My lips curled. "If you were worried, you should have let me run."

His heart hammered now in tandem with mine; our bond ached, stretched taut between us—a gravity all in of itself.

I ignored it.

The breeze lifted my hair, knotting it further as I stuck my hand back out in a rising motion. The weight of the magic was similar to lifting a cart, but I could do it. I had it all now, and I pushed until my temple throbbed.

Just as I was about to snap, from the depths of the furthest mirror pond rose a dragon, glittering and resplendent with black scales like ichor lined with death blue matching her eyes and mine.

She was magnificent and swept over us, gliding through the sky with a great roar, happy to fly free again, even if the blood in her veins was blue instead of red. What mortal would know the difference? The well I pulled from had no bottom now: I had the power of the gods and whatever the primordials left behind.

"Raven." Blackthorn gripped my arm and spun me to face him with more strength than I was ready to face. "Stop."

Every part of him was suddenly, impossibly intoxicating.

"You do not have to be what Fate said."

"They never said what I would be," I whispered, looking at the ground before I took in his eyes again. "It was a king who stands and I don't see one."

"King?" Orion glared.

"Not of the Pantheon." I shrugged; power rolled through my neck with a decisive crack. "If you want to be King of Gods, you'll have to kill me and tear yourself apart because you aren't covered in nearly enough blood to survive the honor."

Orion held me with a treacherous ferocity, torn somewhere between taking me up on the suggestion or tearing me apart on this beach in another way I'd never say no to.

"What?"

"It's a new dawn, one way or another." Some thoughts came back clearly and others disappeared. "I'm riding the dragon to Tyrlas's kingdom where he has a choice to make."

Something shadowed Blackthorn's face. Was it defeat? "Perhaps we should clean up first."

"Here?" I said incredulously. "The mirror ponds are hallowed ground."

"And we're gods?"

I frowned. My head spun. The magic in me was a tidal wave building and crashing, but I needed to go. *We* needed to go.

By the time I answered, he was already splashing water on his face and wringing the blood from his shirt. I sighed and did the same, hoping he might spare me a glance, but the silence was deafening.

Few things interrupted the overwhelming nature of a bond clicking into place between two soul bounds, but resurrection must have been an outlier.

42

[Letter never sent]

[...] Maybe Koros was right.
I didn't deserve the power I had.
The primordials made a mistake.

IF THE GODS WERE alive, the resurrection of a dragon would shake the ground they stood on and send fissures through the Pantheon. The Scribes of Nurem would have called an emergency session on their moon, chanting Priminian prayers over falling sand as they waited for a shifting future to be revealed within it.

Fortunately, all of them were dead and the mortal world hardly blinked. We flew low across the mountain range just over the tips of trees. Rathe's great wings beat against the frigid air with a rush, happy to be freed from her too-long sleep in the primordial pond beside my godhood.

I felt nothing as we soared—not elation, not disappointment, not regret, nor did I feel pain or cold as night fell over the frozen tundra of Miria.

Orion's arms were wrapped around my waist, and both of us were alive. I didn't even have enough mortality to feel the buried guilt and shame.

The godhood had made my decision for me when death was impossible. Numb is what it was to be a god.

I could fell whole armies again, tear down kings, and access the death and power of every soul I'd trapped behind the veil in their mortal afterlife. Controlling it would take patience I hadn't practiced for five hundred years, but I would find it.

How much had I given Blackthorn? I felt complete, but that was impossible. I'd held the starlight in my hands, shoved it through Orion's chest.

Then, I destroyed the weapon meant to kill me with merely a thought and a touch—far more power than I'd ever held. Neither Malcolm nor Koros could do that, even in the depths of their bloodlust and height of their power.

What had I done?

Rathe dropped into a clearing under the mask of night and Orion remained silent.

The bond stretched between us as we set up camp for the last time. It was a rope holding our souls together, burning every time he didn't meet my gaze. I couldn't blame him, but I did warn him.

Foriana wasn't Raven and she never would be again. With my godhood, I saw my weakness. Mortality ruined me and I wouldn't let it happen again because no one else would hold that power over me.

If this wasn't my end, tomorrow in Tyrlas would be my beginning.

I cleared my throat. "One last night in the woods?"

The knight's gaze tore off the dragon curled up under the tree. Her black scales reflected the moonlight from Ore as it waned and I wondered if my prophecy was still written on its shores.

"I'll start the fire," Blackthorn muttered, stalking into the woods.

As he did, I stroked the smooth snout of the dragon—my dragon. She chuffed, steam coming from her nostrils as she closed her eyes and relaxed.

"*Rathe*," I whispered and placed my forehead on hers. Tears welled in my eyes. "I never thought I'd see you again."

She made a chittering noise and nudged my head. I scratched the scales between her eyes and the corner of her mouth.

Rathe was my creation—an abomination of the pixie dragons the elves once tended.

"Does she have a name?" Orion came up behind me. He'd already started the fire. "I don't remember any dragons from the legends of Death."

"Rathe," I muttered and sank next to the fire. Even though the warmth was faint, it was a welcome comfort. "You wouldn't. I tried to erase her. Dragon bones went for a premium and I couldn't bear the idea of her being torn apart and sold. She died in Belfiante with me because I didn't have enough magic to sustain her."

The knight sat next to me, but not close enough to touch. Was he not aching for me the way I ached for him?

Blood peppered his dark blond hair, and his shirt was half-buttoned underneath his coat. The center and neck of the cotton were still stained pink where I'd ripped him open and put him back together just as Koros had done to me.

Guilt tugged at the back of my neck and remained there.

"Am I immortal?" He strained against the stillness of the woods.

"I don't know."

"Can I touch people?" Amber eyes cut to me. "Hug my mother? Hold my niece? Or will I kill them as you would?"

I stared at Orion. The frigid wind blew his hair across his forehead. Each question was a dagger, blunt and destructive.

"You have a niece?"

"Answer me."

"Maybe you should have run faster and left me there because I don't know."

I looked at his hands. The tips of his fingers were bruised, but nothing like the black that had swallowed mine to my elbow.

"You don't know?"

Shame flooded my bones and burned my lungs with every breath. It drowned me. Gods only had the space for one emotion and we bided it, chewed on it, and refused to see the others until their time came.

It separated us from beasts.

"When will you know?"

The fire crackled and sent embers flying into the snow. One landed on my arm, near the scarring from the direwolf, but it turned to ash in seconds.

"When I'm done with Tyrlas, we'll figure it out."

"Would you kill me if I asked?"

"No. With the bond, it'd be like ripping out my own heart."

"Then you're familiar with the pain." Orion stared at the fire and I couldn't deny it. Instead, I answered.

"I'm a coward."

"Yet you asked me to be brave."

"You're a knight of Tyrlas."

His gaze swiveled to mine and I held it. Neither of us blinked and I wished Belfiante never happened. I wished I'd never answered Queen Relia's letter. If I'd just ignored her, I'd be drunk at some tavern, continuing my work of fading into oblivion.

"Not after this . . . I don't know what I am."

I had no answer and hung my head, hands massaging my neck. "How do you feel?"

"Now you ask?"

I didn't know how much I'd given him. It seemed effortless the way he sat in front of the fire, as though the swell of magic wasn't crushing him.

"You seem unchanged except for the blue in your eyes and—"

"My hands?" Orion turned them over before the flames, staring at the bruising. "I was dizzy on the dragon and still feel lightheaded, but otherwise fine—far less cold."

"You're surprised? I said it a hundred times."

He shrugged. "Seemed too convenient."

"Why would I lie about that?"

"It was hard to believe."

"Hard to believe? You were traveling with the Goddess of Death who conjured ghosts and shoved a shard of starlight into her chest, lived, then resurrected a fucking dragon."

"I believe you now." He threw a twig into the fire. "I'm sorry I'm angry, but—"

"Don't apologize. I didn't give you a choice. I was livid for years after Koros changed me." The twig crackled and took flame. "I hated my real father for everything he'd done, but I hated him the most when I realized what immortality meant."

"When did you realize that?"

"His funeral." I looked across the fire. His face had softened. "I went back to help my sister after thirty years and didn't realize how long it had been. I missed her growing up, having a family, and *living* because I was busy in the Pantheon."

"Busy with what?"

"I don't know." I waved the memories away. "Everything before Belfiante was the same. We were in and out of wars with the fae; we were advisors to kingdom courts. And if there wasn't war, we had lavish dinners and festivals that stretched for weeks. And somewhere in the middle, I fell in love with Malcolm."

Orion sighed, breaking another twig and tossing it. "How many times have you married?"

I considered the question. "Four."

"And you weren't able to touch any of them? For centuries?"

A piece of me shivered as I remembered them. The faces I'd dared to commit to, the gods and mortals I'd vowed to love.

"I could touch Malcolm for small amounts of time because his godhood protected him."

Blackthorn looked up at the sky where stars shone between the bare branches. "Am I supposed to feel like retching every hour?"

"It goes away." I yawned. "We'll leave for Tyrlas at dawn. It's a three-hour flight."

"And then what? You have a plan?"

I hesitated, but perhaps the truth was best. "I have a plan. Well, somewhat—it might get complicated. Just . . . don't doubt anything I said to you in the cave tomorrow. I . . . You've seen me in Tyrlas's court?"

A pause, a moment, the memory surfaced and the weight of the last days compounded with force. Yesterday, my arm was broken and we held each other in the hot springs of Belfiante. Hours ago, Orion said he loved me.

"Are we talking about that?" Orion asked quietly, tilting his head, casting a shadow over his face. "Last night?"

My gaze caught his, and for a moment, I couldn't breathe as it all swelled back.

Soul bound.

Now he knew. It wasn't a secret but an unspoken fact between us, and an inevitability.

"Can we get through tomorrow?"

"We have to."

He didn't wait for an answer as he lay down near the fire with his back turned.

"I'm sorry," I whispered.

Never in a million lifetimes did I think I'd be here. I'd been so at peace with death I rarely considered what it would be to live.

Part of me still wanted my end, but power was alluring; power was revenge. When I closed my eyes, I couldn't shake how cold Orion's lifeless face was in my hands or how his blood tasted when my soul cleaved. I would never feel that again.

I destroyed the Scribes of Nurem and half of Linvia when Leander was taken from me. If I had to watch Orion die again, I was sure I'd raze all of Miria trying to destroy myself.

43

Her Royal Highness, Princess Foriana,
is invited to the Vinlian ball
on the 38th day of summer
to usher a fruitful harvest season and a fruitful
peace treaty signed with the Ilverleigh Fae Court.

WE MOUNTED RATHE AS the sky turned from shades of navy blue to vibrant orange; the sky was clear, aside from a few puffy clouds in the south. We grazed the tips of the mountains toward Tyrlas, neither of us saying anything. In the last hour, a snow squall came out of nowhere. Ice pelted my face, and Blackthorn buried his head in my back, clinging to me as he cursed.

Rathe hardly seemed to notice, but she always enjoyed inclement weather. Her wings beat and I trusted her to navigate the wind and white safely.

I'd done everything the King of Tyrlas asked of me. A bargain with the wraith of a god was still a bargain with a god who had no reason to answer to kings.

From the day I killed Koros, I knew what I was to the Pantheon, even when I denied it. It was the taunting of Koros and

Niany and Malcolm—their doubts kept me complacent and broken.

Now I was whole, and they were dead.

I was Queen and I'd show King Tyrlas who I always was and what it meant to restore a god to their full power—then I would show Miria.

Miacor came into view, its gray towers rising first above the winter mist. I guided Rathe to the palace yard as the people below watched, mouths hanging open. We landed smoothly in a circle of frosted hedges and I rubbed her snout, promising we'd be back. We weren't hiding anymore.

Tyrlas smelled the same, like baking almonds, incense, and their overpowering floral soap. Nothing changed in the few weeks we'd been gone except for the layer of snow in the gardens, bare branches, and the white-capped mountains in the distance. Standing out here in the rain with Orion was a lifetime ago.

Even the souls and ghosts took notice as we walked to the palace. A handful glanced over, their forms bristling now that I'd returned. I ignored them, but Orion stopped in his tracks, eyes wide.

Fuck. He could see through the veil.

The Tyrlian palace had a history of being the final battleground for several brutal wars. Worse, the kingdom before Tyrlian conquest did not believe in burying the dead of the enemy or offering any final rites, which was a mistake that only haunted me.

A hundred souls clung to the gardens within the walls because they were never given permission to leave. My stomach lurched. They were all staring at us.

"Is this what you see all the time?" He sucked in a breath as three female ghosts started toward us. "Do you hear them too?"

I stepped directly in front of him, blocking his view as much as I could being half his size.

"Yes. Tyrlas is full of them."

I was close enough to bring my lips to his and forget everything else. I didn't.

"Linvia is empty?"

"Once you get used to the screaming. We need to go before the guards find us."

Orion blinked, focusing on me instead of the roaming specters around us. I grabbed his hand, but he remained planted.

His throat bobbed. "Can I have a pair of gloves?"

My heart cracked and I swallowed the shards as I dug through my coat pocket for a pair that stretched. He took them and to my surprise the seams stayed put.

"I'm ready."

Hand on his hilt, he retreated to his form of Tyrlian knight. Indifference glazed his expression and I could almost see the shadow of the knight I left with as we walked through the stone corridors toward the throne room.

Court was in session; the banality echoed the same as the distinctive clip of my boots.

My lips curved as I took a deep breath and threw open the door, ignoring the guards' hesitation as I buried my doubt and dug out the confidence I needed for the next performance.

Silence fell in a physical hush. All eyes in the room swung to me as the doors creaked. Not one person bowed except the shade standing to the far right of the king, near the last step of the dais.

Beside King Tyrlas sat Nia, the new queen, and hovering over them were his two daughters and several guards I now recognized from the dungeon.

The older daughter was white as a sheet, while the younger retained a blank expression—her eyes stuck on me and unblinking. Did Tyrlas still believe he could shove my godhood into one of them?

Whoever was speaking shuffled aside in their off-gray coat, giving me the room's attention. Were they silenced by the bloodstained clothes or the glowing blue eyes of the restored Goddess of Death? Impossible to know.

"Lady Raven," Tyrlas greeted, clapping his hands together as he rose to his feet. Nia watched me through a slitted glare. "Your eyes are more beautiful than before. Can I be sure you've restored your godhood in full and are ready to continue your service to the Tyrlian throne? I thank you for the shade. It is the start of everything I hope we can achieve together."

"Thank you, Your Majesty." I didn't so much as nod. "If it weren't for you, I might have remained a wraith, but I am restored and ready to serve Tyrlas and the Mirian realm as I see fit."

"Good." He leaned forward, looking between Orion and me, several questions poised on his tongue. "Nia tells me you landed a dragon in my shrubs."

Blackthorn stepped beside me and nodded, grip tight on the pommel of his sword. "It is true, Your Majesty."

"Fascinating."

Tyrlas's head swiveled and the eyes of his daughters widened further as they stepped back. Perhaps they felt the temperature of the room change as ghosts staggered in to watch.

"The dragon has always belonged to the Goddess of Death," I said, taking another step to the dais. "You were reading the wrong histories if it comes as a surprise."

"And my army of shades? Where have you landed? I can be persuasive. Double whatever Verinium wanted."

Chains clinked from behind as guards moved in. Only a few steps, but the threat was clear. I plucked off my gloves, revealing blackened hands and the touch of death the guards might face if they took one more fucking step.

"I will not raise a shade army, nor will I force my godhood on your daughter. My loyalty is and has always been to Miria. Your command would lead to its destruction and I have no mind to grant it."

"Who are you to grant anything, Raven? Without the power of the Pantheon, and absent any power granted by the Scribes of Nurem, you stand in my court, at my request, representing the will of Tyrlas of whom you are a citizen."

"Without the cuffs, am I still yours?"

"You want to play that? Fine." The king waved his arm. "Arrest Sir Blackthorn."

Let them. They have no idea who he is.

I glanced over my shoulder at Orion. His eyes widened, but he appeared otherwise calm. So he'd heard me through the bond—we'd talk about that later, too.

Forcing my expression to strict indifference, I faced the king.

"That is where you're wrong." I crossed my arms and lifted my chin. "You sit on a stolen throne, belonging to a brother you didn't have the balls to kill, *then* you sent a goddess to find parts of herself she hasn't been united with in five hundred years, restoring her to a power beyond your mortal imagination—"

"Oh? You think? And what of the knight? You remember our bargain."

"I do." I nodded. "I held up my end while your queen strung us up and tortured us. Yet here I am, returned to Tyrlas."

He glanced at his queen who sat still upon her own throne, eyes narrowed and her neck red with a rash, as Tyrlas waved another hand and swords moved. Two guards put their blades to Blackthorn's throat.

"Refuse and you know what I'll do. I've given you two options; pick one—either grant your godhood to my daughter, or raise the army. You should care for Sir Blackthorn's life because it also ends his sister's."

"Fortunately, I do not care. I'm above this mortal nonsense." I dismissed it with a wave. "Do what you want to him. He's your dog, not mine."

Anger pulled at the king's temple as he took a step down the dais. Power burned at my fingertips: Death magic, cold and blue, ran circles around my ribs as it gained, waiting to be used.

"If you came here only to deny me, why grant me a shade at all? To save my guard? Surely you have even less of a heart than I, Godkiller."

Not another word. Swords rattled behind me.

Kill him and the guard behind him. I demanded of the shade, sure Orion heard me.

The dead knight's broadsword swung from behind and lopped off the king's head, sending it rolling across the floor in a brilliant display of crimson met with resounding gasps, shouts, and every inch of chaos as his court descended into it.

None of it touched me as the shade beheaded the other guard; the spray of his blood splashed the royals who remained on the dais.

I stood straight as Blackthorn dodged the soldier's steel and met it with his own, resuming his place at my side.

When it had been enough, I lifted my arm and demanded silence by striking the ceiling with a blast of ice-blue death, deafening as a thunderclap.

Queen Nia hardly blinked and Tyrlas's daughters remained frozen in place, blood on their pretty dresses, but no chains met my wrists. Not one soldier even attempted to meet me with steel as the room quieted.

"Sheathe your swords!" I shouted with forced authority, followed by the sound of it. "Tyrlas belongs to you, Queen Nia."

With a long pull of deep blue magic, I withdrew the soul from the shade and released it in a plume of smoke. The body of the soldier crumpled beside King Tyrlas and his other dead guard; the respect of his court was temporary.

"Come after me, even one more time, and I will do the same to you, Nia. Koros, the King of Gods, died at my hand, as did the God of War and a hundred others. Mortals are nothing to me, and I will not play their games if you seek to tear apart the realm as King Tyrlas did."

Now I saw it.

Nia trembled, bottom lip quivering in rage, not fear. She was snarling, face pinched and agitated as her gaze honed in on me. The veins in my arms glowed blue—I was sure I looked every bit as inhuman as I felt.

"Leave Tyrlas alone"—the Queen glowered, lowering her hand from her neck—"or you will regret it."

"No. I'm not done yet. You, *Queen Nia*, killed a man in cold blood and threatened your own knight's life. I also believe it was through your machinations that the king killed Queen Relia because she knew her life was in danger, which is unusual for a queen in a kingdom as fortified as Tyrlas, but we can debate that another time."

"I will not dignify your accusations with a response." Nia lifted her chin as both princesses looked at her, lips thinned, scraping back their emotions. "There is far more I want—"

The echoing sound of someone retching in the corridor drew the hall's attention and my face dropped as another pair of shoes clipped on stone and strode in.

I was the last in the room to turn. He held my gaze for a moment but it dropped quickly when he saw the head of Tyrlas on the floor. Adler was neither surprised nor concerned.

"I'm sorry I'm late." The prince bowed to Nia, not sparing me another glance. "Prince Adler, representing King Donovan of Linvia in negotiations."

"Negotiations?" Nia snapped, her glare cutting as she stood. "What negotiations of Tyrlas concern the fae or Linvia?"

"Certainly the power of the Goddess of Death is a discussion belonging to the realm and not a single kingdom, unless a single kingdom seeks to spark a larger war."

I held my hand up to stop Adler from saying anything else and took a step forward, putting my toes at the last step of the dais where Nia peered down, cropped hair sharpening every feature of her angled face.

"As I was asking before we were interrupted, *Your Majesty*, what do you want? You have the throne of Tyrlas until his heir marries."

Nia brushed me off. "I want you to kneel. If you refuse your own power, recognize mine in the kingdom you're granted citizenship and you will have my protection."

A throaty laugh spilled out of me. "You have no protection to offer me."

Nia took two steps down the dais and I dug my heels in, flipping hair behind my shoulder.

"You, Queen Nia, will kneel before me." I pulled the kernel of nobility from the bottom of my chest where it was buried, while her lip twitched. "I believe *you* will kneel before me—the Queen of Gods, the Pantheon and the sovereign of the Mirian realm. My life does not belong to anyone and I will not waste my death until I've fixed what the gods have broken. Clearly, my work isn't done."

The Queen glowered as the tension in the room expanded. She was almost close enough to wring my neck. "Where was this sense of purpose all those years ago when you razed entire armies and let mortals fight in your wars of gods? Where was it when you let Fortune die and killed everyone else you ever loved?"

"You know nothing of Fortune."

"Don't I, Foriana?"

Nia stood straighter and snapped her fingers. A rage of fire engulfed her. My jaw fell open when a different woman stood before me. A woman I knew nearly as well as myself, with long hair like pulled straw and gold eyes that weren't the only part of Niany she'd inherited.

"Armine," I breathed.

"You weren't the only one who shorn yourself, Godkiller, and you will regret rejecting my offer."

"How? He *killed* you."

"A story for a different time," she answered, waving her hand as several realizations slammed into my memory. My heart collapsed.

"You *knew*," I whispered. My sister, whom I hadn't seen in two hundred years, stared back. My sister who should have been dead; my sister who I *believed* was dead.

My voice rose. "You knew."

Rage boiled, churning and frothing with a thousand unspoken thoughts I choked on.

"What, *sister*, did I know?" A sneer stretched Armine's round cheeks. "Knew that the dog was your soul bound? Knew that you wouldn't recognize me so long as you wore those dastardly cuffs? Of course I knew. Who else would have suggested you kiss the knight? How else would I get you to talk to me if you cared for no one?"

"I should have fucking known," I growled, glaring at the goddess as my breath steadied. Once she was called the Stewardess of Fate, and she hated it. "You always did prefer a face that wasn't your own. What was it father said? You were prettier in the dark? Or were you tired of standing behind us?"

"He only kept you around to see if your next fuck would be politically advantageous."

My voice lowered. "You shouldn't have been able to do any of it, Armine."

"I have my ways." She shrugged, eyes flicking between Orion and I. "Faint, sure, as you've leeched the world of everything, but I've watched the threads of fate for centuries, so I can still see the strong ones."

I shook my head. Emotion swelled—much more and the desperation would spill over. I wanted to strangle her. "Why? Why do this at all?"

"I will have a place in the Pantheon."

I rolled my eyes hard and stared at the fucking ceiling as she continued. The room tilted; I'd fallen into a trap.

"You've always been running and, suddenly, I saw an opportunity. You killed your last soul bound and nearly every god, so I wasn't giving you the chance to escape this time. Not again. That's also why I kept Prince Adler in Linvia—I knew you'd go back. You *always* go back."

"What does Adler have to do with this?"

"You haven't figured it out?" She chortled, tossing her too-blonde hair over her shoulder. "He's your other soul bound—a fae soul bound, somehow."

The room stopped and my ears rang as a snap echoed through my chest. Softer, but sharp and familiar.

"No."

"Yes," she argued back as I tried to press too many thoughts together. "You were too in love with a damn mortal to see it, but I've known since I was betrothed to him. The poor prince has been living in pain since he noticed."

I wouldn't look at Adler.

"How? How is it fucking possible?"

"I thought the great Foriana knew everything." Armine tsked and I was only peripherally aware we had an audience. "Apparently, being father's favorite didn't make you smarter. Like him, you're too obsessed with your own drama to see far beyond—"

"Armine, what are you talking about?" I stepped onto the first step of the dais, ungloved finger pointed at her as she flinched back but didn't relent.

"Did you never find it odd that Koros, the King of Gods, would give the gift of death to the offspring of mortals?"

"Yes." I glared, losing patience as I rolled my neck. Magic was starting to itch again. "I was half-fae and half-mortal. I've always known, but—"

"No, no, no." Armine shook her head with a wide grin. "Apparently, you are half fae and half god. Your godhood only adhered to the mortal part of your soul so you have the power of both."

"I have the power of Death."

She ignored me. "All I want, sister, is a real place in the Pantheon, which Koros never gave me. Give me that and it will be the last thing I ask of you."

"No—"

Armine glared. "You will regret denying me."

I was a conduit who raised a god and controlled all the magic Koros dreamed of holding.

"What is it, Godkiller?" Armine asked, cocking her head to the side, voice too reminiscent of Niany's sugar-coated insults.

"*Foriana*," I spat at her and took a step back, hands dropping to my sides. "Serve Tyrlas, Armine, and learn how to read a map. If you put one foot out of line, I will turn you to nothing, just as I did to Koros and Malcolm."

"Is that a maybe?" She batted her eyelashes as I tugged a glove back over my hand.

"It's whatever you want it to be."

I bit back another insult because I was too tired for this fight.

Then the ground shifted, shaking as if it were about to split. An inhumanely tall man in fine robes strode in through an open door into the court of Tyrlas where the king now lay dead, head only paces from my feet and turning purple while my sister, the new queen, stood over me.

"Excuse me, you can't—" The words died in Armine's throat as Adler moved away from my side and stood between us and the intruder.

"Father," Adler said. Ice dropped down my spine at the word. "Nice of you to join us on this side of the boundary. I've missed your steadfast company and support."

"I have no business with you, Adler." The fae king's hand attempted to push his son out of the way, but Adler didn't move until the king said, "I'm here to speak to Queen Foriana."

I stepped around Blackthorn and peered at the king's inhuman green eyes from over Adler's shoulder. The king was nearly a duplicate of his son and stood even a few inches taller, with only specks of gray in his hair and lines around his eyes.

"He's fine," I said to the prince and I pulled my glove off again. This wasn't the first time I'd stood before the fae king and I had a sinking feeling it wouldn't be the last.

Adler hesitated, shoulders tightening and loosening, before finally stepping aside.

I bowed to the King of Fae. "King Ilverleigh—it's been too long. What business do you have in Tyrlas? We're a bit preoccupied."

The King of Fae glanced at the grotesque head of King Tyrlas and the consequent trail of blood, mingling with his beheaded guard. The edges of it had begun to dry and crack on the stone floor.

"Clearly," the king. Adler flinched, but I did not. "Another god stands beside you? And before you? I thought Death was the last remaining. That is why they call you Godkiller, is it not?"

"It's complicated." I braced my arms. "I'm very busy at the moment trying to ensure a pleasant immortality for myself. What can I help you with?"

"I wanted to invite you to dinner."

"Dinner?"

"Yes, in Ilverleigh, at the palace, before you make any rash decisions for the realm. My son will be your escort since you're clearly acquainted."

The king turned up his nose like he smelled them both on me, which was unlikely given all the blood in the room and in my hair. Maybe that was what he smelled.

I didn't have time for this. "No."

"No?"

"What are you fucking doing?" I ignored Adler's voice as it ran through my head and all the implications that came with it.

"No. Have you not heard the word before?"

The king's face crumpled. "Watch your—"

"You speak to a goddess blessed by the primordials who has extinguished entire fae armies, some by *my* own hand. You watch your tongue with *me*, King Callum Ilverleigh." I took a sharp breath, knowing I needed to get myself under control. A hundred nobles of Tyrlas still stood in the room, eyes wide and jaws dropped; none of them had seen fae before, let alone a prince and the king. "I will agree to dinner at the Pantheon, and your son will be *your* escort in two weeks' time unless there's a better acquaintance to the Mirian realm for Your Majesty."

"Fuck you, Raven."

"You wish," I shot back, waiting for the king to regain himself.

Callum cleared his throat. "I agree to your terms."

"Great." I looked over my shoulder at Armine because I was done. "Good luck, sister."

"Good luck, Foriana." Her voice echoed at my back. "You'll need it more than I do."

I practically ran from the hall with every eye on my back. I'd never wanted this, but I couldn't go back. I lived, and there was only one option. The Pantheon was mine because there wasn't a force in this realm or the next I could stomach answering to.

I rushed through the maze of the palace until I couldn't breathe, then I leaned against the cool stone wall, eyes closed, praying that somewhere in the silence I'd be able to catch my breath again . . . as if magic and fate weren't crushing my ribs.

Then I heard the scuffle of shoes. I peeled one eye open and Orion stalked over, with Adler not far behind.

My eyes drifted up, staring at the ceiling as the two stopped, trapping me against the wall. I wouldn't lower my chin; I would not look at either.

"Now what?" Blackthorn asked, voice dropping to a grating whisper. "You just killed a king, appointed a queen, declared yourself queen, made dinner plans with the King of Fae and stormed out of a hall that isn't your own to go where? The fucking Pantheon?"

"No—I don't know." I groaned, scrubbing my face because I needed my plan to work, even if it wasn't much of a plan and more of hoping my threats were believable. "Not the Pantheon. Not yet."

"Linvia," Adler answered, ignoring how I groaned again and rolled along the wall so my forehead was flush with the stone. "Donovan's swords and rooms are yours as needed. Stay a few days."

"Days?" I said incredulously, panic building in my throat. "Days? The Pantheon—"

"Has been abandoned for almost a hundred years. What is another day or two?"

I spun around. The warmth in Blackthorn's eyes was disarming and chipped some weight from my shoulders.

"You're the one who decided to entertain in three days' time," Adler snapped.

I glared, but it was only half-hearted. "Fine. *Linvia.*"

I was tired—so fucking tired—despite the power twisting through me like a summer storm. I'd used too much of my godhood too soon, and now it roiled my stomach.

"We go by dragon. You can fold your way to the palace or however your fae power works—*if* you haven't spent all of it."

"I'm sorry—dragon?" The prince looked dumbfounded as I rolled my eyes.

"It's a long story about god magic, and primordial pond water."

"Wait—" Orion stepped between us, eyes on Adler. "My sister, where is she?"

"Safe in Linvia. Henry has taken care of her," Adler said evenly. "She'll be at dinner if you wish."

His shoulders fell in relief. "Thank you."

"Thank Raven." Adler smirked but waved his hand and exchanged a glance with me. "She insisted."

I had the misfortune to catch some of the waiting emotion in Blackthorn's eyes I'd been shoving down to get through today. He was meant to be a god, and in this moment, I saw it.

"I'll send for the rest of your family." My voice shrank as my attention pivoted to Adler. "After I speak with Donovan, will your father leave or wage war for what I just did?"

The prince frowned. "He has nothing against the kingdom—likely doesn't even know the name. He'll leave without issue."

"Good." I exhaled, closing my eyes again. I wasn't ready to look at him. "Let's go."

"And Queen Armine?"

"I'll deal with her once I know how. She bites but doesn't have teeth."

Orion followed closely as I barged through the palace, back to the garden where Rathe waited.

44

We landed hours later in a snow-swept field between the palace and the Linvian mountains. Adler and King Donovan greeted us, watching the dragon with awe and curiosity.

"Thank you for your hospitality," I said. My face flushed when Donovan's gaze stopped on my blouse. Both of us were still in our bloodied clothes. It wasn't the first time I'd stood in front of a king, crusted in blood today.

"Anytime, Lady Raven. You've done much for the realm. Dinner and a bed is the least I could do."

King Donovan's voice wavered; he was afraid of me. Forced bravery propped up the long syllables as he stared at the dragon and swallowed. Most of Miria had forgotten dragons were as much a part of our history as the gods, elves, and fae.

"Her name is Rathe."

"Does she need a place to rest? Out of the snow?" the king asked. His brow furrowed as she shook ice from her wing. "I have a large stable we can clear."

"She'd love that." I softened at the kindness as fatigue started to settle in my shoulders.

"Consider it done."

"If you don't mind, Your Majesty. I need some peace and quiet to freshen up before dinner." My eyes snagged on Adler and Orion—two problems I was not solving. "Uninterrupted."

I wasn't supposed to be alive. None of these choices should have been mine and I needed the one thing I knew so I didn't wait for protest. I went straight into the Palace of Niany.

Instead of turning left, I barged down another hallway and raised my fist to Henry's door.

"Raven?" Henry's eyes widened. Worried lines came to a point around his lips. "I was so fucking worried."

He dragged me into his arms, sweeping me from my feet and into the room, not caring I smelled atrocious when he smelled like firewood and warming spices.

"I'm fine. Like always." I stumbled over the words as he set me on my feet and held my face in his warm hands like he couldn't believe me. I laid my hand over his. "Can I use your bath?"

"Of course." Henry disappeared to start the water while I stayed frozen in place, pulling a stray thread from the cuff of my coat as I stared out the window. Dusk crept up and wind pushed snow around the garden below.

I shrugged off the coat and scarf. My fingers played with the buttons of the blouse stained in Orion's blood. I smelled it still: Sharp, sweet iron, punctuating every breath. Death wasn't unfamiliar, but resurrection was—there was always a cost, and if it wasn't my heart or my life, what was it? What couldn't I see?

One button, then another. My heart slipped as I discarded the first blouse on the floor, followed by a second until I stood in the center of the room wearing nothing but my belted pants.

Henry came out of the bath, followed by a cloud of steam. He had a wineglass in hand and I snatched it. The godhood dulled my senses while alcohol dulled my godhood.

"I'll send for a dress," he said, kneeling to untie my boots. Then, he unbuckled my pants as I gulped the wine and watched. We'd been here before too many times.

I stepped out of my boots and pants, clutching his shoulder. Henry stared at me with the same lopsided, rakish smile he had when we first met. Magic buzzed, and everything in me was alight and at odds with how bone-deep exhausted I felt.

He pushed the sleeves of his white shirt to his elbows and took my hand, guiding me to the tub. Steam filled the room. The water was scalding, but it hardly felt lukewarm against my new skin.

"What did I miss?" I asked and the water sluiced while I leaned back and tried to hold my voice steady. The spring garden fresco above was unchanged.

"*Lyra*," Henry chided. "You told me you'd die in Belfiante and since the day you left, I prayed you were wrong."

He sat on a chair beside the tub, brown eyes calm and patient as they always were, but time had refined him to a point.

"I didn't die because I *couldn't*."

"I'm thankful for it, even if you're not."

The panic, the loss, and the twisting knife of love all became a dull ache as the memories of the last day blustered back. I focused on the fresco and the sprays of white magnolias covering a trellis.

"I think I'm restoring the Pantheon."

"Don't worry about it tonight."

"Easy to say." Did he see the difference in my eyes; the glowing blue marked me not as a human—mortal—but a god? "I do have to worry. I invited the fae king to dinner."

"Why?"

"I panicked. It was that or the Ilverleigh court, and you know I'm not setting foot there."

Silence crept into the room as I scrubbed my arms with a bar of soap. The water splashed as the suds loosened the streaks of dried blood. Strong, callused hands brushed my neck, chilled only in contrast to the water as Henry dug his thumbs into my shoulder blades and massaged.

"Lean back."

Giving in to Henry was easy. His hands always knew what I needed. My eyes fluttered closed as he gathered the knotted strands of my black curls and began to comb them as he'd always done on bad nights.

"There was blood on your shirt." He lathered the soap with patience, massaging my scalp as I took a deep breath, closed my eyes to face the memory.

"It was Orion's—the knight. I gave him my father's knife and he was supposed to kill me once I took my godhood back." I trembled, then forced the words out. "I killed him instead. Turned the knife to ash and tore his throat out with my teeth."

"Raven, I—"

"He's fine." My voice iced over. "I gave him part of my godhood. He lived."

"He's a god?"

"Part, at least. I don't know." I opened my eyes. Memories of the cave slammed against it and turned my stomach. I rolled over to the side of the tub, afraid I might vomit.

Henry's hand moved on my back in calming circles. "You said you'd never do that again."

My hands cradled my face as the wave of sick passed.

"I didn't want to. But he—he's my soul bound somehow. And then, in Tyrlas, the Queen is actually my sister, Armine, who seemed to believe Adler is also my soul bound, which should be impossible. I killed my soul bound five *hundred* years ago to keep any of this from happening, and now I—"

"*Lyra.*" Henry's voice soothed a corner, but now I knew Orion—and Adler—the strangling in my chest worsened. I couldn't feel anything more than what I felt for Leander. How could I hold that? How would Miria withstand it?

Henry tugged my hair, forcing my gaze to his. "You weren't happy in exile and what you did in Linvia all those years ago was horrific. You say it's because you loved, but do you know what else you accomplished because you loved?"

"Does it matter?"

"Lean back," he commanded and I obeyed. Deft fingers rinsed the soap from my hair. Bubbles and lavender floated on the surface, clinging to my arms as Henry launched into a list he'd committed to memory in order to win a bet. "You and Leander established a trade treaty that survived the war and every one after. You quelled fifteen rebellions and navigated Linvia and Dover's way to a surplus. Everything he did was aided by *you*. And before Morav, there were a thousand good, lasting things you created. Shall I go on?"

I shrank into the water as his fingers massaged out the last of the soap. Henry's voice lowered again to a tenor, hardly louder than the ripple of water.

"Foria didn't fall because you failed or because you loved too much," he continued.

I tried to swallow the feeling it stirred up because Henry always knew and was happy to remind me.

"Foria fell because a tyrant was determined to embarrass you. Your reign ended after two hundred years, while his collapsed after three because you loved Foria enough to make something lasting."

His hands withdrew and I sat up, knees drawn to my chest while he admired me. He'd only known Raven—the wraith; I was new to him.

"Why couldn't you do that with the Pantheon?" he asked, voice too full of crushing hope for me to stand. "With Koros gone, two immortal soul bounds, why couldn't it be different?"

"I love you, Henry, but I'm too old and I know what I'm capable of." I stared at the space on my arm where the fabric of the glove ended. The black went well beyond it to my elbow. "Everything ends but me."

The faint echo of a knock dragged him to his feet and left me alone for a minute.

Water sloshed as I got out and wrapped myself in a plush towel.

"There's a dress for you on the chair whenever you're ready." Henry hesitated in the doorway. "Are you sure dinner is a good idea? You've been through—"

I brushed past him and sank down before the fireplace, spreading my hair out over my back to dry.

He sat beside me and held out a fresh pair of silk gloves. "So your hands don't stay wet."

"Thank you," I said quietly and laid my head on his shoulder as he set them between us. He watched as I revealed my hands were no longer barely bruised, but entirely overcome.

If the touch of only my fingertip rotted a mortal, I never wanted to remember what the entire weight of my hand would accomplish.

"It's worse," he muttered and I tugged the gloves back on. "Is all of your power back?"

His arm settled around my waist in an embrace so achingly familiar my heart skittered and I lost track of how long we stayed there.

"I suppose. They haven't looked like this since Malcolm and Koros took me to Belfiante."

Henry kissed my forehead, then tilted my chin up where he swept his lips over mine.

"I love you, Raven."

I leaned into the kiss, tasting the sweet wine on his lips as I took my time, but we didn't have forever. I drew back, resting my forehead against his, eyes closed.

This was the only room in all Miria it seemed, so I didn't have to explain myself.

"I love you too," I murmured. Tears prickled my eyes as my body slumped and the truth fell out. "I can't start over. I don't want to."

"Why?" Henry leaned away, but his hand squeezed my arm. "It will be different."

I looked into his eyes and hated time; time was a fucking thief.

"I'm not ready to learn someone else. I'm tired of digging up everything and screaming just to be understood. I'm . . ."

His thumb stroked my jaw. "You get the beauty of something new."

"I never wanted new after Leander. You pulled it out of me."

"I took nothing from you that you didn't want to share." He flashed me a sad smile. It crinkled his eyes and deepened the lines around his lips. "Adler is patient, as I'm sure Orion is too. I know you didn't want this, but a second chance has to be better than death."

"No," I whispered. "My second chance was centuries ago."

His hand fell and mine rested on his chest as I stole another kiss. Nothing else needed to be said, but fatigue tugged at my side. I ignored it and fumbled with the buttons of his shirt until his hand wrapped over mine, stopping me.

"You should get dressed, Raven." The reflection of the fire in his brown eyes brought flecks of green to life, like a lichen on bark. "We have time, *lyra*."

"I don't feel it."

"Well, the last time you said I'd see you tomorrow, I didn't."

"I'm sorry."

"Are you?"

I nodded, blinking away the memory . "I didn't know what else to do but let Tyrlas find me because I'd wasted enough of your time—I wanted you to live."

"Time with you is never wasted."

Henry kissed me again, deep and promising, but it ended too soon. He stood before I did, extending a hand to help me to my feet as I left the towel on the floor.

Like an echo from our younger days, he helped me into the dress. It was a simple black gown—to his chagrin—with a dropped waist and A-line skirt. The back was open, exposing my spine but there was no embellishment, no embroidery, and nothing but stark matte black.

"You're beautiful," he said as he secured the tie on the waist, his finger grazing my spine. He leaned over, lips near the shell of my ear. "The boys won't know what to do with themselves."

"Boys?" I laughed and turned. "One is twelve times your age and the other isn't much younger than you."

"Yes," he agreed and ran his thumb across my bottom lip, "but they don't know what it's like to be loved by you. How it feels to run their hands under your gown and wake up next to a goddess knowing she's chosen you."

He didn't kiss me. Instead, he backed away with his hands at his back because Henry always had a stronger will than I.

"I'll see you at dinner, Lord Baskin."

"Looking forward to it, Lady Raven, or is it Foriana now?"

"Always Raven to you."

With his gentle smile and warm touch seared on my mind, I walked through the palace back to my apartment.

Year 1302, Linvia
Raven is 752

THERE WERE NO LIGHTS on in my apartment at the Linvian Palace as a man named Henry dropped me unceremoniously in an armchair with a laugh.

Only moonlight came through the window in two steady blue streams, though his brown eyes dazzled in it as he looked up from where he crouched, fingers toying with the laces of my boot. He squeezed my ankle.

I should have stopped him before we made it to my room but the young man's eagerness was a weakness of mine.

"May I? I'm a doctor, as I said before."

I cocked my head. "Are you? Surely, I'd remember."

He smiled and undid the lace of my boot anyway. It dropped to the floor with a soft thud. "Well, I've lived many lives, Lady Raven."

"You're twenty-four."

"You remembered."

Henry's hand trailed up my bare foot and stopped at my ankle where he slowly massaged the bone. "It's swollen, my lady. I'm afraid you should stay here a while."

"A shame," I said as his hands traveled further up my calf, a wicked glint in his eye. "I was quite enjoying the dancing."

"Too much, apparently." He massaged my knee. "This bone might be broken too."

"Broken? Are you sure?"

"Well, I'd have to move your dress to know for sure, so I could compare it to the other—as I am a man of science."

Henry's dastardly hands pushed the gown past my knees, continuing to rove and squeeze. His lips parted as he reached my thigh, then his gaze flicked up.

"Broken as I suspected. Moving you from this chair in this terribly dark and silent room would be dangerous."

"You are the doctor."

"I am." His hand let go of my gown, then grabbed my hips and tugged me to the edge. "How do you feel about unconventional treatment, Lady Raven? I could fix your broken leg tonight."

"That's blasphemous magic, Lord Henry."

"The most blasphemous, I assure you."

His hands raked up the skirt again and light fingertips played with the lace edge of my underwear. Without warning, he tugged them off, eyes on mine, waiting for me to stop him, but I wouldn't.

He rose, leaning over, caging me against the back of the chair, lips too close to mine.

"I could leave," he whispered, "but you want to be fucked and I want to know if your cunt is as beautiful as your mouth."

My heart hammered; desire was a torch between my thighs. "And my ankle?"

"I'll start wherever you tell me to."

45

My room in the Linvian palace was exactly as I'd left it. However, clothes had been picked up and the linens had been changed. It was also blissfully empty.

I lay on the bed and closed my eyes. Two hours waited between now and dinner, and I intended to make the most of them—unconscious. I drifted off only to be woken by my name ringing through my head.

"What do you want, Prince?" I snapped. The sun had barely started to set.

"I owe you a conversation."

"What does uninterrupted mean to you?"

"Very little, why?" Someone shifted outside of my door. Fabric rustled. Adler was in the apartment—waiting. Of course he was.

"Where is Blackthorn? I owe him a conversation too."

"He's with his sister presently, but I'd give him several hours this evening if I were you."

"Luckily, you're not."

"Please let me in, Your Majesty."

I stared at the ceiling. The once vibrant white carvings of trees dipped and swirled above, looking more cream than I remembered. Was everything duller?

"Fine," I sighed aloud and the door opened.

I righted myself and wrapped a blanket over my shoulders, covering the bit of cleavage the dress exposed. If I saw any flash of hunger in his eyes, I'd cave and the conversation would veer in another terribly predictable direction.

Adler now wore only a white shirt tucked into black pants. His dark hair was pushed back, emphasizing the freckles on his sharp cheekbones. I hated how handsome he was as he pulled a chair to the bed and sat in front of me, green eyes surveying.

I wanted to be callous and removed like the god I was, but some people were beyond my indifference—like they existed to remind me what it was to be mortal. Had I always felt like this around Adler, or was it apparent now because I knew who he was to me?

"I'm sorry." A nervous hand ran through his hair. I'd never seen Adler less sure of what to say.

"Sorry for what? Hiding the truth?"

He tensed, hands balled into fists as he stared through me. "The same way you kept the truth from Orion or failed to tell me you were part fae? I didn't want you to find out like that either."

"I didn't know it mattered," I mumbled, looking down as I twisted my hands on my lap. "I should be talking to Orion before—"

"I have waited three *hundred* years, Foriana." My gaze snagged on the bottomless fae green, more distracted by the way my name sounded on his lips. "I already told him I'd speak to you. He didn't seem bothered."

"You talked to him about it?"

Adler leaned back, chin tipped to the side. "Why are you surprised? I know why you did what you did, and Orion and I are—we've spent nearly as much time together as you and me. Honestly, if you thought we'd play the jealous soul bounds, you'll have to work harder because I would walk away before I made you choose."

"I wouldn't choose." I pulled at the edge of the blanket, trying to shut out the memory of our night in Avilla. "But I don't know what I want."

His hands took mine. I didn't move. "You wanted to die." Adler strained as he pulled the glove from my left hand and watched my face.

I didn't react. I wasn't sure if I knew what would happen or if I was prepared to watch the prince become a corpse. The glove fell on the bed without a sound as he took my bare palm in his hands and I held my breath.

"Orion said you touched him without gloves. I wanted to see if it was true."

"I've killed armies of fae."

"I know." Adler pulled the other off and it fell on the bed in a whisper of fabric. My nails were still stained with Orion's blood. He traced the lines on my palm with his fingertip. "I was there, standing next to them—only one to survive, if you remember the Battle of Nephrite."

His gaze stayed on mine as he twined his fingers between my knuckles and I shivered. The simple touch melted the parts of me the godhood kept freezing over.

"Why did you wait?"

"Already told you." Adler shifted in the chair; his hands slipped from mine. "First, I was betrothed to Armine—I'd like to know why the fuck she's the Queen of Tyrlas—but I didn't know who you were to me until she suggested it. Centuries ago, I meant to introduce myself at a ball in Linvia, but when I saw you with the Moravian prince and I'd rather you be happy. You'd feel the same."

"Do not presume to know how I'd feel."

He leaned forward, arms draped around the chair as it teetered on two legs. "You are not the cold queen, or the indifferent wraith, you let the kingdoms believe. You've fallen in love with mortals just as I have. Don't you think that makes us more human?"

"You fell for mortals too?"

Adler nodded with a distant expression. "Hard not to when you've tired of the world. They always have a new way of looking at it . . . do you know what I planned to say to you that night?"

"Hello, I'm the Prince of Fae?"

"No," he laughed, crinkling his nose. "I mean, yes, of course—fine. I did plan to take you for a walk in the gardens where I was certain you'd let me under your skirts." He arched an eyebrow, waiting for my reaction. I gave him none. "And then, do you know what I wanted to say when I told you the truth of our bond?"

"What?" I watched the way his freckles lifted as he smiled.

"I was going to say I've waited for you, and continuing to wait would be an honor."

"You think I'd make you wait?"

Adler shrugged. "My cock is convincing, but the soul bond is hard to ignore, even for fae. I'd understand if you're not ready for another change. It doesn't have to be anything, but we both know it wouldn't be true."

I stared at him, searching his eyes for a trick and finding nothing but sincerity. "Maybe we should start with a dance?"

He smiled. "The pleasure would be mine."

The blanket fell from my shoulder and I ignored the way his gaze snagged on my skin, scraping along my collar to the space just above my breasts where my scar had faded. His attention dropped to my poisoned hands he was immune to.

I cleared my throat; his attention snapped back.

"Is that the scar from direwolf?"

"Orion told you."

He nodded, observing. Every wound had now turned into sinewy scars, healed when I was made whole, but memory persisted.

"Orion told me quite a bit. You killed him, brought him to life as a god—all after you'd fucked him then asked him to kill you."

"You would have done the same." I shifted under the accusation. "You know what it's like to live this long—to want out."

"I do," he said, patience softening his voice, but it still had an edge. "I would never ask my soul bound to hold the knife, no matter how dark my world became. Did you know you'd try to kill him?"

I looked at the wall behind him, squeezing my eyes shut, trying not to remember the way Orion's neck had been torn apart, chest open, and the taste of his blood in my mouth.

"I was seventeen when Koros shoved the whole damn thing in my chest . . . and half mortal. They kept me locked in a room for two weeks because I was feral. Until yesterday, I thought I'd controlled it."

"You don't want to rip out my throat now?"

"No more than usual."

Adler stood, kicking the chair back to the wall as he hovered by the door, angling toward me. A knowing expression deepened the lines on his forehead.

"Orion told me to tell you he's in the library and Henry told me to remind you dinner's at seven."

"Thank you."

The door closed with a shudder as I shed the blankets and sighed.

"The offer about my cock still stands: Whenever you want it, Foriana."

I waved away the words and swore I heard his dark laugh through the bond, which would be the death of me.

Adler knew I wanted it.

I'm sure he smelled my arousal—if anything I knew about fae was true—but I couldn't dwell on it; there were far more pressing things to sort out. I was supposed to be dead and instead I was alive with two incomplete bonds after I declared for a crown I never wanted.

I wasn't getting any peace before dinner so I drew on my gloves and left for the library.

The skirt swept the ground with a *swish* as my heels clicked against the marble and echoed through the hollow corridor.

The palace of Linvia shouldn't have felt like home, but the wisps of memories around every corner made it more welcoming than the Pantheon ever was.

The library was on the third floor, tucked away in one of the narrow turrets. Or that's what I thought when I opened the double birch doors. Most of it was the same: Birch shelves were painted white with gold leaf stretching three more stories above. Ladders connected the levels, and wide west-facing windows extended from the floor to the ceiling.

Each table was stacked high with books and Orion hunched over a far table, back to the door, with several open tomes as the gas fixtures above flickered. If he heard me, he'd chosen not to acknowledge me, which was fine. The moment gave me time to admire the way his velvet coat stretched across his back in a shade of green so deep it reminded me of the pine trees in the Linvian forest.

Not entirely contrary to the way he smelled tonight.

"I didn't know you could read," I finally said, softly because I wanted so desperately to return to what we'd been.

"And I didn't know Princess Foriana required child sacrifices from some of the kingdoms." Orion turned around and my breath hitched when his amber eyes caught mine. He was no longer the broken, bloodied man from Belfiante. He looked impossible. Even with the visible scar gracing his neck, every part of him seemed to glow and his features sharpened.

"There's quite a lot you don't know about me, but much of it isn't true."

Orion glanced at the open book. "I'm realizing that. Though I haven't found the short list of atrocities. Is it something you'll point out?"

I followed his amber gaze, threaded with blue. Henry's handwriting crowded several of the margins. "Where did you find these?"

The titles were a mix of mythology and history, with pages opened to several punctuation points in my life . . . including mythos from an old sect of monotheists who believed I survived on the blood of sacrificed children. Another was a history written as I sat across from a master answering his asinine questions—I thought I'd destroyed every copy.

"I asked Adler if he had anything that might help me understand you." Orion looked at the floor. "I need to catch up."

The knight leaned against the table as I drank him in—different and the same. But what could I really know of a man in a month? I knew the answer.

"What do I call you now? Are you still Raven?"

"Raven was a dream I had when I thought I'd put the past behind me." I took a step closer, watching my feet before looking up. "I don't know if that past is still behind me."

"So, Foriana, then?"

The name on his lips didn't sound wrong. It filled the room without a quip or any other titles to hold it in place like he'd forged it himself.

"I'm not mad at you." His fingers tangled in his hair. "I know why you didn't tell me. And you saved my sister's life, so I am grateful. What I don't know is what happens next."

"I don't know either," I admitted, leaning against a painted pillar just in front of him. "I didn't want to get this far."

"Sorry I missed."

I recrossed my arms because every part of me wanted to reach out, to touch him, but a heavy unease percolated between us with words unsaid and unknown.

"I'm sorry I tore your throat out with my teeth and resurrected you as a god. It never worked before."

"And a primordial, right?" He lifted an eyebrow.

Discomfort settled in my chest, this and scratchy, as I looked at my feet.

"Does it bother you I've been speaking to Adler?"

"No." I considered before I looked at him again. "I'm glad for it, but bothered by what I did, shamed. It never worked before and—"

"You regret I'm not Leander."

"No," I said with ferocity. My gaze tightened so he could feel it. I needed him to feel the words. "I would never regret you, nor trade you for another, but I loved him and my heart will always wish we had more time . . . he saved you."

Orion squinted. "How did the ghost of your husband save me? I thought souls couldn't be in the mirror ponds of Belfiante."

"Maybe they make exceptions when a primordial calls. Leander was the one who dragged me out of bloodlust and convinced me to save you the way I tried to save him."

"And the prophecy?"

I shrugged, feeling tired and defeated as another wave of reality struck. "I don't care. I'll ask a seer when I find one, but it changes nothing—filled or not."

"And you'll claim the Pantheon—Queen of Gods? I mean you killed my king in Tyrlas so I'll need another court to serve . . . if you're in need of a knight?"

The parquet floor hadn't been polished in years. "There is a lot I'll have to sort tomorrow."

"You want to enjoy tonight?"

I lifted my eyes to him. "You wanted to talk."

"Does your godhood speak to you?"

"The ghosts do. I'm sure that's what you're hearing."

"Even in Linvia?"

I shook my head. "Screaming is all I can hear in Linvia. Sometimes words come through, but nothing I can't ignore. It just takes time."

"Very well, I'll ignore it . . ." Orion tilted his chin as he looked at me. "If I'm immortal and we're soul bound—"

"Soul bound doesn't have to be a foregone conclusion," I said, voice tight and diplomatic. "You can accept it in your own time. With gods, a sacrifice from us both is required. If it's too much, you or I can—"

"No," he said quickly, catching my apprehension. "I meant what I said in the cave and you did too, unless you changed your mind?"

"What do you want?"

"I want the woman I've come to know these last few weeks. You told me Foriana was different, but she is you."

"She is me," I muttered. "Raven was me without power, without the weight of the godhood. Raven was free and—"

"You told off the King of Fae and executed a mortal king with no consequences—you are not bound to anything. You *are* free."

I gave a half-hearted smile that hardly reached my cheek. "I'm bound to this power, and I will not inflict it on another."

"You inflicted it on me."

"I couldn't lose you."

"And that's why you tried to keep me out?"

The softness of his voice caught on something jagged in my chest. That's what he was afraid of—being left out—alone.

"Yes. No. I—I didn't want to love another mortal, Orion. It's painful enough to know Henry will die and I love him too. When it came to you, I knew what you were when I felt the bond when I . . . I didn't need hope. I needed you to kill me in Belfiante and free Miria from the Pantheon. No one else would have gone to the mirror ponds and here we are."

"Here we are."

He looked at the floor.

I wanted to love him, to be loved by him, but I wasn't sure how much of me was left to love when it had all been chiseled off.

"I want to know *you*," I said with the honesty and rawness of my heart through the strain of building tears. "I'm afraid of what I would do with this power if anything happened to you or Adler. Love turns loss into devastation and now I'm a god with the power to end worlds."

His hand wrapped around mine. "Would you rather face it alone?"

"No." I looked at his smooth face, void of everything except the deepest scar across his cheek. "I've never been good alone."

"Then you won't be."

The words sounded painfully like a promise I didn't want to hear as he pulled me forward. It wasn't magic but something greater—worse—every storm inside of me calmed in his presence and stilled at his touch. This was the inevitable love the gods wrote poems about.

"Are you wearing perfume?"

I cocked my head with a smile as I nudged closer to him, touching my toes to his.

"Gods have a stronger sense of smell."

"What do I smell like to you? Still a dog?"

Shaking my head, curls fell over my shoulder. "You smell like the pine trees of Linvia in the first snow and leather bark."

Orion's hand snaked around my waist and pulled our hips together, his legs hooked around my knees as my whole body flushed. The bond between us was hungry and waiting, like a rope tightening around my heart or a gravity I couldn't escape.

"You smell summer grass in the afternoon, like the meadows in Reen, and oranges."

"Oranges?"

"Oranges," he affirmed and his gaze dropped to my lips just before his swept across them in a slow, measured kiss. I deepened it, tongue plunging and exploring him because we had time now. Nothing was running out because I wouldn't let it.

Soul bound.

His hand trailed my back, exposed in the dress, and pressed my chest to his. Every stroke of his tongue was deeper, more desperate than the last until his hands tugged up my gown, palmed my thighs.

The bond ached between us.

Was he a catalyst or was I the conduit? What does the universe need to wring from us that couldn't have happened before it broke me? I wanted to love him with everything I had left, but what could he love of me?

Orion pulled down the neck of my gown, exposing my breast, which he quickly covered with his mouth. Gods, the way his teeth caught my nipple—with a precision meant to leave me slick with raging desire.

I reached for the edge of his pants and untucked his shirt, fumbling with the buckle of his belt. He lifted me closer again, the friction between us unbearable, but I paused, panting as his teeth scraped my nipple again.

"Are you sure?" I breathed. "This won't—"

He cut me off with a breathless kiss. His pants fell and he sat on the edge of the table, cradling me on his lap against the irresistible hardness of him. Fingers teased the inside of my thigh, pushing my underwear aside as he found the source of my lust. Orion drew back, lips hovering over mine as he pushed one finger in and then another, relentless and punishing, drawing in and out, waiting for my breath to catch as he pulled me closer to the edge.

His gaze flicked over my shoulder and he smiled, quickening the pace as my core tightened and another hand brushed my hair from my shoulder.

Fae green eyes and a wicked smile caught my attention, but I didn't want Orion to stop.

Adler kissed my neck, his arm reaching around my back to grip my hip, holding me steady on the table as warmth built and spread. I was losing control.

"She's dripping, Orion," Adler remarked, his lips at the shell of my ear as he groped my breast and the knight's speed quickened. "I think you need to fuck her with that beautiful cock of yours."

Orion's fingers withdrew as Adler took my breast in his mouth, rolling my nipple over his tongue.

"I think you're right, Prince. She's soaking wet for *us*."

Adler let me go and grabbed Orion's hand where my arousal glistened on his fingertips. He licked it off, sucking Orion's fingers as my hips bucked with pressing need as Orion spread my legs and stroked his cock.

"Fuck." Adler roughly tilted my chin and kissed me, letting me taste my own wetness on his lips as Orion sharply pushed inside me, gliding to the hilt with a desperate groan. Adler squeezed my breast and pushed me forward, allowing Orion even deeper as he stretched me.

"You can fuck our Queen harder than that," Adler said, lips back on the curve of my neck as the knight slammed into me. The desk screeched on the stone, but we didn't move. Not as books scattered and my hands gripped Orion's neck like a lifeline. His amber eyes glittered with every breathless thrust until I hit a crescendo that shifted everything I knew.

This wasn't sex. This was a frenzy, a feral joining and becoming of something more as my whole body tingled and warmed and crashed in a wave of unending pleasure. I couldn't breathe; I couldn't think. Orion Blackthorn filled me, then his whimper of pleasure undid me as Adler's grip tightened. He held me on Orion's cock until my shuddering subsided and I opened my eyes.

Fuck.

I kissed Adler. I kissed Orion. They kissed each other as I caught my breath. *Soul bound.*

How could something I'd done so many times feel so different? Slender fingers reached around my thigh and traced the lingering wetness of my swollen cunt.

"You're not done, Foriana." Adler's voice was a prayer against my temple as he slipped two fingers in and pumped his hand while I kissed Orion and tried to hold on, but the prince was right. His palm slammed against me, and I came again. Hard, splashing both men as I saw fucking stars, and moaned into Orion's mouth for gods that certainly weren't coming.

"That's my girl," one of the men praised.

Which I didn't know, but I leaned my forehead against Orion's and closed my eyes as I caught my breath. Adler's fingers withdrew and his lips trailed my neck and back as he pulled up the top of my dress and tried to put me back together.

"Round two later?" the prince asked as his hand moved away from my side and he stood again, adjusting his pants. "Dinner is in twenty minutes. I came to remind you."

Orion moved me from his lap and set me on the table so he could pull his pants back on. I admired the way both of them were still flushed, undone, and *mine.*

Adler stepped in front of the knight, straightening his jacket before he ran his hands through Orion's hair with a smirk. "You make a stunning god, Sir Blackthorn. Perhaps next time you could fuck me too."

Orion flushed. "We have dinner to get through, don't we?"

Shaking his head, Adler rolled his shoulders and straightened his own shirt, attention directed at me.

"Before Foriana's moans distracted me, I did have something I wanted to say."

"And that is?" I stood up and brushed the creases from my dress.

"King Donovan will want to know what your plans for the Pantheon are." His expression turned serious and sharp so quickly I thought it might hurt my neck. "Raven was an ally, but Queen Foriana is new to him and . . . concerning. You need to calm his fear."

"And if I don't know?"

"Figure something out." Adler leaned against a table. "You didn't seem to have any issue improvising in Tyrlas."

"I always knew what I would say in Tyrlas. He was the man who kept me in cuffs for twenty-six years. You think I didn't dream about the day?"

"And embarrassing my father?"

"More fun than I've had in years." I pulled my shoulders back and lifted my chin. It was rash, but I'd spent years being bossed around by fae following the damage from Malcolm and Koros. Adler's father and I had a storied history I wasn't keen to dissect now.

Orion cleared his throat. "What do you suggest?"

"I would not want to overstep," the prince said.

"Isn't that what you do?" I quipped. "I can think—"

"That was before you called yourself queen in front of an entire court of a Mirian kingdom. Now, I defer to you, *Your Majesty.*"

"What do you think we should do?" I asked, stepping closer to him as he bit his bottom lip, showing off his sharpened teeth.

"We?" Adler's brow lifted. He exchanged a glance with Orion and kicked off the table, moving closer to the knight. "We do go well together."

"I. What should *I* do, Adler?"

The prince frowned and leaned against the table beside Orion. Their shoulders brushed and his green eyes hardened with the pointedness of a fae general rather than the roguish prince.

"Agree only to the reasonable terms set by Donovan," Adler said carefully. "If there is any ambiguity, do not entertain it. King Donovan knows the limits of the Pantheon, as well as your sense of morality. He will not be a problem, but you need his full confidence to get his council's support, and they control his armies and allies. As for my father—he is scared. I hear whispers he's already started to court other Mirian kingdoms for alliances. You need to do the same for the Pantheon."

"I'm not committing to restoring the Pantheon. Not in full."

Adler pulled his shoulders back. "You cannot take back what you said to my father in Tyrlas . . . or to Armine."

"I am the Queen of Gods. That is undisputed, even Armine knows she has no claim."

"Does she?" The lines around Orion's eyes deepened as he tucked his shirt into his pants.

"Yes. She may have found a way to survive, but my sister doesn't want responsibility."

"Fine, we won't worry about her . . . yet," Adler muttered, eyes tight as his mind raced through something. "I also recommend forming your own court and granting Orion and me titles—should you desire—so it's clear where we stand."

"You stand at my side," I said as though it was obvious, "or are you asking Orion be made a prince too? Because I cannot grant you a higher title than the Prince of Fae without sacrificing my own."

Orion's breath stuttered. "It would be an honor, but I don't—"

"Soul bound," I said softly, only looking at the twirling bits of blue in his amber eyes as I stepped closer and caressed his jaw with my hand. "There is nowhere else to be but at my side, Orion Blackthorn. You will be my right hand and commander of the Pantheon. Adler Ilverleigh," I said, dropping my hand to focus on the fae prince beside him, "you will stand on my left, remaining prince of the Ilverleigh Fae Court and hand to the Queen of Gods."

Adler bowed his head. "The honor would be mine."

"Shall we go to dinner?"

Both men nodded and we swiftly left the library. Only one title was unspoken between the three of us. It was a title that meant too much and too little all at once: prince consort. That was a deeper commitment, a meaningful title that would tie us together in ways I couldn't undo.

Only one man ever stood beside me with the designation and it was Malcolm. In my heart, I didn't believe either would betray me the way the God of War had, but in seven hundred years, I'd learned the importance of guarding my heart and my power because time turned us all into villains.

46

I walked into dinner, ready to negotiate with Donovan as the Queen of Gods and heir to a pantheon I wasn't sure I'd resurrect. Instead, every cell in my body and every ounce of magic I had came to an abrupt halt. Air died in my throat and the room shrank to nothing.

Standing near King Donovan was a man I knew. A man with silver hair and an expression so sharp it cut the strongest soldier with a meager glare. It was a man whose shoulders were wide enough to carry the weight of a kingdom without flinching, and hold me against the wall as if I was nothing more than a sack of grain—which is what I meant to him, after everything.

"Lord Wassail," Adler said, stepping around and standing between us. His steady voice sounded distant, as if I were submerged. I clenched my fists, nails leaving marks in my palms through silk. "What are you doing here?"

"King Ilverleigh thought it might be beneficial for me to assist his son in the negotiations with the newly declared Queen of

Gods," Wassail answered; however, his attention didn't waver. Iridescent eyes cut through me; silver hair brushed his shoulders.

Rage.

That was the feeling; it colored every breath I forced myself to take.

I was supposed to say something—every face in the room waited. It wasn't even a large dinner; maybe ten place settings prettied the table, but I couldn't sit through it. Not with Henry beside me, nor Orion or Adler.

"Are you not going to greet your husband?" Malcolm said, cocking his head to the side, sending his hair tumbling as I seethed.

"You died begging like a child." My voice shook as rage swelled and screamed. I angled to step back. "You will *never* be anything to me, Malcolm."

He shrugged and sank into his seat. Orion and Adler bristled as Henry gaped from his place near King Donovan.

They knew only a sliver of what Malcolm had done.

I'd killed him. He'd drowned in his own blood, and I'd fashioned a dagger from the bone of his thigh. This was impossible, and gods, the fucking walls were closing in.

"I am not here for revenge, Foriana."

"How?" It was a whisper.

"That, *Your Majesty*, is a private question." The dead god glowered.

"*How?*" I screeched, unmoving and caring little for decorum. I'd given up everything to kill him, and now I feared I'd do the same again.

"Perhaps I'll tell you when you're calmer."

Pure rage wasn't red like blood; it was white like the deepest throes of bone-shattering pain and silent as it built, waiting for a spark.

"You have made a mistake, Malcolm." Threats turned acidic as my voice graveled. "I've obliterated the Scribes of Nurem, a hundred gods, armies of fae, and my father. I will not rest until your bones are ground to ash."

Malcolm stopped me with a raised hand. "You did kill me, Foriana. King Ilverleigh found a way to bring me back, and here I stand, ready for a good-faith negotiation about the future of Miria, your punishment, the Pantheon—of which I believe I'm still prince consort—"

"*No.*" I stepped back in full. "You will take nothing from me. I will not allow it."

"You believe that?" The rest of the room watched in silence as he let his question fester. "That isn't the Foriana I knew."

All emotion leached from my voice. "The Foriana you knew died on the shore of Belfiante. You held her down and helped my father tear her apart, remember? Or do you only hear me after you've gotten what you wanted?"

The words exploded like a noxious gas and I considered what it was to claim the Pantheon because I couldn't face Malcolm, not like this. No matter who stood at my side.

If I was the true heir, I could run exactly where he couldn't follow before I collapsed in front of the Linvian King. And I would collapse; hate wrung my lungs with a pair of iron fists.

I closed my eyes and exhaled, imagining what it was to walk through the halls of my father's palace—praying I was right. Praying it knew me for who I was: the Queen of Gods and heir to the realm despite my rejection.

The Pantheon would answer my call if Fate wouldn't.

Wind caressed my face in soft silence. The air was warm and fragrant, bereft of any bitter cold or whisper of winter.

I opened one eye first, then the other, with my fists still clenched. Hair caught my eyelashes. I was no longer in the palace, nor in Linvia. I stood in the middle of a spring night, in the center of an overgrown, abandoned garden as power swelled and surged below my skin in licking flames.

Ahead of me was the pristine white of the sprawling palace—the Pantheon. The pillars and most of what had once been recognizable and grandiose were swallowed by nature.

Vines wound around the windows and arches, reclaiming a structure that once had dominion over the realm.

It answered; the Pantheon was mine. Not Malcolm's, not Armine's, nor the ghosts of Koros or Niany.

I surged forward through the overgrowth, up the steps, and into the great opal hall. Once, it had been spectacular, but in the din of night and the bare light of three waning moons, it was dark and haunted by memories and shadows like a relic lost in time.

There were no ghosts here now. Nothing crossed the Pantheon's gates without an invitation, regardless of the veil they belonged behind. Malcolm could not touch me here, nor could the fae king, reality, or anything else I wanted to keep out.

Yet, as I stood, footsteps clipped behind me, running from the garden, up the stairs, before skidding to an abrupt stop on the smooth stone floor.

The outline of Adler stood behind me, in the open archway, catching his breath as he stared, expression haggard.

"I didn't know," he said frantically. His fists were clenched. "You have to believe me. He was an advisor to my father for years. If I knew, I would have—"

"It's fine," I said, but every part of me was unsteady. *Soul bound*. They could call the Pantheon as I did. Anger twitched as I straightened and took one step closer to the fae prince. "You left him with Orion and Henry."

"No." Adler shook his head. "Malcolm left immediately. Orion told me to check on you because he doesn't know anything about his magic. If there is any sign of danger, he will call for you through the bond, I promise."

"Thank you." Rage slipped like water and turned empty and desolate as I turned away from the prince.

Vines burst through the cracking opal floor beneath my feet. The palace may be empty, void of spirits, but whispers of memories remained and clung to every shadow oppressive as smoke.

The Pantheon became mine the moment Koros died. *I* left the Pantheon in disrepair. *I* cut off the magic that kept the gods and palace whole. No one else had the power to do it. This neglect was mine.

The prince followed in silence, looming like a ghost I couldn't disappear.

"You can return to Linvia. I'm fine."

"I'm not leaving you alone in the Pantheon, Foriana." I didn't need to look to know how he stared at me. The heat of his gaze prickled the back of my neck as I walked up marbled steps to another corridor. "What if you gave me a tour? Then I'll go."

I whipped around. "You just want to—"

"*What?*" Adler snapped, a flare of anger in his eyes I'd never seen as he stepped forward, closing some distance between us. "Are you about to accuse me of wanting to see you're actually okay? Wanting to see that you won't scheme your way to a grave because nothing has gone your way in centuries and Malcolm is alive? I care for you and that is the end of it." He ground out. "Show me the palace, Your Majesty."

The ferocity of his tone stunned the argument in my throat. "Follow me," I muttered and began to walk at a clip. The prince jogged to keep up as we went through the hall and past a courtyard into a corridor lined with a hundred lopsided frames. "This is the gallery. Koros kept a painting of every member of the Pantheon here. If any disobeyed him, he'd burn it the next day at the beginning of the session."

I stopped in front of the portrait of Malcolm and bile burned. Of all the gods, how could he be alive? I'd miscalculated everything. Something was wrong. Were the primordials coming back? No. Impossible. If they didn't budge for The War of A Thousand Trees, there was nothing that would call them back.

Adler waited beside me, the warmth a reluctant comfort in the emptiness of my father's palace. I hadn't stood in these halls since the night I killed him.

Adler let me stand another minute, gut roiling, before he leaned over and asked, "What's next?"

I paced to the end of a corridor, which opened into a rotunda. The ceiling flaked off, revealing an old fresco and gold leaf that once said something pertinent in ancient Priminian, but it was gone even before Koros sat the throne.

Adler had been to the Pantheon before.

Many times, in fact. My father invited varying fae nobility throughout his rule. The prince did this only as a favor to distract me and a different emotion started to tangle with the rage and grief.

"I want to see my father's room," I said and he nodded, following me at a small distance as I led us through a winding corridor that opened to a grand marble staircase. A balcony overlooked an open court leading to another hall and the larger ballroom.

The Pantheon was a sprawling maze—a living entity.

There were doubles and triples of every room most palaces only had one of. Somewhere in it were four libraries, five kitchens, two ballrooms, and eight dining rooms—each with a distinct purpose. There were eighteen full apartments for the eighteen members of the Pantheon—a number which came at Niany's insistence—then another seventy rooms, two spring baths, and plenty more I couldn't remember.

Koros' room sat behind a large set of double doors made of granite, suspended by magic. Inside, everything was clean and organized as if he'd never lain dead on the floor, staining it with his blood. The only reminder was a gnarled oak of pure gold, twisting around from the couch and a low table. The branches crowded the ceiling; it couldn't penetrate. Niany's magnolia was closer to the window.

All remnants of blood vanished from the floor, and a fire was stoked in the fireplace as though the room expected me. The furniture was different. It wasn't an array of the airy, gilded pieces he'd once stuffed in every corner. Rather sturdy oak he'd once thumbed his nose at.

My knees disconnected from my body as I peered into the adjoining room. I half expected dusty sheets and his old bed after a hundred years unoccupied, but it wasn't. The sheets were neatly made and the bed frame matched the new furniture in the center room.

"Is someone else here?" Adler asked, glancing around, noticing what I did.

I leaned my head against the wall, folding my fingers into my palm as I steadied the spinning. "No, there's magic here. It's . . . waking up. This isn't Koros' furniture."

"Is it yours?" Adler asked as I turned to watch him. His brow furrowed as he walked to the window where moonlight fell on a garden that might be mistaken for a jungle.

"It knows I'm the heir," I said, running a hand through my hair. "There's one more room I need to check."

With Adler close behind, I continued back through the corridor and down to a final gaping hall. Curiosity had swallowed the rage when wooden doors opened without my touch into a room where the ceilings stretched above and arched like the ancient cathedrals of Dover and Vharos.

I descended the steps into the empty marble room and stopped in the center. A throne sat opposite at the top of the dais of eighteen steps. It was gold and magnificent, untouched and shining even in the sparse light.

No vines broke through the windows; every pane of stained glass was pristine as it had been during the height of Koros' reign. Primordial magic guarded the throne and the Pantheon with the same fervor that maintained the mirror ponds of Belfiante.

Only the rightful heir could sit the gilded chair without succumbing to its power. I'd never tried to sit where Koros did but, inherently, I knew it would welcome me. Some part of him must have always known I would find my way.

I walked forward and stopped at the stone steps, hands at my side. Memories slipped and raged, but the sear of them was blunted when Adler's hand slipped into mine. The magic of the throne hummed like a piece of my godhood as it reached for me.

"It is yours, Foriana."

"I know."

I didn't look at him. I didn't need to. The bond stretched between us. Different from Orion—more strained, more pulsing, more inevitable because it had waited. Because the fae part of me was different and alive when I turned to him.

"Kiss me."

His gaze dropped to my lips at the command and in an instant, we collided.

Adler's tongue plunged into my mouth, and I bit his lip until it drew blood and he moaned. His hands gripped my hair and clawed at my back, trying to pull me closer like we couldn't get near enough to each other in the layers of clothes.

I unbuttoned his shirt in a fever and tore it off, leaving his bare chest exposed and heaving. We were beyond restraint and he was fucking gorgeous, even if he was fae. We parted for a moment, staring at the other. His ears were pointed as he licked the blood from his lip. It covered his teeth and I couldn't deny the way it stirred the heat between my thighs. Gods.

"I held back from you because you didn't know what we were." His hands reached for mine and slowly removed my gloves, discarding them on the floor.

Impossible green eyes flicked to mine and caught the breath in my throat. "As a man who waited three hundred years, I'd happily wait another to kneel before your throne, Foriana."

Impossibly fast and without effort, he'd lifted me into the air, carried me up the stairs of the dais and set me on my father's throne—my throne—where he kissed me like a starved man. I grasped at his bare chest, at his back as his hands, slowly and torturously, pushed up the skirts of my dress, turning desire into pressing need as the fae part of me roared to life more animal than human.

His lips moved lower, first sucking on my neck before he pricked me with his sharp fae teeth. I gasped. He licked the blood and kissed me in a motion that left me reeling, desperate to feel more of him. I should have cared more about the implications, about the mark, but magic hummed between us like a pulse and everything else fell wayside as I squirmed on the gilded throne.

"I need you," I gasped, holding his face in my hands. He flashed me a cocky grin, licking my blood from his teeth as every part of me dissolved into need.

"I did say what I was going to do, Queen Foriana, and I am going to take my fucking time. As you know, fae cannot lie."

He trailed kisses down my collarbone, my breasts, and my stomach as his hands roved my thighs and played with the lacy edge of my underwear. A single teasing finger dipped between, into the wetness.

Warmth flooded at the simple touch, then he withdrew and conjured fire that didn't burn as it flared against the inside of my legs and licked my swollen cunt.

He filled me with three fingers, fire between them warming the walls inside me in a sensation I couldn't find a word for as I arched my back. I needed him, all of him.

"Good girl," he crooned as another finger went in, hot and eager, eliciting a needy moan as his own voice graveled. "Gods, I can't wait to taste you."

I could, I was desperate to feel, but the moment he slid the fabric from my legs and began tracing the inside of my thigh with his tongue, I'd happily spend a lifetime teetering on this edge with him.

He lashed my center and sucked on the most sensitive part of me while I writhed, knuckles white, gripping the pure gold. Pleasure tore through me like a sudden storm and my back arched as I came on his lips. He didn't stop until I cried out a second time, which he cut off with a kiss.

The taste of myself on his lips had my body raging to be a part of him, to feel the fullness of him inside me but he stopped. His chest rising and falling as the pressure of his cock nudged the aching space between my legs. I gripped his pants at the waist as his hand folded over mine.

"I need you," I whimpered again, but something changed in his expression.

"I'm not giving you this cock tonight, Foriana."

"You said whenever I wanted. Is the throne of my father suddenly off-limits?"

He blinked and did not relinquish his grip on my hand. "For how long I've waited, I will not have our first time tainted by Malcolm's memory. When I say I want all of you, I mean your attention and your heart. Use me as you will tonight, but know that when I bind my soul to yours there will be nothing in between. I need to know it's real."

My shoulders slumped. "Do you not trust me? I did what you asked and lived."

"For that, I am grateful." He brushed a fallen curl behind my ear and twirled the length around his finger. "My flirting got ahead of me and I don't know if either of us is thinking clearly."

"Is soul bound not an inevitability?" I whispered, watching the column of his neck.

He leaned forward and kissed me, his thumb running over my neck where he'd bitten me. "I've already marked you, Foriana. You are mine to wait for and I am yours to use."

I gripped his waist and turned us over, shoving him against the throne as I lowered myself onto his lap, grinding my hips into his, delighting in the friction of his length against me even through his pants.

"Then I will torture you."

"As I expected," he said against my lips before I pinned his hands on the arms of the chair, gaining leverage as I ground against him, watching every twist of pleasure and desire in his expression as his fingers dug into my hips.

"I want you." He punctuated with a thrust. "Dripping. All over. Me—*Fuck.*"

Something shook loose. My whole body warmed and shuddered as he moved beneath me until we both cried out, convulsing through the same storm as he fisted my hair and kissed me again.

"Fuck," he mumbled against my lips and tilted his head, nose against my jaw as he ran his tongue over the tender mark he'd left with a lusty groan.

My hands rested on his chest. "You still want to wait?"

Adler gulped, his green eyes bleary. "I do not lie and neither do you."

My hand went to my neck as my skirt fell over his lap. I traced over the tender bite marks. "And this isn't crossing your invisible line?"

"You're my soul bound." He said it so obviously, but I caught the flash of shame in the words. "I couldn't help myself."

"Can I do that to you?"

Adler smiled. "Of course. I've always been yours, and there is no force on this earth or the next that will shake me of my belief."

Every fiber of myself wanted to be tangled and overwhelmed by the fae prince. There was nothing else I thought about but the nagging desire. Waiting would be torture.

Eventually, guilt tugged at my core as the events of the last days crept back up. We dressed and returned to Linvia well after the palace had fallen asleep. Blackthorn slept on the couch and I stared at him, the moment familiar.

I remained the Goddess of Death, but now I was so much more. Queen and a goddess restored, with the power of two soul bounds at my side: one a god and one fae. Nothing would stand in my way—I killed Malcolm once and I'd do it again because I'd live to see Miria's freedom, and maybe it wouldn't kill me.

47

ORANGE SUNLIGHT FILTERED IN through the east side of the Pantheon. It had been four days since Belfiante and Orion was tangled around me as I blinked away sleep and tried to slip out of bed without being noticed.

He cleared his throat and I turned around to see he had one eye open, tracking me. "Where are you going?"

"Can't sleep," I muttered. "I'm going to Rathe."

He grunted, too tired to argue, as I traded my chemise for a dress and padded out of the room.

It was strange to be back in the Pantheon. Since Leander died, I'd only returned a handful of times. Once, I faced my father's wrath against my will, as he berated me in front of his own court of gods from his throne. And then there was the day I killed him.

Since then, the Pantheon fell into disrepair but it started healing the moment I awoke again on the shores of Belfiante. Something larger than Rathe had shifted. Dust disappeared, vines receded, and much of the garden started to look manicured and alive as I remembered.

The roses bloomed midday yesterday, and there was too much to do as I walked along the corridors of my childhood. Memories compounded with grief and elation. Again, I was Queen Foriana, and again, I had to rebuild. This time, though, it would be different. It had to be different.

Power brimmed under my skin, even as my mother's voice nagged at the back of my head about my promise. I didn't want to think about the mortal afterlife. Wasn't surviving this long punishment enough? I had time.

Rathe laid out in the rich green meadow of the Pantheon; the arena was visible in the distance as a series of pillars rising from the ground, mere shadows against the early morning sky transitioning from purple to pink.

I approached, placing my hand on her snout. She cracked open one assessing eye, shook her head, and closed it again with a huff.

She didn't want to ride, but I laid my head on hers.

"You always fucking hated mornings." Rathe chuffed and shook me off. I brushed off my skirt and straightened. "Fine, but we're going later or you don't get a goat."

Her eye opened again at the word.

"You heard me. I'll be back at noon."

Rathe's eye closed again. I wandered toward the arena, fingers running through yellow wildflowers as meadow grass tickled my calves through an overgrown trail that led to what first appeared to be the ruins of an ancient arena.

Every pillar tilted and several crumbled at the top. The gray stone foundation had deteriorated in places and given way to invasive vines, which had claimed several wings of the Pantheon's once grand coliseum. Eventually, the returning magic would bat them back and restore some of its former glory.

Though with a little intention and magic, I might be able to do it faster.

The arena was dug into the meadow, originally built as a fighting pit. Stone stadium seats were added over time, along with suites for nobles, each more elaborate with every passing year through the height of the Pantheon's power—when Koros still cared to impress.

Eventually, the games fell out of favor, but, like most declines, no one noticed until it was too late; I remembered the days fondly.

The patter of my feet on the uneven steps ricocheted through the empty stadium as I followed the bend of it to the royal suite where Koros first introduced me. In those days, a thousand mortals and immortals filled the stands, hoping to see the power of the Pantheon at work.

And they would; Koros always delivered. If the matches weren't good enough, he'd send one of us below to fight and, sometimes, he'd step in and prove he could fell a dragon—then he'd serve it for dinner.

That only happened three times I remembered, but each was enough to quell any rising rebellions.

The once-purple curtains of the royal suite were threadbare and moth-eaten, but below them was an old steel sword, abandoned by one of the last Pantheon knights. It leaned against the wall and I took it in my hands, turning it over.

Time hadn't found it yet. The blade was dull but devoid of rust or weathered scratches. The gold detail in the hilt remained clear: The Pantheon's crest of two torches tied by dragon tails stared at me before I put it back.

"I thought you were with the dragon?" Orion's voice slipped into my thoughts and my head jerked up, looking over the empty arena. I wasn't sure I'd get used to this.

"And I thought you went back to sleep."

I peered over the ledge and saw no one. The bond between Orion and I wasn't complete. There was a corner, one small piece left to slip into place, exclusive and damning to gods. A god's soul bound required a sacrifice of magic willingly given—and blood, but we'd more than crossed the second line.

Historically, gods traded magic and blood with their vows in a ceremony, but as gods became fewer and soul bounds more rare, the practice fell out of favor. Then my war with Koros stole hope.

"Come down here."

"No, come up here."

"Up?" Orion asked, his confusion grazing the back of my neck. *"Any higher and you'll have to rescue me with the damn dragon."*

"She has a name. Where are you?"

"Lost. I was hoping you'd tell me where you were."

I hung my head and laughed. In between the darkest moments, there were always bits of levity. I lived long enough to know, and this was one of those moments I'd cling to because hope was a whisper carried by laughter.

"Find me," I said and the bond went quiet.

A gentle, eternal spring breeze rippled through. I'd left my hair down and it tangled and twisted around my back as I looked out.

Tonight, we'd attend a dinner at King Donovan's invitation. I would announce my intentions for the Pantheon and speak with the other monarchs about what faced us beyond the realm. Somewhere in our bedroom, I had a list of everyone who'd be in attendance, including the Duke of Verinium, as well as the King of Dover and the old Queen of Avilla who had never been fond of me, but she hated Koros more.

Maybe I'd be happy to live a quiet life with the soul bounds Fate had granted me—or maybe it was still my destiny to die so Miria might live.

Or maybe I wanted to be the hand ushering in a new dawn because it now felt achingly possible.

Worn leather and Linvian pine wafted on the edge of the wind before I'd even heard Orion's footsteps. I didn't move, just waited for his arms to wrap around my waist, dragging me into the security of his warm, broad chest.

"You found me."

"It was easy," he said, planting a quick kiss on my hair as he tucked a piece behind my ear. "Is this the infamous Arena of Gods?"

I nodded. "We're standing in the royal suite. If you want, we can restore it and you can lose to me."

His hold on me tightened as a cloud obscured the sun. "So you *are* restoring the Pantheon?"

"Temporarily," I muttered, placing my hand over his and squeezing. "Miria will not be under fae rule, nor the gods' if I can help it. I'm still trying to find a way out."

"And if you can't?"

"Adler's bitterness is wearing off on you."

Orion's finger tipped up my chin and he kissed me. "I think he's right to be concerned. Only a few days ago, you begged me to kill you and instead, you restored yourself, turned me into a god, and we've had the best sex of our lives in the Pantheon. So, has anything ever gone according to your plan?"

I bristled, hands falling to the railing as I looked at the weeds cropping up in the arena sand. "I'll have you know I'm always prepared, and you should not make assumptions about the best sex of my life."

"We have time to change that." His hands dropped to my hips and he turned me to face him. Orion watched my lips as the breeze rustled his hair. "Is the bond supposed to feel suffocating? Or is it because you resurrected me? Ever since the beach, when I'm away from you, Raven, the ache in my chest is unbearable."

I reached up and stroked his face with my bare hand. I'd never get over the feel of his stubble against my fingertips.

"That's how I've felt every moment since you first kissed me. These last weeks have been torture."

Orion's eyes flicked up as his voice turned husky with desire. "Does it get better?"

"I think it only gets bearable"—I rocked on my feet—"but you haven't accepted it yet."

"Haven't I?" His brow quirked up and I sighed. "I could have sworn I've accepted you several times now."

"I didn't want to pressure you."

"Is it pressuring if it will happen, eventually?"

I frowned because I'd said the same to Adler and he still hadn't moved on his opinion but it was different. Orion was so *young*. "Completing a bond requires a sacrifice of magic willingly given and—there's no undoing it ... You haven't even tried to use your magic outside of traveling."

"Maybe this is how I want to learn." He smirked and his hands ran up along my waist, tugging up my dress with his touch. "I'll give you whatever you ask, but it won't be enough when you saved me—"

"I've cursed you, Orion."

He shook his head, blond hair falling into his eyes as he pulled me closer, kissing my forehead with far more sincerity than I deserved. "How do I give myself to you, Foriana?"

I took a deep breath. This, with Orion, was the moment I'd grown up fearing: the last step, the final lock slipping off and crashing to the floor. The moment when I wished Fate would take back something because I'd never given up my power so easily, so quiet.

"Give me your hands," I said, instead of running away.

Orion placed his palms over mine. I wanted to weave my fingers between his and I wanted to scream.

"Close your eyes. Can you feel the power? It's below your lungs, deep in your chest; it hums for most, but—"

"I feel it," he breathed, and something changed in the air—a charge or spark.

"Focus on it, imagine it gathering on your palm—like blood if you'd cut it open. What color is it?"

"My eyes are closed."

"You'll know. I promise."

He inhaled. "White."

Death magic built on my palms near the pressure of his own. Mine was ice blue, and in seconds, it would turn to tar. "Can you feel it?"

"Foriana," he said my name like a prayer as everything around us fell away. "I can feel everything. It's yelling at me—"

I opened my eyes. Blue tendrils tangled with white as our hands glowed and magic dripped to the floor. His was pure blinding white, like lightning.

Every part of me stopped; I blinked.

"Is something wrong?"

The sparks of his magic trailed up our arms in rivulets, tickling my skin as it began to write itself across our souls as it was written in the ages past. I watched with dread.

"Raven?"

I tilted up and kissed him. Something around us sparked as he kissed me back, cautiously at first, and then with the unbridled force of everything Fate had waited for.

His hands grabbed my neck, plunging his tongue deep enough to scrape a moan from me as my hand clawed his shirt and ripped it off.

This wasn't a want but a need . . . a crashing inevitability. My hips rocked into his, and becoming one was a single thought overriding every bit of rationality I'd clung to.

"I need you," he croaked, desperation coloring his voice and igniting.

"You have me," I rasped, hands raking through his hair as he lifted me onto the railing. Shared magic illuminated our arms. Thunder rolled with the sudden onset of a storm, and I jerked back.

Orion stopped. His magic retreated and mine did the same, unwriting itself. "You're not ready."

He brushed my hair away too tenderly. I waited to see any of the lines around his eyes turn scornful.

Thoughts and fears churned. "It's permanent for the gods, Orion. I—I need time."

"You can have all of it, but I still want to fuck you."

A smile curled my lips and there was nothing gentle about the way he fucked me over the Pantheon arena until he cried out my name with shaking knees.

No part of our souls wanted the separation, even as we panted in the other's arms while the flare of light and magic dissipated to nothing.

Orion stroked back my hair and tucked it behind my ear as he kissed me softly, thumb stroking my chin like I was precious to him and not some unbreakable goddess who, weeks ago, said his life meant nothing.

His life was everything now, even with the bond between us still waiting. When I was ready, it would be drawn in the language of the primordials, written over our chests in red like a wound that would never heal. My chest was warm where it wanted to be filled, but an endless lifetime was so much to consider in the wake of settling chaos.

I placed my hand on his chest, wondering what it felt like for him. "Are you sure you can wait?"

His answer was a stolen kiss, lips dancing over mine as if this ache between us was sacred and chaste. "Why are you scared?"

"In a completed bond between gods, our power becomes shared. My father and Niany weren't fated, nor were Malcolm and I. It's power I never conceived, and I—"

Orion's hands squeezed mine. "You don't have to explain yourself."

"I have to explain something." I exhaled and forced myself to say the truth. "You already have a piece of my power and all of my heart. I think sharing any more will take time. Adler did mark me, but it's different with fae. It's symbolic, not—"

Orion's hands found my waist again. "He told me and I understand."

I brushed my hair over my shoulder and tilted my head so he saw the bite marks on my neck where the fae prince had claimed me. His fingers brushed the scar and I shivered.

"Fae mark their soul bounds in blood," I said. "He offered to do the same to you."

"Maybe later," Orion said with a grin and pulled me tight against him. Magic still hummed between us like the first low chords of a song. I'd give in eventually, but the electricity of Orion's magic against mine, the roll of thunder, and a crushing memory of my father took my faith and shook it.

Maybe I was being irrational, but we had time—too much in fact.

"Hate to interrupt." Adler's voice dragged along my neck, surprising me. He'd stayed behind in Linvia. *"But the day is young and there is quite a lot of business to attend to."*

"I think you're jealous."

"Both can be true, just as I can be both right and irrational."

I pulled back and looked out at the arena once more. A breeze swept through, reminding me there's a whole world waiting with a life I never wanted to live.

"We should go back," I said, but the hesitation in my voice was louder. It didn't change the command, of course, but nothing ended here.

Time persisted . . . and so did I.

48

WE RETURNED TO LINVIA at the invitation of King Donovan. Several unsealed crates sat in the main room of my apartment, near the wide windows looking out over the garden blanketed in a thick layer of snow. Only the stone fountain stuck out; the hedges, benches, and everything else were indiscernible lumps of white.

Henry packed away several gowns in one crate, each carefully wrapped in linen. Three more crates were filled with memories I'd discarded in Foria that had found their way to Donovan's archives. I sifted through them as I waited for Orion and Adler.

There were painted dining chairs from the Forian Crystal Palace, stuffed between three tapestries depicting the afterlife, each spun with gold, silver, and a blue thread. The blue dye the artist used came from rare irises that only bloomed for two weeks in the waning spring on the rolling hills near port.

Another crate was partially filled with books on necromancy and the other half held a carefully designed porcelain dining set inlaid with gold and onyx edges shaped in willow branches. Henry also found the Moravian silverware Leander and I had in Dover. My finger traced over the dusted silver and ivory, remembering when it was new.

All the things I'd forgotten and given up, but here they were. They meant nothing when they wouldn't fit in the dusty Tyrlian apartment I'd lived in for a decade . . . but now I had a palace to fill.

A satin dress hugged my hips and matched the silver tiara barely anchored to my hair. The gown was a shade of deep garnet and draped over the angles of my body, doused in dark, embroidered jewels that were sparse on the bodice and pooled at the train.

The door opened and Adler waltzed in with a dumbstruck expression.

"I'm so glad I stole the tiara."

The prince wore a suit in a shade of charcoal so dark it was black in any light that wasn't the sun. He crossed the room and kissed me, drawing me into him as we looked out the window to see it had started snowing again.

Another pair of arms slid around my waist. Orion had shaved and wore a similar suit but in a rich burgundy, layered with a black shirt matching Adler's. The rugged side of Orion is what I'd fallen for, but I could get used to the way Adler dressed him.

Though even as we stood embracing, I couldn't shake off what happened in the Pantheon. Blackthorn hardly touched his magic in the last few days like he were afraid of it.

"Aren't we lucky?" Orion said, drawing me from the intrusive thought with a chaste kiss.

Adler made a noise of agreement.

Did Orion conjure lightning in the arena? It seemed impossible, a figment of my imagination, but it nagged at the back of my neck.

"We should go," I said. My cheeks heated because I was certain Adler smelled my arousal the same as I felt theirs against my body. "I can't stay in here any longer with the two of you looking like this."

Both of them teased me as we wound through the palace into the commotion of the opulent ballroom, which was already filled with guests. Some I recognized, many I didn't. But every face in the room turned as we walked through the wide, arching entrance at the top of the staircase.

I imagined we were quite a sight as we descended. Between the magic that had turned my eyes almost entirely blue, the tangles of it in Orion's, and the size of him beside the fae prince—we looked quite different from the mortals of Miria.

Why did I run away from this? With my godhood, I was everything, and Adler was right. Without Koros, it *could* be different—already the word "queen" felt lighter as if it were mine and mine alone. I'd start the Pantheon from nothing and build the world Leander envisioned.

Gilded wasn't quite the right word for the ballroom of Linvia's palace, but it wasn't wrong. Aside from the white pillars, every wall was gold. Not painted or pressed in gold leaf, but rather covered in pressed, dried leaves that were dipped in gold and preserved in resin.

A hundred gas lanterns hung above, scattering light through gold round globes, where the same leaves were preserved in glass. I admired the room for its tacky creativity; as Niany had once complimented.

The king shouted, calling everyone's attention to the dais he sat on, already drunk before the buffet was uncovered. He stood swaying, entirely reminiscent of his late father.

"Welcome, welcome, to all of my honored guests."

His ivory suit already had a pink wine stain on the sleeve.

"Tonight we recognize and honor a new dawn in Miria and the restoration of our once revered Pantheon." Applause tore through as the king's attention honed in on me—Donovan had no intention of letting me retreat, nor any subtlety. "Queen

Foriana, Goddess of Death, Queen of Gods, and restorer of the Pantheon—heir of Koros. Huzzah! Come to the dais. To you, Your Majesty, we owe many thanks for the protection you will provide for Miria against forces seeking to unseat us."

Adler nudged me as the crowd cleared. I remembered who I was and rolled my shoulders back, walking steadily, feeding on the rapt attention of the ballroom.

Of all the nobility, my attention snagged on Henry. He watched me with a crooked smile as I stood on the dais beside Donovan, no longer the wraith he fell for but something re-born.

"It's an honor to return." I projected with my father's well-practiced soft smile. "I never imagined I'd stand here, be-fore you as Queen Foriana. I look forward to being a steadfast guide and a reliable defense against all threats should you accept the Pantheon's alliance."

"Thank you." Donovan beamed, surveying the room before speaking past me. "The Kingdom of Linvia accepts the Pan-theon's friendship as we had in ages past. A toast—to a new dawn for us all! May it be the brightest yet!"

Glasses chimed, along with several jovial shouts, as I walked back to my soul bounds and the music swelled in a symphony of strings against the chiming notes of a piano.

First, I danced with Adler. He spun me with elegance and a steady leading hand, which happened to be the complete oppo-site of Orion, who tried but fell short and left me out of breath as we fumbled through a single song.

For the minute after, I stood off, downing a glass of wine until someone tapped my shoulder.

"A dance, Lady Raven?"

I turned and there was Henry, hand held out, dressed in his usual finery of an overcoat with woven gold thread and a glimmer in his eyes.

"Of course, Lord Baskin."

It was the same game we used to play. Spinning around the floor, in one another's arms, teasing a kiss but giving none.

"You're stunning this evening." He nipped my ear.

"And you're quite handsome," I whispered, curling my nails into his back. "Do you remember our first dance?"

"Couldn't forget. You meant to twirl away and never speak to me again, but you ran straight into a duke and twisted your ankle somehow."

"You carried me back to my room."

"Very much against your will, if I remember right."

"That was an act."

"I know," Henry murmured and pulled me into him so our chests were flush. Brown eyes stuck to mine. "I was too afraid to be direct because what was a mortal boy like me to a goddess like you?"

"A wraith is what I was."

He kissed me before drawing back as though he remembered himself, but he didn't have to. Miria belonged to me. I would kiss whomever I wanted.

"How do you find the Pantheon, Your Majesty?"

"Empty." I looked past him as the waiting reality ebbed back. I never had the heart to imagine this.

"Empty with two soul bounds?"

"The palace is an island." My eyes flicked to his. "Quite curious, aren't you?"

"It isn't a crime to ask the woman I love questions about her life. Not after I packed up several crates with your stolen possessions—I spent many hours in the dust looking for those."

"Thank you." I tried to find any words I could use, but every expression of gratitude fell terribly short. "I'll have you over for dinner . . . I do miss the way you know me."

"Patience, *lyra*." Henry kissed my forehead, his lips plush and warm as the smell of him pulled me away from reality while we continued to spin across the floor. "There's no rush. Did Adler tell you I gave him my books?"

"Those books are lies." I blushed, and he shook his head as I tried to change his mind. "You left out every bad thing I've done."

Henry shrugged as he spun me out and pulled me back; he smiled as my hand palmed his chest.

"I told you before, I couldn't fit the bad. Adler knows the worst, but it's the good you were best at writing yourself out of."

"You're too soft."

"And you're too hard." He gripped my hand against his heart as the tempo of the music slowed and we swayed. "I am happy you're alive. Do me a favor and enjoy it."

He glanced over my shoulder. I followed his gaze to see Adler holding a second glass of wine and a smile reserved for me.

"I love you, Raven."

"I love you too."

I kissed Henry without abandon, but it was too short for everything we were. Henry stepped back and nudged me toward Adler.

Orion had gone elsewhere, apparently.

I took the other wineglass as the prince's arm snaked around my waist, pulling my back to his chest.

"Everyone is looking at you." His voice was husky as he whispered into the shell of my ear, fingers tracing the bite mark on my neck. Maybe tonight was the night he finally gave in. "Knowing you're mine makes this tolerable, Your Majesty. I miss that sweet—"

A loud commotion disrupted as I gave Adler a small shove, trying to shake the satisfaction off his face. The crowd cleared, revealing Malcolm had returned. Crippling fear crawled up my spine despite the way Adler held me to his chest, and despite the magic coursing through me.

The God of War was nothing to the Goddess of Death restored, but so much of me couldn't remember. It had been too long since I'd leveled battlefields or held the face of a man while he screamed into my palm and turned to ash. That savagery belonged to another woman, a different god who shared my name.

Malcolm stood a head taller than Adler. His silver hair gleamed, contrasting his deep purple coat, as he stalked through the crowd and stood in the center of the room.

His iridescent gaze only saw me as Adler's nails dug into my hip. Everything about Malcolm was overwhelming and impossible.

Anger lined the square face I once loved. What more could I have done to stop this—stop him? I shoved the knife of a god into his heart and cut his head from his shoulders as the sun set in the middle of a Cascaade street. Was that not enough? Did the primordials return and change their minds? Who would fucking appeal for the God of War?

Malcolm should have stayed dead—unless the fae king had more power than I knew.

The god strode across the room, stopping before me with a graceful, mocking bow as he held out his hand. Adler's grip tightened still, nails leaving marks through thin satin. My gaze caught Blackthorn's as the knight—my knight—pushed through the crowd but did not come to my side.

"Surely a dance with your husband can't be out of the question, Foriana," Malcolm said.

I gritted my teeth. Viscous slime crawled over my heart. The room was quiet enough to hear it beat.

"You lost your right to me a long time ago."

The god frowned but didn't move.

"A dance, Your Majesty. All I ask."

I looked at his hand and remembered how it felt around my neck or groping my ass as I finished on his cock. My stomach churned. Once my hands fit in his—*once*.

"No." Defiance tilted my chin. I was the Queen of Gods and he was nothing. "You've had the pleasure more times than you deserve."

"Are you sure you want to do this?" Malcolm purred the warning. Adler's stiff reassurance emboldened me.

The god withdrew his hand and pulled back his shoulders the same as when he stood against my New Mirian banners in the fields of Reen all those years ago.

"Very well."

Malcolm looked past me and gestured to the center of the room, his gaze pointed at King Donovan as he guided the room's attention away from me.

"Do we really all believe this lie? Do you believe Queen Foriana deserves the *honor?* She is the Godkiller and a coward who tried to run from the Pantheon and her duties a thousand times, and yet, here she stands, wearing a crown she was never loyal to."

I pushed away from Adler and stepped into the center of the room. Rage and revenge straightened my spine. If Malcolm wanted to goad me into a performance, then a performance he would get—our disagreements were a script I'd memorized.

"Who are you to talk about loyalty when you serve the fae court?"

"The fae court?" Malcolm laughed coldly and took one step closer. "You're wearing out your knees for the fae prince, Foriana. I see his mark. Do you beg him to choke you, or was that reserved for me?"

Magic simmered against my skin, begging to be released. I took a step closer, nearly jamming my toes against his. My fingertips burned like ice beneath my gloves.

Malcolm continued, "You've always had a soft spot for mortals and misguided souls. Believed you were doing good for them, but were you? Do they know the truth of who you are? That you fight only for yourself? That every kingdom you've had, you lost? You are a tyrant. Koros was right to see it."

"Tyrant?" It was my turn to laugh, cold and cruel with every ounce of a building threat. "You sold yourself out for power. You did it with Koros, with me, and now you do the same with King Ilverleigh. I *never* gave up on Miria."

"Never gave up on Miria?" Malcolm chuffed, and his arms spread, shifting his jacket lapels as he looked at the crowd. It was as though we stood in the middle of a fighting pit where jeers and pageantry mattered instead of a court filled with kings and queens. "Seems a bit rich coming from the woman who has trapped the dead in the afterlife and cut off power for every god but herself. Was that for Miria?"

"You wouldn't understand. What have you come to prove?"

I tried to swallow the burn of magic as familiar eyes stared through me. Now was the wrong time to lose control, but it built like a wave and the dam wouldn't hold. My body remembered the rage he sowed, and centuries vibrated under my skin as I balled my fists.

"I'm here to prove who you are, Foriana—the Goddess of Death—traitor of the Pantheon. And a danger to the realm, responsible for a million million deaths by your own admission."

Malcolm snapped his fingers.

Attention swung to the dais where two men held Henry down before the horrified face of the Linvian King. Royals and nobles watched intently, none as worried as they should have been but to them—gods and their powers were legends and myths.

I couldn't breathe.

Anger churned, white, irrational. They could all touch me, use me, torture *me*—but never Henry.

"Do not harm him if you want to live," I warned as I slid my glove off, stalking toward Malcolm, my arm outstretched, refusing to stand down from the God of War.

Magic built in my palm like ice.

Then I lunged, angling for his face.

Invisible ropes shot out and bound my ankles to the floor, knocking the viscous magic from my hand where it shattered on the marble in shards of poisoned ice, turned black.

Malcolm searched my face and smiled as I teetered in his binds. He hadn't stopped my power. I called even more magic to my hand and used my rage to forge it from blue to black tar capable of poisoning the whole room if I let it swell.

The rattle of chains echoed. Attention swung behind me where Orion and Adler were held at sword-point by two guards, both holding iron cuffs.

"Enough!" Donovan cried, jumping to his feet in front of Henry. "Haven't you proven your point, Lord Wassail? I gave you the cuffs in confidence—"

No.

No. Malcolm will not chain me, not again. I would rather break apart into a thousand pieces than bend for him.

"I'm not done," Malcolm bit out. "The Pantheon's allies deserve to know who Foriana is."

He dropped the hold, his neck straining—I was sure it took everything in him to contain me for that single minute. Malcolm stepped closer and I caught my balance, lowering my arm but doing nothing to tame my raging power.

"Do they know you're barren—"

"Ignore him, Foriana." Adler's voice pleaded as Malcolm cut me open like a knife and carved my heart. *"Orion and I can get out of this. Buy time."*

Malcolm watched me down his nose as I forced my expression to remain steady and unbroken. If I didn't care, I would shove this tar down his throat and claw his lungs from his chest.

"Let. Them. *Go.*"

Death magic dripped to the floor, poignant, deadly sludge, dark as the abyss it came from. All I needed was one more spark. I dared him.

"They are guilty of nothing and you will prove nothing, Malcolm."

My gaze moved to the room as I bit back my rage and addressed the crowd like a monarch.

"If you have doubts, ask me a question and I will answer it. I will tell you about the bad I've committed and the good that I meant to. I only ever cut off the afterlife because *I* was tired of keeping it."

"Yet," Malcolm said, matching my tone, eyes on the bruised black of my raised fingers as we circled the other in the center of the ballroom like hawks, "you have all of it."

Henry gasped and my breath went with his when I saw the sword at his neck, drawing a small crimson bead of blood—one threat. One spark.

Then another motion. A catalyst. The sword slashed his neck and blood spilled like a pitcher tipped over as Henry Baskin collapsed on the dais.

All the air left the room.

This was worse than rage.

Screaming, I lunged for Henry, ignoring everything as I fell to my knees beside him as my tiara clattered to the ground. There was no experience, no amount of practice or life that prepared me for the way his beautiful eyes rolled as he tried to speak. Blood dribbled from the corner of his soft lips.

I crawled the last step because my legs wouldn't make it. Blood kept coming. Why was no one else fucking helping? Why was no one coming? I hauled him onto my lap and brushed a lock of silver-streaked hair aside.

"Don't leave me—"

Henry's eyes widened and in a second—faster than I blinked—every part of him turned to ash and rot as I stared where my ungloved hand had met his skin.

"No. No. *No.* Come back," I choked.

His blood turned black on the marble floor. I grabbed at the lapels of his jacket, but only rot spilled out as I shook it and screamed.

"Come back!"

Even through the ash and blood, his clothes still smelled like dust and tea as I brought his jacket to my nose and tried to wring every moment while his last breath lingered. If I breathed deeply enough, I could pretend we had one last kiss as my tears rolled unabated.

Then Malcolm's voice penetrated, becoming a sword through my heart. My hands shook. I swallowed nausea and grief before it turned into a scream I buried in Henry's clothes.

"Bring him back, Foriana. Show the court."

The god fucking taunted me. We were back in the arena, venerating Koros. I lowered Henry's soiled clothes to the floor, feeling nothing but the raw, iron bite of defeat and grief with no bottom.

I rocked, hair falling forward, catching on the blood and rot that spilled over the steps as every part of me vibrated in the worst kind of rage. I wouldn't bring Henry back. His soul was gone in Linvia, relegated to screaming with the others in an eternity I was helpless to save him from.

There was nothing to retrieve.

Even if I could, I wouldn't.

"Do it, oh Goddess of Death. Raise him."

I stood slowly. Standing still on the dais, Henry's clothes and blood underfoot as I blinked away the film of grief. Rolling my neck, I waited for the vibration, the pull of power that separated man from god and death from life. It was cold and thick, weightless, in the palm of my hand as it reached its final form and I *remembered*.

I charged for Malcolm, arms outstretched, magic on my fingertips, crackling like lightning as my roar filled the room with grief and tangled with the charge of untold, unconfined power in a blinding shade of icy blue.

My feet left the floor only to be stopped. Arms gripped my waist and I cried out. Screaming, thrashing, begging as the grip tightened. Magic bounded from my hands indiscriminately in balls of energy and magic until cuffs clamped around my wrists and froze every ounce of power into utter silence.

No.

My chest constricted. The hold didn't lessen. I was trapped. I thrashed against Orion's broad chest, pounding him with my fists as I cried out and begged him to let me go, to let me kill Malcolm.

What did I have left? Let me kill them all and level Linvia for good.

Orion's arms tightened and jerked me around in time to see Adler throw himself at Malcolm. A white knife flashed in the fae prince's hand.

Malcolm threw him off, sending the prince across the floor as I swallowed a gasp. Losing him or Orion would unwind the last part of me that still held.

"Stop," I tried to yell at him through the bond.

"He hurt you," Adler bit back.

The fae scrambled to his feet, blade in hand as he thrashed toward Malcolm again, dodging one swing and another. Where were the fucking guards?

Malcolm whirled a punch, connecting with Adler's jaw with a force that sent the prince reeling. I screamed. It was the only power I had left so long as Orion held me like this: powerless.

"Let me go, Blackthorn. He won't win."

I was ready to tear the god limb from limb and set fire to his bones when the fae prince lunged a second time with impossible speed. Cutting the god's cheek clean open with a burning hiss that cauterized on contact.

Malcom roared. His primordial sword of feather-light, enchanted iron appeared in his hand and he charged for Adler.

The prince cut for us.

I blinked and we were in the silent hall of the Pantheon, at the foot of the throne.

I pushed off of Orion and staggered to unsteady feet, tears building in my eyes along with the storm of rage and grief ready to explode as I held my wrists out.

"Take them off."

I was drowning, spiraling, still covered in blood and rot and rage. The power built behind my brow like a pulsing headache as I felt too much, too suddenly.

There was nothing about this I wanted, and nothing worth this price. I was deflated and broken apart. Orion wouldn't look at me.

"He did it to keep you from murdering the room," Adler finally said, his voice cracked as his fingers raked through his hair and he paced across the shadows of moonlight in the dead quiet of the Pantheon.

My voice was hoarse. "The room was better dead."

"No."

His green eyes didn't meet mine, but tears watered in them too. The prince looked as haggard and aggrieved as I felt.

"I know why he did it," I snapped, whipping around to level a glare at the knight. "Clearly, I cannot kill anyone here."

"I'm not taking them off."

Blackthorn stared at my hands. They burned now, like they'd been plunged in an ice bath and beaten with a thousand needles.

Adler coughed, voice frenzied. "I need to go back and give Donovan a piece of—"

"No," Orion said, his amber eyes hard on the fae prince. "You lost a friend tonight. Let me. I'll see it's settled."

Something passed between the two of them—a silent conversation. Adler hung his head and Orion disappeared, leaving us alone in abject silence as reality blossomed and the true weight of loss became a suffocating fog.

The prince sank to his knees, head in his hands, as he struggled to breathe. I stood there, numb. What was I supposed to do? Again, I was covered in the blood of a mortal I only wanted to save. I never should have gone to Tyrlas, or Linvia or Belfiante. I should have boarded a ship and never looked back.

A torrent of everything tangled and surged inside me, but none of it moved to emotion because there was too much and the roar of my godhood was too loud in the hollow room.

I wilted beside Adler. My cheek rested against his shoulder, his chin on my head. It wasn't an intimate embrace, but a wordless connection as two wounded souls looked for comfort.

Who would tell Henry's daughters what happened? Should I? No. I couldn't. If they asked me what happened, the words wouldn't come. It was my fault. All of it was my fault because I let him love me. What if his daughters looked so much like him it broke me again? Someone would tell them. It would probably come from a palace guard without emotion.

Was that worse?

I cracked open my eyes, unsure what I was hoping to see, but the glint of something white beside the prince snagged my attention.

"That's my knife."

Adler lifted his head as I reached for the bone-white blade. The hilt was carved with a willow branch. Malcolm's blood dried on it and I wondered if I remembered how it tasted.

"*Miryanai,*" I whispered.

Adler cleared his throat; tears streaked his cheeks. He wiped his face with the sleeve of his jacket before I could reach up. "I didn't know it was yours."

"Made out of Malcolm's bones—named for justice."

"I wish I killed him." He stared at the knife in my hands. The silence of the Pantheon amplified the distance between us, an abyss of loss. "After I helped you steal the other one, I went down before Avilla to see if there were more."

"Why?"

Adler shrugged, leaning back on his hands as he stretched his legs. "Thought maybe I could protect you with it."

"Malcolm shouldn't be alive." I set the knife on the ground again and drew my knees to my chest. "Or Armine."

"Henry should."

The words dangled in the air as Adler sniffled and wiped his nose again. Tears pricked my eyes. Grief started to break out of its cage.

How is Adler the only one whose blood I wasn't covered in? When would it change? It always changed.

Henry's dried, crusting on my dress, but it left a streak on the marble. I stared at it as I curled my body into Adler's and waited for tears to come while he shook.

If I were alone in that ballroom, or if Orion hadn't stopped me, I would have destroyed the Linvian palace. I would have struck Malcolm where he stood and I would have let the magic in my hands turn me entirely into the villain he wanted me to be.

Left alone, I might have leveled Linvia and taken Miria with it.

"Malcolm wanted me to resurrect him."

"You didn't."

"I couldn't." My voice wavered as the truth brushed against it. I'd admitted this to Orion but not to Adler. He could hate me for this if he didn't know. "Souls die in Linvia."

"Why?"

"Me." I raked my hair with my fingers. It was knotted beyond recognition. "The destruction of Linvia and the Scribes of Nurem? That was me. I'd destroyed it all trying to save Leander. Orion spared me from doing worse tonight."

The tips of his fingers found my chin and tipped it up. Then he kissed me too softly, tasting of salt and wine.

My chest caved. I pulled back. Henry was the last man I kissed and now I'd moved on.

"Henry was a good man."

"The best."

I choked and my memory cracked like a dam. Adler pulled me to his chest while I cried and we lost track of time—grieving together in the center of the empty Pantheon until the air crackled and Orion returned.

The knight stood in the doorway of the throne room but didn't move.

"What happened?"

Orion's gaze lifted too slowly; I peeled myself from Adler as we stood up.

"Step away from her, Adler."

"Why?" Adler asked, not moving, arms at his side. "Has something happened?"

Orion's voice was tired and forlorn. He smelled of smoke and metal as he stood on the steps—something had changed. His eyes lifted, streaks of gold crackled in them.

"King Donovan promised his armies to the Pantheon. It's over, Foriana."

"It isn't over," I said, weary. Adler stood beside me. "That's what I wanted. What I asked for. It's the only way to protect Miria from—"

"Step. Away, *Your Highness*," Orion snapped, his voice cold and derelict.

"No." Adler stepped between us. "Tell us what's wrong, Orion."

Lightning struck outside in a great flash of light and Blackthorn didn't blink. My gut twisted. A tear slipped from the knight's scarred cheek, but his gaze didn't leave Adler's.

"Orion, please. Tell me—"

"I said: Step. Away."

A bolt of lightning struck Adler, throwing him into the wall with a rush of energy.

Before I yelled or lunged, another bolt struck the cuffs. Chains stretched from them and anchored me to the floor of the throne room before I could conceive a single strike.

The world stopped with my heart. I should have taken *Miryanai* from Adler and fallen on it when I had the chance.

I lifted my gaze to Orion.

His eyes were overcome with magic I knew too well, magic that illuminated his veins. His chin tilted as the wrong smile curled with my dawning horror.

"The Pantheon would always be your prison, Foriana, and I will always be your king."

"NO!" Adler shouted.

Blackthorn barked out a cold laugh but it wasn't him. With a wave of his arm, he vanished Adler from the Pantheon and my throat closed.

"Worry not, I promised Callum I'd return his son when my daughter had her taste of power."

"Let *him* go."

Another laugh as he crossed his arms and came down the steps, just out of my reach. My heart turned to ice as Koros watched me through the eyes I loved.

"You are always so blinded by your emotions, daughter. You might have won if you hadn't gone back for him, but I knew. *All* of us knew you would claim what you'd always wanted."

There was no bait I was willing to swallow.

"He's in there. I know he is."

"He is," Blackthorn's voice agreed and circled me with a demure grin. "He's banging his soul against mine trying to get back to you, but I'm stronger. I'll always be stronger, little bird. From the moment I knew you'd kill me, I did everything in my power to safeguard my crown from the least deserving."

The floor fell out from under my feet. No longer could I feel the burn of Henry's blood or taste the salt of grief in Adler's kiss as Blackthorn's body bounded up the dais to sit on the throne.

"It was a trap."

Koros leaned forward, resting his elbows on Blackthorn's knees.

"For a second, you won, Foriana. For one shining moment, my godhood was yours and you would've had all the power left behind and taken it all to the grave you thought you'd lie in. But you chose to save him. He wasn't stronger; a mortal soul like any other is just too easy to break. In fact, your sister suspected it at Malcolm's suggestion. Your heart is weak, brittle, and mortal despite everything you've done to it."

"No." I croaked and lifted my chin. The chains rattled. I'd been here before, Koros knew it, but I wouldn't give him the satisfaction of crumbling. "Let me go, let me leave with my soul bound and you'll never see me again. I swear it. The throne is yours if you—"

"You are as much a rake as your mother is, Foriana, and I'd be a fool to believe you."

"Then leave Orion and take what you want as you always have."

"You think that low of me?" He leaned back, lounging on the throne as if my life wasn't ending. "Oh, was this after I *"killed"* you?"

"You never killed me."

I glared and tried to reach for any of my magic, but Koros had strengthened the cuffs. I couldn't conjure so much as a spark. I only felt it build with no release, no outlet. My blood was thick with useless fucking power.

"Well, you were rather convincing when you collapsed in this very room after Belfiante and accused me of murdering *my* daughter before the entire court with no regard for what *I* had lost that day."

My head snapped up. I sharpened as Koros looked down through Orion's eyes. The chains pulled tighter and my shoulders jerked.

"Oh? And what did you fucking lose?"

Bile burned as memories swelled, tasting like blood, sand, and scum water. Koros looked straight at me. The way he held himself in the knight's form was all wrong. His shoulders were too straight and Orion would never fold his hands on his lap, nor smile with such cruelty.

"From that day I was never whole. A part of me was buried there, with you."

"There was no oak tree."

"No," he agreed. "Even in death, without your soul attached, your godhood still found a way to choke me out."

"Go fuck yourself."

Koros paced down the steps again, humming as he looked at me. My seams were coming undone in every way I could imagine. I wasn't fraying but falling. My heart was obliterated and I'd be fooling myself if I ever loved again.

"Raven—"

A flash, a moment, for the briefest second, Orion came through. I watched the lightning return and Koros beat him back, rolling his head as the column of muscle in his neck bulged and strained.

There wasn't a word great enough to hold the grief of watching the man you loved look through you.

I'd never be able to kill my soul bound. Did I trade four days of peace for a lifetime without because I thought I'd thwarted Fate? I never should have fucking gone to Belfiante; I should have run when Orion pleaded. Adler would have found us—we could have been free.

"What do you want?" I choked. "You have me as you've always wanted. Kill me and give this curse to someone else."

"I don't want anyone else. Neither do the primordials."

"They abandoned us."

"You. They abandoned *you* as you methodically executed their creations. Who do you think Vinliana serves? And who else would grant resurrection to Malcolm at Ilverleigh's request? Even he and Armine so refused to see you sit this throne they found an alliance."

No.

Orion—Koros—came toward me, haughtily pushing hair from his lightning-streaked eyes as he stopped within striking distance.

I spat in his face. It collided with his cheek in a splat almost as satisfying as twisting the knife in his heart a century prior.

The god merely frowned and wiped it off with the back of his sleeve.

"This is your punishment, Foriana. For the scribes, for me, for Niany, for everyone that's died at your hands because you thought you were righteous. This is for them. No one but you is fit to serve your sentence. I have no sympathy for the mortal caught in your wake."

Koros stepped around me toward the doors as my heart dragged the floor. The shattered pieces of it would have glittered in the moonlight like slivers of glass if it were a physical thing.

"Tomorrow you'll be presented a contract for your terms of release, but Miria will never be yours."

He walked to the door where I caught Malcom standing in the shadows, leaving me in the center of the throne room still chained.

"No trial?" I squeaked, trying to push false bravado back into my voice. "I'm at least owed that."

There was no bravado. My voice echoed in the hollow room, weak and defeated as Koros took his time turning back.

"A trial won't save you, Foriana. The primordials decided."

He walked away. Brazen heavy footsteps echoed through the marble corridors of the Pantheon that never belonged to me.

The same footsteps I'd memorized, ones that wouldn't walk away from me in a hundred years. Hope trailed off as the door creaked closed leaving me alone in a prison I should have seen.

"You made me this way!" I screamed until my breath gave out and the chains jerked again, tightening. "*En vendie-et ver soo!*"

Without me, you'd be nothing, I shouted after my father in Priminian until my voice dissolved. Then I sank to my knees and stuffed my fist in my mouth, wailing as I rocked because I was well and truly alone.

Malcolm, Armine, Niany—all of them were part of this, part of pushing me here. Tyrlas, Donovan, Callum, Vinliana—each a string Koros pulled to get me where he wanted. He'd offered me a single chance at escape and I couldn't see it.

The prophecy was obvious.

Now I was chained as it began because I thought, maybe, I could be better ... but Koros was right. I was worse. I was always worse. I wanted so deeply to believe this was a beginning the Scribes of Nurem hadn't written it.

He couldn't win. Not again. Koros wasn't all-seeing, I'd defeated him once and I'd do it again. I'd tear this world apart for one more minute with the men whose souls were mirrors to mine.

Miria and the Pantheon would not know peace until I did.

Koros would never be the king who rose from the bones and blood of my grief and weak-willed heart. I wasn't a tool of the Pantheon or a vehicle for prophecy and I would break these chains. I was Foriana—Queen Foriana, the Goddess of Death, and there would be no gods after me.

Year 1334
Raven is 784

A navy blue ocean lapped the crystalline shores of Ore, made of sand like glass pulverized into powder. The tide rose higher than it had in centuries and swallowed the last prophecy the scribes had written.

Fate watched with all of his thousand eyes because, no longer, was there anywhere else to look.

Thank you!

Thank you for reading Who Calls Me Villain. I hope you enjoyed your time in Raven's world. Her story will continue in the second installment and I swear they'll all have their HEA. Follow me on social media for updates, art, and other announcements.

As an indie author, reviews mean the world. They make the countless hours of moving commas around and tearing out my hair worth it. Please take a moment to rate and review on <u>Amazon</u> or <u>Goodreads</u> so more readers can scream with you.

Allison Trebacz is an author who belongs in a forest and lives in a desert. She writes about romance in nearly godless worlds and dreams of being able to wield a sword. For as long as she could remember, she was obsessed with stories about imaginary people in fictional words—clearly, she never grew out of it and has no intention to.

Her natural habitat is a coffeeshop where she can be found hunched over a latte, poking at her computer or in her home, daydreaming of trees and annoying her two cats, dogs, or husband.

Stay up to date on her latest:

Instagram: @allisontrebacz_author
TikTok: @allisonimagining
www.allisonimagining.com

www.ingramcontent.com/pod-product-compliance
Lightning Source LLC
Chambersburg PA
CBHW031150310726
48969CB00001B/29